"GREAT FUN TO READ AND HILARIOUS HAPPENINGS, YET A VERY SERIOUS BOOK. A MUST READ."
—*Tampa Tribune & Times*

"HIAASEN WRITES WITH THE GLEEFUL SOCIAL SCRUTINY OF TOM WOLFE AND THE TWISTED IMAGINATION OF HUNTER S. THOMPSON."
—*Wall Street Journal*

"A WHIZ-BANG STORY...A FINE RETURN TO FORM... ONE OF HIS BEST NOVELS...balancing outrage with humor and playing with both plot and characters like they are shiny silver balls in the pinball machines of life...The master of wacked tales of Florida excess."
—*Detroit News*

"COMICAL AND DARK...The cast of characters in Carl Hiaasen's *SICK PUPPY* makes other fiction rogues galleries seem quaint."
—*Pittsburgh Tribune*

"HIAASEN ONCE AGAIN PRODUCES A DEVILISHLY FUNNY CAPER...In *SICK PUPPY*, he shows himself to be A COMIC WRITER AT THE PEAK OF HIS POWERS."
—*Publishers Weekly*

"BUILDS TO A CRESCENDO THAT CULMINATES IN ONE OF THE MOST SATISFYING, COMPLETE ENDINGS HIAASEN HAS EVER WRITTEN. The rousing conclusion perfectly combines poetic justice, black humor, and action."
—*Ft. Lauderdale Sun-Sentinel*

more ...

Books by Carl Hiaasen

Fiction

Nature Girl
Skinny Dip
Basket Case
Sick Puppy
Lucky You
Stormy Weather
Strip Tease
Native Tongue
Skin Tight
Double Whammy
Tourist Season

For Young Readers

Scat
Flush
Hoot

Nonfiction

The Downhill Lie: A Hacker's Return to a Ruinous Sport

Team Rodent: How Disney Devours the World

Kick Ass: Selected Columns
(edited by Diane Stevenson)

Paradise Screwed: Selected Columns
(edited by Diane Stevenson)

CARL HIAASEN

SICK PUPPY

GRAND CENTRAL
PUBLISHING

NEW YORK   BOSTON

This is a work of fiction. The events described are imaginary; the characters are entirely fictitious and are not intended to represent actual living persons.

However, while most events described in this book are imaginary, the dining habits of the common bovine dung beetle are authentically represented.

Grand Central Publishing Edition

This Grand Central Publishing edition is published in arrangement with Alfred A. Knopf, a division of Random House, Inc.

Grand Central Publishing
Hachette Book Group
1290 Avenue of the Americas
New York, NY 10104

www.HachetteBookGroup.com

Printed in the United States of America

First Grand Central Publishing Paperback Edition: January 2003
First Grand Central Publishing Trade Edition: April 2005
12

Grand Central Publishing is a division of Hachette Book Group, Inc.

The Grand Central Publishing name and logo is a trademark of Hachette Book Group, Inc.

The publisher is not responsible for websites (or their content) that are not owned by the publisher.

ISBN 978-0-446-69568-8
LCCN: 99033435

~ *FOR FENIA,* ~

Η ΜΟΝΑΔΙΚΗ ΜΟΥ ΑΓΑΠΗ

SICK
PUPPY

1

On the morning of April 24, an hour past dawn, a man named Palmer Stoat shot a rare African black rhinoceros. He fired from a distance of thirteen yards and used a Winchester .458, which knocked him flat on his back. The rhinoceros wheeled, as if to charge, before snorting twice and sagging to its knees. Its head came to rest under a spread of palmettos.

Palmer Stoat instructed his guide, a former feed salesman named Durgess, to unpack the camera.

"Let's first make sure she's dead," Durgess said.

"Are you kidding? You see that shot?"

Durgess took the Winchester from his client. He approached the lifeless mass and poked it in the rump with the rifle barrel.

Stoat grinned as he dusted off his mail-order khakis. "Hey, Bungalow Bill, look what I killed!"

While Durgess assembled the video equipment, Stoat inspected his newest trophy, which had cost him thirty thousand dollars, not including ammo and gratuities. When he moved the palmetto fronds away from the rhino's face, he noticed something wrong.

"You ready?" Durgess was wiping down the lens of the video camera.

"Hey, look here." Stoat pointed accusingly.

"I'm lookin'. "

"Care to explain?"

"Explain what? That's a horn," said Durgess.

Stoat gave a yank. It broke off in his hands.

Durgess said, "Now see what you done."

"It's fake, Jethro." Angrily Stoat thrust the molded plastic cone at Durgess.

"The other one's real," Durgess said defensively.

"The other one's a nub!"

"Look, it wasn't my idea."

"You glued a phony horn on my thirty-thousand-dollar rhinoceros. Is that about right?"

Nervously Durgess cracked his knuckles.

"What'd you guys do with the real one?" Stoat demanded.

"Sold it. We cut it off and sold it."

"Perfect."

"They's worth a fortune in Asia. Supposably some kinda magic dick medicine. They say it gives you a boner lasts two days." Durgess shrugged skeptically. "Anyhow, it's serious bucks, Mr. Stoat. That's the program for all our rhinos. Some Chinaman over Panama City buys up the horns."

"You bastards are gypping me."

"Nossir. A jenna-wine African rhinoceros is what the catalog says, and that's what you got."

For a closer look, Stoat knelt in the scrub. The rhino's cranial horn had been taken off cleanly with a saw, leaving an oval abrasion. There the plastic replacement had been attached with white gummy industrial adhesive. A foot or so up the snout was the animal's secondary horn, the caudal, real enough but unimpressive; squat and wart-like in profile.

"The whole idea," Stoat said irritably to Durgess, "was a head mount for my den."

"And that's a helluva head, Mr. Stoat, you gotta admit."

"Except for one tiny detail."

Stoat tossed the fake horn at Durgess. Durgess let it drop to the ground, now sodden with rhino fluids. He said, "I got a taxidermy man does fiberglass on the side, he'll fix you up a new one. Nobody'll know the difference, sir. It'll look just like the real deal."

"Fiberglass."

"Yessir," Durgess said.

"Hell, why not chrome—ever thought of that? Rip the hood ornament off a Cadillac or maybe a 450-SL. Glue it to the tip of that sucker's nose."

Durgess gave Stoat a sullen look. Stoat took the Winchester from the guide and slung it over his shoulder. "Anything else I should know about this animal?"

"Nossir." There was no point telling Stoat that his trophy rhinoceros also had suffered from cataracts on both eyes, which accounted for its lack of alarm at the approach of heavily armed humans. In addition, the animal had spent its entire life as tame as a hamster, the featured attraction of an Arizona roadside zoo.

Stoat said, "Put the camera away. I don't want anybody to see the damn thing like this. You'll get with that fiberglass man right away?"

"First thing tomorrow," Durgess promised.

Palmer Stoat was feeling better. He rubbed a hand across the rhino's bristly plated hide and said, "What a magnificent creature."

Durgess thought: If only I had ten bucks for every time I've heard that line.

Stoat produced two thick cigars and offered one to his faithful guide. "Cohibas," Stoat said, "the genuine article." Theatrically he fired up.

Durgess declined. He grimaced at the acrid comingling of fumes, stogie and rhino piss.

Stoat said, "Tell me something, little bwana."

Oh blow me, Durgess almost said.

"How old you figure this animal to be?"

"I ain't too sure."

Stoat said, "She looks to be in her prime."

"Yeah, she does," said Durgess, thinking: Blind, tame, fat and half-senile—a regular killing machine, all right.

Palmer Stoat continued to admire the carcass, as he felt this was expected of a triumphant hunter. In truth, it was himself he was admiring, as both he and Durgess knew. Stoat patted the flank of the carcass and said to his guide: "Come on, man. I'll buy you a beer."

"Sounds good." Durgess took a portable two-way radio from a pocket of his safari jacket. "First lemme call Asa to bring the flatbed."

Palmer Stoat had more than enough money to go to Africa, but he didn't have the time. That's why he did his big-game hunting at local safari ranches, some legal and some not. This one, located near Ocala, Florida, was called the Wilderness Veldt Plantation. Officially it was a "private game preserve"; unofficially it was a place where rich people went to shoot exotic wild animals. Palmer Stoat had been there twice before, once for a water buffalo and once for a lion. From Fort Lauderdale it wasn't a bad drive, a shade over four hours. The hunts were staged early in the morning, so usually he was home in time for dinner.

As soon as he made the interstate, Stoat got on the phone. He had three cellular lines to his Range Rover, as his professional services were in high demand.

He called Desie and told her about the kill. "It was classic," he said, smacking on the cigar.

"How so?" his wife asked.

"Just being out there in the bush. The sunrise. The mist. The twigs crackling under your boots. I wish you'd come along sometime."

"What did she do?" his wife asked. "When you blasted her, I mean."

"Well—"

"Did she charge?"

"No, Des. Everything was over in a second. It was a clean shot."

Desirata was Palmer Stoat's third wife. She was thirty-two years old, an avid tennis player and an occasional liberal. Stoat's buddies once called her a bunny hugger because she wasn't a fan of blood sports. It all depends on whose blood you're talking about, Stoat had said with a taut laugh.

"I suppose you took video," Desie said to her husband. "Your first endangered species and all."

"As a matter of fact, no. No video."

"Oh, Dick's office called."

Stoat rolled down the window and flicked the ash off his Cuban. "When?"

"Four times," Desie said. "Starting at seven-thirty."

"Next time let the machine pick up."

"I was awake anyway."

Stoat said, "Who in Dick's office?"

"Some woman."

That really narrows it down, Stoat thought. Dick Artemus was the governor of Florida, and he liked to hire women.

Desie said, "Should I make dinner?"

"No, let's you and I go out. To celebrate, OK?"

"Great. I'll wear something dead."

"You're a riot, Alice."

Palmer Stoat phoned Tallahassee and left a message on the voice mail of Lisa June Peterson, an aide to the governor. Many of Dick Artemus's staff members went by three names, a vestige of their college sorority days at FSU. So far, none of them had consented to have sex with Palmer Stoat, but it was still early in the new administration. Eventually they would come to see how clever, powerful and charismatic Stoat was; one of the two or three top lobbyists in the state. Only in politics would a job like that get you laid; no normal women were impressed by what Stoat did for a living, or even much interested in it.

In Wildwood he got on the turnpike and soon afterward stopped at the Okahumpka Service Plaza for a late lunch: Three hamburgers all the way, two bags of french fries and a jumbo vanilla shake. He drove one-handed, stuffing his cheeks. The digital Motorola started ringing, and Stoat checked the caller ID. Hastily he touched the OFF button. The man on the other end was a Miami commissioner, and Stoat had a firm rule against speaking directly with Miami commissioners—those who weren't already under indictment were under investigation, and all telephone lines into City Hall had long ago been tapped. The last thing Palmer Stoat needed was another trip to the grand jury. Who had time for such nonsense?

Somewhere north of Yeehaw Junction, a dirty black pickup truck appeared in the Rover's rear window. The truck came up fast and then settled in, three car lengths behind Stoat's bumper. Stoat was gnawing on fries and gabbing on the phone, so he didn't pay serious attention until an hour or so later, when he noticed the truck was still behind him. Weird, he thought. Southbound traffic was light—why didn't the idiot pass? Stoat punched the Rover up past ninety, but the truck stayed close. Gradually Stoat eased off the accelerator until he coasted down to forty-five; the black pickup remained right there, three lengths behind, as if connected by a tow bar.

Like most affluent white people who owned sport-utility vehicles, Palmer Stoat lived in constant fear of a carjacking. He had been led to understand that luxury 4x4s were the chariots of choice for ruthless black and Latin drug gangs; in such circles a Range Rover was said to be more desirable than a Ferrari. Glare on the truck's windshield made it impossible for Stoat to ascertain the ethnicity of the tailgater, but why take a chance? Stoat groped in the console for the Glock semiautomatic that he'd been given as a Christmas gift by the president of the state Police Benevolent Association. Stoat placed the pistol on his lap. Ahead loomed a slow-moving Airstream travel trailer, as wide as a Mississippi barge and just about as nimble. Stoat accelerated around it and cut back sharply, putting the camper rig between him and the pickup truck. He decided to get off the turnpike at the next exit, to see what the tailgater would do.

The Airstream followed Stoat off the ramp; then came the dirty black pickup. Stoat stiffened at the wheel. The clerk at the tollbooth glanced at the gun between his legs but made no mention of it.

"I'm being followed," Stoat informed her.

"That'll be eight dollars and seventy cents," said the clerk.

"Call the Highway Patrol."

"Yessir. Eight-seventy, please."

"Didn't you hear me?" Stoat asked. He handed the clerk a fifty-dollar bill.

"Have you got something a little smaller?"

"Yeah. Your brain stem," Stoat said. "Now, keep the change and call the goddamn Highway Patrol. There's some lunatic tailgater following me."

The clerk ignored the insult and looked toward the vehicles stacking up behind the Range Rover.

In a low voice, Stoat said: "It's the black pickup truck behind the travel trailer."

"What pickup truck?" asked the clerk.

Palmer Stoat placed the Glock on the dashboard and stepped out of the Rover so he could peek around the Airstream. The next car in line was a station wagon with a square-dance pennant attached to the antenna. The tailgater was gone. "Sonofabitch," Stoat muttered.

The driver of the camper honked. So did another motorist, farther down the line. Stoat got back in the Range Rover. The tollbooth clerk handed him change for the fifty. Dryly she said, "You still want me to call the Highway Patrol?"

"No, thanks."

"How about the CIA?"

Stoat smirked. The little smart-ass didn't know who she was dealing with. "Congratulations, young lady," he told her. "You're about to enter the cold cruel world of the unemployed." Tomorrow he would speak to a man in Tallahassee, and it would be done.

Palmer Stoat found an Exxon station, gassed up, took a leak and then headed back toward the turnpike. All the way to Lauderdale he kept checking his rearview—it was mind-boggling how many people owned black pickups. Had the whole damn world gone redneck? Stoat's nerves were whacked by the time he got home.

They had brought their idea for Shearwater Island to Governor Dick Artemus in glitzy bits and pieces, and he'd liked what he'd heard so far.

A planned seaside community. Beach and boardwalks between the condominium towers. Public parks, kayak tours and a nature trail. Two championship golf courses. A clay pigeon shooting range. A yacht harbor, airstrip and heliport.

But Dick Artemus could not locate Shearwater Island on the wall map of Florida in his office.

That's because it's not called Shearwater Island yet, explained Lisa June Peterson. It's called Toad Island, and it's right there on the Gulf, near the mouth of the Suwannee.

"Have I been there before?" Dick Artemus asked.

"Probably not."

"What does 'Shearwater' mean?"

"It's the name of a bird," Lisa June Peterson said.

"Do they live on the island?" asked the governor. "Is that going to be a problem?"

Lisa June Peterson, having already researched the question, reported that shearwaters were migratory seabirds that preferred the Atlantic coastline.

"But there are other kinds of birds on the island," she added.

"Like what?" Dick Artemus frowned. "Eagles? Don't tell me there's goddamn bald eagles on this island, because that means we got a federal scenario."

"They're doing the survey this week."

"Who!"

"A biological survey. Clapley's people," Lisa June Peterson said. Robert Clapley was the developer who wanted to rename Toad Island and subdivide it. He had contributed most generously to Dick Artemus's gubernatorial campaign.

"There's no votes in bulldozing eagle nests," the governor remarked gravely. "Can we all agree on that?"

"Mr. Clapley is taking every reasonable precaution."

"So what else, Lisa? In fifty words or less." Dick Artemus was famous for his insectine attention span.

His assistant said: "The transportation budget includes funding for a new bridge from the mainland. It passed the Senate, but now Willie Vasquez-Washington is being a prick."

Willie Vasquez-Washington was vice chairman of the House

Appropriations Committee. He and the governor had tangled before.

"What's he want this time?" Dick Artemus said.

"We're not sure."

"You reach out to Palmer?"

"We keep missing each other."

"And I suppose this thing won't fly, this Shearwater Island," the governor said, "without a brand-new bridge."

"The one they've got is sixty years old and wooden," Lisa June Peterson said. "It won't hold a cement truck is what Roothaus says." Roger Roothaus was president of the engineering firm that wanted the contract for designing the new bridge to Toad Island. He, too, had contributed generously to Dick Artemus's gubernatorial campaign. In fact, almost everyone who stood to profit from the development of Shearwater Island had donated money to the governor's election. This, Dick Artemus took for granted.

"So get Palmer to fix the bridge problem," he said.

"Right."

"Anything else?"

"Nothing major. We're anticipating some local opposition," said Lisa June Peterson.

The governor groaned. "People *live* on this island? Christ, nobody told me that."

"Two hundred. Two fifty max."

"Shit," said Dick Artemus.

"They're circulating a petition."

"I guess that means they're not golfers."

"Evidently not," said Lisa June Peterson.

Dick Artemus rose and pulled on his coat. "I'm late, Lisa June. Would you relate all this to Mr. Stoat?"

"As soon as possible," she said.

*   *   *

Twilly had spent the day in Gainesville at the University of Florida veterinary college, reputedly one of the best in the country. Many famous nature parks and zoos, including the one at Walt Disney World, sent their dead animals there to be necropsied. Twilly had gone to deliver a red-shouldered hawk that appeared to have been shot. The bird had fallen on a remote patch of beach at a place called Madeira Bay, in Everglades National Park. Twilly had bubble-wrapped the broken body and placed it on dry ice in a cooler. He'd made the drive from Flamingo to Gainesville in less than seven hours. He hoped the bullet had remained in the bird, because the bullet was a key to resolving the crime.

Which wasn't exactly the same thing as solving it. Knowing the caliber of the weapon would have been useful: something to file away in case the shooter returned to the park and was foolish enough to let himself get stalked, captured and lashed naked for a month to a mangrove tree.

Twilly Spree wasn't a park ranger or a wildlife biologist or even an amateur bird-watcher. He was an unemployed twenty-six-year-old college dropout with a brief but spectacular history of psychological problems. Not incidentally, he also had inherited millions of dollars.

At the veterinary school, Twilly found a young doctor who agreed to do a postmortem on the hawk, which had in fact succumbed to a single gunshot wound. Unfortunately the slug had passed cleanly through the bird's breast, leaving no fragments, no clues, only blood-crusted feathers. Twilly thanked the young doctor for trying. He filled out a form for the U.S. government stating where he had found the dead hawk, and under what circumstances. At the bottom of the paper he signed his name as "Thomas Stearns Eliot, Jr." Then Twilly got in his black pickup truck and drove south. He intended to return directly to the Everglades, where he had been living in a pup tent with a three-legged bobcat.

On the turnpike somewhere south of Kissimmee, Twilly came up behind a pearl-colored Range Rover. Normally he wouldn't have paid attention to the style of the vehicle, but this one had a vanity plate that said in green capital letters: CO-JONES. As Twilly swung into the passing lane, a Burger King hamburger carton flew out the driver's window of the Rover. Next came an empty cup and then a wadded paper napkin, followed by another hamburger carton.

Twilly put a heel on the brake, steered his truck to the shoulder of the highway and waited for a gap in traffic. Then he sprinted into the road and picked up the litter, piece by piece, depositing it in the cab of his truck. Afterward it took him only a few miles to catch up with the pig in the Range Rover; Twilly got behind him and camped there, contemplating his options. He thought about what his therapists would recommend, what his former teachers would say, what his mother would suggest. They were indisputably mature and sensible people, but their advice often proved useless to Twilly Spree. He remained baffled by their outlook on the world, as they were baffled by his.

All Twilly could see of the litterbug was the man's shoulders and the top of his head. To Twilly, it seemed like an exceptionally large head, but possibly this was an illusion caused by the cowboy-style hat. Twilly doubted that an authentic cowboy would be caught dead in a pearl-colored, fifty-thousand-dollar, foreign-made SUV with vanity tags that celebrated the size of his testicles, in *español*. Nor, Twilly thought, would a true cowboy ever toss hamburger wrappers out the window. No, that would be the work of a garden-variety asshole. . . .

Suddenly the Range Rover cut ahead of a slow-moving travel camper, then vectored sharply off the highway at the Yeehaw Junction exit. Twilly followed toward the toll plaza before switching to the exact-change lane, and scooting past. Then he drove across State Road 60 to I-95 and headed at imprudent speeds toward Fort Pierce, where he again hooked up with the turnpike southbound. He parked in the shade of an overpass, raised the hood of the pickup and waited. Twenty minutes later the Rover sped by, and Twilly resumed the pursuit. This time he stayed farther back. He still had no plan but at least he had a clearly defined mission. When the litterbug flicked a cigar butt out the window, Twilly didn't bother to stop. Biodegradable, he thought. Onward and upward.

2

After three glasses of wine, Desie could no longer pretend to be following her husband's account of the canned rhinoceros hunt. Across the table she appraised Palmer Stoat as if he were a mime. His fingers danced and his mouth moved, but nothing he said reached her ears. She observed him in two dimensions, as if he were an image on a television screen: an animated middle-aged man with a slight paunch, thin blond hair, reddish eyebrows, pale skin, upcurled lips and vermilion-splotched cheeks (from too much sun or too much alcohol). Palmer had a soft neck but a strong chiseled chin, the surgical scars invisible in the low light. His teeth were straight and polished, but his smile had a twist of permanent skepticism. To Desie, her husband's nose had always appeared too small for his face; a little girl's nose, really, although he insisted it was the one he'd been born with. His blue eyes also seemed tiny, though quick and bright with self-confidence. His face was, in the way of prosperous ex-jocks, roundish and pre-jowly and companionable. Desie wouldn't have called Stoat a hunk but he was attractive in that gregarious southern frat-boy manner, and he had overwhelmed her with favors and flattery and constant attention. Later she realized that the inexhaustible energy with which Palmer had pursued their courtship was less a display of ardor than an ingrained relentlessness; it was how he went after anything he wanted. They dated for four weeks and then got married on the island of Tortola. Desie supposed she had been in a fog, and now the fog was beginning to lift. What in the world had she done? She pushed the awful question out of her mind, and when she did she was able to hear Palmer's voice again.

"Some creepo was tailing me," he was saying, "for like a hundred miles."

"Why?"

Her husband snorted. "To rob my lily-white ass, that's why."

"This was a black guy?" Desie asked.

"Or a Cuban. I couldn't see which," Stoat said, "but I tell you what, sweets, I was ready for the sonofabitch. Señor Glock was in my lap, locked and loaded."

"On the turnpike, Palmer?"

"He would have been one stone-dead mother."

"Just like your rhino," Desie said. "By the way, are you getting her stuffed like the others?"

"Mounted," Stoat corrected. "And just the head."

"Lovely. We can hang it over the bed."

"Speaking of which, guess what they're doing with rhinoceros horns."

"Who's they?" Desie asked.

"Asians and such."

Desie knew, but she let Palmer tell the story. He concluded with Durgess's fanciful rumor of two-day erections.

"Can you imagine!" Stoat hooted.

Desie shook her head. "Who'd even want one of those?"

"Maybe *you* might, someday." He winked.

Desie glanced around for the waiter. Where was dinner? How could it take so long to boil pasta?

Stoat poured himself another glass of wine. "Rhino horns, Holy Christ on a ten-speed. What next, huh?"

"That's why poachers are killing them off," his wife said.

"Yeah?"

"That's why they're almost extinct. God, Palmer, where have you been?"

"Working for a living. So you can sit home, paint your toenails and learn all about endangered species on the Discovery Channel."

Desie said, "Try the *New York Times*."

"Well, pardon me." Stoat sniffed sarcastically. "I read the newspaper today, oh boy."

This was one of her husband's most annoying habits, dropping the lyrics of old rock songs into everyday conversation. Palmer thought it clever, and perhaps it wouldn't have bothered Desie so much if occasionally he got the words right, but he never did. Though Desie was much younger, she was familiar with the work of Dylan and the Beatles and the Stones, and so on. In college she had worked two summers at a Sam Goody outlet.

To change the subject, she said: "So what did Dick Artemus want?"

"A new bridge." Stoat took a sideways bite from a sourdough roll. "No big deal."

"A bridge to what?"

"Some nowhere bird island over on the Gulf. How about passing the butter?"

Desie said, "Why would the governor want a bridge to nowhere?"

Her husband chuckled, spraying crumbs. "Why does the

governor want *anything*? It's not for me to question, darling. I just take the calls and work my magic."

"A day in the life," said Desie.

"You got it."

Once, as a condition of a probation, Twilly Spree had been ordered to attend a course on "anger management." The class was made up of men and women who had been arrested for outbursts of violence, mostly in domestic situations. There were husbands who'd clobbered their wives, wives who'd clobbered their husbands, and even one grandmother who had clobbered her sixty-two-year-old son for blaspheming during Thanksgiving supper. Others of Twilly's classmates had been in bar fights, gambling frays and bleacher brawls at Miami Dolphins games. Three had shot guns at strangers during traffic altercations and, of those, two had been wounded by return fire. Then there was Twilly.

The instructor of the anger-management course presented himself as a trained psychotherapist. Dr. Boston was his name. On the first day he asked everyone in class to compose a short essay titled "What Makes Me Really, Really Mad." While the students wrote, Dr. Boston went through the stack of manila file folders that had been sent to him by the court. After reading the file of Twilly Spree, Dr. Boston set it aside on a corner of the desk. "Mr. Spree," he said in a level tone. "We're going to take turns sharing our stories. Would you mind going first?"

Twilly stood up and said: "I'm not done with my assignment."

"You may finish it later."

"It's a question of focus, sir. I'm in the middle of a sentence."

Dr. Boston paused. Inadvertently he flicked his eyes to

Twilly's folder. "All right, let's compromise. You go ahead and finish the sentence, and then you can address the class."

Twilly sat down and ended the passage with the words *ankle-deep in the blood of fools!* After a moment's thought, he changed it to *ankle-deep in the evanescing blood of fools!*

He stuck the pencil behind one ear and rose.

Dr. Boston said: "Done? Good. Now please share your story with the rest of us."

"That'll take some time, the whole story will."

"Mr. Spree, just tell us why you're here."

"I blew up my uncle's bank."

Twilly's classmates straightened and turned in their seats.

"A branch," Twilly added, "not the main office."

Dr. Boston said, "Why do you think you did it?"

"Well, I'd found out some things."

"About your uncle."

"About a loan he'd made. A very large loan to some very rotten people."

"Did you try discussing it with your uncle?" asked Dr. Boston.

"About the loan? Several times. He wasn't particularly interested."

"And that made you angry?"

"No, discouraged." Twilly squinted his eyes and locked his hands around the back of his neck. "Disappointed, frustrated, insulted, ashamed—"

"But isn't it fair to say you were angry, too? Wouldn't a person need to be pretty angry to blow up a bank building?"

"No. A person would need to be resolved. That I was."

Dr. Boston felt the amused gaze of the other students, who were awaiting his reaction. He said, "I believe what I'm hearing is some denial. What do the rest of you think?"

Twilly cut in: "I'm not denying anything. I purchased the dynamite. I cut the fuses. I take full responsibility."

Another student asked: "Did anybody get kilt?"

"Of course not," Twilly snapped. "I did it on a Sunday, when the bank was closed. That's my point—if I was really pissed, I would've done it on a Monday morning, and I would've made damn sure my uncle was inside at the time."

Several other probationers nodded in agreement. Dr. Boston said: "Mr. Spree, a person can be very mad without pitching a fit or flying off the handle. Anger is one of those complicated emotions that can be close to the surface or buried deeply, so deeply we often don't recognize it for what it is. What I'm suggesting is that at some subconscious level you must've been extremely angry with your uncle, and probably for reasons that had nothing to do with his banking practices."

Twilly frowned. "You're saying that's not enough?"

"I'm saying—"

"Loaning fourteen million dollars to a rock-mining company that's digging craters in the Amazon River basin. What more did I need?"

Dr. Boston said, "It sounds like you might've had a difficult relationship with your uncle."

"I barely know the man. He lives in Chicago. That's where the bank is."

"How about when you were a boy?"

"Once he took me to a football game."

"Ah. Did something happen that day?"

"Yeah," said Twilly. "One team scored more points than the other team, and then we went home."

Now the class was snickering and it was Dr. Boston's turn to manage his anger.

"Look, it's simple," Twilly said. "I blew up the building to help him grow a conscience, OK? To make him think about the greedy wrongheaded direction his life was heading. I put it all in a letter."

"Yes, the letter's in the file," said Dr. Boston. "But I noticed you didn't sign your name to it."

Twilly spread his hands. "Do I look like an idiot? It's against the law, blowing up financial institutions."

"And just about anything else."

"So I've been advised," Twilly muttered.

"But, still, at a subconscious level—"

"I don't have a subconscious, Doctor. That's what I'm trying to explain. Everything that happens in my brain happens right on the surface, like a stove, where I can see it and feel it and taste the heat." Twilly sat down and began massaging his temples with his fingertips.

Dr. Boston said, "That would make you biologically unique in the species, Mr. Spree, not having a subconscious. Don't you dream in your sleep?"

"Never."

"Seriously."

"Seriously," Twilly said.

"Never once?"

"Not ever in my whole life."

Another probationer waved a hand. "C'mon, man, you never had no nightmares?"

"Nope," Twilly said. "I can't dream. Maybe if I could I wouldn't be here now."

He licked the tip of his pencil and resumed work on the essay, which he submitted to Dr. Boston after class. Dr. Boston did not acknowledge reading Twilly's composition, but the next morning and every morning for the following four weeks, an armed campus security guard was posted in the rear of the classroom. Dr. Boston never again called on Twilly Spree to speak. At the end of the term, Twilly received a notarized certificate saying he'd successfully completed anger-management counseling, and was sent back to his probation officer, who commended him on his progress.

If only they could see me now, Twilly thought. Preparing for a hijack.

First he'd followed the litterbug home, to one of those exclusive islands off Las Olas Boulevard, near the beach. Nice spread the guy had: old two-story Spanish stucco with barrel-tile shingles and vines crawling the walls. The house was on a cul-de-sac, leaving Twilly no safe cover for lurking in his dirty black pickup. So he found a nearby construction site—a mansion going up. The architecture was pre-*Scarface* Medellín, all sharp angles and marble facings and smoked glass. Twilly's truck blended in nicely among the backhoes and cement mixers. Through the twilight he strolled back toward the litterbug's home, where he melted into a hedge of thick ficus to wait. Parked in the driveway next to the Range Rover was a Beemer convertible, top down, which Twilly surmised would belong to the wife, girlfriend or boyfriend. Twilly had a notion that made him smile.

An hour later the litterbug came out the front door. He stood in the amber light under the stucco arch and fired up a cigar. Moments later a woman emerged from the house, slowly backing out and pulling the door shut behind her; bending forward at the waist, as if saying good-bye to a small child or perhaps a dog. As the litterbug and his female companion crossed the driveway, Twilly saw her fanning the air in an exaggerated way, indicating she didn't much care for cigar smoke. This brought another smile to Twilly's face as he slipped from the hedge and hustled back to his truck. They'll be taking the ragtop, he thought. So she can breathe.

Twilly followed the couple to an Italian restaurant on an unscenic stretch of Federal Highway, not far from the seaport. It was a magnificent choice for what Twilly had in mind. Litterbug parked the convertible in true dickhead style, diagonally across two spaces. The strategy was to protect one's expensive luxury import from scratches and dings by preventing common folks from parking next to it. Twilly was elated to witness this selfish stunt. He waited ten minutes after the cigar-smoking man and cigar-hating woman had entered the restaurant, to make sure they'd been seated. Then he sped off on his quest.

Her stage name was Tia and she was already up on their table, already twirling her mail-order ponytail and peeling off her lacy top when the stink hit her like a blast furnace. Damn, she thought, did a sewer pipe break?

And the three guys all grins and high fives, wearing matching dark blue coveralls with filthy sleeves; laughing and smoking and sipping their six-dollar beers and going Tee-uh, izzat how you say it? Kinda name is Tee-uh? And all three of them waving fifties, for God's sake; stinking like buzzard puke and singsonging her name, her stage name, and slipping brand-new fifty-dollar bills into her G-string. So now Tia had a major decision to make, a choice between the unbelievable gutter-rot stench and the unbelievably easy money. And what she did was concentrate mightily on breathing through her mouth, so that after a while the reek didn't seem so unbearable and the truth was, hey, they were nice-enough guys. Regular working stiffs. They even apologized for stinking up the joint. After a few table dances they asked Tia to sit and join them because they had the wildest story for her to hear. Tia said OK, just a minute, and hurried to the dressing room. In her locker she found a handkerchief, upon which she sprinkled expensive Paris perfume, another unwanted gift from another smitten customer. She returned to the table to find an open bottle of the club's priciest champagne, which was almost potable. The crew in the dirty blue coveralls was making a sloppy toast to somebody; clinking their glasses and imploring Tia to sit down, c'mon, sit. Have some bubbly. They couldn't wait to tell her what had happened, all three chattering simultaneously, raising their voices, trying to take charge of the storytelling. Tia, holding the scented hankie under her nose, found herself authentically entertained and of course not believing a word they said, except for the part about their occupations, which they could hardly embellish, given the odor.

How come you don't believe we got our load hijacked! one of them exclaimed.

Because it's ridiculous, said Tia.

Really it was more of a trade, said one of his pals. The young man give us three grand cash and the use of his pickup and told us to meet back here in a hour.

Tia flared her eyebrows. This total stranger, he hands you three thousand bucks and drives off in a—

All fifties, one of the men said, waving a handful of bills. A grand each!

Tia, giggling through the handkerchief: You guys are seriously fulla shit.

No, ma'am, we ain't. We might smell like we are, but we ain't.

The one waving the fattest wad was talking loudest. What we told you, he said, that's the honest-to-God truth of how we come to be here tonight, watchin' you dance. And if you don't believe it, Miz Tee-uh, just come out back to the parkin' lot in about fifteen minutes when the boy gets back.

Maybe I will, said Tia.

But by then she was busy entertaining a table of cable-TV executives, so she missed seeing Twilly Spree drive up to the neon-lit strip club in a full-sized county garbage truck. When Twilly got out, one of the men in blue coveralls tossed him the keys to the black pickup.

"You guys go through all that dough I gave you?" Twilly asked amiably.

"No, but just about."

"And it was worth every dollar, I bet."

"Oh yeah."

Twilly shook hands with each of the men and said good-bye.

"Wait, son, come on inside and have just one beer. We got a lady wants to meet you."

"Rain check," said Twilly.

"No, but see, she don't believe us. She thinks we robbed the bingo hall or somethin'. That's how come you gotta come inside just for a minute, to tell her it's no bullshit, you paid us three grand to rent out the shitwagon."

Twilly smiled. "I don't know what you're talking about."

"Hey, man, where's the load? The truck, it looks empty."

"That's right," Twilly said. "There's nothing to haul to the dump. You guys can go straight on home tonight."

"But what happened to it?"

"Best you don't know."

"Oh Lord," one of the garbagemen muttered to his pals. "This is a crazy-ass boy. He's gone done some crazy-ass thing."

"No," Twilly said, "I believe you'd approve. I really do." Then he drove off, thinking how wrong Dr. Boston had been. Anger wasn't such a complicated emotion.

Palmer Stoat ordered an antipasto salad, garlic rolls, fettuccine Alfredo, a side of meatballs, and before long Desie had to look away, for fear of being sick. He was perspiring, that's how hard he went at the food; droplets of sweat streaking both sides of his jawline. Desie was ashamed of herself for feeling so revulsed; this was her husband, after all. It wasn't as if his personality had transformed after they got married. He was the same man in all respects, two years later. Desie felt guilty about marrying him, guilty about having second thoughts, guilty about the rhinoceros he'd shot dead that morning.

"From here to the salad bar," Stoat was telling her. "That's how close she was."

"And for that you needed a scope?"

"Better safe than sorry. That's Durgess's motto."

Stoat ordered tortoni for dessert. He used a fork to probe the ice cream for fragments of almonds, which he raked into a tidy pattern along the perimeter of the plate. Watching the fastidious ritual plunged Desie deeper into melancholy. Later, while Palmer reviewed the bill, she excused herself and went to the rest room, where she dampened a paper towel to wipe off her lipstick and makeup. She had no idea why, but it made her feel much better. By the time she finished, her husband was gone from the restaurant.

Desie walked outside and was nearly poleaxed by the smell. She cupped her hands to her mouth and looked around for Palmer. He was in the parking lot, beneath a streetlight. As Desie approached him, the odor got worse, and soon she saw why: a sour mound of garbage ten feet high. Desie estimated it to weigh several tons. Palmer Stoat stood at the base of the fetid hill, his eyes fixed lugubriously on the peak.

"Where's the car?" Desie asked with a cough.

Palmer's arms flopped at his sides. He began squeaking like a lost kitten.

"Don't tell me." She struggled not to gag on the stink. "Dammit, Palmer. My Beemer!"

Haltingly he began to circle the rancid dune. He raised an arm, pointing in outraged stupefaction. A cloud of flies buzzed about his face, but he made no effort to shoo them away.

"Goddammit," Desie cried. "Didn't I tell you to put the top up? Didn't I?"

3

Twilly made it back to the Italian restaurant in time for the show. Under the amused supervision of several police officers, a detachment of workers with rakes and shovels had begun the unsavory task of digging out the BMW. This Twilly watched through field glasses from high in a nearby pine tree. There was no sign of the press, which was a shame—here was a story made for TV. Over the rhythmic crunch of digging, Litterbug's voice could be heard admonishing the sanitation workers to be careful, goddamn you, don't scratch the paint! Twilly found it comical, considering the likely extent of the Beemer's contamination. He imagined virgin leather upholstery ripening under an ambrosial lode of orange rinds, cottage cheese, Heineken bottles, coffee grounds, eggshells, crumpled wads of Kleenex, potato skins, sanitary napkins, pizza crust, fish heads, spare ribs, leaky toothpaste tubes, bacon grease, coagulated gravy, cat litter and chicken necks. Twilly wished he could infiltrate the cleanup crew, to see the ghastly sight up close.

Litterbug's wife/girlfriend could be observed pacing, arms folded, beneath a flickering streetlight. Twilly couldn't make out her expression, but the clip in her step suggested impatience. He wondered if she truly cared about the BMW; in any event, the insurance company would buy her a new one. Twilly also thought about the sanitation workers, being called out so late on such a strange job. He had a feeling they might be enjoying themselves, exhuming a fancy red sports car from a heap of refuse, but still he hoped they were getting overtime.

It was quite an extensive operation, and Twilly wondered why he wasn't feeling a commensurate sense of satisfaction. The answer came with a sour jolt as he studied the litterbug through the binoculars; watched the man unwrap a piece of candy—probably an after-dinner mint from the restaurant—then crumple the wrapper and drop it nonchalantly to the ground. The dumb fuckwad didn't get it! Didn't make the link between his piggish misbehavior on the turnpike and the malicious defilement of his automobile. He probably figured it was the random mischief of vandals; a prank.

I should've left a message, Twilly thought glumly. I should've made it crystal clear. He muttered a curse and climbed cautiously through the darkness down the trunk of the tree. By the time he reached the parking lot, the excavation of the car was complete. Litterbug and his wife/girlfriend could be seen leaving in a taxi. The soiled BMW was being hooked to a tow truck, whose burly driver wore a baby blue hospital mask and joked with the sanitation crew, which was shoveling the last dregs into a Dumpster.

Twilly asked one of the cops what had happened to the red convertible.

"Somebody emptied a garbage truck on it," the officer reported with a harsh chuckle.

"Jesus," said Twilly. "Why?"

"Who the fuck knows. It's the sick society we live in."

Twilly said: "I saw all these police cars, I was afraid there was a murder."

"Naw, just some big shot left his ragtop down in the wrong neighborhood."

"He famous or something?"

"I never heard of him before tonight," said the cop, "but obviously he's got some juice. Otherwise I wouldn't be here, I'd be home in my underwear watching basketball. Stand back now."

The tow truck driver was maneuvering out of the parking lot, the cop waving directions. Twilly knew better than to press for the litterbug's name; he didn't need it anyway. He approached one of the sanitation workers and asked if the Beemer was totaled.

"Yeah, and it ain't right. A sweet car like this."

Twilly said, "Completely ruined, huh?"

"You can't never get the interior clean, not after somethin' such as this. We're talkin' about a minimum—I'm guessin' now—four tons of raw garbage." The man stopped working and rested his weight on the stem of the shovel. "I mean, hell, an expensive car like that—why trash it when you can just steal the damn thing? Any fool leaves the convertible top down deserves to lose his wheels. But this? This is evil shit, you ask me. Taking this much trouble to destroy a perfectly splendid vehicle. Deeply evil shit."

"Sick world," Twilly Spree said, in his own defense.

He was born in Key West, where his father had gone to sell commercial waterfront. Little Phil Spree was a real estate specialist. If a property wasn't on the sea or the Gulf, Little Phil wasn't interested. He would buy and sell beach until there was no more beach to buy or sell, then pack up the family and move to another town where, Little Phil typically would exult, "the coast is clear!" Florida has thirteen hundred miles of shoreline, and young Twilly got to savor plenty of it. His mother, who kept out of direct sunlight, wasn't crazy about the tropics. But Little Phil was making excellent money, so Amy Spree basically stayed indoors for eighteen years, tended to her complexion and endeavored to occupy herself with hobbies. She grew bonsai trees. She started writing a romance novel. She learned to play the clarinet. She took up yoga, modern dance and strong martinis. Meanwhile Twilly ran wild, literally. Every free moment was spent outdoors. His parents couldn't imagine what he was up to.

When Twilly was four, Little Phil briefly moved the family to Marco Island, which was famous for its white dune-fringed beaches. The sand was spangled with ornate tropical seashells, which Twilly collected and organized in shoe boxes. Usually he was accompanied by a sitter, hired by his mother to make sure he didn't wander into the Gulf of Mexico and drown. Years later, at age fourteen, Twilly hot-wired a friend's station wagon and drove back to Marco, in order to prowl the shore for shells. He arrived late at night in a howling downpour, and fell asleep in the car. When he awoke at dawn, he comprehended for the first time what his old man did for a living. The island had sprouted skyline; a concrete picket of towering hotels and high-rise condominiums. Waterfront, of course. Twilly fixed his eyes downward and marched the beach, his shoe box under one arm. He hoped he was seeing a mirage, a trick of the fog and clouds, but when he glanced up, the hotels and condos were still there, looming larger than before. As the sun began to rise, the buildings cast tombstone shadows across the sand. Soon Twilly found himself standing in a vast block of shade—shade, on an open beach under a bright clear sky! He sunk to his knees and punched the hard-packed sand with both fists until his knuckles were skinned.

A woman tourist came up to Twilly and told him to stop carrying on, as he was upsetting her children. The woman wore a stretch two-piece swimsuit and spoke with a New England accent. Her toenails were colored magenta and her nose was buttered with zinc oxide and in one hand she brandished an Arthur Hailey paperback. Twilly howled and resumed pummeling the beach. The woman glowered over the rims of her sunglasses. "Young man," she said, "where is your mother?"

Whereupon Twilly whirled and chomped down on her bare foot and didn't let go until a beefy hotel security man came and pried him off. Little Phil arrived later that day with lawyers and a checkbook. On the trip home Twilly had nothing to say to his father. At bedtime Amy Spree went to her son's room and found him mounting a gaily painted human toenail in his seashell display. The next morning she took him to a psychologist for the first time. Twilly was given a battery of tests, none of which pointed toward violent sociopathy. Though Amy Spree was relieved, her husband remained skeptical. "The boy's not right," he would say. Or: "The boy's not all there." Or sometimes: "The boy's playing on the wrong team."

Eventually Twilly tried to talk to his father about Marco Island and other heartaches. He reminded him that Florida for eons had been underwater and was steadily sinking again, the sea and the Gulf rising each year to reclaim the precious shoreline that Little Phil and others were so avidly selling off. So what? Little Phil replied. That's why people got flood insurance. Twilly said, No, Dad, you don't understand. And Little Phil said, Yeah, well, maybe I don't understand geology so good but I understand sales and I understand commissions. And if this goddamn place starts sinking to where I can see it with my own eyes, then me, you and your mother are packin' up and moving to Southern California, where a man can still make a dandy living off oceanfront.

And Twilly said, Forget I even mentioned it.

On the eve of Twilly's eighteenth birthday, Little Phil drove him to a banker's office in Tampa, where it was explained to Twilly that he was about to inherit approximately $5 million from a man he had met only once, Little Phil's father, the late Big Phil. Big Phil Spree made his fortune off copper mines in Montana, and had retired at age sixty to travel the world and play golf. Not long afterward he dropped dead in a sand trap on the sixteenth hole at Spyglass. His will left a third of his money to Little Phil, a third in trust to his only grandchild, Twilly, and a third to the National Rifle Association.

As they walked out of the bank, Little Phil threw an arm around his much taller son and said: "That's a shitload of dough for a young fellow to handle. But I believe I know what your grandfather would have wanted you to do with it."

"Let me guess. Oceanfront?"

"You're a smart one," said Little Phil, beaming.

Twilly shook free. "Mutual funds," he announced.

"What?" Little Phil was aghast.

"Yep."

"Where'd you hear about such nonsense?"

"I read."

"Look around, boy. Hasn't real estate done right by us?" Little Phil rattled off all the fine things in their life, from the swimming pool to the ski boat to the summer time-share in Vermont.

Twilly said: "Blood money."

"Uh?"

"What Grandfather left me is mine, and I'll do what I please with it. That'll be no-load mutuals."

Little Phil grabbed his shoulder. "Lemme see if I understand. I'm offering you a half partnership in a two-hundred-and-twenty-room Ramada at Daytona, *beachside,* but you'd rather stick the cash on that insane roulette wheel otherwise known as the New York Stock Exchange?"

"Yep," said Twilly.

"Well, I always knew you were playing for the wrong team. This ices it," said his father. "Did I mention the motel comes with a liquor license?"

A few months later Little Phil ran off to Santa Monica with a secretary from a title-insurance company. Despite her son's unease in structured settings, Twilly's mother beseeched him to enroll at Florida State University, in the state capital of Tallahassee. There Twilly majored in English for three semesters before dropping out and moving in with a poetry professor, who was finishing a doctorate on T. S. Eliot. She was a dynamic and intelligent woman who took a fervid interest in her new boyfriend, particularly his inheritance. She encouraged him to use the fortune to do good and noble deeds, beginning with the purchase of a snazzy new 280-Z for her garage. Eventually Twilly was spiffed up and presented to the dean of the English department, who proposed the funding of a resident Poet's Chair to be named in honor of Twilly's late grandfather, a man who wouldn't have known W. H. Auden from Dr. Seuss.

Twilly said sure, what the hell, but the gift was never made; not because Twilly welched but because in the interim he was arrested for assault and battery on a state legislator. The man, a Democrat from Sarasota County, had been written up in the news for blocking clean-water reforms while at the same time accepting illicit campaign donations from a cattle ranch that was flushing raw manure into an estuary. Twilly had spotted the legislator in a restaurant and followed him to the rest room. There Twilly shoved him into a stall and lectured him for forty minutes on the immorality of water pollution. In fear the legislator feigned contrition, but Twilly saw through the act. Calmly he unzipped his jeans, pissed prodigiously on the man's Bally loafers and said: "There, that's what your pals on the ranch are doing to Black Drum Bay. How do you like it?"

When a sanitized version of the incident hit the press, the dean of the English department decided it would set a poor precedent to accept grant money from a deranged felon, and broke off contact with Twilly Spree. That was fine with Twilly, for although he enjoyed a good poem, he felt subversion was a worthier cause. It was a view that only hardened as he grew older and met more people like his father.

"Dick says you're the man." Robert Clapley raised his bourbon and gave a nod.

"Dick exaggerates," said Palmer Stoat, well practiced at false modesty.

They were having a late lunch at a walnut-paneled country club in a suburb of Tampa. The governor had set it up.

"Dick's not the only one," Clapley said, "to sing your praises."

"That's very flattering."

"He explained the situation?"

"In a general way," Stoat said. "You need a new bridge."

"Yes, sir. The funding's there, in the Senate bill."

"But you've got a problem in the House."

"I do," Clapley said. "A man named Willie Vasquez-Washington."

Palmer Stoat smiled.

"Have you got any earthly idea," said Clapley, "what he's after?"

"I can find out with a phone call."

"Which will cost me how much?" Clapley asked dryly.

"The call? Nothing. Getting your problem fixed, that'll be a hundred grand. Fifty up front."

"Really. And how much kicks back to your friend Willie?"

Stoat looked surprised. "Not a dime, Bob. May I call you Bob? Willie doesn't need your money, he's got other action—probably some goodies he wants hidden in the budget. We'll work things out, don't worry."

"That's what lobbyists do?"

"Right. That's what you're paying for."

"So the hundred grand. . . ."

"My fee," Stoat said, "and it's a bargain."

"You know, I gave a sweet shitload of money to Dick's campaign. I've never done anything like that before."

"Get used to it, Bob."

Robert Clapley was new to Florida, and new to the land-development business. Palmer Stoat gave him a short course on the politics; most of the cash flying around Tallahassee could be traced to men in Clapley's line of work.

He said, "I tried to reach out to Willie myself."

"Big mistake."

"Well, Mr. Stoat, that's why I'm here. Dick says you're the man." Clapley took out a checkbook and a fountain pen. "I'm curious—is Vasquez-Washington a shine or a spic or what exactly?"

"A little pinch of everything, according to Willie. Calls himself the Rainbow Brother."

"You two get along?" Clapley handed the $50,000 check to Stoat.

"Bob, I get along with everybody. I'm the most likable motherfucker you'll ever meet. Hey, do you hunt?"

"Anything that moves."

"Then I know just the place for you," said Stoat. "They've got every critter known to man."

"How about big cats? I made space for a hide on the wall of my library," Clapley said. "Something spotted would go best with the upholstery. Like maybe a cheetah."

"Name your species, Bob. This place, it's like where Noah parked the ark. They got it all."

Robert Clapley ordered another round of drinks. The waitress brought their rib eyes, and the two men ate in agreeable silence. After a time Clapley said, "I notice you don't ask many questions."

Stoat glanced up from his plate. "I don't *have* many questions." He was chewing as he spoke.

"Don't you want to know what I did before I became a land developer?"

"Not really."

"I was in the import-export business. Electronics."

"Electronics," said Stoat, playing along. Clapley was thirty-five years old and had Yuppie ex-smuggler written all over him. The gold, the deepwater tan, the diamond ear stud, the two-hundred-dollar haircut.

"But everybody said real estate's the smart way to go," Clapley went on, "so a couple years ago I started buying up Toad Island and here we are."

Stoat said, "You're going to lose the 'Toad' part, I hope. Switch to some tropical moth or something."

"A bird. Shearwater. The Shearwater Island Company."

"I like it. Very classy-sounding. And the governor says it's going to be gorgeous. Another Hilton Head, he says."

"It can't lose," said Robert Clapley, "as long as I get my bridge."

"Consider it done, Bob."

"Oh, I will."

Palmer Stoat drained his bourbon and said, "Hey, I finally thought of a question."

Clapley seemed pleased. "Fire away, Mr. Stoat."

"Are you gonna finish that baked potato?"

*　　　*　　　*

That same afternoon, a man named Steven Brinkman was summoned to a cluttered double-wide trailer on Toad Island. Brinkman was a biologist, fresh out of Cornell graduate school, who had been hired as an "environmental specialist" at $41,000 a year by the prestigious engineering firm of Roothaus and Son, designers of highways, bridges, golf communities, office towers, shopping malls, factories and residential subdivisions. Roothaus and Son had been recruited by Robert Clapley to the Shearwater Island project, for which a crucial step was the timely completion of a comprehensive biological survey. Without such a document, the development would be bogged down indefinitely in red tape, at great expense to Clapley.

Brinkman's task was to make a list of species that lived on the small barrier island: plants, insects, birds, amphibians, reptiles and mammals. The job could not be sloppy or hurried, because the government would be doing its own survey, for comparison. Steven Brinkman, in fact, once had been offered a position of staff biologist with the U.S. Army Corps of Engineers, but had chosen the private sector for its higher salaries and broader opportunities for advancement. That was the upside. The downside was having to answer to soulless cretins such as Karl Krimmler, the project supervisor, who would have been rapturous to hear there was no wildlife whatsoever on Toad Island. In nature Krimmler saw neither art nor mystery, only bureaucratic obstacles. A flight of swallowtail butterflies or the chirp of a squirrel could send him into a black funk that lasted for days.

Now Krimmler wedged a phone at one ear and fanned himself with Brinkman's list. Krimmler was an engineer, n'ot a biologist, and he reported directly to Roger Roothaus. It was Roothaus to whom Krimmler was now speaking on the phone.

"Gators?" Krimmler relayed the query to Brinkman.

Brinkman shook his head.

"Bald eagles? *Any* kind of eagles?"

Brinkman said no. Into the phone Krimmler said: "He's sure. No eagles. You want me to read you what he's got? Yeah. No. OK, lemme ask."

To Brinkman then Krimmler explained: "All we're really worried about is endangereds."

"I haven't found any yet."

"You're positive? We don't want any surprises—six months from now, some fucking red-bellied caterpillar turns out to be the last of its race. That we don't need."

Steven Brinkman said: "So far, I haven't found a single endangered species."

To Krimmler this was the happiest of news, and with a satisfied tone he repeated it into the phone. He chuckled at Roothaus's reply, saying, "I know, I know. It's too damn good to be true. But the young man tells me he's sure."

"So far," Brinkman interjected tentatively, "none so far." There was always a chance of the odd burrowing owl or gopher tortoise.

Krimmler glanced up. "Mr. Roothaus wants to know if you've found anything weird. Anything we need to take care of before the eco-pinheads from Fish and Wildlife show up."

Brinkman took a deep breath. It didn't take much to set Krimmler off.

"Well, there's this." The biologist held out his right hand.

Krimmler peered. "The hell is it?" Then, into the phone: "Hold on, Rog."

"It's a toad," Brinkman said.

"Gee, and here I thought it was a baby unicorn. I *know* it's a toad, OK? I know what a goddamn toad looks like. The question is, what kind of goddamn toad, Mr. Brinkman?"

"It's doctor. *Doctor* Brinkman." Some things you couldn't let slide, even at forty-one grand a year.

Krimmler glared. He cupped a hand over the receiver and whispered, "I'm waiting."

"*Bufo quercicus.*"

"Now in English."

"It's an oak toad."

"And?"

"The smallest toad native to North America."

"That I can believe," Krimmler said. "But it's not on the endangered list?"

"No, sir."

"The 'threatened' list?"

"No."

"Any other goddamn lists?"

"None that I'm aware of."

"Then what's the problem?" Into the phone he said, "Hey, Roger, young Dr. Brinkman brought me an adorable baby frog. . . . Well, that's what I'm trying to find out."

Brinkman said, "There's no problem, really, with the oak toads. It's just they're all over the place, by the hundreds. I've never seen so many."

"That would probably explain the name of the island."

"It would," Brinkman said, sheepishly.

The toad in his palm was smaller than a quarter. Its coloration was a mottled gray and brown, with a vertical orange stripe bisecting its back. The toad blinked its shiny eyes and began to squirm. Gently, Brinkman closed his fingers around it.

Krimmler said, "Take your little pal outside before he pees on this fine linoleum. I'll be with you in a second."

Brinkman shut the door behind him. The sun was so bright it made his eyes water. He knelt and placed the diminutive toad on the ground. Immediately it hopped off, into the shade of the trailer.

Five minutes later, Krimmler came down the steps. "Mr.

Roothaus says you're doing a super job. He's a little concerned about those toads, though."

"They're completely harmless," Brinkman said.

"Not necessarily. These days it wouldn't take much to stir up another snail-darter scenario. I mean, if some tree-hugger type really wanted to throw a wrench in this project."

Brinkman said, "I told you, they're not endangered. They don't even take a cute picture."

Krimmler shrugged. "Still and all, we can't be too careful. Where exactly did you find these toads, Dr. Brinkman?"

"All over the island, like I said."

"Uplands or wetlands?"

"Uplands, mostly," said Brinkman.

"Excellent."

"In the flatwood and shrub. There's so many, you'll never catch them all."

"You're absolutely right," Krimmler said. "That's why we're going to bury 'em instead."

4

On the drive to the airport, the man tossed from the Range Rover a styrofoam coffee cup and the cellophane wrapper from a Little Debbie's cinnamon-raisin roll. This happened at eighty miles an hour in breakneck traffic on the interstate, so Twilly was unable to pull over and retrieve the trash. By now he had ditched his dirty black pickup and rented a generic maroon Chevrolet Corsica, of which there were no fewer than half a million on the highways of South Florida during tourist season. Twilly enjoyed feeling inconspicuous behind the wheel; for the sake of appearances, he even spread a road map upside down across his lap. He followed the litterbug all the way to the airport parking garage and, by foot, into the terminal. Twilly shouldn't have been surprised to see the man greeted affectionately at the Delta gate by a top-heavy blond woman with a Gucci overnighter, but Twilly *was* surprised, and a bit pissed off. Why, he didn't know. He drove back to the litterbug's house and waited for the wife/girlfriend to make a move. She came out wearing a short tennis ensemble and carrying not one but three oversized rackets. Twilly watched her slide into a black BMW that her husband/boyfriend must have leased to replace—temporarily, Twilly felt certain—the ruined red one.

After she was gone, Twilly slipped through the hedgerow into the backyard and scoped out the window jambs, which were wired for an alarm. He wasn't concerned. Based on his observations of Litterbug and wife/girlfriend, Twilly had a hunch the alarm wasn't set. And, sure enough, neither of them had remembered to lock the laundry room door, which Twilly nudged open. No sirens, beeps or whistles went off. Twilly stepped inside and listened for a maid or a cook or a nanny. Through a doorway he could see into the kitchen. While there was no sign of movement, Twilly thought he heard breathing.

"Hello?" he called. He had a story ready—county code inspector, checking for hurricane shutters. Saw the door ajar, got worried, et cetera. For the occasion Twilly had worn a thin plain necktie and a white short-sleeved shirt.

"Hello!" he said again, louder.

An enormous jet-black dog trotted around the corner and clamped onto his right calf. It was a Labrador retriever, the largest Twilly had ever seen, with a face as broad as a bear's. Twilly was annoyed with himself for failing to anticipate an oversized house pet, because it fit Litterbug's profile.

He remained motionless and unflinching in the dog's grip. "Bad dog," he said, vainly hoping the animal would be intimidated by his composure. "No!" was Twilly's next try. "Bad boy! Bad boy!" Never before had he been attacked by a dog that didn't growl or even snarl. He took the Labrador by its silky ears. "You made your point. Now let go!"

The dog glanced up with no discernible hostility. Twilly expected to feel more pain, but the Lab actually wasn't biting down very hard; instead it held on with an impassive stubbornness, as if Twilly's hide were a favored old sock.

I haven't got time for games, Twilly thought. Bending over the dog, he locked both arms around its barrel-sized midsection and hoisted it clear off the tile. He suspended the dog in an upside-down hug—its ears slack, hind legs straight in the air—until it let go. When he put the dog down, it seemed more dizzy than enraged. Twilly stroked the crown of its head. Immediately the Lab thumped its tail and rolled over. In the refrigerator Twilly found some cold cuts, which he placed on a platter on the kitchen floor.

Then he went prowling through the house. From a stack of unopened mail in the front hall he determined that the litterbug's name was Palmer Stoat, and that the woman was his wife, Desirata. Twilly moved to the master bedroom, to get a better sense of the relationship. The Stoats had a four-poster bed with a frilly gossamer canopy, which Twilly found excessive. On one nightstand were a novel by Anne Tyler and a stack of magazines: *Town & Country, Gourmet, Vanity Fair* and *Spin*. Twilly concluded that this was Mrs. Stoat's side of the bed. In the top drawer of the nightstand were a half-smoked joint, a tube of Vaseline, a pack of plastic hair clips, and a squeeze bottle of expensive skin moisturizer. On the other nightstand Twilly saw no reading material of any type, a fact that jibed with his impressions of the litterbug. Neatly arranged inside the drawer were a battery-operated nose-hair clipper, a loaded .38-caliber revolver, a Polaroid camera and a stack of snapshots that appeared to have been taken by Palmer Stoat while he was having sex with his wife. Twilly found it significant that in all the photographs Stoat had one-handedly aimed the lens at his own naked body, and that the most to be seen of the wife was an upraised knee or the pale hemisphere of a buttock or a tangle of auburn hair.

From the bedroom Twilly went to the den, a tabernacle of

dead wildlife. The longest wall had been set aside for stuffed animal heads: a Cape buffalo, a bighorn sheep, a mule deer, a bull elk, a timber wolf and a Canadian lynx. Another wall had been dedicated to mounted game fish: a tarpon, a striped marlin, a peacock bass, a cobia and a bonefish scarcely bigger than a banana. Centered on the oak floor was the maned hide of an African lion—utterly pathetic, to Twilly's eye, the whole white-hunter motif.

He placed himself at Stoat's desk, which was strikingly uncluttered. Two photographs stood in identical silver frames; one on the left side, the other on the right side. One picture was of Desirata, waving from the bow of a sailboat. She wore an electric pink swimsuit and her face looked sunburned. The water in the background was too bright and clear to be in Florida; Twilly guessed it was the Bahamas or someplace down in the Caribbean. The other picture on the desk was of the big Labrador retriever in a droopy red Santa cap. The dog's forbearing expression made Twilly laugh out loud.

He listened to Stoat's telephone messages on the answering machine, and jotted some notes. Then he got up to inspect a third wall of the den, a burnished floor-to-ceiling bookcase that was, predictably, devoid of books. Twilly found three thin volumes of golfing wisdom, and a glossy coffee-table opus commemorating the first and last World Series championship of the Florida Marlins baseball franchise. That was it—Palmer Stoat's whole library; not even the obligatory leather-bound set of Faulkner or Steinbeck for decoration. Exquisite tropical mahogany had been used to craft the bookshelves, which Stoat had filled with, of all things, cigar boxes—empty cigar boxes, presumably displayed in a way that would impress other smokers. Montecristo #1, Cohiba, Empress of Cuba Robusto, Don Mateo, Partagas, Licenciados, H. Upmann, Bauzá—Twilly knew nothing about the pedigree of tobacco products, but he realized that for Stoat the empty boxes were trophies, like the stuffed animal heads. Prominently displayed on its own shelf was more proof of the man's fixation: a framed mock cover of *Cigar Aficionado* magazine featuring a nine-by-twelve photograph of Stoat wearing a white tuxedo and puffing a large potent-looking stogie. The dummy caption said "Man of the Year."

Twilly heard a noise at the door and spun around—the Labrador, done with his snack. Twilly said, "Hey, bruiser, come here." The dog gazed around the den at the dead fish and dead mammals, then walked off. Twilly sympathized. A rolling library ladder provided convenient access to the taxidermy. Twilly glided from one mount to the next, using his pocketknife to pry out the glass eyeballs, which he arranged with pupils skyward in a perfect pentagram on Palmer Stoat's desk blotter.

"What is it you want, Willie?"

Palmer Stoat had waited until they reached the back nine before bracing the cagey vice chairman of the House Appropriations Committee.

And Representative Willie Vasquez-Washington replied: "What kind of fool question is that?" He was looking at a four-footer for a double bogey. "Makes you think I want something?"

Stoat shrugged. "Take your time, Willie. I'm on the clock." But he was thinking how he'd undercharged Robert Clapley for the job, because one hundred grand was seeming more and more like a dirt-cheap fee for spending a whole wretched day on the golf course with Willie Vasquez-Washington.

Who, after missing his putt, now asked Palmer Stoat: "Is this about that damn bridge?"

Stoat turned away and rolled his eyes.

"What's the name of that island again?"

"What's the fucking difference, Willie?"

"The governor told me but I forgot."

They rode the cart to the eleventh tee. Stoat hit first, slicing his drive deep into the pines. Willie Vasquez-Washington sculled his shot fifty yards down the right side of the fairway.

What is it you want?

Sometimes Stoat was too direct, Willie thought. The question had sounded so common and venal, the way it came out.

"It's not about wanting, Palmer, it's about needing. There's a neighborhood in my district that needs a community center. A nice auditorium, you know. Day-care facilities. A decent gym for midnight basketball."

"How much?" Stoat asked.

"Nine million, give or take. It was all there in the House version," said Willie Vasquez-Washington, "but for some reason the funding got nuked in the Senate. I think it was those Panhandle Crackers again."

Stoat said, "A community center is a fine idea. Something for the kids."

"Exactly. Something for the kids."

And also something for Willie's wife, who would be appointed executive director of the center at an annual salary of $49,500, plus major-medical and the use of a station wagon. And another something for Willie's best friend, who owned the company that would get the $200,000 drywalling contract for the new building. And another something for the husband of Willie's campaign manager, whose company would be supplying twenty-four-hour security guards for the center. And, last but not least, something for Willie's deadbeat younger brother, who happened to own a bankrupt grocery store on the southwest corner of the proposed site for the community center, a grocery store that would need to be condemned and purchased by the state, for at least five or six times what Willie's brother had paid for it.

None of this would be laid out explicitly for Palmer Stoat, because it wasn't necessary. He didn't need or want the sticky details. He assumed that somebody near and dear to Willie Vasquez-Washington stood to profit from the construction of a new $9 million community center, and he would have been flabbergasted to learn otherwise. Pork was the essential nutrient of politics. Somebody *always* made money, even from the most noble-sounding of tax-supported endeavors. Willie Vasquez-Washington and his pals would get their new community center, and the governor and his pals would get their new bridge to Shearwater Island. A slam dunk, Palmer Stoat believed. He would arrange for Willie's project to be inserted into the next draft of the Senate budget, and from there it would easily pass out of conference committee and go to the governor's desk. And, his private concern for the Shearwater development notwithstanding, Governor Dick Artemus would never in a million years veto the funding for a community center in a poor minority neighborhood, particularly when the elected representative from that district could claim—as Willie Vasquez-Washington had at various times—to be part Afro-American, part Hispanic, part Haitian, part Chinese, and even part Miccosukee. Nobody ever pressed Willie for documentation of his richly textured heritage. Nobody wanted to be the one to ask.

"I'll fix everything tomorrow," Stoat assured Willie Vasquez-Washington. "Listen, I'm kind of late for a meeting at the capitol."

"What're you talkin' about, 'late'? We got eight holes to play." Willie was gesticulating with a three iron. "You can't quit in the middle of a fairway. Specially when I'm down twenty-six bucks!"

"Keep the money, Willie, and the cart, too. I'll walk back." Stoat hung his golf bag over one shoulder and took a beer from the cooler. He gave a genial but firm wave to the vice chairman of the House Appropriations Committee, then began the trudge to the clubhouse.

"Hey, Palmer! One more thing!" Willie Vasquez-Washington called out.

Stoat turned and cupped a hand to his ear. Willie motioned him closer. Stoat cursed sharply under his breath and walked back.

"It's about the name," said Willie, dropping his voice.

"What about it?"

"Didn't you see the name? In the House budget item."

Palmer Stoat said, "I don't read the House budget word for word, Willie. I don't read the Miami phone book word for word, either. So help me out here, OK?"

"The name should be the same in the Senate version. That's all I'm saying."

Stoat had an urge to snatch Willie's three iron and wrap it around his blotched sweaty neck. "What name," he said thinly, "would you like me to put in the Senate bill?"

"The Willie Vasquez-Washington Community Outreach Center."

"Done," said Stoat. Once again he turned for the clubhouse.

"Shouldn't you maybe write it down?"

"No, I'll remember." Stoat thinking: Community *Outreach* Center? Willie's not reaching out, he's just reaching.

"Hey, Palmer, what about your new bridge?"

"I'll fax you the draft language. And it's not *my* bridge." Stoat was moving away briskly now; long purposeful strides.

"What I meant, is it gonna be named after somebody in particular?" Willie called after him. "You want, I could name it after the governor. Or maybe even you!"

"No thanks!" Palmer Stoat shouted pleasantly, but he kept his back to the man and continued walking. "Maggot," he grumbled. "Another greedy little maggot on the make."

*　　*　　*

The human population of Toad Island was 217 and in decline. Repeated efforts had been made to develop the place, and many of its remaining inhabitants were casualties of those doomed enterprises. The unofficial mayor was Nils Fishback, former landscape architect of an ambitious project that had promised three high-rise beachfront condominiums, a total of 660 units, called the Towers of Tarpon Island. (Everyone who sought to develop Toad Island renamed it as the first order of business. In addition to Tarpon Island, it had been incorporated fleetingly as Snook Island, Dolphin Island, Blue Heron Island, White Heron Island, Little Spoonbill Island, Big Spoonbill Island, Sandpiper Key, Sandpiper Cay, Sandpiper Isle and Sandpiper Shoals. The circumstances of failure varied from one busted scheme to the next, but a cheerlessly detailed history was available for scrutiny in the bankruptcy files of the federal courthouse at Gainesville.)

Resistance to the latest Toad Island makeover came from a small core of embittered landholders masquerading as environmentalists. In protest they had begun circulating an impassioned, Thoreau-quoting petition, the true purpose of which was not to protect pristine shores from despoliation but to extort more money from the builders. Among the private-property owners it was strongly felt that Robert Clapley was being stingy about buying them out, and that he could easily afford to overpay for their property, just as previous developers had overpaid previous Toad Island inhabitants. The petition strategy had worked well before, stirring up legitimate conservation organizations and luring big-city editorial writers and columnists to Toad Island's cause. Lacerated by headlines, the developers usually caved in and doubled their offers. There was no reason to believe Clapley wouldn't do the same, to expedite groundbreaking on his luxury resort community.

Fame and seniority handed Nils Fishback the lead role in the anti–Shearwater Island petition drive. He'd bought thirty-three lots there, having invested his life savings—unwisely, it had turned out—during the euphoric first gush of hype for what was then Tarpon Island. It had been Fishback's fantasy to escape Miami and retire to a placid Gulf Coast paradise, surrounded by water. He planned to keep four of the most scenic lots and, using his landscaping earnings from the high-rise project, build a grand plantation-style estate house for himself and his wife. Unfortunately for the Fishbacks, the Towers of Tarpon Island went belly-up shortly after the first slab was poured, due to the unexpected incarceration of its principal backers, two young gentlemen cousins from Barranquilla. At that point, Fishback had decorated only the sixty-by-sixty-foot parcel upon which the Towers of Tarpon Island sales kiosk had been assembled— an admittedly modest landscaping chore, but one for which Nils Fishback nonetheless expected compensation. He was not paid, nor were any of the other subcontractors. Worse: After eight years and three more failed Toad Island ventures, Fishback remained stuck with seventeen barren lots of the original thirty-three. His dream home had never advanced beyond blueprints; Fishback lived alone in the abandoned Tarpon Island sales hut, one of the few company assets in which the U.S. Drug Enforcement Administration showed no interest.

Fishback's wife long ago had given up hope and bolted for the mainland, leaving him with an unhealthy amount of solitude and free time. He went through a stretch of hard drinking, during which he regularly neglected to shave, bathe, floss or change clothes. He commonly passed out for days on the beach, and his skin became as brown and crinkled as a walnut. One morning, while drunkenly urinating off the old wooden bridge, Nils Fishback was approached by an impressionable young feature writer for a St. Petersburg newspaper. The following week, a long story appeared under a headline christening him "The Mayor of Toad Island." Although Fishback could not recall giving the interview, or any of the wild lies he told, he embraced his colorful new title with zest. He grew out his beard and bleached it snowy white, and took to going shirtless and barefoot and sporting bright bandannas. Deftly, Fishback re-created himself as a crusty and reclusive defender of Nature who had settled on the island purely for its grandeur, not to make a real estate killing. He happily posed for photographers, pretending to smooch one of the tiny striped oak toads that had given the place its name. Fishback was always good for a wistful quote or bittersweet adage about the demise of old Florida. For that reason he had been sought out over the years by the *Washington Post, Newsweek,* CNBC and the Turner networks, not to mention local media outlets. In this manner, he had evolved into a regional celebrity eccentric.

In truth, Nils Fishback didn't give a damn what happened to Toad Island or the squirmy creatures that lived there. The most breathtakingly beautiful sight he could imagine in all God's kingdom would be a cashier's check from Robert Clapley's company for the sum of $510,000, which was Fishback's preposterous asking price for his seventeen orphan lots. He would, of course, ecstatically accept half as much and be gone from Toad Island before sunset. He feigned horror when Clapley's crew started bulldozing the toad habitat, but Nils Fishback was secretly delighted. He had never been fond of the toads, especially during mating season when their high-pitched stridulations rang all night long in his skull. Second, and more important, Clapley's mechanized assault on the petite amphibians was potent public-relations ammunition for the petition drive—the man was a monster, was he not? Smushing innocent creatures by the thousands. Fishback kept a Rolodex of media contacts, for precisely such occasions. He would personally lead the TV crews across the old bridge and down the beach road to the site of the massacre, and show them where to set up their cameras. The

Shearwater Island Company couldn't afford such gruesome publicity! Nils Fishback would warn Robert Clapley an hour or so in advance, giving him just enough time to call the bank and get a check cut for the escrow deposit on Fishback's property.

The only question in Fishback's mind was when to pick up the phone. If he waited too long, the toad massacre would be over and there'd be nothing left for the TV people to film. On the other hand, if he intervened too swiftly, the toad infestation would remain substantially undiminished, with the spring breeding season only weeks away.

Fishback stood up and dusted off the seat of his tattered cut-offs. He jerked two beers from the cooler; one he opened, the other he tucked under an arm. Then he ambled down the hill into the trees, where one of the big yellow bulldozers was being refueled. Fishback handed the unopened beer to the driver and said, "How long you boys gonna be at it?"

The driver grunted. "Years, pop. Get used to it."

"No," Fishback said, "I mean this part here." He waved a hand, as bony and gnarled as driftwood. "Buryin' all these damn toads."

The driver's gaze narrowed. "What're you talkin' about?"

"Check out your boots, jocko. That's toad guts, if I'm not mistaken."

The driver stepped back, wiping his soles across the pine needles. "You're fuckin' nuts," he said to the old man.

Fishback sighed impatiently. "Fine. There's no happy hoppers around here. Not a one. So just tell me how long it'll take."

The bulldozer driver glanced appreciatively at the cold beer in his hand. Hell, he thought, the old fart seems harmless enough. Probably just the racket he cares about.

"One week," the driver said to Fishback. "That's what the work order says."

"Perfect." Fishback pointed into the woods. "There's a fresh-water pond a quarter mile or so down that path. Be a good place to dump some dirt. I mean lotsa dirt."

"Yeah?" The driver sounded interested.

Nils Fishback offered a conspiratorial wink. "Oh yeah," he said. "We're talking Toad Central, partner."

5

In the week that followed, a conference committee of the Florida Legislature agreed to appropriate $9.2 million for a neighborhood development project in southwest Miami called the Willie Vasquez-Washington Community Outreach Center. The same committee approved $27.7 million in transportation funds toward the design and construction of an elevated four-lane concrete bridge to replace the creaky two-lane wooden span that connected Toad Island to the mainland. Governor Dick Artemus declared his strong support for both projects, and praised lawmakers for their "bipartisan commitment to progress."

A few days later, as the last of the oak toads were being plowed under, Nils Fishback and twenty-two other signatories of the anti–Shearwater Island petition met with Robert Clapley and his attorneys in a private dining salon at a fashionable Cuban restaurant in Ybor City. A deal was reached in which Clapley would purchase Fishback's seventeen vacant lots for

$19,000 each, which was $16,500 more than Fishback origi-
nally had paid for them. The other Toad Island "protesters" received, and eagerly accepted, comparable offers. They were
flown home on a Gulfstream jet, and the next morning Nils
Fishback called a press conference at the foot of the old wooden
bridge. With a handful of local reporters present, "the mayor"
announced he was terminating the petition drive because the
Shearwater Island Company had "caved in to virtually all our
demands." Wielding a sheath of legal-sized papers, Fishback revealed that Robert Clapley had promised in writing to preserve
the natural character of the barrier island, and had agreed to
provide on-site biologists, botanists and hydrologists to super-
vise all phases of construction. In addition, Clapley had en-
dorsed an ambitious mitigation program that required
replanting three acres of new trees for each acre sacrificed to development. What Nils Fishback didn't tell the press was that
Clapley legally was not compelled to revegetate Toad Island itself, and that the new trees could be put anywhere else in
Florida—including faraway Putnam County, where Clapley
happened to own nine hundred acres of fresh-cut timberland
that needed replanting.

The architect of the mitigation scam was none other than
Palmer Stoat, who'd had a very productive week. The governor's
cronies would be getting their new bridge, Willie Vasquez-
Washington would be getting his new community center, and
that impertinent tollbooth clerk in Yeehaw Junction would be
getting a pink slip. Palmer Stoat flew home from Tallahassee and
drove directly to Swain's, his favorite local cigar bar, to celebrate.
Here he felt vigorous and important among the ruddy young
lawyers and money managers and gallery owners and former pro
athletes. Stoat enjoyed watching them instruct their new girlfriends how to clip the nub oh-so-carefully off a bootleg Boli-
var—the Yuppie foreplay of the nineties. Stoat resented that his

wife wouldn't set foot in Swain's, because she would've looked spectacular sitting there, scissor-legged and preening in one of her tight black cocktail dresses. But Desie claimed to be nauseated by cigars. She nagged him mercilessly for smoking in the house—a vile and toxic habit, she called it. Yet she'd fire up a doobie every time they made love—and did Palmer complain? No, ma'am. Whatever gets you past the night, he'd say cheerfully. And then Desie would say, Just for once shut up, wouldya? And that's the only way she'd do it, with him completely silent in the saddle. The Polaroid routine she'd tolerate, but the moment Palmer blurted a single word, the sex was over. That was Desie's ironclad rule. So he had learned to keep his mouth shut for fifteen or twenty minutes in the bedroom, maybe twice a week. Palmer could handle that. Hell, they were all a little crazy, right? And besides, there were others—the ones up at the capitol, especially—who'd let him talk all he wanted, from start to finish. Like he was calling the Preakness.

The bartender delivered a fresh brandy.

"Where'd this come from?" Stoat asked.

"From the gentleman at the end of the bar."

That was one thing about cigar joints, the customers were all "gentlemen" and "ladies."

"Which one?" said Stoat.

"In the sunglasses."

Young guy in a tropical-print shirt; parrots and palm fronds. Stoat couldn't place the face. Deeply tanned, with long sun-bleached hair and a two-day stubble. Probably an off-duty deck-hand from Bahia Mar or Pier 66, Stoat thought, somebody he'd met on a party yacht.

Stoat raised the brandy and mouthed a thank-you. The boat guy in the sunglasses acknowledged with a wry nod. Stoat turned his attention to an effervescent brunette who wasn't smoking a seven-inch Cuban knockoff so much as fellating it.

And while the woman would hardly be mistaken for a serious cigar connoisseur, her husky giggle indicated an enthusiasm to learn. Stoat was about to introduce himself when the bartender touched his sleeve and passed him a folded cocktail napkin. "The young gentleman in the sunglasses," the bartender said, "he left this for you."

Palmer Stoat opened the note:

Mr. Yee called from Panama City about your "vitamins."
Also, Jorge from Ocean BMW—they'll have another ragtop by
Monday. This time be more careful where you park it!

Stoat's hands were shaky when he put down the napkin. He scanned the bar: no sign of the boat guy. Stoat flipped open his cell phone, dialed the nonlisted number to his den, and punched in the numeric code of his answering machine. The first two messages, recorded on the same morning he'd flown to Tallahassee, were exactly as described in the boat guy's note. Mr. Yee—Durgess's elusive rhino-horn connection—had finally returned Stoat's call. (Without Desie's knowledge, Stoat intended to score some of that magic erection powder; he was scheming some wild recreation for his next business trip.) And the second phone message on the machine was indeed from the BMW salesman, a young go-getter named Jorge Hernandez.

Spooky, Stoat thought. Either the boat guy pirated my phone code or he's been snooping inside my house. Stoat laid a twenty on the bar and raced home. Once inside the front door, he sidestepped the dog and hurried to his den. The room did not appear ransacked, and none of the personal items on his desk had been taken or moved out of place.

Then Palmer Stoat noticed the polished glass eyeballs, arranged in a pentagram star. The geometry was so flawless that it appealed in an occult way to Stoat's obsession with neatness and order. (The inverse manifestation of this fetish was a compulsion to jettison all traces of potential untidiness—every scrap of trash, waste or rubbish—with no regard for the consequences. It's what made Stoat the impenitent litterbug he was.)

So he did not disturb the mystery pentagram. Slowly he raised his face to look at the walls; at the stuffed lynx, the timber wolf, the mule deer, the bighorn ram, the elk, the marlin, the tarpon, the peacock bass. Stoat stared at all of them, but they weren't staring back.

Twilly Spree had a habit of falling in love with any woman who was nice enough to sleep with him. One was named Mae, and she was ten years older. She had straight straw-blond hair, and caramel freckles from her cheeks to her ankles. Her family was wealthy, and she showed an endearing lack of interest in Twilly's inheritance. He likely would have married her, except for the fact she was already married to a businessman in Singapore. Mae filed for divorce three days after meeting Twilly, but the lawyers said it would take years for her to get free, since her spouse avoided the United States and therefore could not be served with papers. Having nothing else to do, Twilly got on a plane and flew to Singapore and met briefly with Mae's husband, who quickly arranged for Twilly to be beaten up, arrested in a brothel and deported. After Twilly was returned to Florida, he said in all innocence to Mae: "What'd you ever see in a creep like that?"

Mae and Twilly lived together five months. She said she wanted him to help her become a free spirit. Twilly had heard the same line from other girlfriends. Without him asking, Mae gave up her bridge league and her Wednesday pedicures and took up the mandolin and bromeliads. Mae's father became concerned and flew down from Sag Harbor to check Twilly out. Mae's father was a retired executive from the Ford Motor Company, and was almost single-handedly responsible for ruining the Mustang. To test Twilly's character, he invited him to a skeet range and placed a 12-gauge Remington in his hands. Twilly knocked down everything they tossed up. Mae's father said, Sure, but can you hunt? He took Twilly to a quail plantation in Alabama, and Twilly shot the first four birds they jumped. Then Twilly set the gun in the grass and said, That's plenty. Mae's father said, What the hell's the matter with you, we're just getting warmed up.

And Twilly said, I can't eat more than four birds so what's the point?

The point, thundered Mae's father, isn't the eating. It's the sport of it!

Is that so? Twilly said.

To shoot something fast and beautiful out of the sky, Mae's father told him. That's the essence of it!

Now I see, said Twilly.

And that evening, as Mae's father's chartered King Air took off from a rural Montgomery airport, somebody hiding in the trees with a semiautomatic rifle neatly stitched an X pattern in one wing, rupturing a fuel bladder and forcing the plane to turn back for an emergency landing. The sniper was never found, but Mae's father went on a minor rampage to the authorities. And while he ultimately failed in his efforts to see Twilly Spree prosecuted, he succeeded in convincing his daughter that she had taken up with a homicidal madman. For a while Twilly missed Mae's company, but he took satisfaction in knowing he'd made his point emphatically with her father, that the man definitely got the connection between his own vanities and the Swiss-cheese holes that appeared in his airplane.

And, really, that was the most Twilly ever hoped for, that the bastards would get the message. Most of them did.

But not the litterbug. Twilly decided he'd been too subtle

with Palmer Stoat; the man needed things spelled out plainly, possibly more than once. For days Twilly tailed him, and wherever Stoat went, he continued to toss garbage out the car window. Twilly was weary of picking up after him.

One afternoon Stoat and his wife returned from a senator's wedding in Jacksonville and found a note under a windshield wiper of the Range Rover. The note said: "Quit trashing the planet, fuckwad." Stoat gave a puzzled shrug and showed Desie. Then he crumpled the note and dropped it on the pavement of the parking garage.

When Stoat sat down in his sport-utility vehicle, he was aghast to find it full of dung beetles. One pullulating mass covered the tops of his shoes, while a second wave advanced up the steering column. Massing on the dashboard was a third platoon, shiny brown shells clacking together like ball bearings.

Despite appearances, dung beetles actually are harmless, providing a unique and invaluable service at the cellar of the food chain; that is, the prodigious consumption of animal waste. Worshiped by ancient Egyptians, the insects are almost as dearly regarded by modern cattle ranchers. In all there are more than seven thousand known species of dung beetles, without which the earth would literally smother in excrement. This true fact would not have been properly appreciated by Palmer Stoat, who couldn't tell a ladybug from a cockroach (which is what he feared had infested his Range Rover). He yelped and slapped at his thighs and burst from the vehicle as if shot from a cannon.

Desie, who had been standing in wait for her husband to unlock the passenger door, observed his athletic exit with high interest. In a flash she produced her cellular phone, but Palmer whisked it from her hand. No cops! he exclaimed. I don't want to read about this in the newspapers. Desie wondered what made him think such nonsense would rate press attention.

On his own phone Palmer Stoat summoned an exterminator,

who used a canister-styled vacuum to remove the bugs from the Range Rover—a total approaching three thousand, had anyone endeavored to count them. To Desie, they sounded like pebbles being sucked through the hose. After consulting an illustrated field guide, the exterminator correctly identified the intruders.

"A what?" Desie asked.

"Dung beetle. A common bovine dung beetle."

"Let me guess," Desie said dryly, "how they get their name."

"Yes, it's true," the exterminator acknowledged.

Stoat scowled. "What're you saying? You saying they eat *shit*?" And still he missed the whole damn point.

The very next afternoon, on his way to the driving range, Stoat tossed a Kentucky Fried Chicken box. At the time, he was stopped for the drawbridge on the Seventeenth Street Causeway in Fort Lauderdale. Stoat casually leaned across the front seat and heaved the chicken box through the passenger window and over the bridge railing. Waiting three cars back in traffic, Twilly Spree watched the whole thing; saw the cardboard box and fluttering napkin and gnawed-on drumsticks and coleslaw cup tumble downward, plopping into the Intracoastal Waterway. That's when Twilly realized that Palmer Stoat was either unfathomably arrogant or unfathomably dim, and in either case was in need of special instruction.

On the morning of May 2, the maid walked into the bedroom and announced that Boodle, the dog, was missing.

"Oh, that's not possible," said Stoat.

Desie pulled on some clothes and tennis shoes and hurried out to search the neighborhood. She was sobbing when she returned, and said to her husband: "This is all your fault."

He tried to hug her but she shook him off. "Honey, please," he said. "Settle down."

"Somebody took him—"

"You don't know that."

"—and it's all your fault."

"Desie, now."

It *was* his fault that she was so jittery. In retrospect, he shouldn't have shown her what had been done to the trophy heads in the den. Yet at the time Stoat was half-wondering if the furtive vandal might be Desie herself; maybe she'd gone postal on him. She definitely was no fan of his big-game hobby—he remembered the grief she'd given him about the rhinoceros kill. And, in truth, it wasn't difficult to envision his wife perched on the library ladder and using one of the sterling lobster forks—a wedding gift from the pari-mutuel industry—to meticulously remove the simulated eyeballs from his hunting trophies.

But Desie couldn't have been the one who had done it. Palmer Stoat knew by her reaction to the macabre pentagram on the desk and the wall of eyeless animal faces. Desie had paled and run from the room. Later she implored her husband to hire some security guards to watch the house; she didn't feel safe there anymore. Stoat said, Don't worry, it's just some local weirdos. Kids from the neighborhood breaking in for kicks, he told her. But privately he suspected that both the glass eyeball episode and the desecration of the BMW were connected to his lobbying business; some disgruntled, semi-twisted shithead of a client . . . or possibly even a jealous competitor. So Stoat had the locks on the house changed, got all new phone numbers, and found an electronics dweeb who came through and swept the place for listening devices. For good measure, he also polygraphed the maid, the gardener and the part-time cook. Desie made her husband promise to set the alarm system every night from then on, and he had done so faithfully. . . .

With the exception of the previous night, when he'd gone to a Republican fund-raiser and gotten so plastered that a cab had to carry him home. The time was 3:00 a.m., an hour at which Stoat could barely identify his own house, much less fit the new key in the door; typing a nonsequential five-digit code on the alarm panel required infinitely too much dexterity.

Still, he couldn't believe somebody had snuck in behind him and grabbed the Labrador. For one thing, Boodle was a hefty load—128 pounds. He had been trained at no small expense to sit, fetch, shake, lie down, heel, and not lope off with strangers. To forcibly abduct the dog, Stoat surmised, would have required more than one able-bodied man.

Then Desie reminded him that Boodle wasn't functioning at full strength. Days earlier he had been rushed into emergency surgery after slurping five of the glass eyeballs from Stoat's desktop. Stoat didn't notice the eyes were missing until the taxidermy man came to repair the mounts. Soon afterward Boodle grew listless and stopped eating. An X ray at the veterinarian's office revealed the glass orbs, lodged in a cluster at the anterior end of the Lab's stomach. Four of them were removed easily during a laparotomy, but the fifth squirted into the intestinal tract, out of the surgeon's reach. Another operation would be needed if Boodle didn't pass the lost eyeball soon. In the meantime the dog remained lethargic, loaded up on heavy antibiotics.

"He's gonna die if we don't get him back," Desie said morosely.

"We'll find him, don't worry." Stoat promised to print up flyers and pass them around the neighborhood.

"And offer a reward," Desie said.

"Of course."

"I mean a *decent* reward, Palmer."

"He'll be fine, sweetie. The maid probably didn't shut the door tight and he just nosed his way out. He's done that before, remember? And he'll be back when he's feeling better and gets hungry, that's my prediction."

Desie said, "Thank you, Dr. Doolittle." She was still annoyed because Palmer had asked the veterinarian to return the glass eyes Boodle had swallowed, so that they could be polished and re-glued into the dead animal heads.

"For God's sake, get some new ones," Desie had beseeched her husband.

"Hell no," he'd said. "This way'll make a better story, you gotta admit."

Of the surgically retrieved eyeballs, one each belonged to the Canadian lynx, the striped marlin, the elk and the mule deer. The still-missing orb had come from the Cape buffalo, Stoat's largest trophy head, so he was especially eager to get it back.

Her own eyes glistening, Desie stalked up to her husband and said: "If that poor dog dies somewhere out there, I'll never forgive you."

"I'm telling you, nobody stole Boodle—"

"Doesn't matter, Palmer. It's your dumb hobby, your dumb dead animals with their dumb fake eyeballs. So it's your damn fault if something happens to that sweet puppy."

As soon as Desie had left the den, Stoat phoned a commercial printer and ordered five hundred flyers bearing a photograph of Boodle, and an offer of $10,000 cash to anyone with information leading to his recovery. Stoat wasn't worried, because he was reasonably sure that none of his enemies, no matter how callous, would go so far as to snatch his pet dog.

The world is a sick place, Stoat thought, but not *that* sick.

Twilly Spree had followed the litterbug's taxi from the party to the house. He parked at the end of the block and watched Palmer Stoat stagger up the driveway. By the time Stoat had inserted the key, Twilly was waiting thirty feet away, behind the trunk of a Malaysian palm. Not only did Stoat neglect to lock the front door behind him, he didn't even shut it halfway. He was still in the hall bathroom, fumbling with his zipper and teetering in front of the toilet, when Twilly walked into the house and removed the dog.

With the Labrador slung fireman-style across his shoulders, Twilly jogged all the way back to the car. The dog didn't try to bite him, and never once even barked. That was encouraging; the big guy was getting the right vibrations. The smart ones'll do that, Twilly thought.

Even after they got to the motel, the Lab stayed quiet. He drank some cold water from the bathtub faucet but ignored a perfectly scrumptious rawhide chew toy.

"What's the matter, sport?" Twilly asked. It was true he often spoke to animals. He didn't see why not. Even the bobcat with which he'd shared a tent in the swamp. *Don't bite me, you little bastard* is what Twilly had advised.

The dog settled in at his feet. Twilly patted its glossy rump and said, "Everything's going to be all right, buddy." He couldn't bring himself to address the animal by the name on its tag—Boodle. It was a quaint synonym for *bribe,* Palmer Stoat at his wittiest.

"From now on," Twilly said to the dog, "you're McGuinn."

The Lab raised its head, which seemed as wide as an anvil.

"After a great guitar player," Twilly explained. The dog uncurled and stretched out on his side. That's when Twilly noticed the tape and bandage. He knelt beside the dog and gingerly peeled the dressing from a shaved patch of belly. Beneath the gauze was a fresh surgical incision, in which Twilly counted twelve steel staples. He pressed the tape back in place and lightly stroked the dog's ribs. It let out one of those heavy sighs that Labs do, but didn't appear to be in pain.

Twilly worried about the wound, wondered what could have gone haywire on such a strapping critter—the gallbladder? Do dogs even *have* gallbladders? I know they get arthritis and heart disease and autoimmune disorders and cancers—for sure, they get cancer. All this was going through Twilly's mind; a juicer commercial on the television and Twilly hunched with his elbows on his knees, on the corner of the bed, with McGuinn snoozing on the burnt-orange shag.

That dog, it had the softest breathing for an animal that size. Twilly had to bend close to hear it, the breathing like a baby's in a crib.

And Twilly thinking: This poor fella's probably on some heavy-duty dope to get past the surgery. That would explain why he'd come along so meekly. And the longer Twilly thought about it, the more certain he became about what to do next: Return to Palmer Stoat's house and find the dog's medicine. Risky—insanely risky—but Twilly had no choice. He wanted nothing bad to happen to McGuinn, who was an innocent.

Master Palmer, though, was something else.

He got fooled. He went back the next night, arriving at the same moment Stoat was driving away, the silhouette of a woman visible beside him in the Range Rover. Twilly assumed it was the wife, assumed the two of them were going to a late dinner.

But it turned out to be one of the maids riding off with the litterbug; he was giving her a lift home. And so Twilly made a mistake that changed everything.

Ever since his previous incursion, the Stoats had been more scrupulous about setting the house alarm. But Twilly decided to hell with it—he'd bust in and grab the dog's pills and run. He'd be in and out and on the road in a minute flat.

The kitchen door was a breeze; a screwdriver did the job and, surprisingly, no alarm sounded. Twilly flipped on the lights and began searching. The kitchen was spacious, newly refurbished in a desert-Southwest motif with earth-tone cabinets and all-stainless appliances. This is what guys like Palmer Stoat do for their new young wives, Twilly thought; kitchens and jewelry are pretty much the upper reach of their imaginations.

He found the dog's medicines on the counter next to the coffee machine: two small prescription bottles and a tube of ointment, all antibiotics, which Twilly put in his pocket. The Lab's leash hung from a hook near the door, so Twilly grabbed that, too. For the daring raid he awarded himself a cold Sam Adams from the refrigerator. When he turned around, there stood Desirata Stoat with the chrome-plated .38 from the bedroom.

"You're the one who stole our dog," she said.

"That's correct."

"Where is he?"

"Safe and sound."

"I said *where*." She cocked the hammer.

"Shoot me, you'll never see McGuinn again."

"Who?"

"That's his new name."

Twilly told Mrs. Stoat he hadn't known about the dog's surgery—not an apology but an explanation for why he was there. "I came back for his medicine. By the way, what happened to him?"

The litterbug's wife said, "You wouldn't believe it if I told you. Put your hands on top of your head."

"I'm sorry, Mrs. Stoat, but that's not how it goes in real life." Twilly took a minute to polish off the beer. "You recycle?" he asked.

Desie motioned toward a closet. Inside was a plastic crate, where Twilly deposited the empty bottle. Then he turned around and calmly snatched the revolver away from the litterbug's wife. He shook out the bullets and put them in the same pocket as the dog's medicine. The gun he placed in a silverware drawer.

Mrs. Stoat lowered her chin and muttered something inaudible. She wore no shoes and a long white T-shirt and pearl earrings, and that was about it. Her arms were as tanned as her legs.

"You're the sicko who put the bugs in my husband's truck?"

"Beetles. Yes."

"And left those nasty notes? And pulled the eyes out of all the animal heads?"

"Correct." Twilly saw no point in mentioning the attack on her red Beemer.

Desie said, "Those were terrible things to do."

"Pretty childish," Twilly conceded.

"What's the matter with you anyway?"

"Evidently I'm working through some anger. How's Palmer holding up?"

"Just fine. He took the maid home and went over to Swain's for a cocktail."

"Ah, the cigar bar." That had been Twilly Spree's original target for the insect infestation, until he'd hit a technical snag in the ventilation system. Also, he had received conflicting scientific opinions about whether dung beetles would actually eat a cured leaf of Cuban tobacco.

"What's your name?" Desie asked.

Twilly laughed and rolled his eyes.

"OK," she said, "you're kidnapping our dog?"

"Your husband's dog."

"I want to come."

Of course Twilly chuckled. She couldn't be serious.

"I need to know what this is all about," she said, "because I don't believe it's money."

"Please."

"I believe it's about Palmer."

"Nice meeting you, Mrs. Stoat."

"It's Desie." She followed Twilly out to the rental car and

hopped in. He told her to get out but she refused, pulling her knees to her chin and wrapping both arms around her legs.

"I'll scream bloody murder. *Worse* than bloody murder," she warned.

Twilly sat down heavily behind the wheel. What a twist of rancid luck that Stoat's wife would turn out to be a head case. A light flicked on in the house across the street. Desie saw it, too, and Twilly expected her to start hollering.

Instead she said: "Here's the situation. Lately I've been having doubts about everything. I need to get away."

"Take a cruise."

"You don't understand."

"The dog'll be fine. You've got my word."

"I'm talking about Palmer," she said. "Me and Palmer."

Twilly was stumped. He couldn't think of anything else to do but drive.

"I'm not very proud of myself," she was saying, "but I married the man, basically, for security. Which is a nice way of saying I married him for the dough. Maybe I didn't realize that at the time, or maybe I did."

"Desie?"

"What."

"Do I look like Montel Williams?"

"I'm sorry—God, you're right. Listen to me go on."

Twilly found his way to the interstate. He was worried about McGuinn. He wondered how often the dog needed the pills, wondering if it was time for a walk.

"I'll let you see the dog, Mrs. Stoat, just so you know he's all right. Then I'm taking you back home."

"Don't," Desie said. "Please."

"And here's what I want you to tell your husband—"

"There's a cop."

"Yes, I see him."

"You're doing seventy."

"Sixty-six. Now here's what you tell Palmer: 'A dangerous drug-crazed outlaw has kidnapped your beloved pet, and he won't give him back until you do exactly what he says.' Can you handle that?"

Desie stared in a distracted way out the window.

Twilly said: "Are you listening? I want you to tell your husband I'm a violent bipolar sociopathic lunatic. Tell him I'm capable of anything."

"But you're not."

He was tempted to recite a complete list of personal felonies, but he thought it might freak her into jumping from the car. "I blew up my uncle's bank," he volunteered.

"What for?"

"Does it matter? A bombing is a bombing."

Desie said, "You'll have to do better than that. I still don't believe you're nuts."

Twilly sighed. "What do you and Palmer talk about—politics? Television? Repression in Tibet?"

"Shopping." Desie spoke with no trace of shame or irony. "He's got a keen interest in automobiles and fine clothes. Though I suppose that doesn't count for much in your social circle."

"I have no social circle."

"And he also plays a little golf," Desie said, "when he's not hunting."

"You play golf, too?"

"Exactly twice in my life. We're members at Otter Glen."

"How nice for you," Twilly said. "Ever see any otters out there?"

"Nope."

"Ever wonder why?"

"Not really," Desirata Stoat said.

Back in the motel room, McGuinn-Boodle was happy to see her. Twilly tried to play vet but the dog kept spitting out the pills. It turned into quite a comic scene. Finally Desie shooed Twilly aside and took over. She slipped one of the big white tablets under McGuinn's tongue while she massaged his throat. Serenely the Labrador swallowed the pill. When Twilly tried to duplicate Desie's technique, the pill came shooting out at him.

She said, "I'd say that clinches it."

"No, you *cannot* come along."

"But I'm the only one who can give him the medicine. Yesterday he nearly took off Palmer's thumb."

"I'll get the hang of it," Twilly said.

After Desie got the dog to gulp the second pill, she asked Twilly about the new name.

"After a musician I'm fond of. Roger McGuinn."

She said, "You're way too young to be fond of Roger McGuinn."

"You know about him?" Twilly was thrilled.

"Sure. Maestro of the twelve-string. 'Eight Miles High,' 'Mr. Spaceman,' and so on."

"Fantastic!" Twilly said. "And how old are *you*?"

"Old enough." Desie gave him the knowing older-woman smile. She didn't mention her summer stints at Sam Goody's.

Twilly noticed she was stroking McGuinn with one hand and twisting the tail of her T-shirt with the other. Finally she got around to the big question.

"Tell me exactly what you want from my husband."

"I want him to clean up his act."

"Do what?"

"He's a loathsome pig. Everywhere he goes he leaves a trail of litter."

Desie said, "That's it?"

"I want him to get the message, that's all. I want to see shame in his eyes. Beyond that, hell, I don't know." Twilly tugged a thin blanket off the bed and tossed it to her. "Cover up, Desie. I can see your butt."

She said, "You're aiming low, Mr. Spaceman."

"How do you mean?"

"You know who my husband is? You have any idea what he does for a living?"

"No," Twilly said, "but the governor's office was on his answer machine the other night."

"Exactly, there you go—the governor himself. Probably calling about that ridiculous bridge."

"What bridge?" asked Twilly.

Desie got cross-legged on the floor, with the blanket across her lap. "Let me tell you some stories," she said, "about Palmer Stoat."

"No, ma'am, I'm taking you home."

But he didn't.

6

Twilly drove all night with the woman and the dog. They arrived at Toad Island shortly before dawn. Twilly parked on the beach and rolled down the windows.

"What are we doing here?" Desie said.

Twilly closed his eyes. He didn't open them again until he heard gulls piping and felt the sun on his neck. The Gulf was lead gray and slick. In the distance he saw Desie strolling the white ribbon of sand, the hulking black McGuinn at her side; above them were seabirds, carping. Twilly got out and stretched. He shed his clothes and plunged into the chilly water and swam out two hundred yards. From there he had a mariner's perspective of the island, its modest breadth and altitude and scraggled green ripeness, as it might have appeared long ago. Of course Twilly understood the terrible significance of a new bridge. He could almost hear his father's voice, rising giddily at the prospects. That this scrubby shoal had been targeted for development wasn't at all shocking to Twilly. The only genuine surprise was that somebody hadn't fucked it up sooner.

He breaststroked to shore. He stepped into his jeans and sat, dripping, on the hood of the rental car. When Desie returned, she said: "Boodle wanted to jump in and swim. That means he's feeling better."

Twilly gave her a reproachful look.

"McGuinn, I mean," she said. "So, is this what you expected to find?"

"It's nice."

"You think Governor Dick owns this whole island?"

"If not him, then some of his pals."

"How many people," Desie said, "you figure they want to cram out here? All total."

"I don't know. Couple thousand at least."

"That explains why they need a bigger bridge."

"Oh yes. Trucks, bulldozers, backhoes, cement mixers, cranes, gasoline tankers, cars and bingo buses." Twilly blinked up at the clouds. "I'm just guessing, Mrs. Stoat. I'm just going by history."

Desie said, "McGuinn found a man passed out on the beach. He didn't look too good."

"The unconscious seldom do."

"Not a bum. A regular-looking guy."

Twilly said, "I guess you want me to go have a look. Is that the idea?"

He slid off the car and headed down the shore. Desie whistled for the dog, and off they went. The passed-out man was in the same position in which she'd found him—flat on his back, pale hands interlocked in funereal calm across his chest. The man's mouth hung open and he was snorting like a broken diesel. A gleaming stellate dollop of seagull shit decorated his forehead; one eye was nearly swollen shut, and on the same cheek was a nasty sand-crusted laceration. Nearby lay a shoe and an empty vodka bottle.

Tail swishing, McGuinn inspected the passed-out man while Twilly Spree shook him by the shoulder. The man woke up hacking. He whispered "No" when Twilly asked if he needed an ambulance.

When Desie knelt beside him, he said, "I got drunk and fell off a bulldozer."

"That's a good one."

"I wish it weren't true." The man wiped his sleeve across the poop on his forehead. He grimaced when McGuinn wet-nosed the swollen side of his face.

"What's your name?" Desie asked.

"Brinkman." With Twilly's assistance, the man sat up. "Dr. Steven Brinkman," he said.

"What kind of doctor?"

Brinkman finally noticed what Desie was wearing—the long T-shirt and pearl earrings and nothing else—and became visibly flustered. The big Labrador retriever was also making him jumpy, snuffling in his most personal crevices.

"Are you an M.D.?" Desie said.

"Uh, no. What I am—I'm a field biologist."

Twilly stiffened. "What're you doing out here on the island?"

"This is where I work."

"For who?" Twilly demanded. "The Army Corps? Fish and Wildlife?"

Brinkman said, "Not exactly."

Twilly took him by the arm, hauled him to his feet and marched him up a grassy dune. "You and I need to talk."

Dr. Brinkman was not the only one who'd had a rough night. Palmer Stoat had relaxed to sloppy excess at Swain's bar, then

wound up at a small party in the owner's private salon with two
bottles of Dom, a box of H. Upmann's straight off a boat from
Varadero, and a call girl who made Stoat show his voter's card,
because she only did registered Republicans. Stoat was so be-
witched by the woman's ideological fervency that he couldn't
properly concentrate on the sex. Eventually the halting encounter dissolved into a philosophical colloquy that lasted into
the wee hours and left Stoat more exhausted than a routine
night of illicit intercourse. He crept home with a monstrous
headache and collapsed in one of the guest rooms, so as not to
alert Desirata, whom he presumed to be slumbering alone in the
marital bed.

Stoat slept past noon and woke up to a grim hangover and a
silent house. Spears of sunlight slanted harshly through the Bahamas shutters. Stoat buried his face in a pillow and thought
again of the voluble prostitute at Swain's. To meet someone with
genuine political ideals was a rarity in Stoat's line of work; as a
lobbyist he had long ago concluded there was no difference in
how Democrats and Republicans conducted the business of
government. The game stayed the same: It was always about favors and friends, and who controlled the dough. Party labels
were merely a way to keep track of the teams; issues were mostly
smoke and vaudeville. Nobody believed in anything except
hanging on to power, whatever it took. So, at election time,
Palmer Stoat always advised his clients to hedge generously by
donating large sums to all sides. The strategy was as immensely
pragmatic as it was cynical. Stoat himself was registered independent, but he hadn't stepped inside a voting booth in fourteen
years. He couldn't take the concept seriously; he knew too
much.

Yet it was refreshing to hear the call girl go on so earnestly
about the failure of affirmative action and the merit of prayer in
public schools and the dangerous liberal assault on the Second

Amendment. None of those subjects affected Palmer Stoat's life to the point that he'd formed actual opinions, but it was entertaining to meet someone who had, someone with no covert political agenda.

If only he'd been able to screw her, Erika the call girl. Or was it Estelle? Brightly Stoat thought: Now there's a candidate for an evening of fine wine and rhino powder. He reminded himself to reach out once more to the mysterious Mr. Yee in Panama City.

The ring of the telephone cleaved Stoat's cranium like a cutlass, and he lunged for the receiver. The sound of his wife's voice befuddled him. Maybe he was in the wrong house! If so, how had Desie found him?

"I didn't want you to worry," she was saying on the other end.

"Right." Stoat bolted upright and looked around the room, which he was relieved to recognize.

"I can explain," Desie was saying, an odd jittery edge in her tone.

"OK."

"But not right now," she said.

"Fine."

"Aren't you going to ask if I'm all right?"

"Yes, sweetie. I've been, huh, out of my mind wondering where you went."

An unreadable pause on the other end. Then, too sweetly, Desie saying, "Palmer?"

"Yes, hon."

"You didn't even know I was gone, did you?"

"Sure I did. It's just . . . see, I got home late and crashed in one of the guest bedrooms—"

"Sixteen hours."

"—so I wouldn't wake you up."

"Sixteen bloody hours!"

Stoat said, "What?"

"That's how long it's been."

"Christ. Where? Tell me what happened."

"You just got up, didn't you? Unbelievable." Now Desie sounded disgusted. "You were so smashed, you never bothered to check in the bedroom."

"Desie, I'll come get you right now. Tell me where."

But when she told him, he thought she was joking.

"An Amoco station in Bronson? Where the hell's Bronson?"

"Not far from Gainesville," Desie said. "That's where you should send the plane to pick me up."

"Now hold on—"

"It doesn't need to be, like, a jet. I'm sure one of your rich big-shot clients has something they can loan out. Did I mention I was kidnapped?"

Stoat felt bilious and fevered. Bobbling the phone, he sagged back on the pillows.

"It *was* a kidnapping, sort of," Desie was saying. "It's a long freaky story, Palmer."

"OK."

"But I did find Boodle."

"Hey, that's great." Stoat had almost forgotten about the missing dog. "How's the big guy doin'?"

"Fine. But there's a slight problem."

Stoat grunted. "Why am I not surprised."

Desie said, "I'll tell you everything when I see you."

"In Bronson," Stoat said weakly.

"No, Gainesville. Remember?"

"Right. Where I send the private plane."

Once they got some black coffee into Dr. Brinkman, he was able to pull himself together for a short tour of soon-to-be Shearwater Island.

Here's where the yacht harbor will be dredged. There's where the golf courses go. That's being cleared for the airstrip. And, everywhere else: homesites.

"Houses?" Desie asked.

"Very expensive houses," Brinkman said. "But also condominiums and town homes and even some year-round rentals. Duplexes and triplexes."

Twilly pulled off the road into the shade of some pine trees. "What's the tallest building they've got in the plans?" he asked Brinkman.

"Sixteen stories. There'll be one at each end of the island."

"Assholes," Twilly muttered.

Desie remarked on the multitude of peeling, bleached-out signs advertising other past projects. Brinkman said they'd all gone bust.

"But these new fellows have serious capital and serious financing," he added. "This time I think it's a done deal."

"Provided they get their bridge," said Twilly.

"Obviously."

"And your job here," Desie said to the biologist, "is what exactly?"

Brinkman told them about the field survey. "Basically a complete inventory," he explained, "of every living plant, animal and insect species on the island."

"Wow," said Desie.

Twilly snickered contemptuously. "Fuck 'wow.' Dr. Steve, please tell Mrs. Stoat why she shouldn't be so impressed."

"Well, because. . . ." Brinkman looked uncomfortable. "Because it's fairly routine, a survey like this. More bureaucracy than science, if you want the truth. Sure, it makes us appear responsible and concerned, but the purpose isn't to figure out what trees and animals to save. The purpose is to make sure the developers don't run into a snail-darter type of crisis."

Desie looked to Twilly for elaboration.

"Endangered species," he told her. "That would be a show-stopper, am I right, Dr. Steve? Shut down the whole works."

Brinkman nodded emphatically.

"And I'm guessing," Twilly continued, "that you finished your field study this week, and didn't come across anything like a snail darter or a spotted owl on this entire island. Nothing so rare that it would get in the way of the building permits. And I'm also guessing that's why you went out and got plastered last night, because you'd secretly been hoping to come across something, anything, to block this project—even an endangered gnat. Because you're probably a decent human being at heart, and you know exactly what's going to happen out here once these bastards get rolling."

In a voice raw with sadness, Brinkman said, "It's already started."

Then he took them into the upland woods to see what had become of the oak toads. Right away McGuinn started digging.

"Make him stop," Brinkman implored.

Desie hooked the dog to his leash and tugged him along. Twilly Spree walked ahead, kicking at the fresh-churned dirt, following the checkerboard tread marks of a large earth-moving machine. When they reached the area where the bulldozers were parked, Brinkman pointed and said: "That's the one I fell from. I was trying to get the darn thing started."

"What for?" Desie asked.

"I was drunk."

"That, we've established."

"I had a notion to destroy Mr. Clapley's billboard."

Twilly said, "He's the main guy?"

"Mr. Shearwater Island himself," said Brinkman. "Robert Clapley. I've never met the man, but he put up a huge sales sign. You must've seen it when you came across the old bridge. I suppose I was wondering what it might look like, that goddamn billboard, all busted to splinters."

Twilly said, "I could be persuaded to wonder the same thing."

"What about the frogs?" Desie asked. McGuinn was on the prowl again, jerking her around like a puppet.

"Toads." Steven Brinkman made a sweeping notion with one arm. "They buried them."

"Nice," said Twilly.

"Because Clapley's people got it into their heads that they might be a problem later on, when the crews started clearing the island. They were afraid somebody like the Sierra Club would make a stink with the newspapers, because the toads were so small and there were so many. So Clapley's people decided to bulldoze 'em in advance, to play it safe."

Desie was watching Twilly closely. She said: "He's making this up, right?"

"I wish."

She said, "No, it's too awful."

"Well," said Brinkman, "you didn't hear it from me. We never spoke, OK?" He turned his back on them and slowly made his way into the pines. He walked with his head down, pausing every few steps as if he was searching for something.

Twilly said to Desie: "I've seen enough."

"You think he was on the level? I say he's still drunk."

"Turn the dog loose."

"I will not."

He pried the leash from her fist and unclipped it from McGuinn's collar. The Lab bounded to a hillock of freshly turned soil and began digging exuberantly, his shiny black rump waggling high. After a minute or so, Twilly told Desie to call him back. Twilly went over to the place where McGuinn had been digging and, with the toe of a shoe, finished the hole. Then he reached down and picked up a pearly gelatinous clot of mushed toads.

"Come here, Mrs. Stoat."

"No, I don't think so."

"You wanted proof, didn't you?"

But she was already running, McGuinn at her heels.

Later, in the car, Twilly told Desie it was time for her to go home. She wasn't prepared to argue. He dropped her at a gas station in Bronson and gave her two fifties for breakfast and clothes and a cab ride to Gainesville. So she wouldn't be walking around half-naked, Twilly purchased a plastic raincoat from a vending machine. The raincoat was bright yellow and folded into a kit no larger than a pack of Camels. Desie unwrapped it and, without a word, slipped it on.

Twilly walked her to the telephone booth and put a quarter in her right hand. He said, "I'll be on my way now."

"Can't I say good-bye to Bood—I mean, McGuinn?"

"You two already said your good-byes."

"Now, remember the trick I showed you to give him his pills. The roast-beef trick. He's partial to rare."

"We'll manage," Twilly said.

"And keep him out of the water until those stitches are healed."

"Don't worry," he said.

Desie caught her reflection in the cracked glass door of the phone booth. With a frail laugh, she said, "God, I'm a mess. I look like a drowned canary." She was stalling because she couldn't make sense of her feelings; because she didn't want to go home to her wealthy powerful husband. She wanted to stay with the edgy young criminal who had broken into her home and abducted her pet dog. Well, of course she did. Wouldn't any normal, settled, well-adjusted wife feel the same way?

"You're serious about this?" she said to Twilly.

He was incredulous at the question. "You saw what I saw. Hell yes, I'm serious."

"But you'll go to jail."

"That all depends."

Desie said, "I don't even know your name."

Twilly smiled. "Yes, you do. It's printed on the car-rental receipt, the one you swiped out of the glove compartment last night in Fort Pierce."

She reddened. "Oops."

As Twilly turned away, Desie reached for his arm. She said, "Before I go home, I want to be sure. That was no joke back there? They deliberately buried all those harmless little—"

"Yeah, they did."

"God. What kind of people would do something like that?"

"Ask your husband," said Twilly, pulling free.

7

The airplane was a twin-engine Beech. When Desie stepped aboard, the pilot asked, "Where's your friend?"

Desie was flustered; she thought he meant the kidnapper.

"The dog," said the pilot. "Mr. Stoat said you were traveling with a dog."

"He was mistaken. I'm alone."

The plane took off and banked to the west. Desie expected it to turn southbound, but it didn't. Squinting into the sun, she leaned forward and tried to raise her voice above the engines.

"Where are you going?"

"One more stop," the pilot said over his shoulder. "Panama City."

"What for?" Desie asked, but he didn't hear her.

It was a choppy and uncomfortable flight, more than an hour, and Desie was steaming by the time they got there. Palmer should have come up on the plane to pick her up; that's what a husband ought to do when his wife is freed from a kidnapping.

At the least, he should have directed the pilot to bring her straight home, instead of making her sit through a bumpy add-on leg. Desie assumed Palmer was taking advantage of the plane's availability to pick up one of his big-shot cronies, thereby saving a few bucks on a separate charter. She wondered who'd be riding with her on the return trip to Lauderdale, and hoped it wasn't some asshole mayor or senator. Some of Palmer's lobbying clients were tolerable in small doses, but Desie couldn't stand the politicians with whom her husband avidly fraternized. Even Dick Artemus, the undeniably charismatic governor, had managed to repulse Desie with a distasteful ethnic joke within moments of being introduced; Desie had been poised to launch a margarita in his face when Palmer intervened, steering her to a neutral corner.

But no other passenger boarded the Beechcraft in Panama City. The pilot stepped off briefly and returned carrying a Nike shoe box, which he asked Desie to hold during the flight.

"What's inside?" she said.

"I don't know, ma'am, but Mr. Stoat said to take special care with it. He said it's real valuable."

Through the window Desie saw a gray Cadillac parked on the tarmac near the Butler Aviation Terminal. Standing by the driver's side of the car was a middle-aged Asian man in a raspberry-colored golf shirt and shiny brown slacks. The man was counting through a stack of cash, which he placed into a billfold. Once the plane began to taxi, the Asian man glanced up and waved, presumably at the pilot.

Desie waited until they were airborne before opening the shoe box. Inside was an opaque Tupperware container filled with a fine light-colored powder. Desie would have guessed it was cake mix, except for the odd musky smell. She snapped the lid on the container and set it back in the box and began to wonder, irritably, if her husband had gone into the narcotics business.

Palmer Stoat didn't fly to Gainesville to meet Desie because Robert Clapley unexpectedly had phoned to congratulate him for icing the funds to build the new Toad Island bridge. In the course of the conversation Clapley mentioned he was headed to a friend's farm near Lake Okeechobee for some off-road bird shooting, and he'd be delighted if Stoat joined him.

"Oh, and I've got the rest of your money," Clapley added.

Stoat took the interstate to U.S. 27 and sped north toward Clewiston. An hour later he located Clapley, waiting in a field of bare dirt that not so long ago had been a tomato patch. The field had been baited heavily with seeds, and all that remained for the two hunters was to wait for the doves to show up. It wasn't much of a challenge but that was fine with Palmer Stoat, who hadn't yet shaken the bleary bone-ache from his hangover. Clapley set up a roomy canvas shooting blind and broke out a bottle of expensive scotch. With a matching flourish, Stoat produced two large cigars from a pocket of his hunting vest. The men drank and puffed and told pussy-related lies until the birds started arriving. The blind was spacious enough for both men to fire their shotguns simultaneously, and in only two hours they shot forty-one doves, very few of which were actually airborne at the time. The rest of the doves were on the ground, obliviously pecking up birdseed, when they got blasted. The men didn't even need a retriever, since the doves all succumbed within twenty yards of the portable blind, where the bulk of the food had been sprinkled.

At dusk the men quit shooting and removed their earmuffs. Clapley began picking up the small ruffled bodies and dropping them in a camo duffel. Behind him walked the wobbly Stoat, his shotgun propped butt-first across his shoulder.

"How many a these tasty little gumdrops you want?" Clapley asked.

"Not many, Bob. Just enough for me and the wife."

Later, when he got home and began to sober up, Stoat realized that Robert Clapley had forgotten to give him the $50,000 check.

When Desie arrived, Palmer was plucking the birds in the kitchen. He got up to hug her but she ducked out of reach.

He said, "Tell me what happened, sweetie. Are you all right?"

"Like you care."

And so it went for nearly an hour—Stoat apologizing for coming home so bombed the previous night that he'd failed to notice Desie was missing; apologizing for not being on the airplane to meet her in Gainesville; apologizing for not personally picking her up at the Fort Lauderdale airport (although he'd sent a chauffeured Town Car!); apologizing for failing to comment upon her odd attire—baggy sweatpants and an orange mesh University of Florida football jersey, purchased in haste at a campus bookstore; apologizing for not inquiring sooner if the deranged kidnapper had raped her or roughed her up; and, finally, apologizing for stacking dead doves on the kitchen table.

Then Desie said: "Aren't you even going to ask about Boodle?"

So Stoat apologized again, this time for not being properly concerned about the abducted family pet.

"Where is he, hon?"

"The kidnapper's still got him," Desie announced.

"Oh, this is crazy."

"You're not going to like it."

"How much does he want?" Stoat asked.

"He's not after money."

"Then what?"

Desie repeated what the strange young dognapper had instructed her to say. She omitted the fact that she was the one who'd tipped him off to the Shearwater project.

When Stoat heard the kidnapper's demand, he cackled.

"Palmer, the man is *serious.*"

"Really."

"You'd better do what he wants."

"Or what," said Stoat. "He's going to kill my dog? My *dog?*"

"He says he will."

Again Stoat chuckled, and resumed cleaning the birds. "Come on, Des. The sickest bastard in the whole world isn't going to hurt a Labrador retriever. Especially Boodle—everybody falls head over heels for Boodle."

Exhausted though she was, Desie couldn't help but watch as her husband meticulously tugged out the gray feathers one by one and placed them in a soft velvety pile. Naked, the doves looked too scrawny to eat. The breasts were gaunt and the flesh was pocked unattractively with purple-tinged holes from the shotgun pellets.

He said, "Oh, I almost forgot—the package from Panama City?"

"On the porch," Desie said. "What is it, anyway?"

"Stationery."

"In Tupperware?"

"Oh . . . well, yeah," her husband stammered. "Keeps out the humidity. It's good stuff. Embossed."

"Cut the crap, Palmer. It's powder."

"You opened it!"

"Yeah. My husband the smack dealer. No wonder you didn't want it sent by regular mail."

Stoat threw back his head and laughed. "Heroin? Now you think I'm moving heroin! Oh, that's priceless."

"Then what is it?" Desie demanded angrily. "What's in the Tupperware? Tell me, Palmer."

So he did, adding: "But I wanted it to be a surprise."

She stared at him. "Rhino sex powder."

"Hon, they don't always shoot the animals to get the horns. That's a common myth."

"You're unbelievable," Desie said.

"I just thought it might liven things up for you and me. Hey, can it hurt to try?"

Wordlessly she stood up and went to the bedroom.

"Aren't you hungry?" Stoat called hopefully after her. "Marisa's firing up the barbecue."

It took another forty-five minutes to finish with the heads and the skins of the birds. Not wishing to stink up his garbage can with the innards, he wrapped them in butcher paper and carried it across the backyard, through the hedge, to the well-manicured property of his neighbors, the Clarks, where he dumped the whole mess in the goldfish pond. Ned and Susan Clark, Stoat happened to know, were on a gambling cruise to Nassau.

After Stoat returned to the house, he sent the cook home, stored the doves in the refrigerator, stood for a long time under a hot shower and pondered what to do about Desirata. He didn't believe the kidnap story but took it as proof that something was seriously amiss, something was unraveling inside her mind. Maybe she'd run off with some guy on a whim, then changed her mind. Or maybe she'd simply freaked out and bolted. Manic depression, multiple-personality syndrome— Stoat had heard of these illnesses but was unclear about the symptoms. This much was true: Given the hinky events of the past twenty-four hours, he had come to suspect that his own un-happy spouse had conspired in the defacing of his prize taxidermy, the trashing of the red BMW, and even the infesting of his luxury sport-utility vehicle with shit-eating insects.

A cry for help, Palmer Stoat figured. Obviously the kid's got some loose shingles.

But whatever weird was happening within Desie, it was the part of her yarn about the dog that Stoat couldn't sort out. What had she done with poor Boodle, and why?

He toweled off and crawled into bed. He felt her go tense when he slipped an arm around her waist.

"You OK?" he asked.

"Never felt better."

"You smell good."

"Compared to a sack of dead pigeons, I hope so."

"I know you're upset, sweetie. I think we should talk."

"Well, I think we should be calling the police." Desie knew he wouldn't do it, but she was ticked off that he hadn't raised the prospect. What concerned husband wouldn't at least consider notifying the authorities after an intruder breaks into his home and takes off with his wife! So maybe it hadn't been a *real* kidnapping (since it was Desie's idea to go), but Palmer didn't know that.

He said, "Sweetie, we can't possibly get the police involved."

"Why not? You said he'll never hurt the dog, so what've we got to lose?"

"Because it'll be all over the TV and the newspapers, that's why. My clients rely on me to be low-profile and discreet," he explained. "This would be a disaster, Desie. I'd be a laughingstock. 'Dognapper Targets Prominent Lobbyist.' Jesus Hubbard Christ, can you imagine the headlines?"

She squirmed out of his embrace.

Stoat said, "Honestly, how could I show my face in Tallahassee or Washington? A story like that, I'm telling you, it might turn up in a Letterman monologue. Try to understand what that could do to my business."

"Fine," she said curtly.

"Don't worry. We'll get our puppy back."

"Then you'll do what this maniac wants. It's the only way," she said.

With an exaggerated sigh, Palmer rolled on his back. "It's *not* the only way. Trust me."

Desie turned to face him. "Please just do what he says."

"You can't be serious."

She said, "It's just a bridge, Palmer. One lousy bridge to one lousy little island. They'll get by fine without it."

"You don't know what you're talking about. Besides, it's already done. I couldn't stop it even if I wanted to, which I don't."

"Don't lie to me. Not about this."

Stoat sucked in his breath, wondering: What the hell does she mean by *that*?

Desie said what she'd been told to say by the dognapper: "Your buddy Governor Dick—he hasn't signed the budget bill yet, has he? Tell him to veto the money for the bridge."

"OK, that's it." Stoat sat up and reached for the lamp. "Darling, you've obviously lost your goddamned mind."

She closed her eyes but kept her cheek to the pillow. "Otherwise we'll never see the dog again," she said. "The lunatic has already changed his name, Palmer. He calls him McGuinn."

"Yeah. Whatever." What a whacked-out imagination she has, Stoat thought. He'd had no idea.

Desie stiffened beside him. "So you think I'm out of my mind? Isn't that what you just said?"

Palmer bowed his head and gingerly massaged his tender temples. "Look, Des, let's please finish talking about this tomorrow. I'm having a tough day's night."

His wife groaned in exasperation and rolled over.

*　　　*　　　*

Robert Clapley celebrated in his own special style. He returned with his share of the dove kill to the oceanfront condominium his company owned in Palm Beach. There he cooked the birds in a light wine sauce and lovingly served them to Katya and Tish, whom Clapley half-whimsically referred to as Barbie One and Barbie Two. Katya was from Russia; Tish was from the Czech Republic. They were both five ten and weighed approximately 130 pounds. Clapley didn't know their last names, or their true ages, and didn't ask. He had met them six months earlier on South Beach, at an all-night party thrown by a bisexual German real estate tycoon. The women told Clapley they were models and had come to Miami for new career opportunities. Steady fashion work was hard to come by in Eastern Europe, and the pay was lousy compared with that in France or the States. Robert Clapley thought Katya and Tish looked a bit flashy for big-time modeling, but they were plenty attractive enough for him. The fellow who'd thrown the party had taken Clapley aside and confided that it was he who had purchased the transatlantic plane tickets for Katya and Tish, and half a dozen other women who were exceptionally eager to come to America. The man had chosen them from an array of more than one hundred who had appeared on an audition videotape mailed to him by a "talent agency" in Moscow.

"But don't get the wrong idea, Bob. These girls are *not* common prostitutes," the man had assured Clapley.

No, Katya and Tish were not common. Within a week Clapley had installed them in one of his part-time residences, the sixteenth-floor Palm Beach condo, which featured a seven-jet Jacuzzi, a Bose sound system, and a million-dollar view of the Atlantic Ocean from every room. Katya and Tish were in heaven, and demonstrated their gratitude to Clapley with ferocious ardor. Occasionally they would go out to actual modeling tryouts, but for the most part they filled their days with swimming, sunning, shopping and watching American soap operas. When eventually it came time for their visas to expire, Katya and Tish were crestfallen. They appealed to their generous new boyfriend, Bob, who suggested he might be able to fix their immigration problems in exchange for a favor; not a small favor, though.

Robert Clapley had been the youngest of five children, and the only boy. At some point in an otherwise unremarkable childhood, young Bob had developed a somewhat unnatural interest in Barbie dolls, which his sisters collected like marbles. In fact there were so many Barbies and Barbie playhouses and Barbie wardrobes in the Clapley household that Robert's sisters never seemed to notice when one or two of the dolls went missing, and in any case wouldn't have thought to accuse their meek little brother. Robert's attraction to the Barbies was more than a fleeting puerile curiosity; three of the voluptuous eleven-and-a-half-inch icons—Wedding Day Barbie, Cinderella Barbie and Disco Barbie (plus assorted costumes)—covertly accompanied Clapley when he went off to college at age eighteen. Later, running dope twice monthly from Cartagena to South Bimini, Clapley was never without his favorite Live-Action Barbie, zipped snugly into the fur-lined pocket of his leather flight jacket.

What did he so adore about the plastic dolls? Their pneumatic and shapely flawlessness, to be sure. Each Barbie was dependably perfect to the eye and feel. That Clapley's obsession had an eccentric sexual component, there was no doubt, but he would have argued on the side of harmless fantasy over perversion. And indeed he treated the toy Barbies with the utmost veneration and civility, undressing them only long enough to change (or iron) their exquisite miniature outfits. Innocent or not, Robert Clapley knew enough to guard his secret; who would have understood? Clapley himself was vexed by the doll fixation, and as he got older began to doubt he would ever outgrow it—until he met Katya and Tish. Instantaneously the future appeared to Clapley in dual thunderbolts of lust. The statuesque immigrants represented a luminous opportunity for a therapeutic breakthrough; the transcendence of appetites from toy to flesh, from Barbie worship to Barbie carnality. In other words: from boy to man.

So strong was their desire to remain in the United States (and retain twenty-four-hour spa privileges at Robert Clapley's condominium tower), that Katya and Tish weren't completely unreceptive to his ambitiously twisted proposal. Matching the hair was a cinch; the blond hue of Clapley's choosing came in a brand-name bottle. The surgery, however—to begin with identically sized breast implants—was the cause of some trepidation for the two women.

There's absolutely nothing to worry about! Clapley insisted. America has the best doctors in the world!

Ultimately, Katya and Tish were persuaded to go along, cajoled and flattered and spoiled as they were by their enthusiastic young host. And Clapley was enthralled to observe the concurrent transformations, each cosmetic refinement bringing him closer to his dream of living live-in Barbies. No, it wouldn't be long now!

He sat at the head of the dinner table, sipping a chardonnay and beaming as Katya and Tish hungrily hacked at the scorched little bird carcasses. Palmer Stoat seems like a fellow who would appreciate this setup, Clapley thought cheerily. I can't wait to see his face when I introduce him to the girls.

And Stoat, like every man who'd recently met Katya and Tish, undoubtedly would lean over to his host and whisper: Wow, Bob, are those really twins?

And Robert Clapley would smile and answer the way he always did.

No, but they will be soon.

* * *

Vecker Darby's house blew up and burned down while Twilly Spree was asleep. Twilly would notice the photograph in the newspaper two days later, and sleep just as soundly that night. "Justice," he'd mutter to McGuinn, whose chin rested on his knee. "Justice, boy. That's all it is." The dog would sleep fine, too.

They were parked in palmetto scrub off a dirt road near Zolfo Springs when Vecker Darby came into their lives. It was close to midnight. Presumably, Desirata Stoat was home in Fort Lauderdale with her worthless dickhead of a husband, and Twilly found himself thinking about her. He was sitting in the rental car with an empty pizza box on his lap. McGuinn already had downed supper, four heaping cups of premium dry dog food; Desie had strictly instructed Twilly on which brand to purchase. Vet's orders, she'd said. Typically, McGuinn wolfed the whole pile in about fourteen seconds. Afterward Twilly would sneak out the antibiotic pills, each concealed in a square-folded slice of rare roast beef, which McGuinn eagerly inhaled.

Twilly had the radio turned up loud for Derek and the Dominoes, so at first he didn't hear Vecker Darby's flatbed truck. Certainly he didn't see it, as Vecker Darby was driving without headlights. Twilly was drumming his fingertips on the pizza box and wondering if, in retrospect, he'd been too hasty in his decision to ditch Mrs. Stoat in Bronson. Not that she would run to the cops; he had a strong feeling she wouldn't. No, what bothered Twilly was how he sort of missed her. She was good company; plus, she had a lovely laugh. The dog was terrific, a real champ, but he didn't light up the car the way Desie Stoat did.

I wonder if I'll ever see her again, Twilly thought.

When the song ended, he turned off the radio. That's when he heard the truck nearby—specifically, the grinding hydraulics of the flatbed being tilted. McGuinn raised his huge black head and barked. Hush! Twilly whispered. He slipped from the car and circled back through the scrub until he gained a clear view of the truck and what the driver was doing. As the incline of the flatbed steepened, the truck's unbound cargo began sliding off the back—assorted barrels, drums, tanks and cylinders, tumbling one after another down a gentle mossy embankment toward the banks of the Peace River, where Twilly Spree had hoped to spend a soothing, restful night.

The driver, whose name Twilly wouldn't learn until he saw it in the paper, didn't bother to watch his own handiwork. He leaned one hip against the fender and smoked a cigarette and waited until the whole load went down the slope. Then he lowered the flatbed, climbed in the cab and drove the five miles home. Vecker Darby was still in the shower when Twilly hotwired the truck and raced back to the river to retrieve the barrels, drums, tanks and cylinders. Two hours later, when Twilly returned, Vecker Darby was sleeping in his favorite Naugahyde recliner with six empty Coors cans at his feet and the Playboy Channel blaring on the television.

He failed to awaken when one of the bedroom windows was pried open and the screen was cut, and therefore didn't see the broken-off end of a plastic rain gutter being inserted into his house by a stranger clad in Vecker Darby's own canary yellow hazmat moon suit (which Vecker Darby almost never wore but stored faithfully under the seat of his truck, in case of encountering an EPA inspector).

Nor did Vecker Darby awaken during the following ninety minutes, during which approximately 197 gallons of virulent and combustible fluids were funneled from barrels, drums, tanks and cylinders directly into the house. The resulting toxic soup contained the ingredients of xylene, benzyl phythlate, methanol, toluene, ethyl benzene, ethylene oxide and common formaldehyde, any of which would have caused a grave and lasting damage to the Peace River. The risk to an occupied home dwelling was equally dire but would prove far more spectacular, visually.

What finally aroused Vecker Darby from sleep were the caustic fumes. He arose, coughing violently and keenly aware that something was amiss. He fully intended to exit the premises, after first emptying his bloated bladder of beer. Conceivably, he would have survived a brief detour to the bathroom had he not (out of dull, brainless habit) lighted up a Marlboro on the way.

From the stark photograph in the Fort Myers *News Press,* it appeared that Vecker Darby's house had burned all the way to the slab. He had lived alone in what was once a small orange grove, miles out of town, so that no one became aware of the inferno until it was spotted by the pilot of a commercial jetliner. By the time the fire engines arrived, even the victim's flatbed truck had melted to a skeletal husk. The newspaper article identified Vecker Darby as the owner of a private waste-disposal firm, servicing industrial clients from Sarasota to Naples. Farther down the story, it was noted that the late Mr. Darby had once paid a $275 fine for illegally dumping used hypodermics, surgical dressings and other contaminated hospital waste in a public Dumpster behind a Cape Coral kindergarten.

Twilly Spree read the article about Vecker Darby while standing at a pay phone in the Seminole Indian service plaza on the cross-state expressway known as Alligator Alley. Twilly was waiting to call Desie Stoat at the prearranged hour. She picked up on the second ring.

"Twilly?"

It was the first time he'd heard her say his name, and it gave him an odd, though not uneasy, feeling.

"Yeah, it's me," Twilly said. "Can you talk?"

"Just for a minute."

"Did you inform your husband of the threat?"

"I did, yes."

"And?"

"He doesn't believe it," Desie said.

"Doesn't believe what—that I'll assassinate his dog?"

From Desie's end came a perturbed sigh. "Palmer doesn't believe you've got the dog, Twilly. He doesn't believe there was a kidnapping. He doesn't even believe there's a *you*. He thinks I flipped my wig and made up the whole story."

"Don't tell me this."

"We had a terrible fight. He wants me to see a shrink."

Twilly said, "But his dog's missing! What does he say about that?"

"He thinks I sent Boodle to my mother's."

"Jesus, what for?"

"All the way to Georgia."

Twilly said, "You're married to a jackass."

Desie said, "I gotta go."

"I'll call back in two days. Meanwhile, tell your husband to watch for a FedEx delivery."

"Oh no. What're you going to do now?"

"Make him a believer," Twilly said.

Desirata Brock was born in Memphis and raised in Atlanta. Her mother was a pediatrician and her father was a mechanic for Delta Air Lines. Desie attended Georgia State University with the plan of becoming a schoolteacher but was sidetracked in her senior year by her engagement to a professional basketball player named Gorbak Didovlic, who stood a shade over seven feet tall and spoke no English.

Dido, as he was known in the NBA, was a rookie backup center for the Atlanta Hawks. He had spotted Desie on a tennis court and sent one of the Hawks trainers to get her phone number. Dido was considerate enough to bring a Serbo-Croatian interpreter along on their first two dates, but the third time Dido arrived alone at Desie's apartment. They went to dinner and then to a club. Dido was surprisingly garrulous, and although Desie could understand nothing he said, she sensed in his impenetrably consonanted monologues a quaint sort of immigrant innocence. It wouldn't be the last time she misread a man.

Shortly after one in the morning, Desie tapped on the face of her wristwatch to show Dido it was time to leave. He took her home, walked her to the doorstep and kissed her tenderly on the crown of her head, the only part of her body that he could reach with his lips, without dropping to one knee. Then he placed his enormous slender hands on her shoulders and began speaking in a hushed, ardent tone. Desie, who was exhausted, nodded and smiled warmly and murmured all-purpose responses like "That's so sweet," or "I know what you mean." But in fact she hadn't a clue what Dido meant, for the next morning a large diamond engagement ring was delivered to her door. It arrived with a note; two notes actually—Dido's original, scribbled in pencil on notepaper bearing the Reebok logo, and the laborious translation, which said: "I am so very happy you are to be my wife. Our life together will be full of many funs and pleasures. Thank you plenty for saying yes. Your truest love, Gorbak."

Desie was stunned to learn that Dido had proposed marriage, and even more stunned to find out she had accepted. But that's what Dido insisted had happened, and Desie took the man at his word; it seemed romantic, in a quirky sitcom way. She dropped out of college with the idea of accompanying her new fiancé on the NBA tour. She imagined that traveling with Dido would be an exciting way to see the country's greatest cities; in particular, she was looking forward to New York, Boston and Chicago. But through his Serbian interpreter (whom the Hawks provided to Dido on a full-time basis), Dido explained to Desie that wives and girlfriends weren't allowed to accompany basketball players on the road. He would, however, be "plenty much happy" if she attended all the home games in Atlanta. "Is better that way," the interpreter added. "Also, you can stay in school and get smartened." Desie wasn't entirely sure it was Dido talking, but she told the interpreter she'd think about it.

The first basketball game she attended was a kick. January

something, 1988. For a while Desie saved the ticket stub in her antique sewing box. The Hawks beat the Chicago Bulls 107–103. Dido played most of the third quarter and blocked four shots. Desie got to sit close to courtside, in a section with the other wives and girlfriends. Most of them, like her, were young and exceptionally attractive. At halftime the women laughed and gossiped. Desie didn't follow professional basketball, and so was unaware how huge the sport was becoming. One of the Hawks wives pointed out a prematurely bald Chicago player, practicing jump shots, and said he was paid more than $5 million a year, not including endorsement fees. Desie was astounded. She wondered aloud how much Dido was making, and one of the Hawks wives (who memorized all the team stats) was pleased to inform her. It was a truly boggling sum of money for a twenty-two-year-old man, or for anybody. Desie did the arithmetic in her head: Dido's salary worked out to $10,500 *per game.*

"See that ring on your finger?" the Hawks wife said, lifting Desie's left hand. "One night's work. And that's if he got it retail."

Desie didn't return to college. Dido set her up in a bigger apartment in the Buckhead area, bought her a Firebird convertible (two nights' work, at least) and arranged for private tennis lessons at a nearby country club. Reebok supplied free shoes.

The engagement lasted a day shy of three months. It ended when Desie decided on a whim to fly to Detroit, of all places, to surprise Dido on the road for his birthday. When she knocked on his door at the Ritz-Carlton, she was met by a raven-haired woman wearing chrome hoop earrings and latex bicycle pants, and no top. Tattooed on the woman's left breast was a grinning skull with a cowboy hat.

The topless visitor turned out to be a local exotic dancer who spoke fluent Serbo-Croatian, in addition to English. One of the

Pistons players had introduced her to Dido at a bachelor party. Desie chatted politely with the woman until Dido returned from the basketball game. Unfortunately, he had sent his interpreter home early—reasoning there'd be no need, with a bilingual stripper—so Dido found himself mostly lost during Desie's agitated discourse. Certainly her mood needed no translation; Dido had picked up on the anger even before she'd flushed her diamond engagement ring down the toilet.

He tried to make up after the team returned to Atlanta, but Desie refused to see him. She moved out of the Buckhead apartment and went to stay with her parents. One day, when Dido showed up at the house, Desie turned the garden hose on him. Being rejected sent him into a glum frame of mind that deleteriously affected his already marginal performance on the basketball court. One wretched night, filling in for a flu-bound Moses Malone, Dido scored only three points, snagged precisely one rebound, turned the ball over five times and fouled out by the middle of the third quarter. The following morning he was traded to the Golden State Warriors, and Desie never saw him again, not even on television.

Oh, you'll find somebody new, her mother assured her. You just got off on the wrong foot.

But Desie couldn't seem to find the right one. In her twenties she was engaged three other times but never married. Twice she returned the rings without rancor, but one she kept. It had been given to her by a fiancé named Andrew Beck, with whom Desie was nearly in love. Andrew Beck produced and directed campaign commercials for political candidates, but his background was as an artist. For years he had seriously painted and sculpted and nearly starved. Then he got into television and became wealthy, as were all of Desie's fiancés. She told herself this was coincidence but knew better. In any case, she felt strongly about Andrew, who had a dreamily creative and distant side. Desie was captivated, as she'd never before been with a man who was even slightly enigmatic. Andrew couldn't stand politics and generally detested the senators and congressmen who paid so exorbitantly for his image-shaping skills. Desie came to admire Andrew for hating his own work—only a highly principled man would stand up and admit to wasting his God-given talent on something so shallow, manipulative and deceptive as a thirty-second campaign commercial.

The downside of Andrew Beck's commendable candor was that he often went around brooding and depressed. Desie blamed herself for what happened next. She had persuaded Andrew to see a psychologist, who urged him to seek an outlet for releasing his inner fountain of angst. Andrew chose body piercing and embarked on a zealous program of self-mutilation. He began with three small holes in each earlobe and advanced quickly to the eyebrows, one cheek and both nostrils. And he didn't stop there. He wore studs and pegs made only of the finest silver, and before long he bristled from so many man-made orifices that commercial air travel became impractical, due to delays caused by the metal detectors. With each new attachment Andrew's visage became more grotesque, although it didn't seem to bother his politician clients; Andrew's professional services were in greater demand than ever. Desie, on the other hand, could hardly bear to look at him. She held out hope that it was just a phase, even after Andrew got his tongue pierced to accommodate a size 4/0 tarpon hook. Desie appreciated the symbolism but not the tactile effect. In fact, sex with Andrew had already become too much of an obstacle course, body ornaments snagging and jabbing her at the most inopportune moments.

But she cared for him so she kept trying, until the evening he showed up with a tiny fourteen-karat Cupid's arrow pinned through the folds of his scrotum. It was then Desie realized there was no saving the relationship, and she moved home with her folks. She hung on to the engagement ring not for sentimental reasons, but because she feared Andrew Beck might otherwise put it to some perversely self-decorative use.

Less than a week later, Desie got a phone call from Palmer Stoat. She had met him only once, during an editing session at Andrew's studio. Andrew had been videotaping trial campaign spots for a man named Dick Artemus, who was planning to run for the governorship of Florida. Palmer Stoat had accompanied Artemus to Atlanta, and sat beside him while the "Vote for Dick" commercials were screened. Desie was there to prevent Andrew from offending Artemus (whom he abhorred) and thereby pissing away a $175,000 production contract.

In the studio Stoat began flirting with Desie, until she made it plain she was spoken for. Stoat apologized convincingly and didn't say another word, although he hardly took his eyes off her all afternoon. Desie never did figure out how he learned so quickly of her breakup with Andrew Beck, but Palmer wasted no time with phone calls, flowers and first-class plane tickets. Initially Desie put him off but in the end he wore her down with his slick enthusiasm—she had always been a sucker for pampering and flattery, and Palmer was a virtuoso. Desie's parents seemed to adore him (which should have been a warning signal) and urged her to give the nice young gentleman a fair chance. Only later, when she'd married Palmer and moved away to Fort Lauderdale, did it occur to Desie that her folks had been trying to nudge her out of the house. (Two days after the wedding, her father brought in a team of carpenters to convert her bedroom into a gym.)

She couldn't deny that Stoat treated her well: the Beemer, the canal-front house off Las Olas, all the shopping she could stand. And while the physical relationship between Desie and her husband wasn't acrobatic or fiery, it was mostly pleasurable. Morphologically, Palmer was a bit doughy for Desie's taste, but at least he didn't look like a damn Christmas tree when he took off his clothes. Not one of Palmer's pallid body parts was pierced, pinned or spangled, which was a treat for his new bride. It was nice, if not exactly rapturous, to make love without fear of puncture or abrasion.

Desie felt so liberated that on their honeymoon night in Tortola she was able to remain aroused—and not dissolve into giggles—when Palmer panted into her ear: "Come on, baby, light my candle."

"Fire," she whispered gently.

"What?"

"It's 'fire,' honey. The song goes, 'Come on, baby, light my fire.' "

"No way. I saw that fella do a show down at Dinner Key before he croaked—"

"Palmer," Desie said, changing the subject, "can I get on top now?"

It was three months before he brought the Polaroid camera into bed. Desie went along but she didn't approve—the flash was annoying, as were Palmer's stage directions. Moreover, the snapshots came out so blurry and shabbily composed that she couldn't understand how her husband found them titillating. Did that make him a weirdo? After being with Andrew Beck, nothing short of a medieval mace and chain-mail suit would have seemed kinky to Desie.

She did, however, draw the line at cigars. Palmer wanted her to try one in the bedroom, before and possibly during sex.

"No chance," Desie said.

"It's that goddamn Bill Clinton, isn't it? Him and his twisted bimbos, they've given the whole cigar scene a bad name. Honest, Des, all I want you to do is *smoke* one."

"The answer is no, and it's got nothing to do with the president."

"Then what?" Palmer Stoat rattled off the names of several cigar-puffing movie starlets. "Come on," he pleaded, "it's a very erotic look."

"It's a very stupid look. Not to mention the nausea that goes with it."

"Oh, Desie, *please.*"

"They cause cancer, you know," she said. "Tumors in the soft palate. You find *that* erotic, Palmer?"

He never again mentioned cigar sex. But now: rhinoceros horns. Desie was appalled. Killing one was bad enough, but this!

Admittedly, she and Palmer hadn't been making love so often. Desie knew why she wasn't feeling amorous—she wasn't happy with herself or the marriage; wasn't even certain she still *liked* her husband all that much. And she was aware he seemed to have lost interest, as well. Maybe he kept girlfriends in Tallahassee and Washington, or maybe he didn't. Maybe he was being truthful when he said that the only reason he'd purchased the black-market rhino powder was to rekindle their romance.

Desie didn't know what to do. Materially she had secured a good comfortable life; she was scared to think of starting over. But the emptiness in her heart was scary, too; scarier by the day. She didn't view herself as one of those wives who could accept a marital chill as inevitable; pretend it wasn't there, distract themselves with spas and overseas travel and home-improvement projects.

Or perhaps she could. To Desie, being alone sounded less appealing than being in a not-so-torrid marriage. Some of her friends had it worse; they had husbands who didn't give a shit. At least Palmer was trying, or appearing to try. His hope for a two-day erection was either endearing or idiotic, depending on his true motives.

In any case, Desie was so infuriated by the way he ridiculed her kidnap story that she ordered him to sleep in one of the guest rooms.

"I'll find you a shrink. The best in town," Palmer Stoat told her. "Please, Des. You're just a little confused."

"I prefer to stay confused," she said, "for now." Firmly she closed the bedroom door in his face.

All of a sudden McGuinn quit eating and became lethargic. At first Twilly didn't know why. Then he found the lint-covered cluster of antibiotic pills on the car floor, beneath the backseat. All this time the dog had been pretending to swallow—scarfing down the roast beef envelopes while somehow concealing the chalky tablets under his tongue. Then, when Twilly wasn't looking, he'd spit them out.

So the stubborn mutt probably has a post-op infection, Twilly thought. From the phone book he picked a nearby veterinarian's office. There the receptionist took out a clipboard and asked him some questions.

"Name of the pet?"

Twilly told her.

"Breed?"

"Labrador retriever."

"Age?"

"Five," Twilly guessed.

"Weight?"

"One twenty. Maybe heavier."

"Is he neutered?"

"Check for yourself."

"No thanks," the receptionist said.

"See? Balls."

"Why don't you have him lie down again, Mr. Spree."

"Down, boy," Twilly said obediently.

"Would you like us to go ahead and neuter him?"

"I'm not the one you should be asking," said Twilly.

"We've got a special this month on cats and dogs," the receptionist told him. "You get a twenty-five-dollar rebate from the Humane Society."

"Is that twenty-five per testicle?"

"No, Mr. Spree."

Twilly sensed the Lab gazing up at him. "Cats and dogs only?"

"That's right."

"Too bad."

The receptionist ignored his last remark. A tall frizzy-haired woman in a pink lab coat came out to collect McGuinn. Twilly followed her to an examination room and together they hoisted the dog onto a stainless-steel table. In came the veterinarian, a slightly built fellow in his sixties. He had a reddish gray mustache and wore thick-rimmed eyeglasses, and he didn't say much. He listened to McGuinn's heartbeat, palpated his abdomen and examined the sutures.

Without looking up, the doctor asked, "What was the reason for the surgery?"

Twilly said, "I don't know." Desie had promised to tell him, but never did.

"I don't understand. Isn't this your dog?"

"Actually, I just found him a few days ago."

"Then how do you know his name?"

"I had to call him something besides 'boy.'"

The veterinarian turned and eyed Twilly dubiously. Twilly made up a story about finding the Labrador wandering the shoulder of Interstate 75 near Sarasota. He assured the veterinarian he was taking an advertisement in the local newspaper, in the hopes of locating the dog's owner.

"No rabies tags?" the veterinarian asked.

"No, sir."

"No collar?"

"Nope," Twilly said. The collar and the tag were in the car.

"A dog like this—it seems hard to believe. This animal has champion bloodlines."

"I sure wouldn't know about that."

The veterinarian stroked McGuinn's snout. "Somebody cared enough to take him in for surgery. Doesn't make any sense they'd abandon him afterward. Not to me, it doesn't."

Twilly shrugged. "Humans are hard to figure. The point is, I care about him, too. Otherwise I wouldn't be here."

"No, I suppose not."

"I got worried when he stopped eating."

"Yes, it's good you brought him in." The veterinarian lifted McGuinn's upper lip and peered at the pale gums. "Mr. Spree, do you mind waiting in the other room?"

Twilly returned to the reception area and took a seat across from two maternal-looking women, each with an obese cat on her lap. Next to Twilly sat a sharp-featured man clutching a brushed leather valise, from which a small shaggy head—no larger than an apple—would emerge intermittently. Its moist brown eyes would dart edgily about the room until the man whispered something, and then the tiny canine head would pop out of sight.

The sharp-featured man noticed Twilly staring, then pulled the valise protectively to his chest. Abruptly he got up and moved three chairs away.

"So," Twilly said affably, "what's your hamster's name?"

The young man snatched up a veterinary magazine and pretended to read. The other pet owners seemed equally disinclined to chat. Twilly assumed they disapproved of his attire—he was shirtless and barefoot, and wore only a pair of old chinos. The rest of his clothes were at a laundromat down the street.

"Ah well," he said, and folded his arms. Before long he fell asleep and, as always, did not dream. He awoke to see the face of the frizzy-haired woman in the pink lab coat.

"Mr. Spree? Mr. Spree?"

"Yes. Sorry."

"Dr. Whitcomb needs to see you right away."

Twilly rose so fast, it made him wobbly. "Is something wrong?" he asked the woman in pink.

"Please. Come right now."

The dog predated Desirata. It was a gift from Dag Magnusson, president of the Magnusson Phosphate Company, who knew that Palmer Stoat loved to hunt. Dag Magnusson had purchased the dog from a breeder of field-trial champion Labradors in Hibbing, Minnesota. The one selected by Dag Magnusson was the pick of the litter and cost fifteen hundred dollars. Stoat named him Boodle as an inside joke, although the dog technically wasn't a bribe but rather a reward for arranging one.

Dag Magnusson had sought out Stoat because a Magnusson mine in Polk County was about to be shut down by the EPA for polluting a community lake with chemical runoff. The chemical was so vile that it exterminated all life-forms larger than amoebas, and the government was contemplating a whopping six-figure fine against Magnusson Phosphate, in addition to padlocking the facility. The situation was so politically touchy— and the lake so odiferously befouled—that not even the sluttiest congressman could be induced to intervene.

So Palmer Stoat tried another approach. He put Dag Magnusson in touch with a regional EPA administrator who was known to have a weak spot for trout fishing. Dag Magnusson invited the EPA man to accompany him on a trip to a private stretch of blue-ribbon river in western Montana, and it was there the lucky fellow nailed his first twenty-inch rainbow. The fish had barely stopped flopping when the EPA quietly began settling its differences with Magnusson Phosphate, which ultimately agreed to pay a $3,900 fine and erect large warning signs on the shores of the poisoned lake in Polk County. Dag Magnusson was delighted with the outcome, and decided that Palmer Stoat deserved something more than his customarily exorbitant fee.

Hence the dog. Stoat's wife at the time (his second) protested, but to no avail. The wife's name was Abbie, and she had no patience for puppy piddle or puppy poop. Few humans are able to resist the spunky charms of a six-week-old Labrador retriever, but Abbie could and did. She was resolutely not, by her own admission, "an animal person." She felt that anything with fur belonged on a hanger, not under the dining room table licking her pedicured toes. Abbie's attitude toward the puppy was so glacially resentful that it alarmed her husband, who was amused, if not smitten, by his rambunctious new pooch. Palmer Stoat had been mentally compiling reasons to divorce Abbie, and her aversion to Boodle immediately vaulted to the top of his list (replacing, temporarily, her aversion to oral-genital contact).

In the end, Stoat was able to turn his wife's dislike of the puppy to his own legal advantage. One evening he returned home from Tallahassee to find Abbie hysterically flogging the young dog with a rolled-up copy of *Women's Wear Daily*. Boodle was nearly a year old and already ninety-plus pounds, so he wasn't the least bit harmed or even unnerved by Abbie's outburst (and failed to make a connection between the spanking and the coral red Rossetti sling-back that had become his newest chew toy). The dog thought Abbie was playing, and throughout the attack he kept wagging his truncheon-like tail in appreciation of the rare display of attention. Palmer Stoat burst into the laundry room and wrested the rolled-up fashion magazine from his wife's fist. Within a week he presented her with divorce papers. Abbie signed without a fight, rather than face the lurid accusations of animal cruelty that her husband had vowed to publicize.

After she was gone, Stoat briefly set out to make a hunting dog of his blood-champion Lab. Boodle proved excellent at fetching but not so good at retrieving. He could find a downed mallard in the thickest cattails but invariably he kept swimming. By the time Stoat and his hunting companions chased down the dog, there was too little remaining of the bedraggled game bird to cook. Stoat went through half a dozen Labrador trainers before giving up on Boodle; the retrieval talents for which his canine lineage was famous obviously had skipped a generation. Stoat consigned the dog to household-protection duties, for which he seemed well suited, given his daunting size and midnight blackness.

So Boodle had settled in as lord of the manor. Stoat was undeniably fond of the animal, and enjoyed the company on those rare nights he wasn't away traveling, or drinking at Swain's. To his delight Stoat also discovered that, unlike the vanquished Abbie, most women adored large huggable dogs and were attracted to men who owned them. Boodle (Palmer Stoat would brag to his buddies) turned out to be a "big-time chick magnet." Certainly it had worked on Desie, who'd fallen instantly for the dog. Naïvely she had regarded Boodle's exuberantly sunny disposition as a positive reflection on his master. Such a happy pooch, she reasoned, could only have been raised by a patient, caring, unselfish man. Desie believed you could tell as much about a potential suitor from his pet as from his automobile, wardrobe and CD collection. Boodle being a riotously content and gentle dog, it seemed unthinkable that Palmer Stoat could be a conniving shitweasel.

Although Desie's view of her husband had grown darker after their marriage, her affection for the dog had deepened. Now Boodle/McGuinn was in the custody of a disturbed young man who might or might not prove to be a maniac, and Desie couldn't convince her husband that it was true. Several days passed before the envelope arrived via Federal Express late one afternoon. Desie wondered what Twilly Spree possibly could have sent that would "make a believer" of her doubting husband. A photograph of the dog, she guessed; the dog depicted in obvious jeopardy. But how—tethered to a railroad crossing? Tied up with a revolver pressed to his head? Desie cringed at the possibilities.

Palmer's flight from Tallahassee was late, so he didn't arrive home until half past eleven, after Desie was in bed. She heard him go into the den, where she'd left the package; heard him open the top drawer of his desk, where he kept the gold-plated scissors. For several moments she heard nothing else, and then came a quavering bleat that didn't sound anything like her husband, though it was.

Desie ran to the den and found him standing away from the desk, pointing spasmodically with the scissors.

"What is it, Palmer?"

"Eeeaaaaaahhh!" he cried.

Desie stepped forward to see what was in the FedEx envelope. At first she thought it was just a sock, a thin, shiny wrinkled black sock, but that wouldn't make any sense. Desie picked up the velvety thing and suddenly it looked familiar, and then she let out a cry of her own.

It was the severed ear of a dog, a large dog. A large black Labrador.

Desie dropped the thing, and it landed like a dead bat on the pale carpet. "Jesus!" she gasped.

Her flushed and trembling husband bolted for the bathroom. Desie pounded furiously on the door. "Now do you believe me?" she shouted over the roar of retching. "How about it, Palmer? Do you believe me now, you smart-assed sonofabitch?"

9

Twilly missed McGuinn. Missed the sound of his panting, the musky warmth of his fur.

It's only a dog, he thought. I got through my whole childhood without so much as a goldfish for a pet, so why all the guilt over a damn dog?

For two days Twilly Spree drove, scouting the likeliest locations. Okeechobee Road in west Dade. Sunrise Boulevard in Fort Lauderdale. Dixie Highway in North Miami. U.S. 1 from Kendall Drive to Florida City. And all the time he was missing McGuinn.

I'm going soft, Twilly grumbled. I'm definitely slipping here.

On the third day, after finally finding what he needed, he returned to the veterinary clinic. The frizzy-haired lady in pink met him in the reception area and took him to Dr. Whitcomb's private office. The veterinarian, who was on the telephone, motioned Twilly to a chair. The lady in pink closed the door on her way out.

As soon as Dr. Whitcomb hung up, Twilly said: "Well?"

"Yes. You ought to have a look." The veterinarian took a small round object from the top drawer. He handed it to Twilly, who rolled it in the palm of his hand. Seeing the object on an X ray was one thing; holding it was something else, a handful of guilt.

It was a glass eye from the stuffed head of an animal.

"And you've got no idea," Dr. Whitcomb was saying, "how your dog came to ingest something like this?"

"Beats me," Twilly lied. "I told you, I just found him a few days ago."

"Labs'll eat just about anything," the doctor remarked.

"Evidently."

Now Twilly knew the truth: He was the one responsible for the dog's sickness. If he hadn't removed the eyeballs from Palmer Stoat's taxidermy, McGuinn wouldn't have found the damn things and swallowed them.

Twilly wondered why Desie hadn't told him. He might've returned the dog to Stoat if he'd known the truth about the surgery. Now he felt purely rotten.

"A glass eye," Dr. Whitcomb was saying, "imagine that."

"And it got stuck inside him?"

"Basically, yes. Pretty far down the chute, too."

Twilly said, "God. The poor guy needed another operation?"

"No, Mr. Spree. A laxative."

The door swung open and McGuinn clambered into the office, trailing his leash. Excitedly he whirled around twice before burrowing his snout in Twilly's crotch, the customary Labrador greeting.

"A very potent laxative," Dr. Whitcomb added, "and plenty of it."

Twilly found himself hugging the dog fiercely. He could feel McGuinn's tongue, as thick as a cow's, lathering his right ear.

"You sure he'll be OK?"

"Fine," said Dr. Whitcomb, "but pretty soon he'll need those staples taken out of his belly."

From a damp crumple of cash Twilly counted out a thousand dollars in fifties, which he handed to the veterinarian.

"No, Mr. Spree, this is way too much."

"It is not."

"But—"

"Don't argue, just take it. Maybe next time somebody can't afford to pay, then. . . ."

"That's a good idea," said Dr. Whitcomb. "Thank you."

He followed Twilly and McGuinn to the parking lot, where the dog methodically peed on the tires of five late-model cars, including the doctor's.

"Can I ask a favor?" the veterinarian said. "It's about that fake eyeball. Mr. Spree, would you mind if I kept it for my collection?"

"That depends," said Twilly, "on the collection."

"Weird Things Dogs Eat," Dr. Whitcomb said. "I've got doorstops, earrings, fountain pens, cigarette lighters, car keys. This one Lab—Rachel was her name—she swallowed a cellular phone! And here's the funny part: It kept ringing inside her stomach. That's how her owners figured out what'd happened."

Twilly reached into his shirt for Palmer Stoat's Cape buffalo eye. He tossed it underhand to the veterinarian. "It's all yours, Doc."

Dr. Whitcomb looked amused as he fingered the glossy orb. "Crazy dog. How'd you suppose he got hold of something like this?"

Twilly shrugged. "Crazy damn dog," he said.

Why couldn't he stop thinking of Desie?

Her neck, in particular—the pale snowy slope between her pearl-spangled earlobe and her collarbone. Twilly had a grand weakness for the female neck. The last time he'd seen one as alluring as Desie's, it nearly got him killed.

The neck had been attached to a woman named Lucy, and Twilly didn't know about the pharmaceuticals and the booze and the bipolar disorder. All he knew was that Lucy had an indisputably fabulous neck, and that she freely let him nuzzle her there. She was also nice enough to have sex with him, which meant he quickly fell in love with her and moved in. They had known each other sixteen days.

Lucy, it turned out, was not well. She took lots of self-prescribed medicine and washed it down with Bombay gin. Some nights she was the happiest person on the planet, a joy to behold. And some nights she was a skank monster, violent and paranoid and gun-crazy. Twilly had never known a woman so fond of handguns. Lucy owned several, mostly semiautomatics. "My father was a policeman," she would say by way of explanation. Whenever Twilly came across one of Lucy's firearms, he would secretly take it from the house and throw it down a nearby manhole. But she always seemed to have another at the ready; where she hid all those guns was a mystery. Sometimes she shot at the telephone; sometimes it was the television. Once she shot the bagel toaster while Twilly was fixing breakfast. Another time she shot out her personal computer because one of her drug connections had e-mailed to say he was out of Percocet. That was the same afternoon she ran next door and shot her neighbor's scarlet macaw for squawking during her nap time (Lucy needed lots of naps). The police took Lucy downtown but no charges were filed, since she promptly reimbursed the grief-stricken bird owner and agreed to undergo counseling. There the therapists found Lucy to be a model of stability—engaging and self-aware and repentant. Happy, too. One of the happiest patients they'd ever seen. But of course they didn't have to live with her.

To Lucy's credit, she never purposely tried to shoot Twilly, although on several occasions she nearly hit him by accident. For all her vast gun-handling experience, she was a surprisingly lousy shot. Yet during fourteen hair-raising weeks under the same roof, Twilly's fear of taking a bullet was outweighed by his neck-nuzzling lust. It was, he realized later, another appalling example of his own deficient judgment.

Twilly never knew which Lucy was coming through the front door until he leaned down to kiss her neck, which was the first thing he always did. If it was Happy Lucy, she would sigh and press close against him. If it was Bipolar Lucy, she would shove him away and beeline for the medicine cabinet, and then the gin. Later a loaded handgun or two might appear. Most boyfriends would have wisely bolted after the first drunken shooting episode, but Twilly stayed. He was infatuated with the Happy Lucy. He truly believed he could mend her. Whenever Bipolar Lucy surfaced, Twilly declined to do the sensible thing, which was run like a scalded gerbil. Instead he hovered at the scene, endeavoring to soothe and coax and *communicate*. He was always trying to talk Lucy down; he dearly wanted to be the one to catch her when she fell. And that's how he nearly died.

Lucy worked at an acupuncture clinic, keeping the books. One day the doctor caught her in an error—a minor mathematical transposition that resulted in a $3.60 overstatement of the accounts receivable. The doctor made a remark that Lucy deemed unfairly harsh, and she arrived home in a moist-eyed fury that told Twilly she'd stopped for cocktails and toot along the way. For once he knew better than to attempt a neck nuzzle. Lucy disappeared into the bathroom and emerged five minutes later, naked, with an empty pharmacy bottle clenched in her teeth and a 9-mm Beretta in her right hand. Twilly, who remembered she was left-handed, prudently stepped back while she did her Elvis routine, shooting up the TV and the stereo and even the Mr. Coffee. Many rounds were required, due to Lucy's poor marksmanship, yet there was little risk of anyone calling the police. Lucy considerately used a muzzle suppressor to mute the gunshots.

Twilly made a practice of counting, so he'd know when the clip was empty. His near-fatal mistake that night was assuming Lucy was too fucked up to reload. After she'd exhausted herself and collapsed in bed, Twilly waited patiently for her ragged and fitful snoring. Then he slipped beneath the sheets, enfolded her in his arms and held her as still as a baby for a long time. Soon her breathing became soft and regular. Through his shirt Twilly could feel the steel coldness of the Beretta, which Lucy continued to clutch with both hands between her breasts. The snout of the silencer pressed ominously against Twilly's ribs, but he wasn't afraid. He thought the gun was empty; he clearly remembered Lucy pulling the trigger over and over until the only noise from the gun was a dull click. He didn't know about the spare clip that she'd stashed inside a tampon box under the bathroom sink.

So on Twilly's part it was carelessness, embracing an unconscious dope-addled psychotic without first confiscating her weapon. His second mistake was succumbing at the worst possible moment to raw desire. By chance Twilly had aligned his comforting hug of Lucy in such a way that his chin came to rest on one of her shoulders. He calculated that a slight turn of the head could put his lips in direct contact with her bare silken neck, and this proved blissfully true.

And perhaps if Twilly had stopped there—perhaps if he'd been content with a chaste and feathery peck—then he wouldn't have ended up on a stretcher in the emergency room. But Lucy's neck was a truly glorious sight and, gun or no gun, Twilly could not resist kissing it. The sensation (or possibly it was the sound of ardent smacking) jarred Lucy from her turbulent, gargoyle-filled stupor. She stiffened in Twilly's arms, opened one blood-shot eye and emitted a hollow startled cry. Then she pulled the trigger, and drifted back to sleep.

The bullet furrowed along Twilly's chest, rattling across his rib cage as if it were a washboard, then exiting above the collar-bone. So copious and darkly hued was the seepage of blood that Twilly feared he might be mortally wounded. He snatched the top sheet off the bed (rearranging the zonked Lucy) and knot-ted it around his thorax; a full body tourniquet. Then he drove to the nearest hospital, informing the doctors that he'd acciden-tally shot himself while cleaning a pistol. X rays showed that Lucy's slug had missed puncturing a jugular vein—and likely killing Twilly Spree—by scarcely two inches.

She hadn't meant to shoot him; she was scared, that's all, and too ripped to recognize him.

Twilly never told Lucy what she'd done. He did not return to the house, and never saw her again. More than a year had passed since the shooting, and during that time Twilly had avoided all lip-to-neck contact, the experience being indelibly connected to the muffled thump of a Beretta. Even in the throes of lovemak-ing, he remained scrupulous about the location of his kisses, and banished all thoughts of delicious forays into the nape region.

Until he met Desie. Twilly wanted very much to see the in-triguing Mrs. Stoat again, despite the imminent risk of arrest and imprisonment. He wanted not only to be near her but to apolo-gize for leaving the glass eyeballs lying around for McGuinn to swallow; wanted her to know how remorseful he felt.

The dog was the connection, the link to Desie. Having the dog beside him buoyed Twilly's spirits and gave him something resembling hope. So what if Desie was married to an irre-deemably soulless pig? Everybody makes mistakes, Twilly thought. Look at me.

*   *   *

McGuinn instantly knew something was wrong—he could smell it in the car. His nose twitched and the hair bristled on his withers.

"Chill out," Twilly said.

But the beast hurdled into the backseat and started digging frenetically at the upholstery.

"Oh stop," said Twilly.

McGuinn was trying to claw through the cushions and get into the trunk of the car.

"No!" Twilly commanded. "Bad boy!" Finally he was forced to pull off the road and park. He snatched the end of McGuinn's leash and gave a stiff yank.

"You wanna see? OK, fine." Twilly got out, pulling the dog behind him. "You're not gonna like it, sport. That, I can promise."

He popped open the trunk and McGuinn charged forward. Just as suddenly he drew back, his legs splaying crookedly, like a moose on thin ice. He let out a puppy noise, half bark and half whimper.

Twilly said, "I warned you, dummy."

Inside the car trunk was a dead Labrador retriever. Twilly had found it in south Miami-Dade County at the intersection of 152nd Street and U.S. 1, where it had been struck by a car. The dog couldn't have been dead more than two hours when Twilly spotted it in the median, bundled it in bubble wrap and placed it on a makeshift bed of dry ice in the rental car. The dog wasn't as hefty as McGuinn, but Twilly thought it would do fine; correct species, correct color phase.

Before spotting the black Lab, Twilly had searched 220 miles of highway and counted thirty-seven other dog carcasses—mostly mutts, but also a golden retriever, two Irish setters, a yellow Lab and a pair of purebred Jack Russell terriers with matching rhinestone collars. The Russells had perished side by side in a school zone on Coconut Grove's busy Bayshore Drive. Twilly speculated it might have been a double suicide, if dogs were capable of such plotting. Evidence of a cold and heartless master was the fact that the two stumpy bodies of the Russells lay uncollected in the roadway; they would have easily fit in a grocery bag. It took Twilly twenty minutes to bury the dogs between the roots of an ancient banyan tree. Before that, he had jotted down the numbers off the rabies tags, so that someday—when he had more time—he could track down the owner of the terriers and ruin his or her day.

The roadkill Lab wore no tags or identification collar. Twilly was saddened to think it might be a stray, but he would have been equally depressed to know it was somebody's beloved pet; a child's best buddy, or an old widow's faithful companion. A dead dog was just a sad thing, period. Twilly didn't feel good about what he had to do, but the animal was long past suffering and the cause seemed worthy.

McGuinn was pacing behind the rental car. He whined and kept his head low, and every few steps he would glance apprehensively toward the trunk, as if expecting the dead Lab to spring out and attack. Twilly calmed McGuinn and put him in the front seat. As an extra precaution, Twilly tethered the leash to the steering wheel. Then he walked back to the rear of the car and snapped open his pocketknife, a splendid three-inch Al Mar from Japan. The blade was wicked enough to shave tinsel.

Twilly was glad the dead dog's eyes were shut. He stroked its silky brow and said: "Better it's me than the damn buzzards." Afterward he tucked the severed ear in his back pocket and drove around Miami until he spotted a FedEx truck on the Don Shula Expressway. For a two-hundred-dollar tip the driver was pleased to pull over for an unscheduled pickup.

10

The king-sized hot tub was outdoors, on the scalloped balcony of Robert Clapley's beachfront condominium. All four of them peeled off their clothes and slipped into the water—Clapley, Katya, Tish and Palmer Stoat, who needed three cognacs to relax. Stoat was self-conscious about his pudginess, and slightly creeped out by the two Barbies; he wished Clapley hadn't told him the details.

"Twins!" Clapley had chortled.

"No kidding."

"Identical twins—in time for next Christmas!"

"They speak English, Bob?"

"Damn little," Clapley had replied, "and I intend to keep it that way."

Now one of the Barbies was attempting to straddle Stoat in a balmy swirl beneath tropical stars, and Stoat caught himself peeking under her immense high-floating breasts for telltale surgical scars. Gradually the cognac began to soothe him.

"In Moscow," Clapley was saying, "there's a school where they go to become world-class fellatrixes."

"A what?"

"Blow-job artists," Clapley explained. "An actual school—you hear what I'm saying!"

"Oh, I hear you." Stoat thinking: They can hear you all the way to St. Augustine, dipshit.

Robert Clapley got very loud when he was coked up and drunk. "I'd like to be there for final exams!" he said with a salacious grunt. "I'd like to personally grade *those* SATs—"

"Which one's from Russia?" Stoat inquired.

Clapley pointed at the Barbie now laboring to wrap her legs around Stoat's waist. "Yours!" he said. "You old horndog!"

"And she . . . went . . . to . . . this . . . 'school'?"

"She's the one who told me about it. Isn't that right, Katya? Show Mr. Stoat what you learned."

"Me, too!" exclaimed Tish. Her vast bosom pushed a wake like a shrimp trawler as she sloshed across the tub to join her future twin. They spread Palmer Stoat's legs and, with merry jostling, squeezed between them.

He said, "Really, Bob."

Robert Clapley laughed. "I should get the camcorder!"

"Not unless you want to see it in pieces." Normally Stoat was more of a sport, but not tonight. Desie was heavy on his mind; also, the severed dog ear that had been delivered by the FedEx man.

Clapley said, "You need to relax, kiddo."

"I just stopped by to talk some business, Bob. I didn't mean to make an evening of it."

"Hell, we can chat later. How often in a guy's lifetime does he have a chance to get sucked off by two semi-identical six-foot dolls? I'm guessing this isn't a weekly event for you, Palmer, so please shut the hell up and enjoy. I need to make a couple calls."

Clapley climbed agilely out of the tub. Stoat could hear him talking on the phone but couldn't see over the tops of the two Barbies, each of whose head was stacked with at least one linear foot of shiny bleached hair. The women tugged and stroked and prodded at Palmer Stoat until finally, not wishing to seem the ungrateful guest, he closed his eyes and submitted. He enjoyed the moment, but not so much that he forgot his reason for being there.

By the time Clapley finished his calls, the Barbies were done, out of the tub and in the shower. Stoat floated back with his legs extended, frog-like. He pretended to gaze at the stars.

Clapley said, "How'd you like that twin sandwich?"

Stoat whistled appreciatively. "Blond sugar, like the song says."

"Yea, brother." Clapley was too trashed to dispute the lyric. "Listen, I know why you're here."

Stoat slowly righted himself, tucking his pink knees beneath him. How could Robert Clapley know! Was it possible, Stoat wondered, that the maniacal ear-mutilating dognapper had contacted his client?

Clapley said, "I believe I still owe you some money."

"Yeah, you do." Stoat was much relieved.

They moved to the den, both wearing long towels and matching terry-cloth bath slippers. Clapley sat behind a glass-topped desk and opened his checkbook.

"It completely slipped my mind," he said, "last time you were here."

"That's quite all right, Bob."

"Now . . . how much was it?"

"Fifty thousand," Stoat replied, thinking: Asshole. He knows damn well how much.

"Fifty? Boy, that's a shitload of shotgun shells."

Clapley, alluding to the bird-hunting trip. That and the kinky

Barbie action was aimed at hustling a discount, Stoat concluded. Well, Bobby boy, you can bite me.

Robert Clapley waited a couple beats, but Stoat retained his anticipatory demeanor.

"Right. Fifty it is." Clapley strained to sound gracious.

Palmer Stoat enjoyed watching the man write out the check. Clapley's discomfiture was manifest, and Stoat didn't mind prolonging it. An important principle was at stake; a matter of respect. Stoat considered himself a professional, and in the lobbyist trade a pro didn't tolerate being jerked around for his fee, particularly by baby-faced ex-smugglers with Barbie fetishes. Stoat had come to Clapley's condo intending to warn him of a temporary snag with the Toad Island bridge appropriation. Stoat had been prepared to let Clapley hold the balance of his fee until the situation with the extortionist dognapper got resolved. But Clapley had so annoyed Palmer Stoat with his coy cheapness—*"how much was it?"*—that Stoat changed his mind about the money. He'd pocket it and say nothing. Besides, if Desie left him—as she'd threatened to do if Stoat didn't meet the dognapper's demands—he would be needing the extra fifty grand (and more) for divorce lawyers.

"Here you go." Clapley capped his Mont Blanc and slid the check toward Stoat.

"Thanks, Bob." Stoat's smile could have passed for sincere. He didn't take the check immediately, but left it lying faceup on the glass desktop.

Clapley said, "Dick was right about you."

"Dick has his moments."

"So, when's he supposed to sign the budget?"

"Week or two, I expect," Stoat said.

"Fan-fucking-tastic. The sooner they can get started on the new bridge, the sooner I can slap together some model homes."

One of the Barbies walked in carrying a tray with two cognacs and two large cigars. She was wearing a blood-red catalog-style teddy with lacy bra cups. Clapley whistled when she leaned over to set down the drinks.

"Thank you, *darling*," he said in a leering tone. Then, to Palmer Stoat: "Hey, how'd you like that double-barreled hummer in the hot tub?"

"Great." Stoat thinking: Christ, how many times do I have to say it? "One of the great blow jobs of all time, Bob."

"And all because she buckled down and stayed in school. You know what they say, Palmer: A tongue is a terrible thing to waste." Clapley winked at the departing Barbie, who responded with a perky four-fingered wave. After she closed the door, he said, "That was Katya. I dream of the day when I can't tell 'em apart."

"Shouldn't be long now," Stoat said, encouragingly.

They spent a few ceremonial moments clipping and lighting the cigars. Then Robert Clapley raised his glass in a toast.

"To Shearwater Island," he said.

"Amen," said Palmer Stoat.

"And good company."

"The best, Bob."

They sipped cognac and blew smoke rings toward the ceiling. Clapley told a crude joke about a nearsighted rabbi. Stoat told one about a farsighted cheerleader. Again Clapley raised his drink.

"Here's to doing business again one day, you and me."

"Anytime," Stoat said, thinking: It'll be sooner than you think, dipshit.

As soon as Palmer had left for Palm Beach, Desie opened the freezer and removed the plastic Baggie containing the dog ear. She examined it with a mixture of revulsion and forensic curiosity. The ear didn't seem large enough to be one of Boodle's, but she couldn't be certain. That it belonged to a big black dog was indisputable. If that dog turned out to be hers, then Twilly Spree was a savage monster and Desie had horribly misjudged him.

Equally mortifying was her own culpability in the crime. After all, it was she who'd told Twilly about what was happening at Toad Island; it was she who'd given him the crazy idea of saving the place. Why? Because she'd wanted to see the smugness wiped off her husband's face, wanted to appraise Palmer's reaction when one of his slick fixes went awry. But how could she have known that young Twilly Spree would carry things so far?

Desie returned the dog ear to the freezer—placing it out of sight, behind a half-gallon of rum raisin ice cream—and went to draw a hot bath. At noon the maid knocked on the door and said a "Mister Ezra Pound" was on the telephone. Desie asked the maid to hand her the portable.

It was Twilly's voice on the other end. "Well, does he believe it now?"

Desie said, "I'd say so, judging by the way he hurled his dinner. Where are you?"

"Not far."

"Please tell me it's not Boodle's ear."

"The name's McGuinn, remember?"

"But it's not his ear, is it? God, please don't say you sliced off that poor dog's ear. Not over a bunch of dead toads."

Twilly said, "I didn't. I would never."

"I *knew* it."

"But this isn't about toads, it's about pillage. We're dealing with an immoral, unforgivable crime." Twilly sighed in frustration. "Don't you read the papers, Mrs. Stoat? Can't you see who's running the show?"

Desie said, "Take it easy." The last thing she wanted to do was set him off.

"Now I've got a question for you," Twilly said. "Why didn't you tell me the truth about your dog?"

"Uh-oh," said Desie.

Twilly recounted the visit to the veterinarian, and the unsavory retrieval of the glass buffalo eye.

"It wasn't your fault. He'll eat anything," Desie said.

"It most certainly *was* my fault."

"How's he doing now? That's the important thing."

"He seems OK," Twilly said, "but he misses you."

"I miss him, too."

"How much?" asked Twilly. "What I mean is, do you want to see him?"

"Yes!"

"That way, you can count his ears. See for yourself that I'm no puppy slasher."

"Of course I want to see him." Desie climbed out of the water and put on a robe, switching hands with the phone. "Where are you now?" she asked Twilly again.

"But you can't tell your dickhead husband, OK? He's got to believe it's McGuinn's ear, or the whole plan goes bust. Can you promise me? Because if Palmer finds out the truth, neither of you will ever see this animal again. I won't hurt him, Mrs. Stoat, I'm sure you already figured that out. But I swear to God you'll never lay eyes on him again."

Desie knew he wasn't bluffing. She knew he was angry enough to punish her husband, and that he wouldn't stop with snatching the family pet. She said, "Twilly, I won't tell him about the ear. Look, I've trusted you. Now it's your turn to trust me."

Still dripping from the bath, she padded to the kitchen and got a notepad. Twilly made her read back his directions after she'd jotted them down.

"Can I bring you anything?" she said.

There was a pause on the line. "Yes, I'd like a book."

"Poetry?" Desie, thinking of his Ezra Pound approach.

"I'm not in the mood. But anything by John D. MacDonald would be terrific. And also some Tic Tacs. Spearmint, if it's not too much trouble."

Desie caught herself smiling. "No trouble," she said. Something brushed her bare toes and she jumped—it was only the maid, diligently mopping the drops on the kitchen tile.

"How do you know McGuinn misses me?"

"Sometimes he gets mopey," Twilly said.

"Maybe it's Palmer he misses."

"Be serious. I'll see you later."

"Wait. About this ear—what do I do with it?"

"Whatever you want," said Twilly. "Hang it on the Christmas tree, for all I care. Or nail it to the wall, with the rest of your husband's dead animal parts."

Desie thought: Boy, he *is* in a shitty mood.

She said, "I'm just curious. If it's not Boodle's—"

"McGuinn!"

"Sorry. If it's not *McGuinn's* ear—"

"And it's not. Didn't I tell you?"

"Right, you did," Desie said. "And that's why I can't help being curious. Anybody would—a gross item like this arrives on your doorstep. But now I'm thinking: Do I really want to know where it came from?"

"You do not," said Twilly Spree. "Definitely not."

Dick Artemus had known Palmer Stoat three years. They'd first met on a quail-hunting plantation in Thomasville, Georgia, across the state line from Tallahassee. At the time, Dick Artemus was the mayor of Jacksonville, and also the multimillionaire owner of seven Toyota dealerships, all prosperous. For the usual reasons he decided he needed to be governor of Florida, and methodically began ingratiating himself with all the major players in state politics. One was Palmer Stoat, the well-known lobbyist, problem fixer and deal broker.

Stoat had been ambivalent about meeting Dick Artemus, as he'd recently purchased a Toyota Land Cruiser that had given him nothing but grief. One of the electric windows shorted out, the CD player got jammed on Cat Stevens, and the four-wheel drive functioned only in reverse. These annoyances were brought to Dick Artemus's attention by a mutual acquaintance of Palmer Stoat, and two days later a flatbed hauling a brand-new Land Cruiser pulled into Stoat's driveway. The next morning, Stoat chartered a plane for Thomasville.

The quails were so quick that he actually managed to hit a few. Another pleasant surprise was Dick Artemus, who turned out to be glib, sufficiently charming and presentable, with the obligatory flawless dentition and mane of silver-gray hair. The man could actually win this thing, Palmer Stoat thought—Artemus was three inches taller and ten times better-looking than any of the Democrats.

In Stoat's occupation it was unwise to take sides (because one never knew when the political tides might change), but he discreetly arranged introductions between Dick Artemus and Florida's heaviest campaign donors, most of whom happened to be Stoat's clients from industry, real estate and agriculture. They were favorably impressed by the handsome automobile tycoon. By midsummer, two months before the Republican primary, Dick Artemus had collected more than $4 million in contributions, much of it traceable and even legitimate. He went on to capture the general election by a breezy margin of 200,000 votes.

Dick Artemus never forgot the value of Palmer Stoat's early

guidance, because Palmer Stoat wouldn't let him forget. Usually it was the lobbyist who needed a favor but occasionally the governor himself made the phone call. They cut back on the weekend hunting trips, as both men agreed it would be imprudent to be seen spending time together. Stoat couldn't afford to piss off the Democrats, while Dick Artemus couldn't afford to be branded the stooge of some oily wheeler-dealer lobbyist. The two remained friendly, if not close. When (after less than a year!) Palmer Stoat traded in the Toyota for a new Range Rover, Dick Artemus diplomatically hid his disappointment. He had reelection to worry about; he would need Stoat's connections.

So naturally the governor said yes when Palmer called to request a rare meeting alone. Lisa June Peterson, the aide who took the call, knew it was a serious matter because Stoat didn't try to flirt with her over the phone, or invite her out for drinks, or ask for her dress size so he could buy her a little something the next time he was in Milan. No, Palmer Stoat sounded more tense and distracted than Lisa June Peterson had ever heard him.

Dick Artemus set up one of his famous private lunches at the governor's mansion, and made sure Stoat arrived through the service entrance, out of view of visitors and journalists. The menu featured sautéed baby lobsters, quite illegal to possess, which had been confiscated from poachers by the marine patrol in Key Largo and then transported by state helicopter to Tallahassee. (Anyone who asked questions was told the undersized crustaceans were being donated to the kitchen of a local church orphanage, and on infrequent occasions—when the governor had a prior dinner commitment, for example—that act of charity would actually come to pass.)

The lobsters were so runty that Palmer Stoat immediately abandoned the fork and went to his fingers. Dick Artemus couldn't help but notice how Stoat delicately stacked the empty carapaces on his butter plate, a display of meticulousness that contrasted oddly with his wet sloppy chewing.

"The bridge," Stoat said, after his second glass of wine.

"Which bridge?"

"Toad Island. The Shearwater project." Stoat had a baby lobster plugged in each cheek. It made him appear mottled and goggle-eyed, like a grouper.

Dick Artemus said, "What's the problem, Palmer? The bridge money is in the budget—it's a done deal."

"Well, I need you to undo it."

"Is this a joke?"

"No," Stoat said, "it's a matter of life and death."

"That's not good enough," said the governor.

"Dick, you've got to veto the bridge."

"You're completely insane."

"No, you listen up." Palmer Stoat wiped his butter-slick hands on a linen napkin and slugged down the rest of his wine. Then he told Dick Artemus the whole story about the missing dog; about the deranged lunatic who broke into his house and stole Boodle and vowed to murder the animal if Robert Clapley got that new bridge; about how Desie was threatening to leave him if he didn't do what the dognapper demanded; about how he couldn't afford another costly divorce, couldn't afford to have a humiliating story like this splashed all over the newspapers and television; and, finally, about how much he loved his big dopey pooch and didn't want him to die.

The governor replied with a murmur of disappointment. "It's that fucking Willie Vasquez-Washington, isn't it? He wants something else from me."

Palmer Stoat rose off his chair. "You think I'd make up something like this—a *dog* abduction, for Chrissake!—to cover for a greedy two-bit cocksucker like Willie V? He's nothing to me, Dick, a jigaboo gnat on the fucking windshield of life!"

"OK, keep it down." Three hundred Brownie scouts were touring the governor's mansion, and Dick Artemus preferred that their tender ears be spared Stoat's profane braying.

"This is my reputation I'm talking about," Stoat continued. "My marriage, my financial situation, my whole future—"

"What kind of dog?" the governor asked.

"Black Lab."

Dick Artemus smiled fondly. "Aw, they're great. I've had three of 'em."

"Then you know," Stoat said.

"Yeah, yeah. I sure loved those hounds, Palmer, but I wouldn't have tanked a twenty-eight-million-dollar public works project for one. I mean, there's love and then there's love." The governor raised his palms.

Stoat said, "I'm not talking about *killing* the bridge project, my friend. You sign a line-item veto next week. Maybe Clapley screams and hollers for a little while. Same for Roothaus. My crazy dognapper reads in the papers how the Shearwater deal is suddenly DOA, and he lets Boodle go free and everything's hunky-dory."

"Boodle?" Dick Artemus said quizzically.

"That's his name—long story. Anyhow, soon as I get back my dog, here's what you should do, Dick. You call the legislature back to Tallahassee for a special session."

"All for a bridge? You can't be serious. I'll get slaughtered by the press."

In agitation Stoat lunged for a fresh bottle of wine. "Dick, in the immortal words of Jethro Tull, sometimes you're as thick as a stick."

The governor glanced at his wristwatch and said, "How about cutting to the chase."

"OK," said Stoat. "You're not calling a special session for one lousy bridge, you're calling it for *education*. You aren't happy with how your colleagues in the House and Senate hacked up your education package—"

"That's the truth."

"—and so you're bringing them back to Tallahassee to finish the job, on behalf of all the children of Florida. You say they deserve bigger classrooms, more teachers, newer books, and so on. You follow me?"

The governor grinned. "Let me guess. Robert Clapley intends to build a public school on Shearwater Island."

"I expect he'll be receptive to the idea, yes."

"But school buses are heavy vehicles, aren't they?"

"Especially when they're full, that's absolutely right." Palmer Stoat was pleased. There was hope yet for Dick Artemus. "You can't have a bus loaded with innocent little kids going back and forth across the bay on a rickety old bridge."

"Too dangerous," the governor agreed.

"Risky as hell. And how can you put a price tag on a child's safety?"

"You can't," said Dick Artemus.

Stoat's voice rose melodramatically to the occasion. "Try telling Mom and Dad that little Jimmy doesn't deserve a safe new bridge for his first school bus ride to Shearwater Elementary. See if they don't think twenty-eight million dollars is a small price to pay. . . ."

The governor's eyes twinkled. "You're a stone genius, Palmer."

"Not so fast. We've got lots of phone calls to make."

The governor canted one eyebrow. "We?"

"Hell, Dick, you *said* you liked dogs."

This is craziness, thought Dick Artemus, whacko world. That he was even considering such a scheme was a measure of how desperately he wanted to keep Palmer Stoat on his side.

Said the governor: "I assume Bob Clapley's on board for all this nonsense."

"Oh, I'll handle Clapley," Stoat said with the flick of a hand. "He doesn't give a damn how he gets the bridge, as long as he gets it. Don't you worry about Clapley."

"Fine, then."

"In fact, I'd keep my distance from him until we get this ironed out."

"You're the man, Palmer."

They talked about basketball and hunting and women until they were done with dessert, homemade pecan pie topped with vanilla ice cream. Stoat was putting on his coat when the governor said: "Your kooky dognapper—how do you know he's not fulla shit?"

"Because he sent me a goddamn ear, that's how," Stoat said. "An ear off a real dog."

The governor was dumbfounded. "Yours?"

"I don't know for sure. It's very possible," Stoat acknowledged, "but even if it isn't Boodle's ear, you see what I'm up against. He hacked the damn thing off a dog, *some* dog *somewhere*. That's the point. An actual ear, Dick, which he then sent to me via Federal fucking Express. Just so you appreciate what we're dealing with."

"Yes. I get the picture." The governor looked shaken. He was thinking: Again with the "we"?

11

Palmer took Desie to a seafood restaurant on Las Olas Boulevard, where she was so distracted by his table manners that she hardly ate a bite. He'd ordered two dozen oysters, slurping them with such sibilant exuberance that customers at nearby tables had fallen silent in disgust. Now Palmer was arranging the empty oyster shells around the rim of his plate, six identical piles of four. He was chattering away, seemingly unaware of his deviant tidying. Desie was as perplexed as she was embarrassed. Wasn't this the same slob who had, on the drive to the restaurant, lobbed an empty coffee cup and three handfuls of junk mail out of the Range Rover? Desie didn't know the clinical name of her husband's disorder, but the symptoms were not subtle; anything he couldn't eat, drink or reorganize got chucked.

"You're not listening to me," said Palmer Stoat.

"Sorry."

"What're you staring at?"

"Nothing."

"Is there something wrong with your scrod?"

"It's fine, Palmer. Go on, now. Tell me what Dick said."

"He said he'll do it."

"Are you serious?" Desie had assumed there was no chance.

"For me, he'll do it," said Stoat self-importantly. "He'll kill the bridge."

"That's fantastic."

"Yeah, well, it's gonna cost me big-time. Bob Clapley'll want my testicles on a key chain before this is over, and he won't be alone. Twenty-eight million bucks buys an army of enemies, Des."

She said, "What's more important—another stupid golf resort or saving your dog's life?"

"Fine. Fine. When do we get the big guy back?"

"When it makes the newspapers, about the bridge veto. That's when the kidnapper will let Boodle go. He said he'll be in touch in the meantime."

"Wonderful." Stoat signaled for the check. "Too bad you didn't get his name."

"Palmer, he's a criminal. They don't give out business cards." Desie didn't understand why she continued to protect Twilly Spree, but it was no time to change her story.

Stoat said, "I'm just curious is all. It's gotta be somebody who knows me. Somebody I pissed off somewhere up the line. *Seriously* pissed off, to break into my house and snatch my goddamn Labrador."

"What's the difference?" she said. "You said everything's set. Governor Dick's going to do what you asked, then we get Boodle back and all the fuss is over. Right?"

"That would be the plan," said her husband. Then, turning to the waiter: "Could you please see that my wife's entrée is taken off our bill? The scrod was so freezer-burned she couldn't eat it."

"For heaven's sake," Desie said.

Driving home, Palmer slid his free hand beneath her skirt. "You proud of me?" he asked.

"I am." Involuntarily she pressed her knees together.

"How proud?"

Desie felt her chest tighten. She locked her eyes straight ahead, as if watching the traffic.

"Proud enough for a little you-know-what?"

"Palmer." But she was leaden with guilt. Of course she'd have sex with him tonight—after what he'd done for the dog, how could she say no?

"It's been a couple of weeks," he noted.

"I know. A rough couple of weeks."

"For both of us, sweetheart. So how about it? Lilac candles. A bottle of French wine—"

"Sounds nice," said Desie.

"—and maybe a spoonful of rhino dust for some extra-special excitement."

"No!"

"Des, come on."

"No way, Palmer. *No way!*" She removed his hand from inside her panties and told him to mind the road. It took three traffic lights for Stoat to compose himself and rally for the salvage operation.

"You're right," he said to Desie. "Forget the rhino horn, forget I even mentioned it. I'm sorry."

"Promise me you'll throw it away."

"I promise," Stoat lied. Already he was thinking about the intriguing call girl he'd met the other night at Swain's, the one who fucked only Republicans. Certainly *she* would have no liberal qualms about aphrodisiacs harvested from endangered species.

Nor would Roberta, the free-spirited, prodigiously implanted blonde who was Stoat's occasional travel companion. For the promise of a new and improved orgasm, Roberta would've killed the rhinoceros with her own bare hands.

But to his wife, Palmer Stoat declared: "I'll toss the stuff first thing in the morning."

"Thank you."

With a sly sideways glance, he said: "Does that mean we're still on for later?"

"I suppose." Desie turned her head, pretending to scout the bikinis in the display window of a beachwear shop. She felt the spiderish return of Palmer's fingers between her legs. He left them there after the light turned green.

"You look soooooo gorgeous tonight," he said. "I can't wait to see the pictures!"

Lord, Desie thought. The shutterbug routine again.

"Palmer, I'm not really in the mood."

"Since when? Come on, darling, learn to relax."

Stoat stopped at a convenience store, where he purchased three packs of Polaroid film. He compulsively tore them open inside the truck, throwing the empty boxes into the parking lot. Desie got out and retrieved each one, much to her husband's consternation.

"What's gotten into you?" he demanded.

"Just drive," she told him. "Just take me home."

So we can get it over with.

That night Twilly Spree was pulled over by a policeman on Route A1A in the snowbird community of Lauderdale-by-the-Sea. Twilly thought he knew why: There had been another incident of anger mismanagement, this one involving four college students, two personal watercrafts and a large volume of beer.

It had happened after Twilly returned the rented Chevrolet Corsica and transferred McGuinn to the black pickup truck. Twilly was minding his own affairs, waiting in traffic on the Commercial Boulevard drawbridge, when he noticed two Jet Skis racing at break-ass speed down the Intracoastal Waterway. One Jet Ski was white with bright blue stripes; the other was white with red stripes. Each carried a matching pair of riders— a young stud at the helm with a young babe behind him, arms locked around his waist. They were jumping the wakes of yachts, buzzing the sailboats, spraying the bait netters and otherwise announcing their drunken idiocy to the world. Such brain-dead antics were so commonplace among water bikers that it was hardly noteworthy, and Twilly Spree would have paid no further attention except that the drawbridge was still up and he was stuck for entertainment. Besides, there was a better-than-average chance that the bozos would crash their noisy toys head-on into the seawall at fifty miles per hour—and Twilly was always eager to see Darwin vindicated in such cinematic style.

Back and forth the Jet Skis went, bitch-howling like runaway chain saws. A frightened pelican took off from a piling, and instantly both water bikes lit out in a deafening pursuit. Twilly jumped from his truck and ran to the bridge rail. McGuinn poked his snout out the window and whined.

It was over in less than a minute. At first the bird flew low to the water, struggling to gain speed. The Jet Ski riders came swiftly from behind, the afternoon rays glinting off their beer cans. All four kids let loose at the same time, just as the pelican began its ascent. Three of the cans missed the bird, but one struck the crook of a wing. The exploding cartwheel of gold mist told Twilly the beer can was full, as heavy as a rock. The pelican went down in an ungainly spin, landing backward with its beak agape. The water bikers circled the splash once and then sped off, up the Intracoastal in a frothy streak. They were too far away for Twilly to see if they were laughing, but he chose to assume they were. He watched a river taxi retrieve the injured pelican, which was flogging the water with its good wing, trying to lift off.

Twilly got in his truck and turned up the radio and scratched McGuinn under the chin and waited for the bridge to go down. Then he shot free of the traffic and drove north like a psychopath along the waterfront, searching for the marina where the water bikers had put in. At dusk he finally caught up with them, at a public wharf in Pompano Beach. They were winching the Jet Skis up on a tandem trailer that was hitched to a black Cadillac Seville coupe, new but dirty from a long road trip. The expensive car, which bore Maryland license tags, probably belonged to somebody's father. The kids obviously were on spring break from college, and even more obviously drunk. The two young studs had put in some serious gym time, and they wore mesh tank tops to advertise the results. Their girlfriends were both slender and brunette, possibly sisters, and too cadaverously pale for the neon thongs they wore. Their bare bike-wrinkled butt cheeks looked like pita loaves.

Twilly's initial impulse was to ram the Cadillac so hard that it would roll in reverse down the boat ramp. That way he could sink the car and the Jet Skis and all cash and valuables therein. Unfortunately, the Caddy substantially outweighed Twilly's pickup truck, making such an impact problematic. Twilly didn't give a hoot about himself, but there was McGuinn to consider—the last thing the poor dog needed was whiplash.

And besides, Twilly reasoned to himself, what would be accomplished by petty property destruction? The insurance company would replace the luxury coupe and the Jet Skis, and no important lessons would have been learned. The water bikers would fail to see any connection between the vandalism against their belongings and their cruel attack on the pelican. To Twilly, that was unacceptable. Vengeance, he believed, ought never to be ambiguous.

So he clipped McGuinn to the leash and got out of the truck. The two tipsy college girls spotted the huge dog and scampered over, their sandals flopping on the asphalt. They knelt beside McGuinn, cooing and giggling while he licked their salty sunburned faces. This, Twilly had counted on, as Labrador retrievers were magnets for children and women. The beefy college boyfriends wandered up with an air of sullen, incipient jealousy; as trashed as they were, they still resented not being the center of attention. While the girls fawned over the dog, Twilly struck up a conversation with the boyfriends about their nifty water bikes—how fast they went, how much they cost, what kind of mileage they got. The two guys loosened up quickly and started to brag about how their Jet Skis had been illegally modified to go much faster than the factory recommended. Twilly asked if he could have a close-up look. He told them he'd never ridden one before, but said it looked like a blast. And the boyfriends said sure, come on.

Twilly asked the girlfriends if they'd mind keeping an eye on the dog, and they said: Mind? We wanna take him home to Ocean City with us! What's his name, anyway?

Beowulf, said Twilly.

Aw, thassadorable, said one of the girlfriends.

As Twilly followed the boyfriends across the parking lot toward the Cadillac with the tandem trailer, he asked if there was an extra beer in the cooler. And that was the last thing the girlfriends remembered overhearing until Twilly returned a few minutes later and took the dog by the leash. The college girls hugged "Beowulf" and crooned their smoochy good-byes. Then they wobbled to their feet and glanced around for their boyfriends, at which point Twilly Spree lowered his voice and said: "I saw what you dipshits did to that pelican."

"Uh?" said one of the girlfriends.

The other grabbed her elbow and said, "Whadhesay?"

"Don't ever come back here," Twilly advised. "Not ever. Now go call the fire department. Hurry."

The trunk of the Cadillac was open. So was the cooler inside. The boyfriends were stretched out on the ground, faceup at a forty-five-degree angle to each other; like the hands of a broken clock. One had a fractured cheekbone, denoted by a rising purple bruise. The other had a severely dislocated jaw, also festooned with an angry raw contusion. Nearby lay two misshapen Budweiser cans, fizzing beer bubbles on the pavement. The drunken girlfriends began to wail, and from the cooler they frantically scooped bare handfuls of ice cubes, which they attempted to affix on the lumpy wounds of their drunken boyfriends. The college girls were so absorbed in first aid that they didn't notice the two water bikes smoldering ominously on the trailer, soon to burst into flames.

As much as he would've enjoyed it, Twilly Spree didn't wait around for the fire. Later, when the flashing blue police lights appeared in his rearview mirror, he concluded that the two girlfriends hadn't been quite as intoxicated as he thought. He figured they'd taken note of his pickup truck, perhaps even memorizing the license plate. It was a dispiriting turn of events, for Twilly couldn't afford to go back to jail. Not now anyway; not with the Toad Island mission unresolved. The timing of his outburst against the young pelican molesters couldn't have been worse, and he was mad at himself for losing control. Again.

The Lauderdale-by-the-Sea police officer was a polite young fellow not much older than Twilly. He stood back from the truck, peering into the cab and shining a powerful flashlight on McGuinn, who started barking theatrically. The officer seemed relieved that it was a dog and not a large dark-skinned person sharing the front seat with Twilly. He asked Twilly to step out and show his driver's license. Twilly did as he was told. He easily could have disarmed and outrun the young cop, but he couldn't abandon McGuinn. No, they were going down together, man and beast.

The policeman said: "Sir, I noticed you were driving erratically."

Twilly was elated—a routine traffic stop! "Yes. Yes, I *was* driving erratically!"

"Is there a reason?"

"Yes, sir. I accidentally dropped a Liv-A-Snap on my lap, and the dog went for it." This was the absolute truth. "At that moment," Twilly said, "I'm sure I began driving erratically."

"It's a big dog you got there," the officer allowed.

"And rambunctious," added Twilly. "I'm sorry if we alarmed you."

"Mind taking a Breathalyzer?"

"Not at all."

"Because I definitely smell beer."

"I didn't drink it. It got spilled on me," Twilly said, without elaboration.

He passed the breath test with flying colors. The young policeman got on the radio to check for outstanding warrants, but Twilly came up clean. The officer walked back to the truck and gave it a once-over with the flashlight, the beam of which settled upon an old steamer trunk in the cargo bed.

"Mind if I look inside?" the policeman asked.

"I'd rather you didn't," Twilly said.

"Whatcha got in there?"

"You'd never believe it."

"I can call in a K-9 unit, Mr. Spree. If you want to do this the hard way."

"K-9s in Lauderdale-by-the-Sea," Twilly marveled. "What are they sniffing for, bootleg Metamucil?"

A second squad car brought a trained German shepherd named Spike. Twilly and McGuinn were ordered to stand back and observe. Twilly spied the Labrador looking up at him querulously. "You're right," Twilly muttered to the dog. "I'm an asshole."

The young cop lowered the tailgate, and the trained German shepherd sprung into the bed of the pickup. One whiff at the steamer chest and Spike went white-eyed—yapping, snapping, scratching at the locks, turning circles.

"God Almighty," said the K-9 cop.

"I got the trunk at a yard sale," Twilly said. "They said it came over on the *Queen Mary.*" True enough.

"The hell you got in there, son?"

Twilly sighed. He approached the pickup and said, "May I?"

"Do it," said the younger cop.

Twilly flipped the latches and opened the lid of the chest. When Spike the drug-sniffing shepherd saw what was inside, he vaulted off the tailgate and bounded, whimpering, into the cage of his master's squad car. Both policemen trained their lights on the contents of the steamer trunk.

The K-9 cop, trying not to sound shocked: "What's the story here?"

"It's dead," said Twilly.

"I'm listening."

"That's just ice, dry ice. It's not dope."

"What a helpful guy," said the K-9 cop.

"There's no law against possessing a dead dog," Twilly asserted, although he wasn't certain.

The officers stared at the roadkill Labrador. One of them said: "Happened to the ear?"

"Vulture," replied Twilly.

"So, why are you driving around with this . . . this item in your truck?" the younger cop asked.

"Because he's a deeply twisted fuckhead?" the K-9 officer suggested.

"I'm on my way to bury it," Twilly explained.

"Where?"

"The beach."

"Let me guess. Because Labs love the water?"

Twilly nodded. "Something like that."

The younger cop said nothing as he wrote Twilly a ticket for improper lane changing. Nor did he reply when Twilly asked if he'd ever lost a beloved pet himself.

"Look, this is *not* what you think," Twilly persisted. "He got hit by a car. He deserves a decent burial."

"Whatever." The young policeman handed him the ticket. "You can pay by mail."

"I don't blame you for being suspicious."

The K-9 officer said, "On the off chance you're telling the truth, don't try to bury this damn thing on the public beach."

"Why not? Is there a law against it?"

"I don't know and I don't care. Understand?"

The younger cop bent to stroke McGuinn's neck. "If I stop your truck again," he said to Twilly, "and there's *two* dead dogs inside, I'm going to shoot your ass. Law or no law."

"Your candor is appreciated," Twilly said.

After the policemen left, he drove south along A1A to Fort Lauderdale, where he parked across from Bahia Mar. He hoisted the steamer trunk out of his truck and, walking backward, dragged it along the sand. He stopped behind the Yankee Clipper Hotel and dug for more than an hour with his bare hands. No one stopped to ask what he was doing but around the steamer trunk a small crowd of curious tourists gathered, many of them Europeans. They acted as if they anticipated entertainment; a magic act, perhaps, or a busker! Twilly opened the lid to show them what was inside before he covered it up with sand. Afterward one of the tourists, a slight gray-bearded man, stepped up to the fresh grave and said a prayer in Danish. Soon he was joined by the others, each murmuring reverently in their native tongue. Twilly was deeply moved. He hugged the Dane, and then each of the other tourists one by one. Then he stripped off his clothes and dove into the ocean. When he got out of the water, he was alone on the beach.

He picked up Desie on Federal Highway, at the south end of the New River Tunnel.

"A really super idea," she remarked when she got in the truck. "They think I'm a hooker, standing out here on the corner. I had a dozen guys stop and ask how much for a blow job."

"What did you tell them?"

"Very funny."

"Well," said Twilly, "you don't look like a hooker."

"Aw, what a sweet thing to say."

"Aren't we the sarcastic one?"

"Sorry," Desie said, "but I had a shitty day. And a fairly shitty night, too, come to think of it. Where's my dog?"

"Someplace safe."

"No more games, Twilly. Please."

"I had to be sure you came alone."

"Another vote of confidence. What're you staring at?"

"Nothing."

"Blue jeans, sandals and a Donna Karan pullover—is that what streetwalkers are wearing these days?"

Twilly said, "You look great. That's what I'm staring at."

"Well, don't." Self-consciously she pulled her hair back into a ponytail, tucking it into a blue elastic band. This gave Twilly quite a lovely angle on her neck.

"What's in the shopping bag, Mrs. Stoat?"

When she showed him, he broke into a grin. It was a paper-back edition of *The Dreadful Lemon Sky,* a box of Tic Tacs, a jumbo bag of Liv-A-Snaps and a compact disc called *Back From Rio,* a solo album by Roger McGuinn, the dog's namesake.

Twilly slipped the CD into his dashboard stereo. "This is an extremely nice surprise. Thank you."

"Welcome."

"What's the matter?"

"Nothing." Desie sniffled. "Everything." She was biting her lower lip.

"I'll shut up now," said Twilly. But they weren't even halfway to Miami Beach when he noticed her left foot tapping in time to the music. Twilly thought: She'll be all right. And it was nice with her sitting beside him again.

He'd reserved two ocean-view rooms at the Delano. Desie was incredulous. "The dog gets his own?" she asked in the elevator.

"The dog snores," Twilly explained, "and also farts."

"How'd you sneak him past the front desk?"

"Kate Moss is staying here."

"Go on," Desie said.

"She and her actor boyfriend. What's his name—Johnny Damon?"

"Johnny Depp."

"Right," Twilly said. "This is Johnny's dog. Johnny doesn't go anywhere without him. Johnny and the dog are inseparable."

"And they went for that?"

"Seemed to."

"Lord," said Desie.

The elevator was lit in red but the rooms were done entirely in white, top to bottom. McGuinn was so excited to see Desie that he dribbled pee on the alabaster tile. She took a white towel from the white bathroom and got on her knees to wipe up

McGuinn's piddle. The dog thought she wanted to play—he flattened to a half crouch and began to bark uproariously.

"Hush!" Desie said, but she was soon laughing and rolling around on the floor with the dog. She noticed that the surgical staples had been removed from his belly.

"He's doing fine," said Twilly.

"Is he taking his pills?"

"No problemo."

"Roast beef?"

"No, he got hip to that. Now we're doing pork chops."

Desie went to the minibar, which was also white. She was reaching for a Diet Coke when she noticed it—a plastic Baggie. She picked it up, recognized what was inside and hastily put it back, between the table wafers and the Toblerone chocolate bar. With a gasp she said, "My God, Twilly."

He plopped down helplessly on the corner of the bed. McGuinn trotted to the other side of the room and tentatively positioned himself by the door.

"Where did it come from?" Desie asked.

"Same place as the ear."

Desie closed the door of the minibar.

"Don't worry," Twilly said, "I didn't kill anything. He was dead when I found him."

"On the road?" Desie spoke so softly that Twilly could barely hear her. "Did you find him on the road?"

"Yep."

Her eyes cut back toward the minibar. "What a weird coincidence, huh? Another black Lab."

"No coincidence. I was looking for one. I drove all over creation."

Desie sighed. "That's what I was afraid of."

"Well, what the hell was I supposed to do?" Twilly rose from the bed and began to pace. "And it worked, didn't it? The Great White Hunter fell for it."

"Yes, he did."

"Right, so don't give me that what-a-poor-sick-soul-you-are look. The animal was already dead, OK? He didn't need the ear anymore!"

Desie motioned him to sit down. She joined him on the bed and said, "Calm down, for heaven's sake. I'm surprised is all. I'm not being judgmental."

"Good."

"It's just . . . I thought the ear was enough. I mean, I thought it worked like a charm. Governor Dick did what you wanted, didn't he? He vetoed the Shearwater bridge."

"Well, speaking from experience, it never hurts"—Twilly shooting to his feet again—"it never hurts to add an exclamation point."

"All right."

"So there's no ambiguity, no confusion whatsoever."

Desie said, "I understand."

"Excellent. Now, we'll need a cigar box."

"OK."

"A special cigar box," Twilly said. "Are you going to help me or not?"

"Would you please chill out? Of course I'll help. But first—"

"What?"

"First, I think I know somebody," Desie said, turning toward the door, "who needs a nice long w-a-l-k. . . ."

McGuinn's ebony ears shot up and his tail began flogging the tile.

12

I spoke to the governor."

Jesus, that wasn't what Palmer Stoat wanted to hear from Robert Clapley; not while Stoat was tied to a bar stool, trussed up with an electrical cord in his own kitchen, the maid off for the day and a blond stranger with a stubby-barreled gun standing over him.

And Robert Clapley pacing back and forth, saying things such as: "Palmer, you are a fuckweasel of the lowest order. Is that not true?"

This, less than two hours after Stoat had phoned Clapley to break the news about the governor's intention to veto the Shearwater Island bridge appropriation. Stoat, laying it off on Willie Vasquez-Washington—that sneaky spade/spic/redskin!—Stoat claiming it was Willie backing out of the deal, busting the governor's balls to make him sign some bullshit budget rider guaranteeing minority contractors for the new Miami baseball stadium. Haitian plasterers, Cuban drywallers, Miccosukee plumbers—God only knows what all Willie was demanding! Stoat telling Clapley: It's race politics, Bob. Amateur hour. Has nothing to do with you or me.

And Clapley, going ballistic (as Stoat had anticipated), hollering into the phone about betrayal, low-life double cross, revenge. And Stoat meanwhile working to soothe his young client, saying he had a plan to save the bridge. Wouldn't be easy, Stoat had confided, but he was pretty sure he could pull it off. Then telling Clapley about the special session of the legislature that Dick Artemus had planned—for beefing up the education budget, Stoat had explained. There'd be tons of dough to go around, too, plenty for Clapley's bridge. All he had to do was build an elementary school on Shearwater Island.

"Name it after yourself!" Stoat had enthused.

On the other end of the line there was a long silence that should have given Stoat the jitters, but it didn't. Then Robert Clapley saying, in a tone that was far too level: "A school."

You bet, Stoat had said. Don't you see, Bob? A school needs school buses, and a school bus cannot possibly cross that creaky old wooden bridge to the island. So they'll just have to build you a new one. They can't possibly say no!

More silence on Clapley's end, then what sounded like a grunt—and Stoat still not picking up on the inclemency of the situation.

"I think this is perfectly doable, Bob. I believe I can set this up."

And Clapley, still in a monotone: "For how much?"

"Another fifty ought to do it."

"Another fifty."

"Plus expenses. There'll be some travel," Stoat had added. "And some dinners, I expect."

"Let me get back to you, Palmer."

Which were Robert Clapley's last words on the matter, until

he showed up unannounced at Stoat's house. Him and the freak in the houndstooth checked suit. The man was short and broadly constructed, with incongruously moussed-up hair—dyed, too, because the ends were egg white and spiky, giving the effect of quills. Clapley's man looked like he had a blond porcupine stapled to his skull.

Stoat had opened the front door and in they came. Before greetings could be exchanged, the spiky blond man had whipped out a stubby pistol, bound Stoat to the bar stool and dragged the bar stool into the kitchen. There Robert Clapley paced in front of the bay window, his diamond ear stud glinting when he spun on his heels.

He began by addressing Stoat as follows: "Palmer, you are a world-class turd fondler."

And so on, ending with: "I spoke to the governor."

"Oh." Stoat experienced a liquid flutter far, far down in his colon. He went icy at the prospect of being shot point-blank, which now seemed likely. Bitterly he thought of the Glock in the Range Rover's glove compartment, and of the .38 in his bedroom, both useless in his singular moment of dire peril.

"Dick told me everything," Clapley was saying. "Told me this was entirely your idea, the veto, on account of your fucking dog got kidnapped by some mystery maniac. Can this possibly be true? Of course not. There's no earthly way."

Stoat said, "The guy sent me an ear."

"Do tell." Robert Clapley put his tan face close to Stoat's. He wore a mocking smile. Palmer Stoat was struck—no, overwhelmed—by Clapley's cologne, which smelled like a fruit salad gone bad.

"The dog's ear, Bob. The guy cut it off and sent it to me."

Clapley chuckled harshly and moved away. "Yeah, Dick told me all about that, the FedEx delivery. I say it's bullshit. *Creative* bullshit, Palmer, but bullshit nonetheless. I say you're nothing but a world-class turd fondler who's making up stories in order to shake me down for an extra fifty large. Please give me one good reason not to trust my instincts."

Then, as if on impulse, Blond Porcupine Man seized a handful of Stoat's hair, jerked back his head, pried open his mouth, inserted something warm and soft, closed his mouth and then continued to hold his jaws shut. This was achieved, with viselike effect, by placing a thumb beneath Palmer Stoat's surgically resculpted chin, and a stiff finger inside each nostril.

Robert Clapley saying: "Before I became a real estate developer, I was engaged in another line of work—not exporting VCRs, either, as you've probably figured out. Mr. Gash here was on my payroll, Palmer. I'm sure even you can figure out what he did for me, job description–wise. Nod if you understand."

It wasn't easy, with Mr. Gash clamping his face, but Stoat managed to nod. He was also desperately trying not to throw up, as he would likely choke to death on his own trapped vomit. The gag reflex had been triggered when the small soft object Mr. Gash had dropped into Stoat's mouth began to squirm; when Stoat finally identified the odd tickling sensation as movement—ambulation, it felt like, something crawling across his tongue, moistly nosing into the pouch of his right cheek. Stoat's doll-sized blue eyes puckered into a squint, and with a violent moan he began shaking his head.

Robert Clapley said to Mr. Gash: "Aw, let him go."

And Mr. Gash released Stoat's face, allowing him to unhinge his jaws and expel (in addition to the tuna casserole he'd eaten for lunch) a live baby rat. The rat was dappled pink and nearly hairless, no bigger than a Vienna sausage. It landed unharmed on the kitchen counter, next to a bottle of Tabasco sauce, and began to creep away.

Later, after Stoat finished hacking and splurting, Clapley placed a hand on the back of his neck. "That's a little something from the old days, the rat-in-the-mouth number. Worked then, works now."

"Lets you know we're serious." The first utterance by Mr. Gash. He had a deceptive voice, as mild as a chaplain's, and it sent a frigid bolt up Stoat's spine.

Clapley said, "Palmer, I assume you've now got something to say. Help me fill in the missing pieces."

And Stoat, who had never before faced torture or death, willed himself to swallow. He grimaced at the taste of his own bile, spit copiously on the tile and croaked: "The freezer. Look in the goddamn freezer." Jerking his chin toward the huge custom Sub-Zero that Desie had picked out for the kitchen.

Mr. Gash opened the door, peeked inside, turned to Clapley and shrugged.

Stoat blurted: "Behind the ice cream!" Praying that Desie hadn't moved the damn thing, or thrown it in the trash.

Mr. Gash, reaching into the freezer compartment and moving things around, taking things out—a pair of steaks, a box of frozen peas, a do-it-yourself pizza, a carton of rum raisin—dropping them on the floor. Then giving a barely audible "Hmmmm," and withdrawing from the freezer the clear Baggie containing the dog ear.

"See!" cried Stoat.

Mr. Gash tapped the frosty ear into the palm of his hand. He examined it closely, holding it to the light as if it were an autumn leaf, or a shred of rare parchment.

Then he turned and said: "Yeah, it's real. But so fucking what?"

But Robert Clapley knew what the severed ear in the freezer meant. It meant that Palmer Stoat (turd fondler though he was) was telling the truth about the dognapping. Stoat was capable of many tawdry things, Clapley knew, but hacking off a dog's ear wasn't one of them. A fellow like Mr. Gash, he might do it on a friendly bet. But not Stoat; not for fifty grand, or five hundred grand. He couldn't hurt a puppy dog, his or anybody else's.

So Robert Clapley told Mr. Gash to untie Stoat, then allowed the sweaty wretch a few moments to freshen up and get dressed. When Stoat finally emerged from the bathroom—his face puffy and damp—Clapley motioned him to take a seat. Mr. Gash was gone.

"Now, Palmer," Clapley said. "Why don't you start at chapter one."

So Stoat told him the whole story. Afterward, Clapley rocked back and folded his arms. "See, this is exactly why I'll never have kids. Never! Because the world's such a diseased and perverted place. This is one of the sickest goddamn things I ever heard of, this business with the ear."

"Yeah," said Stoat without much fervor. In his cheeks he could still feel the tickle of Clapley's rat.

And Clapley ranted on: "Stealing and mutilating a man's dog, Jesus Christ, this must be one diseased cocksucker. And you've got no idea who he is?"

"No, Bob."

"Or where he is?"

"Nope."

"What about your wife?"

"She's met him. He grabbed her, too," Stoat said, "but he let her go."

Robert Clapley frowned. "I wonder why he did that. Let her go, I mean."

"Beats me." Stoat was exhausted. He wanted this creep out of his house.

"Would you mind if I spoke to Mrs. Stoat?"

"She's not here now."

"Then whenever."

Stoat said, "Why?"

"To find out as much as possible about your sicko dognapper. So I'll know what I'm up against."

"Up against, *when?*"

"When I send Mr. Gash after him, Palmer. Don't be such a chowderhead." Clapley smiled matter-of-factly and tapped his knuckles on the kitchen table. "When I send Mr. Gash to go find this deranged bastard and kill him."

Stoat nodded as if the plan was not only logical but routine—anything to please Clapley and hasten his departure, leaving Stoat free to go get drunk. He was so shaken and wrung-out that he could barely restrain himself from fleeing the house at a dead run. And, Christ, now the man was talking about *murder.*

"One thing I've learned about the world," Clapley was saying, "is that shitheads like this won't go away. They say they will but they never do. Suppose Dick vetoes my bridge, and this pervo puppy-slasher actually frees your dog, or what's left of your dog. What d'you think happens as soon as he finds out we're getting the bridge anyway?"

Stoat said, "OK, I see your point."

"He'll pull some other crazy stunt."

"Probably."

"Not only inconvenient to me but very expensive."

"Not to mention vicious," said Stoat.

"So the only sensible thing to do, Palmer, is waste the fucker. As we used to say in the old days."

"Did you tell that to the governor?"

"Oh sure. He said he'd loan me his MAC-10." Robert Clapley drummed the table impatiently. "What the hell's the matter with you? *No,* I didn't tell the governor."

Clapley informed Stoat that he, too, was a dog lover at heart. He would go along with the veto scam so that Stoat's Labrador retriever might be saved, and also to buy Mr. Gash some time to get a bead on this lunatic kidnapper.

"But I'm not building any elementary schools on Shearwater Island, not with my hard-laundered money. I made this crystal clear to our friend Governor Dick, and he said not to worry. He said it's all for show, the school item, and nobody'll remember to check on it later, after the bridge is up."

Stoat said, "The governor's right. They'll forget about it."

"So we'll get this little problem straightened out. I'm not concerned about that," said Clapley, "but I am disappointed in you, Palmer. After all I've done for you, the dove hunt and the free pussy and so forth. . . ."

"You're right, Bob. I should've told you as soon as it happened."

"Oh, not telling me was disappointing enough. But on top of it all you try to rip me off . . . that takes kryptonite balls! Not just blaming Rainbow Willie for the veto but exploiting the dog situation for your own gain—I mean, that's about the lowest thing imaginable."

Stoat said, miserably, "I'm sorry." He should have had a backup plan; should have guessed that the hotheaded Clapley might contact the governor directly; should have known that Dick Artemus would've ignored Stoat's instructions and taken Clapley's phone call, Clapley being a platinum-plated campaign donor and Dick being an obsequious glad-handing maggot.

"I thought it was all bullshit, until I saw the ear." Clapley pointed solemnly toward the freezer. "I thought, Hell, Palmer's gotta be making it up, that weirdness about the dog ear. A fifty-thousand-dollar line of bullshit is what I figured. But you weren't making it up."

"I'm afraid not."

"Which makes it worse. Which makes *you* worse," Clapley said. "Worse than the worst of turd fondlers, is this not true?"

Stoat, dull-eyed and slump-shouldered: "What do you want from me, Bob?"

"Fifty thousand bucks' worth of fun," Clapley replied without hesitation. "Let's start with a cheetah for the wall. I remember you told me about a place where I could shoot one. A place right here in Florida, so I wouldn't have to fly to Bumfuck, Africa, or wherever."

"Yes. It's called the Wilderness Veldt Plantation."

"Where you got your black rhino!"

"Right," Stoat said.

"So how about let's go there on a cheetah hunt. All expenses paid by you."

"No problem, Bob." Stoat thinking: Easy enough. One phone call to Durgess. "It'll take a little time to set up," he told Clapley, "in case they don't have a cat on the property. Then they'll have to order one."

"All the way from Africa? That could be months."

"No, no. They get 'em from zoos, circuses, private collectors. Two-day air freight. Three tops."

Robert Clapley said, "I want a goody."

"Of course."

"A prime pelt."

"Guaranteed." Stoat was dying for a drink and a cigar at Swain's. Something to kill the reek of fear, and also the aftertaste of rodent. Maybe Estelle the Republican prostitute would be there to listen to his tale of terror.

"A cheetah would be fantastic, really fantastic," Robert Clapley was saying.

"I'll call you soon with the details."

"Terrific. Now, what else?"

Stoat shook his head helplessly. "What else do you want?"

"Something for the Barbies. Something special."

Stoat sagged in relief. "I've got just the thing." Opening a cupboard and removing the opaque Tupperware container; popping the lid and showing Clapley what was inside.

"Is that what I think it is?" Clapley wasn't pleased. "I hauled all kinds a shit in my day, but I never used the stuff. As a matter of policy, Palmer."

"It's not dope, Bob. It's rhinoceros horn. Powdered rhinoceros horn."

"Wow." Clapley, leaning closer, using a pinkie finger to touch the fine grains. "I heard about this," he said.

"The Barbies will love you for it. And love you and love you and love you." Stoat winked.

"No shit?"

"Magical erections, amigo. I want a full report."

Stoat inwardly congratulated himself for remembering about the rhino powder. Now he and Clapley were back to being buddies, almost. Clapley closed the Tupperware and tucked it like a football under one arm. Palmer Stoat felt a wave of liberation as he escorted him to the door.

"What exactly do I do with this stuff?" Clapley was saying. "Snort it or smoke it, or what?"

"Put some in your wine," Stoat advised. "You drink wine? Sprinkle some in there." That's what the Chinese man in Panama City had instructed.

"But how much? How much should I use?" asked Clapley.

Palmer Stoat didn't know the answer; he'd forgotten to question Mr. Yee about dosages. So Stoat told Clapley: "Normally I'd say a tablespoon, but for you, two. One for each Barbie."

Clapley laughed. "Well, I *do* try not to play favorites."

"Exactly!" Now Stoat was laughing, too.

"Good night, Palmer. Sorry if Mr. Gash gave you a fright, but it's important to get these things out in the open."

"Speaking of which"—Stoat, giving a worried backward glance over his shoulder—"I almost forgot, Bob. What about that damn rat?"

"Oh, you keep it," said Clapley amiably. "It's yours."

*　　*　　*

Contrary to popular assumption, Lisa June Peterson was not sleeping with her boss. To be sure, she had been hired by Dick Artemus with that in mind. The three names, the long straw-blond hair, the impeccable Tri Delt credentials from Florida State—she was everything the new governor desired in a junior staff assistant. But his lubricious plans for Lisa June had been derailed by her unexpected and dazzling competency, which made her too valuable to be a mistress. Dick Artemus was not a brilliant man but he appreciated talent, especially talent that made him look good. Lisa June was meticulous, quick-thinking and intuitive, and she advanced quickly to the important position of executive assistant—gatekeeper to the governor's office. Nobody got a personal audience with Dick Artemus unless Lisa June Peterson checked off on it. No phone call reached the governor's desk without ringing first at Lisa June's. And, consequently, it was largely because of her that Dick Artemus's office appeared to run smoothly.

He would have been disappointed to know that Lisa June Peterson's fierce and protective efficiency had nothing to do with loyalty. She was assiduous and responsible by nature. It was not the rare honor of working for a governor that had drawn her to the job but rather a keen and calculating curiosity. Lisa June wanted to learn how government really worked, wanted to know who held the true power, and how they'd gotten it. She was looking down the road—long after Dick Artemus had returned to his Toyota tent jamborees in Jacksonville—to a day when she herself could be a serious player, putting to good use all the tricks she'd learned, all the contacts she'd made while babysitting Governor Dick. . . .

"Where do you see yourself, hon?" he'd ask her now and then.

And she would answer: "Someday I'd like to be a lobbyist."

Dick Artemus would crinkle his face as if he'd just stepped in dog shit, as if lobbying was the most loathsome job in the universe. Lisa June Peterson was always tempted to say something sarcastic about the lustrous ethical standards of your average car salesman. . . .

But she held her tongue, and took the calls. For someone who professed to despise lobbyists, the new governor counted plenty of them as friends. And they were (Lisa June was the first to admit) a mostly purulent lot. Neggy Keele, the NRA's seedy point man in Tallahassee, sprung instantly to mind. So did Carl Bandsaw, the pinstriped hustler who represented sugarcane growers and phosphate miners. And then there was sweaty-faced Palmer Stoat, the boss hog of them all. No cause was too abhorrent for Stoat—he'd work for anybody and anything, if the price was right. In addition to the requisite lack of a conscience, Stoat had been blessed with a monumental ego; he was openly proud of what he did. He considered it prestigious, the fixing of deals.

Other lobbyists didn't try to sleep with Lisa June Peterson because they assumed she was sleeping with the governor. Dick Artemus did nothing to discourage the rumor, nor did Lisa June herself. It made life easier, not having to fend off so many drooling scumbags. Palmer Stoat was the only one who didn't seem to care. In fact, he often hinted to Lisa June that he and the governor had "shared" other women, as if inviting her to join some exclusive club. She declined firmly but without reproach. In two years Dick Artemus himself had made only one drunken pass at Lisa June Peterson, late one evening when she was alone at her desk. He had come at her from behind, reaching around and cupping both hands on her breasts. Lisa June hadn't protested or squirmed or yelled—she had simply put down the telephone and said: "You've got sixty seconds, Governor."

"To do what?" Dick Artemus had asked, his breath sour and boozy.

"Touch 'em," Lisa June had said, "and you'd better make the most of it, because this is all you'll ever get from me. No blow jobs, no hand jobs, no intercourse, nothing. This is it, Governor, your one minute of glory. Fondle away."

He had recoiled as if he'd stuck his hands in a nest of yellow jackets, then shakily retreated to the executive toilet until Lisa June Peterson went home. To the governor's vast relief, she never mentioned the incident again. Nor did she interfere with, or comment upon, his many liaisons with other staff members. Dick Artemus mistook Lisa June's silence for discretion, when in truth it was plain disinterest. She was no more surprised or appalled by the governor's oafish behavior than she was by that of legislators, cabinet members or (yes) lobbyists. Far from being dispirited by their aggregate sliminess, Lisa June Peterson found in it a cause for hope. She could run circles around these lecherous, easily distracted clowns, and in time she would.

Until then, she would continue to watch, listen and learn. Every morning she arrived at work at eight sharp, poised and cordial and always prepared—as she was on this day, one of the rare days when Dick Artemus had beaten her to the office. He was waiting at his desk when she brought him a cup of coffee. He asked her to close the door and sit down.

"I've got a little problem, Lisa June."

He always used both names.

"Yes, sir?"

"I need to find a man that's been missing awhile."

Lisa June said, "I'll call FDLE right away."

That was the Florida Department of Law Enforcement, the state equivalent of the FBI.

The governor shook his head. "Naw, there's a better way to handle this. If I give you a name, can you get me some information?"

"Certainly."

"Take as much time as you need. The whole day," Dick Artemus said. "It's real important, Lisa June."

He told her the man's name, and what he'd done. She looked surprised.

"I've never heard of him," she said.

"It was before your time, hon."

"But, still. . . ."

"Ancient history," said the governor. "When were you born?"

"Nineteen seventy-five."

Dick Artemus smiled. "Sweet Jesus, you weren't even out of diapers when it happened."

Lisa June Peterson spent the morning at the state archives, her lunch break on the telephone, and the afternoon in the morgue of the Tallahassee *Democrat*. That evening she returned to the governor's office with two cardboard boxes of files and newspaper clippings.

"It's all old stuff," she reported. "Too old. He could be dead by now."

"Oh, I seriously doubt it. Who could find out for us?" asked Dick Artemus. "Who would know where he might be?"

Lisa June passed the governor a sheet of paper. It was the copy of a letter from a Highway Patrolman to his troop commander, a seemingly routine request for transfer. In red ink Lisa June had circled the name at the bottom of the letter.

"*He* could probably find out," she said, "and he's still with the department."

"Good," said the governor. "Anything else I oughta know?"

"Yes, there is." Lisa June Peterson handed him a copy of another letter. This one was signed by the man himself.

Dick Artemus read it and said: "Excellent. This is excellent. Thank you, Lisa June."

"You're welcome."

She went home, showered, skipped dinner, got into bed and

lay there all night with her eyes wide open. She couldn't stop thinking about the missing man, wondering why Dick Artemus wanted to find him after so many years.

Car salesman turned governor.

How it fried Dick Artemus to hear himself described that way, the snotty implication being that all car salesmen were cagey and duplicitous, unworthy of holding public office. At first Dick Artemus had fought back, pridefully pointing out that his dealerships sold only Toyotas, the most popular and reliable automobile on the face of the planet. A quality vehicle, he'd said. Top-rated by all the important consumer magazines!

But the governor's media advisers told him he sounded not only petty but self-promotional, and that folks who loved their new Camry did not necessarily love the guy who'd sold it to them. The media advisers told Dick Artemus that the best thing he could do for his future political career was make voters *forget* he'd ever been a car salesman (not that the Democrats would ever let them forget). Take the high road, the media advisers told Dick Artemus. Act gubernatorial.

So Dick Artemus dutifully had programmed himself not to respond to the jokes and jabs about his past life, though it wasn't easy. He was a proud fellow. Moreover, he believed he wouldn't have made it to the governor's mansion had it not been for all those hard sweaty Florida summers on automobile lots. That's where you learned your people skills, Dick Artemus would tell his staff. That's where you learned your sincerity and your flattery and your graciousness. That's where you learned to smile until your cheeks cramped and your gums dried out.

Running for public office was a cakewalk, Dick Artemus liked to say, compared to moving 107 light pickups in one year (which he had done, single-handedly, in 1988). Even after winning the election, the new governor frequently found himself falling back on his proven Toyota-selling techniques when dealing with balky lobbyists, legislators and constituents. Wasn't politics all about persuasion? And wasn't that what Dick Artemus had been doing his entire adult life, persuading reluctant and suspicious people to overextend themselves?

While Dick Artemus felt unprepared for some facets of his job, he remained confident in his ability to sell anybody anything. (In interviews he insisted on describing himself as "a people person's people person," though the phrase induced muted groans from his staff.) The governor's abiding faith in his own charms led to many private meetings at the mansion. One-on-one, he liked to say, that's how I do business. And even his most cynical aides admitted that Dick Artemus was the best they'd ever seen, one-on-one. He could talk the fleas off a dog, they'd say. He could talk the buzzards off a shit wagon.

And talking was what Dick Artemus was doing now. Loosening his necktie, rolling up his cuffs, relaxing in a leather chair in his private study, the tall hardwood shelves lined with books he'd never cracked. Talking one-on-one to a black man wearing the stiff gray uniform of the state Highway Patrol. Sewn on one shoulder of the uniform was a patch depicting a ripe Florida orange, a pleasing sunburst of color to take a tourist's mind off the $180 speeding ticket he was being written.

The black trooper sitting in the governor's study had a strong handsome face and broad shoulders. He looked to be in his late forties or early fifties, wisps of silver visible in his short-cropped hair.

Dick Artemus said, "Well? Has it changed much since you worked here?" He was referring to the governor's mansion.

"Not much," the trooper said, with a polite smile.

"You're a lieutenant now?"

"Yes, sir."

"That's impressive," said the governor. Both of them knew why: The Highway Patrol was not famous for promoting minorities.

"Your wife?"

"She's fine, sir."

"She was a trooper, too?"

"That's right."

"Never went back?"

"No, sir."

Dick Artemus nodded to show his approval. "One in the family's enough. It's dangerous as hell out there on the road."

As if the lieutenant needed reminding.

"Which is why I asked you to stop by, Jim"—as if the trooper had a choice—"for this private chat," said the governor. "I've got a problem that needs to be handled quickly and quietly. A delicate situation involving a highly unstable individual—a nutcase, if I can be blunt—who's on the loose out there . . . *somewhere.*" Dick Artemus motioned somberly toward the window.

The trooper's expression never changed, but the governor sensed an onset of discomfort, a newfound wariness in the man's gaze. Artemus picked up on it immediately; he'd encountered the same vibe a thousand times before, with customers at Dick's Toyota Land, USA.

"What I'm about to tell you," the governor said, leaning forward, "must remain in the strictest confidence."

The trooper, whose name was Jim Tile, said, "Of course."

And Dick Artemus told him the story, almost the whole story, about the young man who'd kidnapped Palmer Stoat's dog and FedExed him one of the ears, in order to stop a new bridge from being built to a place called Toad Island.

"Or Shearwater, which is the developer's Yuppie-ass name for it," the governor added. "Point is, I didn't call you here to talk about rescuing some jerkoff lobbyist's dog—that's been taken care of. The problem is this young man, who has the potential—and I'm no shrink—but I'd say he's got the potential to hurt or even kill someone if we don't find him fast."

"And then what?" asked the black trooper.

"Get him some help, of course. Professional help, Lieutenant Tile. That's what the young man needs."

"Do you know his name?"

"Nope," said the governor.

"What he looks like?"

"We can find out. He was seen in a bar called Swain's, down in Lauderdale."

"Where is he now? What's the best guess?"

"No earthly idea, my friend." Dick Artemus was amused by the trooper's straight-faced questions, entertained by the charade.

Jim Tile said, "Then there's not much I can do."

"Is that so." The governor, smiling now. Not the car-lot smile, either, or the campaign smile. This was the OK-let's-cut-the-bullshit smile. "Look here, Jim, you know damn well what I need you to do."

The trooper momentarily glanced away. Dick Artemus could see the cable-thick cords of his neck go tight.

"So, tell me. How is our former governor these days? And don't say, 'Which one?' You *know* which one. The crazy one. Clinton Tyree."

"I don't know, sir. I haven't spoken to him in at least a year, probably longer."

"But you do know where to find him?"

"No, sir," said Jim Tile. Technically it was the truth. He knew *how* to find the ex-governor, but not *where*.

Dick Artemus got up, stretched his arms and ambled to the window. "The old-timers still talk about him around here. He wasn't even in office, what, two years, before he disappeared.

And still he's the one they always talk about. 'Where is he?' 'What's he done now?' 'Did they catch him yet?' 'You think he's still alive?' Man, it's the crazy fuckers that always capture the public imagination, huh? What is old Clint calling himself these days?"

The black trooper said, "I don't know. I call him Governor."

He said it so deadpan that Dick Artemus whipped around. And what Dick Artemus saw in Jim Tile's expression was worse than distrust, or even disliking. It was a bloodless and humiliating indifference.

"Look here, Jim, you were here when it happened. You were his bodyguard, for God's sake."

"And his friend."

"You bet," said the governor, "his friend, of course. When I say 'crazy,' you know what I mean. There's good crazy and bad crazy. And this kid who's hacking up Labrador retrievers to make a political statement, that's the bad kind of crazy."

"I'm sure you'll find him, sir." Jim Tile rose from the chair. He was several inches taller than Dick Artemus, big hair and all.

But the governor, selling hard, pressed on. "Skunk," he said, "I believe that's what he calls himself. Or is it Skink? See, Lieutenant, I've done my homework. Because I was as curious as anybody, hearing all this talk, all the rumors. You know he never even sat for a portrait? In the whole mansion there's nothing, not a picture or a plaque—nothing—to show he ever lived here. So hell, yes, I was curious."

Jim Tile said, "Sir, I'm sorry but I ought to be going. I teach a DUI school downtown that starts in twenty minutes."

"This'll take only five." Dick Artemus casually sidled in front of the door. "This Toad Island bridge, it's a twenty-eight-million-dollar item. The folks who want those contracts gave quite a bit of money to my campaign. So it's gonna get done, this damn bridge, one way or another. You can bet the farm on that.

Now—about this crazy boy, he's got the potential to make some ugly headlines, and that I don't need. Neither do my loyal friends at the future Shearwater Island resort.

"But even worse, I get the distinct feeling this boy's whacko behavior has put his own welfare in jeopardy. This information goes no further than you and me, Lieutenant. All I'll say is this: Some of the characters involved in this project aren't so nice. Am I proud to be their choice for governor?" Dick Artemus snorted. "That's a whole 'nother issue. But for now, I need to make sure nothing awful happens to this crazy dognapper, because, a, no young man deserves to die over something stupid like this and, b, that would be one ugly headline. A goddamn nightmare of a headline, can we all agree on that?"

The trooper said, "You really think they'd murder him?"

"Fucking A. And if he's half as crazy as I think, he won't go quietly. He'll make a big splash, like all these nutty ecoterrorists. And then Shearwater gets on the front pages, and before long some prick reporter follows the trail of slime directly to yours truly. Who, by the way, is hoping to be reelected in a couple years."

"Sir, I see your problem," Jim Tile said.

"Good."

"But he won't do it. Assuming I can even find him—in a million years I don't think he'd ever agree to help."

"And I think you're wrong." Dick Artemus walked to a maple credenza and picked up a brown office envelope. Both ends were taped shut. "Give this to the former governor, please. That's all I'm asking, Jim. Just make sure it reaches him, and then you're free of the whole mess. Whatever he decides, he decides. It's all laid out for him in black and white."

The governor handed the envelope to the trooper. "This is not a request, Lieutenant."

"Yes, sir, I know. I'll do what I can." Jim Tile spoke with such a blazing lack of enthusiasm that Dick Artemus abandoned his plans for an inducement: A job offer is what he'd been prepared to offer. An opportunity for the trooper to get off the highway and rest his tired middle-aged butt. Step out of the hot polyester uniform and into a nice suit. Return to the governor's mansion and ride security.

But Dick Artemus didn't waste his time trolling the idea by Jim Tile. He knew a cold customer when he saw one. The lieutenant would do what he was asked, but he would act strictly out of duty. Nothing more. The man had no interest in hitching his future to the governor's star, one-on-one.

"The truth is," Dick Artemus said, "after all I've heard, I'd like to meet your legendary friend someday myself. Under different circumstances, of course."

"I'll be sure to pass that along."

After the trooper was gone, the governor poured himself some fine bourbon and sat back to reflect on simpler times, when the worst thing he had to do was sell cherry-red pinstriping to helpless widows in two-door Corollas.

13

Estella was the name.

"Would you care for a drink?" asked Palmer Stoat. Then, to the bartender: "A vodka martini for my gorgeous guest."

The prostitute smiled tolerantly. "I remember you, too."

"I'm glad, Estella."

"You were quite the chatty one." She wore a violet cocktail dress and matching stockings. "You told me about a fishing trip with George Bush."

"Yes, that's right," Stoat said. "And you said he was the most underrated president since Hoover."

"He got a bum rap in the media, Bush did. Because he wasn't a smoothy, some TV glamour boy with big teeth." Estella's lipstick was a shade or two darker than her cocktail dress. She had nice skin and wore little makeup. Her hair, however, was myriad shades of blond. "I would've done him for free," she confided, "just to say thanks, Mr. Commander in

Chief, for the Gulf War. He did a helluva number on those shitbird Iraqis."

Stoat said, "Plus he's a very nice guy. Very down-to-earth." Estella slid closer to the bar. "I saw him lose a hundred-pound tarpon at the boat," said Stoat. "The line snagged on the propeller and that's all she wrote. And he was such a damn good sport about it."

"Doesn't surprise me one bit." The prostitute plucked the cigar from Stoat's mouth and took a couple of dainty puffs. "How about President Reagan?" she asked. "Ever meet him?"

Man oh man, thought Stoat. This is just what the doctor ordered. "Several times," he said matter-of-factly to Estella. "Talk about impressive. Talk about charisma."

She returned the cigar, slipping it between his lips. "Tell me some stories, Palmer."

He felt a small hand settle confidently between his legs. To hell with Robert Clapley and Porcupine Head, Stoat thought. To hell with the dognapper and the Shearwater bridge. Even Desie—where the hell had *she* gone today? Well, to hell with her, too.

Because Stoat was at Swain's now, buzzing sweetly in a familiar cloud of blue haze, alcohol and perfume. He leaned close to the call girl and said: "Ronnie once told me a dirty joke."

Another self-aggrandizing lie. Reagan had never spoken so much as a word to him. "Wanna hear it?"

Estella was practically straddling Palmer Stoat now, the bar stool listing precariously. "Tell me!" She nudged him purposefully with a breast. "Come on, you, tell me!"

But as Stoat struggled to remember the punch line to the joke about the horny one-eyed parrot, the bartender (who'd told Stoat the joke in the first place) touched his sleeve and said: "Sorry to bother you, but this just came by courier."

Which highly annoyed Stoat, as Estella's hand was now tugging on a part of him that craved tugging. Stoat was ready to wave off the bartender when he noticed what the man was holding: a cigar box. Even through the smoke Stoat recognized the distinctively ornate label, the official seal of the Republic of Cuba, and of course could not suppress his excitement.

Pulling away from the call girl, even as her fingers worked on his zipper. Reaching across the bar for the cigar box, assuming it to be a gift from a grateful client. Thinking of how many years he'd been trying to get a line on this particular blend. Already imagining the best place to display the box in his bookcase, among his other treasures.

Stoat taking the box with both hands and noticing first that the seal had been broken, and, second, that the box seemed too light.

Setting it on the polished oak bar and opening the lid—Estella watching, her chin on his shoulder—to find no cigars inside the box, not a single one.

Only the paw of an animal; a black shorthaired dog paw, severed neatly at the bone.

"What's that?" The prostitute craned to see.

Stoat was dumbstruck with disgust, the lunatic once again violating his sanctum.

"Lemme look," Estella said, releasing the tab on Stoat's zipper and extending the same inquisitive hand—she was a nimble one, Stoat had to admit—for the cigar box.

"Don't," he warned, too late.

Now she had the ghastly curio out of the box, turning it first one way and then another; tracing her painted fingernails around the velvety paw pads, playfully flicking at the sharp dewclaw.

"Palmer, is this some sorta joke? This can't be real."

Stoat clutched lugubriously at his drink. "I gotta go."

"Wow." Now Estella the prostitute was stroking the severed paw gently, as if it were alive. "Sure *feels* real," she remarked.

"Put it back, please. Back in the box."

"Holy Christ, Palmer!" In newfound revulsion she dropped the furry thing. It fell with a sploosh, stump-first into his brandy; lifeless doggy toenails hooking on the rim of the glass. Palmer Stoat snatched up the Cuban cigar box and made for the door.

Desie asked to see where he had buried the dead Labrador.

Twilly said, "You don't believe me."

"I believe you."

"No, you don't."

So they drove all the way back to Lauderdale. McGuinn rode in the bed of the pickup. The rush of seventy-mile-per-hour wind on the interstate made his ears stand out like bat wings. Desie said she wished she had a camera. Every time she spun around to look at the dog, Twilly got an amber glimpse of her neckline in the sodium streetlights. He liked the fact she wanted to see for herself about the other dog. Of course she would—after all, she was married to a compulsive bullshit artist. Why would she believe anything said to her by any man?

The beach behind the Yankee Clipper was nearly deserted, cast in a pinkish all-night dusk by the lights of the old hotel. The breeze had stiffened, and with it the splash and hiss of the surf. Twilly led Desie to the grave.

He said, "I suppose you want me to dig it up."

"That won't be necessary."

McGuinn sniffed intently at the fresh-turned sand.

"Ten bucks says he pees on it," Twilly said.

McGuinn cocked his head, as if he understood, and began circling a target zone.

"No!" Desie snatched up the leash and tugged the dog away from the grave. "This is so sad," she said.

"Yes."

"Didn't it creep you out? Cutting off the ear and the paw—"

"It's getting late, Mrs. Stoat. Time for you to go home."

"I left my purse at the Delano."

"We'll mail it to you," Twilly said.

"With my car keys and my house keys."

"Anything else?"

"Yes. My birth-control pills."

And I had to ask, Twilly thought. He nearly dozed off on the drive back to Miami Beach. Up in the hotel room he decided on a scalding shower, to rouse himself for more driving. From the bathroom he called to Desie: "Phone your husband and tell him you're on the way."

When Twilly came out, he found her in the white bed with the white covers pulled up to her throat. She said, "I'm afraid I got sand in your sheets. What time is it?"

"One-fifteen."

"I think I want to stay."

"I think I want you to stay."

"You're in no shape to drive."

"That's the only reason?"

"That's what I'm telling myself, yes."

"All right, stay. Because I'm in no shape to drive."

"Thank you," Desie said. "But no sex."

"Furthest thing from my mind."

Then McGuinn jumped on the bed and began licking her chin. Twilly said, "I could demand equal time."

"He's just a dog," said Desie. "You're a crazed felon."

"Move over."

That's how they spent the night, the three of them under a blanket at the Delano; Desie sandwiched in the middle. She awoke at dawn to husky dog breath, McGuinn's bullish head on the pillow beside her. Desie tried to turn over but she couldn't—

Twilly's face was buried in the crook of her neck, his lips pressed softly against her skin. She didn't know it but he was dreaming. For the first time ever.

Mr. Gash had spent the day listening to 911 tapes. He couldn't get enough of them. Off late-night television he had mail-ordered *The World's Most Bloodcurdling Emergency Calls*, Volumes 1–3. The recordings had been tape-recorded by police departments all over the country, and somebody had gotten the slick idea to compile them into a Best of 911 series and sell them on cassettes and CDs. Only the *F* word was edited out, to protect children who might be listening.

CALLER: 911? 911?

DISPATCHER: This is the police department. Do you have an emergency?

CALLER: Yeah, my one brother, he's stabbing the shit out of my other brother.

DISPATCHER: A stabbing, did you say?

CALLER: Yeah, you better send somebody out here fast. There's [bleeping] blood all over the drapes. He's gone crazy, you got to send somebody fast, fore he goes and kills us all.

DISPATCHER: Could you describe the weapon, ma'am?

CALLER: It's a knife, for Christ's sake. A huge [bleeping] butcher knife. It's got a wood handle and at the other end it's real pointy. Get the picture?

DISPATCHER: OK, OK, settle down. Where's your brother at now?

CALLER: On the floor. Where the hell do you think he's at? He's on the floor bleeding to death. He looks like a piece of [bleeping] Swiss cheese, except with catsup.

DISPATCHER: No, the brother with the butcher knife. Where's he at?

CALLER: In the kitchen. Probably getting another goddamn beer. Are you guys coming? 'Cause if you're not, just let me know so I can go ahead and slit my throat. To save my drunken crazy-ass brother the trouble.

DISPATCHER: Easy now, we've got units on the way. Can you stay on the phone? Are you in a safe place?

CALLER: Safe? Oh Christ, yeah. I'm locked in the [bleeping] bathroom of a double-wide house trailer, it's like Fort [bleeping] Knox in here. I'm snug as a bug in a goddamned rug—what's the matter with you people! Hell no, I'm not safe. A cat fart could knock down this whole damn place. . . .

DISPATCHER: Ma'am, try to stay calm.

CALLER: Oh Jesus, that's him! I hear him outside!! Clete, you back off from here! You leave me be, else I'm tellin' Mama what you did to Lippy, I swear to God! Don't you . . . now don't you dare open this door! Clete . . . goddammit, I got the cops on the phone—no! I told you no—

DISPATCHER: Ma'am, is that him? Is that your brother you're talking to?

CALLER: No, it's Garth [bleeping] Brooks. What's the matter with you morons—hey, Clete, stop that shit right now! No, no . . . put that thing down, you hear? Put it away!!!!

DISPATCHER: Ma'am? Hello? Are you all right?

Mr. Gash was exhilarated by the sound of fear in human voices. Fury, panic, despair—it was all there on the 911 calls, the full cycle of primal desperation.

Daddy's on a rampage.

Baby's in the swimming pool.

Momma took some pills.

There's a stranger at the bedroom window.

And yet, somehow, somebody makes it to a telephone and phones for help.

To Mr. Gash, this was better than theater, better than literature, better than music. True life is what it was; true life unspooling. He never tired of the 911 tapes. He even redubbed his favorites and set them to classical music—Mahler for domestic disputes, Tchaikovsky for cardiac arrests, and so on.

The emergency tapes kept his mind off the grinding traffic, and he listened to them all the way to Toad Island, the morning after he'd roughed up Palmer Stoat. For the long drive north, Mr. Gash had selected the *Best-of-House-Fire Calls*, with background accompaniment by Shostakovich.

DISPATCHER: Is there an emergency?

CALLER: Hurry! My house is on fire! It's on fire!

DISPATCHER: Where are you, sir?

CALLER: Inside! Inside the house!

DISPATCHER: Where inside the house?

CALLER: The bedroom, I'm pretty sure! Hurry, man, it's all on fire! Everything!

DISPATCHER: The trucks are on the way—

CALLER: I was basing under the Christmas tree, see—

DISPATCHER: Sir, you need to exit the dwelling immediately.

CALLER: Freebasing, see? And somehow, man, I don't know what happened but all of a sudden there's a flash and the tree's lit up, I mean big-time. Next thing, all the Christmas presents, they're on fire, too, and before long the whole scene is smoke. . . .

DISPATCHER: Sir, you need to get out of the house immediately. Right now.

CALLER: You hurry, that's the main thing. Hurry! 'Cause I
     don't have a goddamn clue where "out" is. You under-
     stand what I'm saying. I am one lost mother[bleeper],
     OK?

The tapes were aural tapestry to Mr. Gash. From a lone
scream he could fully visualize the interior of a house, its bare
halls and cluttered bedrooms; the faded carpets and the functional furniture, the oversized paintings and tense-looking family photographs. And of course he could see the orange flames
licking at the walls.

"Ouch," he said aloud as he drove.

Toad Island was the logical place to start hunting for the man
he was supposed to murder. Possibly the fellow lived there, or at
least must have visited the place. Why else would he give two
shits about Robert Clapley's bridge?

Mr. Gash's first stop was the home of Nils Fishback, the island's self-crowned "mayor" and Clapley's onetime political ad-
versary. Clapley had told Mr. Gash it was Fishback who'd know
the inside dope on any malcontents among the residents.

"Get off my damn property!" was Nils Fishback's intemper-
ate greeting to Mr. Gash.

"Mr. Clapley sent me."

"What for?" Fishback demanded. "What's with the hair,
jocko—you from England or somethin'?"

The old man was stationed on the front lawn. He was shoe-
less and shirtless, a bandanna knotted around his neck. The
bandanna was milky yellow, as was Fishback's long beard and
also his toenails. He appeared not to have bathed for some time.

"Can't you tell I'm busy?" Fishback pointed at a moving van
in the driveway. Two beefy men were lugging a long plaid sofa
up the ramp to the truck.

Mr. Gash said: "This'll only take a minute."

"I don't have a minute."

"What you don't have," said Mr. Gash, "is manners."

He intercepted the two movers and advised them to take a thirty-minute break. Then he grabbed Nils Fishback by one of his bony elbows and dragged him into the house and tied his ankles and wrists with a Dacron curtain sash and pushed him into a bathtub. After a short search Mr. Gash found a bar of Dial antiperspirant soap, untouched, which he forcefully inserted into Fishback's mouth.

"You probably feel like puking," Mr. Gash said, "but of course you can't."

From the tub Fishback stared up with wild, horsey eyes.

"Here's what I need from you," said Mr. Gash. He was hovering, a gun held loosely in one hand.

"There's a man causing Mr. Clapley lots of grief over the new bridge. What I need to know, 'Mr. Mayor,' is who would do something like this? Somebody out here on the island is my guess. Some creep trying to squeeze more money from my good friend Mr. Clapley."

Nils Fishback shook his head frantically. Mr. Gash laughed. He had been made aware of Fishback's lucrative real estate sellout. "Oh, I know it's not you," he told the old man. "From what I hear, you got no complaints. You made out like a bandit on this deal."

Now Fishback was nodding. Mr. Gash set the handgun on the toilet seat and took out a penknife, which he used to pry the cake of Dial from Fishback's mouth. The soap came out embedded with expensive porcelain bridgework. Immediately the mayor wriggled upright and began vomiting in his own lap. Mr. Gash turned on the shower, picked up his gun and left the bathroom.

When Nils Fishback emerged, he was the consummate host, all southern graciousness and hospitality. He fixed fresh coffee and powdered doughnuts for Mr. Gash, and told him of a rumor going around the island.

"About a guy who works for Roothaus, Clapley's engineering firm. This guy's all—what is it they say these days?—*conflicted* about his job. He's been getting drunked up at night, roamin' around saying it's a damn crime, what Clapley's set to do to this island."

"Crime?" Mr. Gash was amused.

"Crime against nature, the young man said. I believe he's some kind a biologist." Nils Fishback paused to readjust his dental bridge. Slivers of orange soap were visible between his front teeth.

He said, "Tree-hugger type, that's the rumor."

"But he works for Roothaus," said Mr. Gash, "who works for Clapley. Ha!" Mr. Gash knit his brow. "What ever happened to good old-fashioned loyalty? This is excellent coffee, by the way."

Fishback said: "Thanks. The young fella's name is Brinkman or Brickman. Somethin' like that. They say he's a doctor of biology."

"I appreciate the information."

Fishback fingered his sodden beard apprehensively. "Keep in mind, it's only a rumor. I don't wanna see nobody get hurt, because there might be nothin' to it. People say all kinds a crazy shit when they drink."

Mr. Gash rose and handed his empty cup to Fishback. "Well, these sorts of stories need to be checked out. Where you moving to, Mayor?"

"Vegas."

"Whoa. Land of opportunity."

"No, it's just I got sinus problems."

Mr. Gash smiled encouragingly. "You'll love it there."

* * *

Krimmler had warned Dr. Steven Brinkman to curtail his drinking, but it wasn't easy. Brinkman was depressed so much of the time. He had nearly completed the biological survey of Toad Island without documenting one endangered species. That was splendid tidings for Roger Roothaus and Robert Clapley, but not for the remaining wildlife; not for the ospreys or the raccoons, not for the gray squirrels or the brown tree snails, not for the whip-tailed lizards or the western sandpipers. Because now, Brinkman knew, there was no way to block the Shearwater resort. The creeps who'd bulldozed the tiny oak toads would do the same to all other creatures in their path, and no law or authority could stop them. So Dr. Brinkman's exhaustively detailed catalog of Toad Island's birds, mammals, reptiles, amphibians, insects and flora was for all practical purposes a death list, or that's how the young biologist had come to think of it.

Sometimes, at night, he would sneak into the construction trailer to brood over the impressive Shearwater mock-up—how verdant and woody the layout looked in miniature! But Brinkman knew it was an illusion created by those two immense golf courses—a wild, rolling splash of green rimmed by houses and condos, a chemical hue of emerald found nowhere in nature. And the suckers were lining up to buy! Occasionally Brinkman would crouch by the scale model in mordant contemplation of Clapley's "nature trail"—a linear quarter-mile trek through a scraggle of pines at the north hook of the island. And there was the scenic little saltwater creek, for kayaks and canoes. In the mock-up the creek was painted sky blue, but in real life (Brinkman knew) the water would be tea-colored and silted. A school of mullet would be cause for great excitement. Meanwhile Clapley's people would be leveling hundreds of acres for homesites, parking lots, the airstrip, the heliport and that frigging shooting range; they'd be dredging pristine estuary for the yacht harbor and water-sports complex and desalinization plants. Along the beach rose the dreaded high-rises; on the model, each sixteen-story tower was the size of a pack of Marlboro mediums.

Steven Brinkman felt awful about his complicity in the Shearwater juggernaut, and about his career calling in general. Go with the private sector—that's what his old man had advised him. His old man, who'd spent twenty-six years with the U.S. Forest Service and had nothing positive to say about government work. If I had it to do all over again, he'd grumble, I'd jump on that job with the timber company. Private sector, son, all the way!

And though it was the handsome salary that had induced Steven Brinkman to sign on with Roger Roothaus, he also honestly thought he could make a difference. Fresh out of school, he naïvely believed it was possible to find middle ground between the granola-head bunny lovers and the ruthless corporate despoilers. He believed science and common sense could bring both sides together, believed wholeheartedly in the future of "environmental engineering."

Then they put him to work counting butterflies and toads and field mice. And before long, Brinkman was also counting the days until he could go home. He didn't want to be on Toad Island when the clearing started. And he would never return afterward, to see if it ended up looking like the scale model.

For living quarters, Roothaus had provided a secondhand Winnebago but Steven Brinkman rarely used it, choosing instead to sleep under the stars in the doomed woods. Here he could drink recklessly without drawing Krimmler's ire. Most evenings he'd build a campfire and play R.E.M. on the small boom box that his sister had given him. The locals had long ago pegged Brinkman as a flake, and let him be.

Rarely was his outdoor solitude interrupted by anything noisier than a hoot owl, so he was therefore surprised to see a stocky stranger clomping into his camp. The man's blond hair was eccentrically spiked, but it was the houndstooth suit that put Brinkman on edge, even after half a quart of Stoli.

"I'm looking for a dog," the man announced, in a voice that was almost soothing.

Brinkman tottered to his feet. "Who're you?"

"A black Labrador retriever is what I'm looking for."

Brinkman shrugged. "No dog here."

"Possibly with one ear cut off. I don't suppose you'd know anything about that."

"No—"

In a flash the man pinned him against the trunk of a pine tree. "I work for Mr. Robert Clapley," he said.

"Me, too," said Brinkman. "What's the matter with you?"

"Are you Steven Brinkman?"

"Dr. Brinkman. Yeah, now—"

"The troublemaker?"

Brinkman struggled to break free. "What? I'm a field biologist."

The spiky-haired man grabbed him by the throat. "Where's the goddamn dog, *Doctor*?"

Brinkman spluttered a protest but Clapley's man knocked him down with a punch to the gut. "Jesus, you don't know what I'm talking about," the man said disgustedly. He kicked through the campsite, swearing. "You don't have the goddamn dog. You're not the one."

"No." Brinkman was on his knees, gasping.

"But you're still a troublemaker. Mr. Clapley doesn't like troublemakers." The man took out a pistol. "And you're trashed on top of it. Not good."

Brinkman fearfully threw up his dirt-smeared palms. "There was a guy here, a couple days ago. He had a black Lab."

"Go on." The man brushed a moth off his lapel.

"On the beach. Guy my age. Very tan. He had a big black Lab."

"How many ears?"

"Two, I think." Brinkman was pretty sure he would've remembered otherwise.

"What else, doctor?"

The man placed the gun to Brinkman's temple. Brinkman had been drinking so heavily that he couldn't even pee in his pants, couldn't make neurotransmitter contact with his own bladder.

He said, "The guy drove a black pickup truck. And there was a woman."

"What'd she look like?"

"Beautiful," Brinkman said. "Outstanding." The Stoli was kicking in magnificently.

The spiky-haired man whacked him with the butt of the pistol. " 'Beautiful' covers a lot of territory, doesn't it?"

Brinkman tried to collect himself. He felt a warm bubble of blood between his eyebrows. "She was a brunette, in her early thirties. Hair so long"—Brinkman, using both hands to indicate the length—"and the dog seemed to be hers. The Lab."

"So they weren't, like, a couple."

"Is it Mr. Clapley's dog? Those people—did they steal it?"

The man in the checked suit smirked. "Do I look like a person who wastes his time chasing lost pets? Seriously? Would I need a gun for that? Here, whistle dick, have another drink."

He shoved the Stoli bottle at Steven Brinkman, who took a swig and pondered what the blond man had said. He was a professional killer, of course. Clapley had sent him to the island to murder somebody, over something to do with a dog. Brinkman was too drunk to find it anything but hilarious, and he began to giggle.

The man said, "Shut up and tell me the guy's name."

"He never said." Again Brinkman felt the cold poke of the gun barrel against his temple. "They never gave their names. Neither one," he told the spiky-haired man. "Why would I lie?"

"I intend to find out."

Then, as sometimes happened with vodka, Steven Brinkman experienced a precipitous mood plunge. He remembered that he'd sort of liked the tan young man and the outstandingly beautiful woman with the friendly black dog. They had seemed entirely sympathetic and properly appalled about what was happening out here; the burying of the toads, for instance. Not everyone cared about toads.

And now here I am, Brinkman thought morosely, ratting them out to some punk-headed hit man. Just like I ratted out *Bufo quercicus* to Krimmler. Ratted out the whole blessed island. What a cowardly dork I am! Brinkman grieved.

"The name," said the killer. "I'm counting to six."

"Six?" Brinkman blurted.

"It's a lucky number for me. Three is another good one," the killer said. "Want me to count to three instead? One . . . two . . ."

Brinkman wrapped one hand around the gun barrel. "Look, I don't know the guy's name, but I know where he's camping tonight."

"That would be progress." Clapley's man holstered the gun and motioned for Brinkman to lead the way.

The biologist picked up a gas lantern and set off through the woods, though not stealthily. He was exceedingly tipsy and barely able to hoist his feet, much less direct them on a course. As he plowed ahead, pinballing off tree trunks and stumbling through scrub, Brinkman heard the blond stranger cursing bitterly from behind. Undoubtedly the pine boughs and thorny vines were taking a nappy toll on the houndstooth suit.

Brinkman's idea—it would hardly qualify as a plan—was to

tromp along until he found a clearing in which he could wheel around and clobber Clapley's man with the lantern. Only fine vodka could have imbued Brinkman with such grandiose estimations of his own strength and agility, but the anger in his heart was true and untainted. The spiky-headed intruder had become an ideally crude and lethal symbol for Shearwater and its attendant evils. Wouldn't it be cool to knock out the bastard and turn him over to the cops? And then? Sit back and watch Robert Clapley squirm, trying to explain such shenanigans to the media—a hired thug with a gun, turned loose to hunt down "troublemakers" on the island! Brinkman grinned, somewhat prematurely, at the headline.

Suddenly he found himself stepping out of the pines and into a broad opening, which filled with the lantern's pale yellow light. Brinkman saw squat machines, furrows and mounds of dry dirt—and, beneath his boots, a corrugated track. He knew where he was; a good place to do it, too. He gulped for the cool salty air and quickened his pace.

"Hey, shithead." It was Clapley's man.

Dr. Brinkman didn't turn all the way around, but from the corner of an eye he spotted the shadow—a flickery figure projected by lantern light on the blade of a bulldozer, like a puppet on a wall.

"Hey, you think this is funny?"

Clapley's man, striding faster now, coming up behind him. Dr. Brinkman deliberately slowed his pace, laboring to clear the buzz from his head, straining to gauge the proximity of the killer's footsteps, knowing the timing of this grand move had to be absolutely flawless . . . flawless timing, unfortunately, not being a typical side effect of massive vodka consumption.

So that when Steven Brinkman spun and swung the hefty lantern, Clapley's man was still five yards from reaching him, and safely out of range. Centrifugal physics whirled Brinkman almost 360 degrees, an involuntary rotation halted only by the force of the lantern striking the tire of a four-ton backhoe. Brinkman saw a white-pink flash and then a bright blue flash, heard one sharp pop and then another louder one—the lantern exploding, followed by something else. Brinkman went down in darkness, finding it fascinating (in a way that only a drunk man could) to feel the onrushing dampness of his own blood yet no pain from the bullet. He tried to run without getting up, his legs cycling haplessly in the dirt until he was breathless.

The clearing had become shockingly silent, and Brinkman momentarily rejoiced in the possibility that Clapley's man had taken him for dead and run off. But then Brinkman heard the bulldozer start, backfiring once before lurching into gear. Then he knew. Even with his brain awash in Stoli, he knew what was coming next; knew he should have been terrified to the marrow. But Steven Brinkman mainly felt tired, so tired and chilly and wet that all he wanted now was to sleep. Anyplace would do, anyplace where he could lie down would be dandy. Even someplace deep in the ground, among tiny man-mulched toads.

14

Twilly dreamed about Marco Island. He dreamed he was a boy, jogging the bone white beach and calling out for his father. The long strand of shore was stacked as far as he could see with ghastly high-rise apartments and condominiums. The structures rose supernaturally into the clouds, blocking the sunshine and casting immense chilly shadows over the beach where young Twilly ran, a shoe box full of seashells tucked under his arm.

In the dream, the first he could ever remember, Twilly heard Little Phil from somewhere on the far side of the high-rises; a voice echoing gaily along the concrete canyon. Twilly kept running, searching for a way between the buildings. But there was no path, no alley, no beckoning sliver of light: Each tower abutted the next, forming a steep unbroken wall—infinitely high, infinitely long—that served to blockade the island's entire shore.

Twilly Spree ran and ran, shouting his father's name. Above

the boy's head flew laughing gulls and ring-billed gulls and sand-wich terns, and around his bare legs skittered sanderlings and dowitchers and plovers. He noticed the tide was rising uncom-monly fast, so he ran harder, kicking up soft splashes. In the dream Twilly couldn't make out his father's words, but the tone suggested that Little Phil was not addressing his lost son but closing a real-estate deal; Twilly recognized the counterfeit buoyancy and contrived friendliness.

Still the boy ran hard, for the beach was disappearing beneath him. The salt water had reached his ankles—shockingly cold, too cold for swimming—and Twilly dropped the shoe box so he could pump with both arms to make himself run faster. The sting of the salt caused his eyes to well up, and the shoreline ahead grew blurry. In the dream Twilly wondered how the tide could be racing in so swiftly, because there was no storm push-ing behind it, not the smallest breath of wind. Beyond, the water lay as flat and featureless as polished glass!

Yet now it was rising to Twilly's kneecaps, and running had become impossible. The boy was seized by a paralyzing chill, as if a spike of ice had been hammered into his spine. Through the blur he could make out the W-shaped silhouettes of seabirds wheeling and slanting and skimming insanely above the roiled foam. He wondered why the birds didn't simply fly upward and away, far out to the Gulf, but instead they went crashing blindly into the monolith of buildings; dull concussions of feather and bone. In wild whirling torrents the birds smashed themselves into windowpanes and balconies and awnings and sliding doors, and before long the façades of the hulking high-rises were freck-led top to bottom with bloody smudges. Twilly Spree no longer heard his father's voice.

In the dream he squeezed his eyes closed so that he would no longer see the birds dying. He stopped trying to move his legs because the water had reached his waist, water so frigid that it would surely kill him in minutes. Twilly wondered how the sea could be so unbearably chilly—in southern Florida! Latitude twenty-six degrees!—but then the answer came to him, and so simple. The water was cold because there was no sun to warm it; because the goddamned skyscrapers on the beach had blotted out every ray of sunlight, leaving the Gulf in a perpetual unholy shade. So it got plenty cold. Sure it did.

Twilly decided to float. In the dream the water was up to his armpits and he was fighting so frantically to catch his breath that he was making weird peeping noises, like a tree frog. Not acceptable, nossir! Floating—now there's a nifty idea. Float on my back, let the tide carry me up to one of these buildings, where I'll just climb outta this freezing soup. And keep climbing as high and as long as it takes to get dry, climbing like the clever little froggy I am. Water's gotta lay down sometime, right?

In the dream Twilly opened his stinging eyelids and began to float, yipping for breath. He drifted up to a condo, maybe a thousand stories tall, and hooked his arms over a balcony rail. He hung there hoping to regain some strength. Bobbing all around him in the foam were the bodies of seabirds, tawny clumps with rent beaks, clenched yellow claws, disheveled red-smeared plumage. . . .

The boy struggled to hoist himself out of the frigid water and onto the dry terrace. He raised his chin to the rail but that was as high as he got, because standing there in baggy wet Jockey shorts on the balcony was his father, Little Phil. Cupped in his outstretched palms were hundreds of tiny striped toads, bug-eyed and bubble-cheeked, peeping with such ungodly shrillness that it hurt Twilly Spree's ears.

And in the dream he cried out. He shut his eyes and let go of the rail and fell back into the flow, the current spinning him like a sodden chunk of timber. Something soft touched his cheek and he swiped at it, thinking it was a dead sandpiper or a gull.

But it wasn't. It was Desie's hand. Twilly opened his eyes and could not believe where he was: lying warm in her arms. He could hear her heart.

"Everything's all right now," she told him.

"Yes." He felt a light kiss on his forehead.

"You're shaking."

He said, "So that's what they call dreaming."

"Let me get you another blanket."

"No, don't move."

"All right," Desie said.

"I don't want you to go."

"All right."

"I mean *ever*," Twilly said.

"Oh."

"Consider it. Please."

The house was dark and silent. No one had set the alarm. Palmer Stoat opened the door. He called out Desie's name and started flipping on light switches. He checked the master bedroom, the guest bedrooms, the porch, the whole house. His wife wasn't home, and Stoat was miffed. He was eager to show her the latest atrocity—the dog paw in the Cuban cigar box. He wanted to sit her down and make her recall every detail about the crazy man who'd snatched Boodle. And he wanted her to tell it all to that sadistic porcupine-haired goon of Robert Clapley's, so then the dognapper could be hunted down.

And killed.

"I want him dead."

Palmer Stoat, hollow-eyed in front of the bathroom mirror. He looked like hell. His face was splotchy, his hair mussed into damp wisps. In the bright vanity lights he could even see the shiny crease on his chin where the surgeon had inserted the rubber implant.

"I want him dead." Stoat said the words aloud, to hear how severe it sounded. Truly he *did* want the man killed . . . whacked, snuffed, offed, done, whatever guys like Mr. Gash called it. The man deserved to die, this young smart-ass, for interfering with the $28 million bridge deal that Palmer Stoat had so skillfully orchestrated; for abducting good-natured Boodle; for using severed dog parts as a lever of extortion; for mucking up Palmer Stoat's marriage . . . how, Stoat wasn't sure. But ever since she'd encountered the dognapper, Desie had been acting oddly. Case in point: Here it was ten-thirty at night and she wasn't home. Mrs. Palmer Stoat, not home!

He stalked to the den and took his throne among the glass-eyed game fish and gaping animal heads. He dialed the governor's mansion and demanded to speak to Dick Artemus. A valet named Sean—Oh perfect! It had to be a Sean!—informed Stoat that the governor had gone to bed early and could not be disturbed, which meant Dick Artemus was off screwing Lisa June Peterson or one of his other triple-named ex–sorority sister aides. Palmer Stoat, who eyed the cigar box on the desk in front of him, believed the arrival of the paw merited a personal conversation with Florida's governor. Stoat felt it was vital for Dick Artemus to know that the dognapper was keeping on the pressure. Stoat felt Governor Dick needed reminding to veto the Shearwater bridge as soon as possible, and to make damn sure it hit the newspapers so the dognapper would see it.

But no—protective, diligent young Sean wouldn't put the call through to the fornicating ex–Toyota salesman!

"What's your full given name, son!" Palmer Stoat thundered over the phone.

"Sean David Gallagher."

"And do you enjoy working at the governor's mansion? Because one word from me about your obstinate attitude and you'll be back at the fucking Pizza Hut, Windexing the sneeze hood over the salad bar. You follow, son?"

"I'll give Governor Artemus your message, Mr. Stoat."

"Do that, sport."

"And I'll also say hi to my father for you."

"Your father?" Stoat sniffed. "Who the hell's your father?"

"Johnny Gallagher. He's Speaker Pro Tem of the House."

"Oh. Right." Palmer Stoat mumbled something conciliatory and hung up. Goddamn kids these days, he fumed, can't even get a job without the old man's juice.

Stoat opened the cigar box and peeked again at the dog paw. "Jesus, what next," he said, slapping the lid shut.

He tried to remember what the guy had looked like that night at Swain's, passing him that snarky note. The suntan, the flowered shirt. . . . Stoat had figured the guy for a boat bum, a mate on a yacht. But the face? He was young, Stoat remembered. But the bar had been smoky, Stoat had been half-trashed, and the kid had been wearing dark shades, so . . . no luck with the face. Desie was the one nasty Mr. Gash should consult. She's the one who'd spent time with the dognapper.

But the thought of Mr. Gash alone with Desirata made Palmer Stoat cringe. What a scary little prick he was! Stoat wondered if the disgusting baby rat was still alive—mewling and crawling half-blind through his cereal cupboard, no doubt! It was unbelievable. Shocking, really. One of the most powerful human beings in the state of Florida, and here his lofty shining universe had been reduced to a tabloid freak show—dog dismemberers and Barbie-doll fetishists and armed punk-haired sadists who crammed rodents down his gullet!

Thank God they didn't know about it, all those people who feared and needed and sucked up to Palmer Stoat, big-time lobbyist. All those important men and women clogging up his voice mail in Tallahassee . . . the mayor of Orlando, seeking Stoat's deft hand in obtaining $45 million in federal highway funds—Disney World, demanding yet another exit off Interstate 4; the president of a slot-machine company, imploring Stoat to arrange a private dinner with the chief of the Seminole Indian tribe; a United States congresswoman from West Palm Beach, begging for box seats to the Marlins home opener (not for her personally, but for five sugar-company executives who'd persuaded their Jamaican and Haitian cane pickers to donate generously—well beyond their means, in fact—to the congresswoman's reelection account).

That was Palmer Stoat's world. Those were his people. This other sicko shit, it had to stop. It *would* stop, too, once Porcupine Head tracked down the creep who was holding poor Boodle.

Stoat opened the top drawer of his desk and found a favorite stack of sex Polaroids. He had taken them in Paris, while he and Desie were on a weeklong junket paid for by a multinational rock-mining conglomerate. There wasn't much of Desie to be seen in the photographs—here a thigh, there a shoulder—but it was enough to give her husband a pang in his heart and a tingle in his groin. Where the hell was she?

Palmer Stoat noticed the message light blinking on his answering machine. He punched the PLAY button and leaned back. The first message was from Robert Clapley, sounding uncharacteristically edgy and out of breath.

"It's about that rhino powder," he said on the tape. "Call me right away, Palmer. Soon as you get this message!"

The second call, thirty minutes later, also from Clapley: "Palmer, you there? I gotta talk to you. It's the Barbies, they're. . . . Call me, OK? No matter how late."

The third message on Stoat's machine was from Desie. When he heard her voice, he quickly rocked forward and turned up the volume.

"Palmer, I'm all right. I'm going to be gone for a few days. I just need some time away. Please don't worry, uh . . . we'll talk when I get home, OK?"

She didn't sound upset or frightened. She sounded perfectly calm. But there was something quite alarming on the tape—a noise in the background. It happened the moment before Desie said good-bye.

Palmer Stoat listened to the message three times, to be sure. The noise was familiar and unmistakable: a dog barking.

Not just any dog, either. It was Boodle.

Stoat moaned and pressed his fleshy knuckles to his forehead. Now the sick bastard had gone and snatched his wife!

Again.

On a warm breezy morning in late April, twelve Japanese men and women stepped from an air-conditioned charter bus that had parked on the shoulder of a two-lane road in North Key Largo. The travelers paired off and climbed into half a dozen candy-colored canoes. Under a creamy porcelain sky they began paddling down a winding creek called Steamboat toward Barnes Sound, where they planned to eat box lunches and turn around. The entire trip was supposed to take four hours, but the canoeists went missing for almost three days. Eventually they were found trudging along County Road 905 in the dead of night and, except for a few scrapes and insect bites, were all found to be in excellent health. Oddly, though, they refused to tell police what had happened to them, and fled from reporters seeking interviews.

The men and women were employed by MatsibuCom, one of Tokyo's most prolific construction companies. Timber being scarce and exorbitant in Japan, MatsibuCom imported millions of board feet annually from the United States; specifically, Montana and Idaho, where entire mountains had been clear-cut, essentially razed down to dusty bald domes, for the purpose of enhancing Tokyo's skyline and, not incidentally, MatsibuCom's profit margin. Having weathered Asia's financial upheaval in relatively robust shape, the company rewarded a dozen of its top executives with a group vacation to Florida. They would begin the week at unavoidable Walt Disney World and finish down in the Keys, at the upscale (and safely Republican) Ocean Reef Club. Ironically, the MatsibuCom executives expressed an interest in ecotourism activities, and so the Steamboat Creek canoe trip was arranged. The men and women were told they might come across manatees, indigo snakes, bald eagles and perhaps even the elusive North American crocodile (which lived in the mangrove lakes and grew to a length of fourteen feet). Many rolls of film were purchased in anticipation.

When the Japanese failed to return on time from the expedition, an intense search was launched using ultralight planes, airboats, skiffs and swamp buggies. Governor Dick Artemus even dispatched a pair of state helicopters to assist (a modest favor, in his view, compared to the free membership he'd been given at Ocean Reef on the day of his inauguration). Meanwhile, Florida tourism officials gloomily pondered how many millennia it would take for the industry to recover if it came to pass that twelve foreign business executives had been devoured by crocodiles—or perished under some equally horrific circumstances—while vacationing in the Sunshine State.

Publicly, authorities stuck to the theory that the Japanese visitors were "lost" in the mangrove creek system, although reporters found no shortage of locals who were both skeptical and happy to be quoted. Steamboat Creek was about as complicated to navigate as Interstate 95, and a thousand times safer. Fear of foul play rose with the ominous discovery of the missing canoes, shot full of holes and strung together with blue ski rope. The canoes had been hung off the Card Sound Bridge to dangle and spin high over the Intracoastal Waterway, like the baubled tail of an oversized kite. Boaters stopped to snap pictures until police showed up and hastily cut down the rope. The spectacle of the bullet-riddled boats all but vanquished hopes that the Matsibu-Com executives would be found safe. It now appeared that they'd been abducted by either psychopaths or terrorists—a far more devastating scenario, publicity-wise, than a simple crocodile attack. A dour-faced contingent from the Japanese consulate in Miami arrived by private jet at Ocean Reef, where they were given a suite of waterfront rooms and unlimited long-distance privileges. Meanwhile, in Washington, a team of FBI forensic experts already had packed for the trip to Florida—they awaited only the somber phone call, reporting that the decomposing bodies had been located.

Then the dozen Japanese canoeists surprised everybody by turning up alive, unharmed and closemouthed. By daybreak on April 30, the MatsibuCom men and women were on a chartered Gulfstream 5, speeding back to Tokyo. The local press milked what it could from the ecotour-gone-awry angle, but in the absence of first-person quotes (and corpses), the story faded quickly from the headlines.

Lt. Jim Tile had heard about it before it made the TV news; the state Highway Patrol sent five road troopers and its top K-9 unit to join the search for the important visitors. The discovery of the canoes—and the emphatic manner in which they'd been sabotaged and strung up for display—confirmed Jim Tile's suspicions about the incident on Steamboat Creek. He was hopeful the Japanese would remain silent, so that no other authorities would make the connection. Obviously Dick Artemus had not. Jim Tile purposely hadn't shared his theory about the ecotour abduction with the governor during their brief meeting in Tallahassee.

That afternoon, though, the trooper dialed the voice-mail number they customarily used to trade messages—he and his friend, the long-ago governor—and was annoyed to find the line disconnected. So he packed an overnight bag, kissed Brenda good-bye and drove south nonstop, virtually the full length of the state. The sun had been up an hour by the time he arrived at the gatehouse of the Ocean Reef Club in North Key Largo. The trooper was admitted to the premises by a surly young security guard who apparently had failed the rudimentary knuckle-dragging literacy quiz required to join regular police departments. The guard reluctantly escorted Jim Tile to the club's executive offices, where—after producing a letter of introduction from the attorney general—the trooper was permitted to examine a roll of film that had been found in a camera bag left behind by one of the Japanese canoeists.

The film had been developed into a black-and-white contact sheet by the local sheriff's lab technician, who had understandably failed to recognize its evidentiary value: Thirty-five of the thirty-six frames were dominated by a blurred finger in the foreground—not an uncommon phenomenon, when a 35-mm camera was placed in the excitable hands of a tourist. But, to Jim Tile, the finger in the snapshots from Steamboat Creek did not appear to be the wayward pinkie of a slightly built Japanese business executive, but rather the fleshy, hairy, crooked, scarred-up middle digit of a six-foot-six Anglo-American hermit with a furious sense of humor.

The last photograph on the roll, the only photograph without the finger, was of equal interest to the trooper. He turned to the slug-like security guard and said: "Does the club have a boat I can borrow? A skiff would do fine."

"We keep a twelve-footer tied up at the marina. But I can't letcha take it out by yourself. That'd be 'gainst policy."

Jim Tile folded the contact sheet and slipped it into a brown office envelope, the same envelope Dick Artemus had handed to him at the governor's mansion.

"So, where's the marina?" the trooper asked the security guard.

"You ain't authorized."

"I know. That's why you're coming with me."

It was a shallow-draft johnboat, powered by a fifteen-horse outboard. The guard, whose name was Gale, cranked the engine on the third pull. Over his ill-fitting uniform he buckled a bright orange life vest, and told Jim Tile to do the same.

"Policy," Gale explained.

"Fair enough."

"Kin you swim?"

"Yep," said the trooper.

"No shit? I thought black guys couldn't swim."

"Where you from, Gale?"

"Lake City."

"Lake City, Florida."

"Is they another one?"

"And you never met a black person that could swim?"

"Sure, in the catfish ponds and so forth. But I'm talking about the ocean, man. *Salt* water."

"And that's a different deal?"

"Way different," the guard said matter-of-factly. "That's how come the life jackets."

They crossed Card Sound behind a northerly breeze, the johnboat's squared-off hull slapping on the brows of the waves. Gale entered the mouth of Steamboat Creek at full throttle but slowed beneath the low bridge.

He said to the trooper, up in the bow: "How far you need to go?"

"I'll tell you when we get there, Gale."

"Is that a .357 you got?"

"It is."

"I don't got my carry permit yet. But at home I keep a Smith .38 by the bed."

"Good choice," said Jim Tile.

"I b'lieve I'll get somethin' heavier for the streets."

"See the eagle? Up there in the top of that tree." The trooper pointed.

"Cool!" exclaimed Gale the security guard. "Now for that, you need a pump gun, twenty-gauge minimum. . . . Hey, I gotta stop'n take a leak."

"Then stop," said Jim Tile.

"I drank about a gallon of Sanka this morning and I'm fit to 'splode."

"Anywhere's fine, Gale."

The guard cut the engine and the boat coasted silently in the milky green water. Gale removed the life vest and modestly turned around to urinate off the stern. The featherweight boat swung sidelong in the current, and at that moment an ill-timed gust of wind disrupted Gale's golden outflow, blowing it back on the front of his uniform. He let out a yowl and clumsily zipped himself up.

"Goddammit. *That* won't work." He started the engine and idled the nose of the boat into the trees, up against the bank. Stepping out, he snagged one foot on a barnacled root and nearly went down. "Be right back," he told the state trooper.

"Take your time, Gale."

To escape the messy effect of the breeze, the security guard clomped twenty yards into the woods before choosing a spot to unzip. He was midstream—and pissing gloriously, like a stallion—when he heard the *chuk-a-chuk* of the outboard motor. Gale strained to halt his mighty cascade, tucked in his pecker and charged back toward the water's edge. When he got there, the johnboat was gone.

Jim Tile headed down Steamboat Creek at half throttle. A school of finger mullet scattered in silvery streaks ahead of the bow. From behind he heard Gale the security guard bellowing hoarsely in the mangroves. He hoped the young man wouldn't do something completely idiotic, such as attempt to *walk* out.

As he followed the creek, the trooper closely scanned the shoreline along both sides. He wasn't expecting an obvious sign; a flotilla of searchers had been up and down the waterway and found nothing. Jim Tile knew his friend would be careful not to leave tracks. The trooper shed the life vest and reached inside his shirt, where he'd hidden the brown envelope. He took out the contact sheet and glanced once more at frame 36.

The photo had been snapped with the camera pointed aimlessly downward, as if the shutter had been triggered by mistake. And even though the picture was underlit and out of focus, Jim Tile could make out a patch of water, a three-pronged mangrove sprout and—wedged in the trident-like root—a soda-pop can. Schweppes, it looked like.

A Schweppes ginger ale, of all the unlikely brands.

At least it was *something*. Jim Tile started scouring the waterline for cans, and he found plenty: Coke, Diet Coke, Pepsi, Diet Pepsi, Mountain Dew, Dr Pepper, Orange Crush, Budweiser, Busch, Colt .45, Michelob—it was sickening. People are such slobs, the trooper thought, trashing such a fine and unspoiled place. Who could be so inexcusably disrespectful of God's creation? Jim Tile had grown up in neighborhoods where there was more broken glass than grass on the ground, but his mother would've knocked him on his scrawny black butt if she'd caught him throwing a soda can anywhere but in a trash bin. . . .

The trooper had twisted the throttle down so that the johnboat was barely cutting a wake. Back and forth across the creek he tacked, scooping up floating cans where he saw them; easy to spot, glinting in the bright sun. But no Schweppes. Jim Tile felt foolish for chasing such a weak clue—he knew that weather skidded flotsam all over these creeks. And if the tide rose too high, the trident-shaped mangrove bud would be submerged anyway; invisible. The trooper crumpled the photographic contact sheet and shoved it into his pocket.

Still he kept searching the banks, mechanically collecting other cans and bottles and paper cups. Soon the inside of the johnboat began to look like a Dumpster. He was turning a wide bend in the creek when something caught his attention—not a ginger-ale can or a three-pronged mangrove sprout, but a slash of canary yellow paint. It appeared as a subtle vector across a cluster of tubular stalks, a yard above the waterline, where somebody had dragged something heavy and brightly painted into the trees. Something like a canoe.

Jim Tile tied off the bow and rolled up his trousers and pulled off his shoes. He bird-stepped from the johnboat and gingerly made his way into the snarl of trees. His left foot poked something smooth and metallic: The Schweppes can from the photograph, trapped beneath the surface by its mangrove talon. The trooper moved ahead, excruciatingly, the soles of his feet rasped by roots and shards of broken mollusks. He slipped repeatedly, and twice nearly pitched onto his face. Jim Tile was aware that he sounded like a herd of drunken buffalo, and not for a moment did he entertain the fantasy that he could sneak up on the governor. It would have been impossible, even on dry land.

The trees thinned and the trooper found a bleached rocky ridge that led him to the edge of a shallow tannic-looking lake. He realized he had stumbled into the federal crocodile refuge, a fact that impelled him to sit down, slap the spiders off his ankles and reconsider the practical boundaries of friendship.

Jim Tile was parched, exhausted, well lacerated—and no great fan of carnivorous reptiles. He rose with rictus-grim determination. Rocking on tender feet, he cupped both hands to his mouth.

"HEY!" he yelled out across the lake. "IT'S ME!"

High overhead, a lone osprey piped.

"I'M TOO OLD FOR THIS SHIT!" Jim Tile shouted.

Nothing.

"YOU HEAR ME? GODDAMN CROCODILES—YOU THINK THAT'S FUNNY? I GOT A WIFE, GOVERNOR! I GOT PERSONAL RESPONSIBILITIES!"

The trooper was shouting nearly at the top of his lungs.

"COME ON OUT, MAN, I'M SERIOUS! SERIOUS AS A FUCKING HEART ATTACK! YOU COME OUT!"

Jim Tile sucked in his breath and sat down again. He folded both arms across his knees and rested his head. He would've strangled a nun for a drop of warm ginger ale.

Then came the gunshot, followed by two, three, four more. The trooper raised up and smiled.

"Melodramatic sonofabitch," he said.

The man whom Jim Tile had been sent to find was almost sixty now, but he stood formidably erect and broad-shouldered. Beneath a thin plastic shower cap his pate gleamed egg pink and freshly shorn. He had taken to wearing a kilt and little else; a kilt fashioned from a checkered racing flag. Jiffy Lube 300, the man said, I sort of stole it. He offered no explanation whatsoever for the origin of his weapon, an AK-47.

The man had grown out his silver beard in two extravagant tendrils, one blossoming from each cheek. The coils hung like vines down his broad leathery chest, and were so intricately braided that Jim Tile wondered if a woman had done it. Fastened by a ribbon to the end of each braid was the hooked beak of a large bird. Vultures, the man acknowledged. Big fuckers, too. His tangled eyebrows were canted at a familiar angle of disapproval, and somewhere he had gotten himself a new glass eye. This one had a crimson iris, as stunning as a fresh-bloomed hibiscus. Jim Tile found the effect disarming, and somewhat creepy.

The one-eyed kilted man had once been a popular and nationally famous figure, a war hero turned political crusader; brash, incorruptible and of course doomed to fail. It was Jim Tile who had driven the limousine that finally carried the man away from the governor's mansion, away from Tallahassee and a creeping volcanic insanity. It was Jim Tile who had delivered him—his ranting friend—into a private and sometimes violent wilderness, and who had endeavored for more than two decades to keep track of him, watch over him, stop him when he needed to be stopped.

The trooper had done the best he could, but there had been the occasional, unpreventable eruption. Gunplay. Arson. Wanton destruction of property. Even homicide—yes, his friend had killed a few men since leaving Tallahassee. Jim Tile was sure of it. He was equally sure the men must have behaved very badly, and that in any case the Lord, above all, was best qualified to judge Clinton Tyree. That day would come soon enough. In the meantime, Jim Tile would remain recklessly loyal to the man now known as "Skink."

"How's your lovely bride?"

"Just fine," the trooper replied.

"Still like your steaks scorched?" The ex-governor was bending over a crude fire pit, flames flicking perilously at the ringlets of his beard.

Jim Tile said, "What's on the menu tonight?" It was a most necessary question; his friend's dining habits were eclectic in the extreme.

"Prime filet of llama!"

"Llama," said the trooper, pensively. "Should I even ask?"

"A circus came to town. I swear to God, up in Naranja, a genuine carny."

"Uh-oh."

"Not what you think," Skink said. "Poor thing fell off a truck ramp and fractured both front legs. The girl who owned the critter, she didn't have the heart to put it down herself."

"I get the picture."

"So I did it as a favor. Plus you know how I feel about wasting meat."

Jim Tile said, "What in the world were you doing at a circus?"

Skink grinned; the same charming matinee-idol grin that had gotten him elected. "Romance, Lieutenant. It didn't last long, but it was fairly wonderful for a while."

"She do the beard?"

"Yessir. You like it?" Skink stroked his lush silvery braids. "The beaks were my touch. They're fresh."

"So I noticed."

"Had a little run-in with these two birds. They took an unhealthy interest in my llama."

Jim Tile shook his head. "But you know the law on buzzards. They're protected."

"Not too effectively, in my experience." Skink flipped the steaks in the pan and stepped back from the sizzle. He used a corner of the kilt to wipe a spatter of hot grease off his glass eye. "You're here about the Japanese, right?"

"No," said the trooper, "but I am curious."

"You know who they worked for? MatsibuCom, those greedy, forest-nuking, river-wrecking bastards. But they're strong little buggers, one-on-one, even the ladies. Fiberglass canoes are heavier than you think, Jim. Two miles they hauled 'em on their shoulders, through some pretty thick cover."

"What exactly did you do to those folks, Governor?"

"Nothing. We talked. We hiked. Went for a ride. Nibbled on some llama cutlets. I showed them a few sights, too. Immature bald eagle. Butterfly hatch. Baby crocs." Skink shrugged. "I believe I broadened their horizons."

"They didn't have much to say when they got back."

"I should hope not. I explained to them how seriously I value my privacy. Hey, all we got for refreshments is good old H-two-oh. That OK?"

"Perfect," said Jim Tile. It had been a long time since he had seen the man so talkative. "It's nice to find you in a civilized mood."

"Afterglow, brother." Skink spoke wistfully. "The Human Slinky—that was her circus name. Said she was limber in places other women don't even have places. She made me laugh, Jim. I've gotten to where that counts more than . . . well, that other stuff. Which means I'm either getting real old or real smart. Brenda make you laugh?"

"All the time."

"Fantastic. How about we shut up now and eat?"

Cooked well done, the llama tasted fine. After lunch Skink snatched up his assault rifle and led the trooper at a brisk pace down a sparse trail, past an abandoned cockfighting ring and across County 905 to his new base camp. He had set it up in the buggy shade of an ancient mangrove canopy, within earshot of the ocean. There was no tent but there was a genuine NASCAR Dodge, number 77, blue and gold and plastered bumper-to-bumper with colorful decals: Purolator, Delco, Firestone, Rain-X, Autolite, Bose, BellSouth, Outback Steak House, Sudafed and more. The governor caught Jim Tile staring and said: "From that obscene racetrack up in Homestead. Fifty million dollars of tax money they spent. The car came from there."

"You swiped it."

"Correct."

"Because . . ."

"The godawful noise, Jim. You could hear it all the way across

Card Sound. Gave me the worst migraine—you know how I get."

Dumbstruck, the trooper walked a circle around the stolen stock car.

"It's just the body," Skink said. "No engine block or tranny."

"Then how'd you manage?"

"It was on an eighteen-wheeler. The crew parked it behind the Mutineer after the race—the dopes, though I guess they were bright enough to win. They hung the checkered flag off the CB antenna, bless their little hillbilly hearts." Skink paused to admire his new kilt. "Anyhow, the car is where I sleep these days."

The auto theft was one more thing Jim Tile wished he didn't know about. "Where's the truck rig?" he asked uneasily.

"Farther down the shore, toward the abandoned marina. That's where I keep all my books, except for the Graham Greene. Those, I'm traveling with." Skink slid his butt up on the shiny hood of the NASCAR Dodge. Idly he twirled the buzzard beaks on the ends of his beard. "So let's hear the bad news, Jim."

The trooper eyed him squarely. "They want you to hunt down a man. Some wild young kid who's hiding out in the boonies. Seems he reminds them of a junior Clinton Tyree."

"They being . . ."

"Our current governor, the Honorable Dick Artemus."

Skink snorted. "Never heard of him."

"Well, he's heard of you. Wants to meet you someday."

At this, Skink hooted. The trooper went on: "This boy they want you to find, he's been trying to stop a new bridge from getting built."

"I expect he's got a name."

"Unknown."

"Where are they putting this bridge?"

"Place called Toad Island, up on the Gulf. The boy's kidnapped the pet dog of some important guy, some asshole buddy of the governor. And now the governor's pal is receiving pooch parts via Federal Express."

Skink's eyebrows arched. "FedEx? That could run into some money, depending on the size of the animal."

"It's a Labrador, I'm told." Jim Tile reached for his friend's canteen and took a swig of water. "The point is, Governor Artemus is keen on getting this bridge built—"

"Like I care—"

"—and he wants this disturbed young fellow tracked down and apprehended at your earliest convenience. Please don't look at me that way."

Skink said, "I'm no damn bounty hunter."

"I'm aware of that."

"And, furthermore, I wouldn't know Dick Artemus from an elephant hemorrhoid. I don't give two shits about him and I don't give two shits about his bridge, though I do feel badly about the dismembered canine. Now"—Skink, boosting himself off the hood of the race car—"you may return to Tallahassee, my large Negro friend, and advise the governor to go fuck himself, repeatedly and without lubricants, at my behest."

"Not so fast." The trooper reached under his shirt for the brown envelope, damp with sweat. "He told me to give this to you. He thought it might change your mind. I'm afraid he's right."

"What the hell is it?"

"See for yourself."

"You peeked?"

"Certainly," said Jim Tile.

Inside the envelope was a single piece of paper, to which The Honorable Richard Artemus had been wise enough not to affix his name. The man known as Skink read the paper twice, silently. He looked up and said, "The bastard might be bluffing."

"He might be."

"On the other hand. . . ." Skink turned, and for several moments he gazed off through the mangroves, toward the sounds of the waves on the coral. "Goddammit, Jim."

"Yeah."

"I don't see another way but to do this thing."

"Not one you could live with, I agree."

"So now what?"

"Take me back to wherever the hell I parked that little boat. I'll go up to Ocean Reef and make some calls. Then we'll meet up tonight outside the Last Chance, say ten o'clock."

"All right." For once Skink sounded old and worn-out. He slung the AK-47 over his shoulder and adjusted his shower cap.

Jim Tile said, "I got a feeling you'll get another uninvited guest today. A fat-assed Cracker rent-a-badge—Gale would be his name. He'll be lost and thirsty and chewed up, and he'll be screaming bloody murder about some crazy nigger cop ditching him on Steamboat Creek. Otherwise he's mostly harmless."

"I'll show him the way to the road."

"I'd appreciate that, Governor."

On the trek out, the two men came across a full-grown crocodile with a blue heron clamped in its jaws. The beast lay in the reeds on the edge of a brackish pond, its massive corrugated tail blocking Skink's footpath. He stopped to watch, motioning for the trooper to do the same. The idea of using their guns would not have occurred to either man. Respectfully they waited while the reptile, spraying feathers, gulped down the magnificent stilt-legged bird.

"A sad sight," whispered Skink, "but also a beautiful one. Because you and I and the six billion other selfish members of our species didn't interfere."

"Honestly, I wouldn't dream of it."

Jim Tile was relieved when the crocodile skidded off the

muddy bank and into the lake. Twenty minutes later the two men reached the johnboat. Skink held it steady while the trooper climbed in. The motor was cold and didn't crank until the fifth pull. Skink eased the bow away from the mangroves and gave a light push.

"See you tonight," he said.

"Wait, there's one more thing," said Jim Tile. The engine coughed and stopped. The boat began to drift, slowly.

Skink said, "Tell me later, Jim."

"No, I need to tell you now. Artemus says somebody else is out hunting for this boy. Somebody bad."

"Imagine that."

"Well, you need to know." The trooper waved. "Ten o'clock sharp?"

Skink nodded heavily. "With bells on." He bent over and plucked the Schweppes can out of the roots. He tossed it into the johnboat, where it clattered against the others.

The trooper chuckled. "Nice shot." He jerked the starter cord and the outboard motor hiccuped to life.

Skink stood on the shore, twirling his twin buzzard beaks. "Jim, I'm sorry. I truly am."

"For what, Governor?"

"For whatever's coming," he said. "I'm sorry in advance." Then he turned and splashed into the trees.

15

As agreed, Governor Dick Artemus vetoed from the state budget all $27.7 million set aside for "the Toad Island–Shearwater bridge and highway-improvement project." Other funds blocked by the governor included $17.5 million for the construction and promotion of a Southern Bowler's Hall of Fame in Zolfo Springs; $14.2 million for the "agronomic testing" of a technique to genetically remove the navel-like aperture from navel oranges; $2.6 million to rebuild Aqua Quake, a simulated tidal-wave attraction owned by the uncle of a state senator, and destroyed in a fire of dubious origin; and $375,000 to commence a captive breeding program for the endangered rose-bellied salamander, of which only seven specimens (all males) were known to survive.

In all, Dick Artemus used a line-item veto to eliminate more than $75 million in boondoggles. Except for the Toad Island bridge, all had been proposed by Democrats. Among the items *not* vetoed by the governor were numerous frivolities initiated by his fellow Republicans, including: $24.2 million to redesign a private golf course in Sarasota, ostensibly to attract a PGA tournament but in truth to spruce up the back nine for the chairman of the House Appropriations Committee, who owned three prime lots along the fourteenth fairway; $8.4 million for the purchase of an abandoned South Dade tomato farm liberally appraised at $561,000, purportedly to expand the crucial buffer around Everglades National Park, but actually to enrich the absentee owners of the property, who had contributed magnanimously to the state Republican Committee; $19.1 million to pave and widen to six lanes a gravel road leading to a 312-acre cow pasture in Collier County, said pasture being the as-yet-unannounced future site of a mammoth outlet mall, its silent developer partners including the wife, sister-in-law and niece of the Republican Speaker of the House.

None of the pet projects overlooked by Governor Dick Artemus made the newspapers, but the vetoes did. Desie found the list in the Fort Lauderdale *Sun-Sentinel*, beneath the following headline:

GOVERNOR AXES $75 MILLION FROM BUDGET
DECLARES WAR ON POLITICAL "PORK"

Desie read the story aloud to Twilly Spree in the truck.

"Be happy," she told him. "You did it. The bridge is history."

Twilly said, "We'll see." He held one hand on the steering wheel and one hand out the window of the pickup, cupping air. He nodded when Desie asked if he was still thinking about the dream.

She said, "You know what a psychologist would say? A psychologist would say you had a breakthrough."

"Anything's possible." Twilly didn't seem unhappy or upset; only absorbed.

Desie said, "Do you remember asking me to stay?"

"Yes."

"Why did you?"

"Because I was scared."

"Of what—more dreams?"

Twilly smiled. "No, not dreams." He adjusted the rearview to check on McGuinn, riding in the bed of the truck. "You think he's OK back there?"

"Oh, he's loving life," Desie said.

"I think he ought to be riding with us."

"Twilly, he's in heaven."

"But what if it starts to rain—"

"He's a Labrador!"

"But he's been sick. He shouldn't be out in the weather."

Twilly parked on the shoulder and brought McGuinn into the cab, between him and Desie. It proved to be a cramped arrangement, made worse by an onset of canine flatulence.

"From the dog food," Desie explained. "Liver-flavored is the worst."

Twilly grimaced. He got off at the next exit and stopped at a Buick dealership, where he traded in the pickup truck on a 1992 Roadmaster station wagon. The entire transaction took twenty-one minutes, Twilly making up the difference in cash that he peeled from a wad in his denim jacket. Desie watched, intrigued.

"This is the largest domestic passenger vehicle ever manufactured in the United States," Twilly announced, loading McGuinn into the cavernous rear compartment. "Now you can fart all you want."

And off they went again.

Desie almost asked where Twilly had gotten the money, but it didn't matter. He could've robbed a church and still she wouldn't have wanted to go home. She understood him no better than she understood herself, but she felt unaccountably comfortable at his side. Sometimes she caught him glancing sideways at her—it was a look no other man had ever given her, a combination of naked desire, penetrating curiosity and also sadness. Finally she said: "What in the world is going through your head?"

"How beautiful you are."

"Please."

"OK. How much I want to sleep with you?"

"No, Twilly. There's more."

"You're right. I keep forgetting how complicated I am." He took a slow breath and interlocked both hands at the top of the steering wheel. "What I'm thinking," he said, "is how much I *want* to need you."

"That's a better answer," Desie said. "Not as flattering as the others, but a little more original."

"What if it's the truth?"

"And what if I feel the same way?"

Twilly let out a soft whistle.

"Exactly," she said.

"So we're both off the rails."

"A case could be made, yes."

He was silent for several miles. Then he said: "Just for the record, I *do* want to sleep with you."

"Oh, I know." Desie tried not to look pleased.

"What are your views on that?"

"We'll discuss it later," she said, "when you-know-who is asleep." She cut her eyes toward the rear of the station wagon.

"The dog?" Twilly said.

"My *husband's* dog. I'd feel weird doing it in front of him—cheating on his master."

"He licks his butt in front of *us*."

"This isn't about modesty, it's about guilt. And let's talk about something else," Desie said, "such as: Where the heck are we going?"

"I don't know. I'm just following this car."

"Why?" Desie said. It was a cobalt four-door Lexus with a Michigan license plate. "May I ask why?"

"Because I can't help myself," said Twilly. "About twenty miles back she tossed a cigarette, a lit cigarette. With piney woods on both sides of the road!"

"So she's an idiot. So what?"

"Luckily it landed in a puddle. Otherwise there could've been a fire."

Swell, Desie thought, I'm riding with Smokey the Bear.

"All right, Twilly, she threw a cigarette," Desie said, "and the point of following her is. . . ."

Inside the blue Lexus was only one person, the driver, a woman with an alarming electric mane of curly hair. She appeared to be yakking on a cellular phone.

Desie said: "You do this often—stalk total strangers?"

"The woods look dry."

"Twilly, there's lots of dumb people in this world and you can't be mad at all of 'em."

"Thanks, Mom."

"Please don't tailgate."

Twilly pointed. "Did you see that?"

Desie had seen it: the woman in the Lexus, tossing another smoldering butt. Twilly's fists were clamped on the steering wheel, and the cords of his neck stood out like cables, yet no trace of anger was visible in his face. What frightened Desie was the gelid calm in his eyes.

She heard him say, "I bet that car's got a huge gas tank."

"Twilly, you can't possibly go through life like this."

She was digging her fingernails into the armrest. They were

inches from the bumper of the Lexus. If the idiot woman touched the brakes, they'd all be dead.

Desie said, "You think you can *fix* these people? You think you can actually teach 'em something?"

"Call me an optimist."

"Look at her, for God's sake. She's in a whole different world. Another universe."

Gradually Twilly slid back a couple of car lengths.

Desie said, "I'm an expert, remember? I'm married to one of them."

"And it never makes you mad?"

"Twilly, it made me nuts. That's why I'm here with you," she said. "But now you've got me so scared I'm about to wet my pants, so please back off. Forget about her."

Twilly shifted restlessly. The driver of the Lexus had no clue; her tangly head, wreathed in smoke, bobbed and twitched as she chattered into the phone.

"Please." Desie touched his wrist.

"OK."

He eased off the gas. The cobalt Lexus began to pull away, and as it did a can of Sprite flew out the window and bounced into the scrub. Desie sighed defeatedly. Twilly stomped the accelerator and the station wagon shot forward. He got tight on the bumper again, this time punching the horn.

"Jesus," Desie gasped. "I can practically see her dandruff."

"Well, I believe she finally knows we're here."

The woman in the Lexus anxiously fumbled with the rearview mirror, which had been angled downward for makeup application instead of traffic visibility.

"Moment of truth," Twilly announced.

"I'm begging you," Desie said. Ahead of them, the idiot driver was now frantically jerking the Lexus all over the road.

Twilly wore a wistful expression. "Admit it," he said to Desie.

"It would be a glorious sight, that car going up in flames—and her hopping around like a cricket in the firelight, screeching into that damn phone. . . ."

"Don't do this," Desie said.

"But you can see it, can't you? How such an idea might take hold—after what she's done?"

"Yes, I understand. I'm angry, too." Which was true. And the scene Twilly described would not have been completely unsatisfying, Desie had to admit. But, God, it was nuts. . . .

The Lexus began to slow down, and so did Twilly. The curly-haired woman clumsily veered onto the shoulder, gravel flying. Desie's pulse pounded at her temples, and her mouth felt like dry clay. She could feel the car shudder when Twilly pumped the brakes. Groggily, McGuinn sat up, anticipating a walk.

The Roadmaster eased up alongside the Lexus. The driver cowered behind the wheel. She wore enormous rectangular sunglasses, which spared Desie from seeing the dread in her eyes.

Twilly glowered at the woman but abruptly turned away. Desie watched him draw a deep breath. She was holding hers.

Then, to her surprise, the station wagon began to roll. "Maybe some other time," Twilly said quietly.

Desie leaned across and kissed him. "It's all right."

"Honey, where's the Tom Petty CD?"

"Right here."

She felt a rush as Twilly gunned the big car toward the interstate. He cranked up the music.

" 'One foot in the grave,' " he sang.

" 'And one foot on the pedal,' " sang Desirata Stoat. She was glad to be with a man who got the words right.

"This is all your fault," said Robert Clapley.

"I beg your pardon."

"You're the one who gave me that shit."

"In the first place," said Palmer Stoat, "it was for *you* to use, not the girls. That's my understanding of powdered rhinoceros horn, Bob. It's a male stimulant. In the second place, only a certifiable moron would smoke the stuff—you mix it in your drink. You know, like NutraSweet?"

They were in the doorway of the master bedroom at Clapley's Palm Beach condominium, which reeked of garlic and hashish and stale sweat. The place was a wreck. The mirror hung crooked and cracked, and the king-sized mattress lay half on the floor; the silk bedsheets were knotted in a sticky-looking heap. Above the headboard, the walls were marked with greasy partial imprints of hands and feet and buttocks.

"Fucking olive oil," Robert Clapley growled. "And I mean *fucking* olive oil."

"What else they were taking," Stoat asked, "besides the rhino powder?"

"Hash, ecstasy, God knows what—trust me, you'd need a moon suit to go in their bathroom." Clapley laughed mirthlessly. "Some asshole they met at the spa sent up some Quaaludes. When's the last time you ever *saw* an actual Quaalude, Palmer? You can't find that shit in a pharmaceutical museum."

The men moved to the bay window that overlooked the sundeck, where Katya and Tish floated toe-to-toe in the Jacuzzi, with their eyes closed. Today they did not look much like Barbie dolls. They looked like whored-up junkies. In fact they were so blotched and bloated and unappetizing that Palmer Stoat almost felt sorry for Robert Clapley—almost, but not quite. This was, after all, the same prick who'd called him a turd fondler; the same prick who'd threatened him and brought that psycho Porcupine Head into his home. Therefore it was impossible for Stoat to be wholly sympathetic to Clapley's predicament.

"Where does it stand now, Bob? Between you and the twins."

"Limp is how it stands," Clapley said. Nervously he tightened the sash on his bathrobe. Stoat noticed a fresh scab on one earlobe, where once there had been a diamond stud.

"Here's the thing. The last couple days were wild, real carny stuff," said Clapley. "Truth is, the rhino horn didn't do a damn thing for me except ruin a perfectly good bourbon. But the girls, Palmer, they think it's some kind of supercharged jingle crack. . . ."

"But they were stoned, anyway."

"The point is," Clapley said, raising a hand, "the point is, they think it was the rhinoceros powder that gave 'em the big wet high. They *believe*, Palmer, and that's ninety percent of what dope is about: believing in it. And these are not—let me remind you, pardner—these are not the most sophisticated ladies you'll ever meet. They escape from a dull, cold, miserable place and end up in beautiful sunny South Florida, a.k.a. paradise. Everything's supposed to be new and exciting here. Everything's supposed to be better. Not just the weather but the drugs and the cock and the parties. The whole nine yards."

Through the tinted glass Stoat studied the two nude women in the tub, their impossibly round implants poking out of the water like shiny harbor buoys. The bright sun was brutally harsh on their facial features; puffy eyelids, puffy lips. Their sodden, matted hair looked like clumps of blond sargassum—Stoat could see by the dark roots it was time for refresher dye jobs. He heard Clapley say: "They want more."

"They used it all up?"

Clapley nodded grimly. "And now they want more."

"Bob, that shit is extremely hard to come by."

"I can imagine."

"No, you can't. You have no idea."

"Problem is, they're supposed to get their chins done next

week," Robert Clapley said. "I've got the top chin guy in the whole goddamn world flying in first-class from São Paulo. But the girls—get this—first thing this morning they announce: No more sex and no more surgery and no more Barbie wardrobe until we get rhino dust. That's what they call it, rhino dust."

"How adorable." Palmer Stoat, stroking his own artificially sculpted chin. "My advice, Bob? Deport these ingrates straight back to the motherland, then get on with your life."

Clapley looked pained. "You don't understand. I had plans for these two. I had a timetable."

"Bob, you can always find new Barbies to climb your little staircase to heaven. Florida's crawling with 'em."

"Not like these. Not twins."

"But they're *not* really twins, for Christ's sake—"

Robert Clapley seized Stoat's arm. "I have too much invested here. And not just time and money, Palmer. This is an important project to me. *They*"—jerking his head toward the hot tub—"are important to me."

A project, Stoat mused. Like customizing Chevys.

"Christmas," Clapley was saying. "We're right on schedule to be finished by the Christmas holidays—everything, head to toe. That's how close we are."

"They're hookers, Bob. They'll do whatever you tell them."

"Not anymore." Clapley wheeled away from the window. "Not without the rhino dust."

Palmer Stoat followed him into the living room. "I'll make some calls. I can't promise anything."

"Thank you." Clapley sagged into an overstuffed chair.

"But I'm not responsible for what might happen. They could croak smoking that stuff. They could fall down dead right before your eyes. Where'd they get such a damn fool idea?"

"TV probably. For some reason they decided to put the shit

in a pipe. They were sucking it out of a glass pipe. Then they were sucking on me—"

"Enough. I get the picture," Stoat said.

"Then Spa Boy showed up and they were sucking on him, and he was sucking on them. . . ." Robert Clapley clicked his teeth. "Oh, it was a regular tropical suckfest, Palmer. You should've been here."

"No thanks. I had my own excitement."

"Yeah?" Clapley gave a halfhearted leer.

"That's what I need to talk to you about. The dognapper."

"What now?"

"He sent me a paw," Stoat said, "in a Cuban cigar box."

Clapley grunted. "To go with the ear? Man, that's cold."

"Here's what else, Bob. He's got my wife."

"Still? I thought—didn't you tell me he let her go?"

"He did," said Stoat. "But he got her again."

"How, for God's sake?"

"Who knows. Point is, he's most definitely got her."

"Plus the dog?" Clapley asked.

"That's right."

"Damn." Clapley looked exasperated. "What a sick fucking world. Sick, sick, sick."

"Speaking of which," said Palmer Stoat, "your charming Mr. Gash—where might he be, Bob?"

"Shearwater Island, last I heard. Hunting for the sicko dognapper."

Palmer Stoat said, "Call him off, please."

"What for?"

"I don't want him anywhere near my wife. Call him off until this puppy-slicing freak lets her go."

"What if he doesn't let her go?"

"He will," Stoat said. "Governor Dick vetoed your twenty-eight-million-dollar bridge. It was in the papers this morning."

The veto was a very sore subject with Clapley. "You're damn lucky to be alive," he reminded Palmer Stoat.

"I know, I know. The point is, Bob, that's all the dognapper guy asked for—the veto. So now he'll think he won."

Clapley fidgeted impatiently. "And you're saying this twerp is as good as his word. Some demented fruitcake who's mailing you chunks of your pet dog—him you trust. Is that about the size of it?"

"Look, I want him out of the picture as much as you do. Once Desie's free, then Mr. Gash can go do his thing and you can get on with Shearwater. Just give it a couple days, that's all I'm asking. Until she's home safe and sound."

"The dog, too?" Robert Clapley said. "Or should I say, what's left of the dog."

Stoat ignored the snideness. "When does Mr. Gash usually check in?"

"When there's a result to report."

"Next time he calls—"

"I'll be sure to relay your concerns," Clapley said, "and in the meantime, you'll make inquiries about purchasing another rhinoceros horn."

Stoat nodded. "If I find one, it won't be cheap."

"When did perfection ever come cheap?" Clapley smiled wearily. "Do your best, Palmer."

A commotion arose from outside, on the deck. Clapley hurried to the door, Stoat at his heels. The two Barbies were fighting in the Jacuzzi, throwing punches and shrieking in two thickly dissonant tongues. As Clapley waded haplessly into the hot tub, Palmer Stoat could not help but reflect once more on the seedy, disturbing downturn his own life had taken. Here he was, standing in the scorching sun like a eunuch servant, obediently holding a silk robe for a man—his own client!—who had filled both pockets with dolls. Not only dolls but a tiny hand mirror and makeup kits and a hairbrush, too!

Stoat held the miniature brush, no larger than a stick of Dentyne, in the palm of one hand. The bristles were exquisitely fine and the handle—my God, could it possibly be? Stoat squinted in amazement. Pearl!

Slowly he looked up, beyond the sordid tumble of yowling flesh in the Jacuzzi, toward the tranquil gem blue of the Atlantic. What's happening to this country of ours? Stoat wondered ruefully. What's happening to me?

16

No, Mr. Gash was not a patient man.

And Toad Island was a drag; no trace of the dick-faced boy he was supposed to murder.

After much searching, Mr. Gash located a tolerable motel on the mainland. He chose not to call Robert Clapley, as there was nothing to report except for the drunken biologist whom Mr. Gash had shot and buried with the backhoe. No bonus points there.

So Mr. Gash got in his car and returned to Toad Island. All morning he drove back and forth across the old bridge, with a favorite 911 compilation in the tape deck: *Snipers in the Workplace*, accompanied by an overdub of Tchaikovsky's Symphony no. 3 in D Major.

CALLER: It's Tim! Tim from the ramp! He's gone totally batshit! He's shooting all the goddamned supervisors!
DISPATCHER: What's your last name, Tim?
CALLER: I AM NOT TIM! Tim's the shooter!!!

DISPATCHER: You say he's got a gun?

CALLER: Hell yes. He's got, like, FIVE guns! You better send some cops fast!

DISPATCHER: Sir? Sir?

CALLER: You hear that? Holy Christ.

DISPATCHER: Was that gunfire?

CALLER: Well, it ain't the [bleeping] Fourth a July. Is somebody on the way yet?

DISPATCHER: Yes, sir, we've got units en route. Could you give me a description of the suspect?

CALLER: He's about six two, two hundred forty pounds, dark curly hair.

DISPATCHER: What's his full name?

CALLER: Hell, I got no idea. He doesn't even work for me, OK? Tim is all I know—Tim, the day-shift loading-ramp guy.

DISPATCHER: Does he have any—sir, you there? Sir?

CALLER: Yeah, I'm still here. Can't you hear all those shots? Don't you understand what's going on here? All [bleeping] hell is breaking loose. The man is runnin' from office to office, poppin' the supervisors—

DISPATCHER: Does this Tim have any distinguishing features, any scars or tattoos?

CALLER: No, lady, but he won't be hard to pick out. He'll be the only one with five smoking handguns. In fact, he'll be the only one here with a pulse, if the cops don't show up real soon. . . . Oh Jesus!

DISPATCHER: Sir?

CALLER: Hey there, Timmy boy! . . . Howzit goin', bro? . . . Yeah, it's me. . . . Oh, just catchin' a few z's here in the old broom closet. . . . So how's it going? Man, you look really stressed—

DISPATCHER: Sir, please don't hang up. Sir?

Mr. Gash was buoyed by the panic that infused the tape recording; it connected him to a more familiar realm, and temporarily relieved his sense of dreary isolation on Toad Island. Back and forth across the bridge he went, reasoning that it was the best way to monitor who was coming and going. No cars or trucks could slip past, while small boats approaching from the mainland would be visible from the low span.

But even with his 911 emergency tapes in the car, Mr. Gash found himself battling boredom and impatience. Part of him wanted to bag the Clapley job and rush home to his comfortable apartment on South Beach, where he could change to a clean houndstooth suit and get some sushi on Lincoln Road and then head to the clubs, scouting for girls. One was never enough for Mr. Gash. Oh, he was way past one-on-one. Two was all right but three was even better. In his apartment Mr. Gash had a custom-made bed, double the width of a standard king. Bolted into the overhead ceiling beams was a pulley rig, to which was attached a harness made of the choicest green iguana hides. A furniture upholsterer on Washington Avenue had tailored the lizard-skin harness to fit Mr. Gash's block-like torso; first-rate work, too, and reasonably priced.

That's what Mr. Gash was daydreaming about doing—dangling from his ceiling above three writhing long-legged women, one of them wielding platinum ice tongs—when a station wagon carrying a large dog sped past going the other direction, across the bridge toward the island. Mr. Gash was sniggering as he wheeled around to follow. He could see the dog's pitch-black head jutting from a window; Mr. Gash was almost certain it was a Labrador. And, from a quarter of a mile away, Mr. Gash counted only one black ear flapping in the wind.

Bingo! he thought, and eagerly stepped on the gas.

The dog, it turned out, was a black Labrador retriever. Both ears, however, were intact—the one invisible to Mr. Gash had merely been turned inside out. The dog's name was Howard and he belonged to Ann and Larry Dooling of Reston, Virginia. They did not resemble the young couple described to Mr. Gash by the fatally dweebish Dr. Brinkman. The Doolings were in their mid-sixties; she was retired from the Smithsonian, he from the U.S. Commerce Department. They had come to Florida for the sunshine, and to Toad Island in particular for the beach, where Mr. Gash had approached them on the pretense of seeking directions. Once he determined they were tourist goobs, not ecoterrorists or dognapping extortionists, he endeavored to terminate the conversation and clear out.

But Larry Dooling slapped a cold sweaty Budweiser in his hand and said: "We been all over this damn state, looking for a decent beach. By 'decent,' I mean peaceful and quiet."

"The brochures," chimed Ann Dooling, "are *very* misleading."

Howard the dog sniffed the tops of Mr. Gash's shoes while Larry Dooling recounted the many beaches in Florida that had disappointed them on their travels. "Fort Lauderdale, of course—just try to find a parking space there, I dare ya'. Miami we steered clear of. Vero was OK but they had a shark warning posted, so we couldn't swim. Palm Beach, it was poison jellyfish. And what possessed us to take a chance on Daytona, I'll never know."

"Don't forget Clearwater," interjected Ann Dooling. "What a zoo—all those college kids!"

The couple's voices bore like titanium augers into Mr. Gash's skull. When the woman remarked for the third time upon his "modern hairstyle," Mr. Gash enthusiastically immersed himself in another daydream. He imagined the Doolings writhing from toxic jellyfish stings; imagined he was listening to them not on a sunny beach but in the cool dark privacy of his own apartment, in 5.1 Dolby Surround sound.

He imagined the Doolings on a 911 emergency tape.

"Aren't you warm in that suit?" Ann Dooling asked.

Oh, part of him wanted to peel off the houndstooth coat and let the Doolings eyeball his gun; wanted to watch their jaws drop as he snatched it from the holster and leveled it to their shiny cocoa-buttered foreheads—the yappy goobs rendered speechless at last. . . .

But it was broad daylight and nearby on the sand were children playing Frisbee. So Mr. Gash tossed his beer can, turned away and tromped disgustedly to the car.

He made it halfway across the old bridge when he spotted another station wagon coming fast the other way; a Buick Roadmaster woody, the mother of all wagons, carrying another couple, another black dog with its head out the window.

Mr. Gash reflexively braked. Then he thought: Fuck *that*. I'm all tapped out on tourists today. What he needed now was a stack of porny magazines and a bottle of Meyer's. So he kept driving, away from Toad Island.

Tomorrow, Mr. Gash told himself. Tomorrow I'll come back to check out the Roadmaster.

In the spring of 1966, two brothers went to Vietnam. One came back a hero, the other came back a casualty. Doyle Tyree was riding in an army Jeep when it turned over, ten miles outside of Nha Trang. The driver, a sergeant, died instantly. Doyle Tyree suffered a broken leg and grave head injuries, and he was airlifted stateside to spend six weeks in a VA hospital. To his everlasting torment, the Jeep accident had not been caused by hostile fire but by recklessness. He and his sergeant had polished off a case of Hong Kong ale and decided to go carp fishing in a flooded rice paddy—carp fishing after dark in a combat zone! All because Doyle Tyree was homesick for Florida and worried

out of his mind about his little brother, Clint, who was playing
sniper somewhere out in the steamy highland fog, among the
Cong and the leeches and the cobras.

They had grown up on a fine little bass lake, all the Tyree
boys, but it was Doyle and Clint who could never get enough of
the place—after school and Saturday mornings, and Sundays,
too, when church let out. And it wasn't the fishing so much as
the good hours together and the unbroken peace—the breeze
bending the cattails, the sunlight shimmering the slick-flat
water, the turtles on the logs and the gators in the lilies and the
querulous calls of the meadowlarks drifting down from the pas-
tures. Doyle Tyree was wretched with longing and loneliness
when he suggested to his sergeant that they go carp fishing that
evening, not even knowing if there *were* carp or any other damn
fish in the flooded-out rice paddy; knowing only that in the twilight it reminded him of the lake back home. So they'd cut down
bamboo shoots for poles and bowed sewing needles into hooks
and for bait swiped a bread loaf from the mess, then grabbed up
their remaining bottles of ale—bitter and piss-warm, but who
cared?—and set off to catch some major motherfucking carps.
The dirt road was unlit and potholed but ultimately it was the
damn goat that did the job, some sleepy peasant's runaway goat.
When the sergeant swerved to avoid it, the Jeep flipped (as those
army Jeeps would do) and kept on flipping until an ox-drawn
wagon stopped it as conclusively as a concrete wall.

And Doyle Tyree awoke in a chilly white room in Atlanta,
Georgia, with steel pins in his femur and a plate in his head and
more guilt and shame on his twenty-five-year-old soul than
seemed bearable. He asked to return to duty in Vietnam, which
was not unusual for soldiers injured under such circumstances,
but the request was turned down and he was handed an honorable discharge. So back to Florida he went, to wait for his heroic
little brother. Only after Clint returned safely from the jungle,

only after they'd hugged and laughed and spent a misty morning on the family lake, only then did Doyle Tyree allow the breakdown to begin. Within a week he was gone, and nobody knew where.

It was many years before his brother found him. By then Clinton Tyree was governor and had at his disposal the entire state law-enforcement infrastructure, which on occasion displayed bursts of efficiency. The governor's brother, who had been using the name of his dead sergeant from Vietnam, was unmasked by a sharp-eyed clerk during a routine fingerprint screen. The fingerprint data located Doyle Tyree in an Orlando jail cell, where he was doing thirty days for trespassing. He had been arrested after pitching his sleeping bag and firing up a Sterno camp stove inside the tower of Cinderella's Castle at Walt Disney World—the thirty-sixth time it had happened during a two-year stretch. Disney police figured Doyle Tyree for a wino, but in fact he had not swallowed a drop of alcohol since that night outside of Nha Trang. He was bailed out of the Orlando jail, bathed, shaved, dressed up and brought to Tallahassee on a government plane.

For Clinton Tyree, the reunion was agony. Doyle grasped his hand and for a moment the dead-looking eyes seemed to spark, but he uttered not one word for the full hour they were together at the governor's mansion; sat ramrod-straight on the edge of the leather sofa and stared blankly at the sprig of mint floating in his iced tea. Eventually Clinton Tyree said, "Doyle, for God's sake, what can I do to help?"

Doyle Tyree took from his brother's breast pocket a ballpoint pen—a cheap give-away souvenir, imprinted with the state seal—and wrote something in tiny block letters on the skin of his own bare arm. Doyle Tyree pressed so forcefully that each new letter drew from his flesh a drop of dark blood. What he wrote was: PUT ME SOMEWHERE SAFE.

A week later, he began work as the keeper of a small light-house at Peregrine Bay, not far from Hobe Sound. The red-striped tower, a feature tourist attraction of the Peregrine Bay State Park, had not been functional for almost four decades, and it had no more need of a live-in keeper than would a mau-soleum. But it was indeed a safe place for the governor's unrav-eled brother, whose hiring at a modest $17,300 a year was the one and only act of nepotism committed by Clinton Tyree.

Who scrupulously made note of it in his personal files, to which he attached a copy of Doyle Tyree's military and medical records. Also attached was the letter Clinton himself had written to the di-vision of parks, politely requesting a position for his brother.

The letter was one of the documents that Lisa June Peterson had dutifully shown to her boss, Dick Artemus, the current gov-ernor of Florida, upon delivering the boxes of background ma-terial about Clinton Tyree. Lisa June Peterson had also reported that the name Doyle Tyree continued to appear on the state pay-roll—at his original salary—suggesting that he was still en-camped at the top of the Peregrine Bay lighthouse.

Which Dick Artemus was now threatening to condemn and demolish if Clinton Tyree turned him down and refused to go after the deranged young extortionist who was cutting up dogs in protest of the Shearwater project.

That was the ball-grabbing gist of the unsigned demand de-livered by Lt. Jim Tile to the man now known as Skink: "Your poor, derelict, mentally unhinged brother will be tossed out on the street unless you do as I say. Sorry, Governor Tyree, but these are lean times in government," the letter had said. "What with cutbacks in the Park Service—there's simply no slack in the budget, no extra money to pay for a seldom-seen keeper of a de-funct lighthouse.

"Unless you agree to help."

So he did.

Lisa June Peterson had become uncharacteristically intrigued by the subject of her research, the only man ever to quit the governorship of Florida. She'd devoured the old newspaper clippings that charted Clinton Tyree's rise and fall—from charismatic star athlete and decorated-veteran candidate to baleful subversive and party outcast. If half the quotes attributed to the man were accurate, Lisa June mused, then quitting had probably saved his life. Somebody surely would've assassinated him otherwise. It was one thing to recite the standard gospel of environmentalism—for heaven's sake, even the Republicans had learned to rhapsodize about the Everglades!—but to rail so vituperatively against growth in a state owned and operated by banks, builders and real-estate developers. . . .

Political suicide, marveled Lisa June Peterson. The man would've had more success trying to legalize LSD.

To an avid student of government, Clinton Tyree's stay in Tallahassee was as fascinating as it was brief. He was probably right about almost everything, thought Lisa June Peterson, yet he did almost everything wrong. He cursed at press conferences. He gave radical speeches, quoting from Dylan, John Lennon and Lenny Bruce. He let himself go, shambling barefoot and unshaven around the capitol. As popular as Clinton Tyree had been with the common folk of Florida, he'd stood no chance—none whatsoever—of disabling the machinery of greed and converting the legislature to a body of foresight and honest ethics. It was boggling to think a sane person would even try.

But perhaps Tyree was not sane. Look at his brother, thought Lisa June Peterson; maybe it runs in the family. Look at the way the governor had blown town, fleeing the capitol after his Cabinet had betrayed him by closing a wildlife preserve and selling the seaside property to well-connected developers. So swift and complete was Tyree's disappearance that people initially thought he'd been kidnapped or murdered, or even had done himself in—until the letter of resignation arrived, the angry slash of a signature verified by FBI experts. Lisa June Peterson had made two photocopies of the historic missive; one for Dick Artemus and one for her scrapbook.

For a short while after Clinton Tyree vanished, the newspapers had been full of gossip and speculation. Then nothing. Not a single journalist had been able to find him for an interview or a photograph. Over the years his name had popped up intermittently in the files of the state Department of Law Enforcement—purported sightings in connection with certain crimes, some quite bizarre. But Lisa June Peterson had found no record of an arrest, and in fact no solid proof of the ex-governor's involvement. Yet the mere idea he was still alive, brooding in some gnarly wilderness hermitage, was beguiling.

I'd give anything to meet him, Lisa June thought. I'd love to find out if he really snapped.

Never would she have guessed what her boss wanted with her research. She didn't know Dick Artemus had stayed up until 4:00 a.m. one night, grubbing through the documents and clippings until he seized with excitement upon the tragic story of Doyle Tyree, the ex-governor's brother. Nor did Lisa June Peterson know about the unsigned communiqué given by her boss to the black state trooper, or the icy nature of her boss's threat.

And so she was unaware of the event she had set in motion: a man coming wounded and bitter out of deep swamp; a man such as she had never known, or imagined.

"Money is no object," Palmer Stoat said into the phone.

On the other end was Durgess. "This ain't only about money. It's about major jail time."

"The Chinaman hung up on me."

"Yessir. He don't like telephones."

"One lousy horn is all I need," Stoat said. "Can't you reach out to him? Tell him the money's no object."

Durgess said, "You gotta understand, it's not been a good year for the rhino trade. Some of the boys we normally use, they got busted and went to jail."

"Does he know who I am? The Chinaman," said Stoat, "does he know how well connected I am?"

"Sir, you shot the last rhino we had on-site. Used to be Mr. Yee could do business direct with Africa, but Africa's shut down for a couple months. Africa got too hot."

Palmer Stoat paused to light up an H. Upmann, only to find the taste metallic and sugary. It was then he remembered, with revulsion, the cherry cough drop in his cheek. Violently he spit the lozenge onto his desk.

"You mean to tell me," he said to Durgess, "that for the obscene price of fifty thousand dollars, your intrepid Mr. Yee cannot locate one single solitary rhinoceros horn anywhere on planet Earth?"

"I didn't say that," said Durgess. "There's a private zoo in Argentina wants to sell us an old male that's all broke down with arthritis."

"And he's still got his horns?"

"Damn well better," Durgess said.

"Perfect. How soon can you get him?"

"We're workin' on it. They tell me a month or so."

"Not good enough," Stoat said.

"Lemme see what I can do."

"Hey, while I got you on the line"—Stoat, giving the Upmann another try—"how's my head mount coming? Did you get with your fiberglass guy?"

"He's on the case," Durgess said. "Says it'll look better'n the real thing, time he gets done. Nobody'll know it's fake except you and me."

"I can't wait," Palmer Stoat said. "I can't wait to see that magnificent beast on the wall."

"You bet."

Stoat failed to detect the mockery in Durgess's tone, and he hung up, satisfied that he'd lit a blaze under the guide's slothful butt. Stoat fastidiously nubbed the ash of his cigar and went to shower. He carried a portable phone into the bathroom, in case Desie called from Hostage World, wherever. . . .

The lights went out while Stoat had a head covered with shampoo lather. He groped in the dark, cursing and spitting flecks of soapy foam, until he found the shower knobs. When he tried to open the door, it wouldn't budge. He leaned a shoulder to the glass, with no better result.

Through stinging eyes Stoat saw a hulking shadow on the other side of the shower door. A cry died in his throat as he thought: Mr. Gash again. Who else could it be?

Then the glass disintegrated, an earsplitting echo off the imported Italian marble. The door fell in pieces around Stoat's bare feet. Afterward the only sound in the bathroom was his own stark, rapid breathing. He felt a stinging sensation on his right leg, and a warm trickling toward his ankle.

The shadow no longer loomed face-to-face; now it was seated on the toilet, evidently evacuating its bowels.

"Mr. Gash?" The words came out of Palmer Stoat in a choke.

"Wrong," the shadow said.

"Then who are you?"

"Your friend Dick sent me," the shadow man said. "Dick the governor. Something about a missing pooch."

"Yes!"

"Suppose you tell me."

"Now? Here?"

The lights came on. Palmer Stoat squinted, raising one hand to his brow. With the other hand he covered his shrunken genitals. Broken glass lay everywhere; it was a miracle he'd only been nicked.

"Start talking," said the shadow man. "Hurry, soldier, life is passing us by."

As Stoat's eyes adjusted, the broad-shouldered figure on the toilet came into focus. He had sun-beaten features and a silvery beard, exotically platted into two long strands. Tied to each of the strands was a beak, yellow and stained like old parchment. The man wore ancient mud-caked boots and a dirty orange rain jacket. Bunched at his ankles was a legless checkered garment that might have been a kilt. On his head the man wore a cheap plastic shower cap, through which shone a shiny bald scalp. Something was odd about his eyes, but Stoat couldn't decide what it was.

"Do you have a name?" he asked.

"Call me captain." The visitor spoke in a low rumble, like oncoming thunder.

"All right, *captain*." Stoat didn't feel quite so terrified, with the guy sitting where he was. "Why didn't you just ring the doorbell?" Stoat said. "Why break into the house? And why'd you bust the shower door?"

"To put you in the proper frame of mind," the man replied. "Also, I was in the mood for some serious goddamn noise."

"Dick Artemus sent you?"

"Sort of."

"Why—to get my dog back?"

"That's right. I'm from Animal Control." The man barked sarcastically.

Palmer Stoat fought to stay calm. Considering the political stakes, it almost made sense that Governor Dick would recruit his own tracker to take care of the dognapper—maybe not to kill him but certainly to stop him before he caused more trouble. But where had the governor found such a crazed and reckless brute? Stoat wondered. He was like Grizzly Adams on PCP.

Stoat asked: "Are you a manhunter?"

"More like a shit scraper," the visitor replied, "and I'm starting with you."

"Look, I'll tell you the whole story, everything, but first let me towel off and put on some clothes. Please."

"Nope. You stay right there." The man rose and reached for the toilet paper. "In my experience," he said, hoisting his checkered kilt, "men who are buck naked and scared nutless tend to be more forthcoming. They tend to have better memories. So let's hear your sad doggy story."

Stoat realized what was bothering him about the manhunter's eyes: They didn't match. The left eyeball was artificial and featured a brilliant crimson iris. Stoat wondered where one would procure such a spooky item, and why.

"Are you going to start talking," the man said, "or just stand there looking ridiculous."

Palmer Stoat talked and talked, nude and dripping in the shower stall amid the broken glass. He talked until the dripping stopped and he had completely dried. He told the one-eyed stranger everything he thought might help in the manhunt—about the tailgater in the black pickup truck; about the cruel trashing of Desie's Beemer convertible; about the break-in at his house and the perverse defacing of his trophy taxidermy; about the swarm of dung beetles set loose inside his sports-utility vehicle; about Boodle's abduction and the ensuing eco-extortion demand; about the resort project turning Toad Island into Shearwater Island, and the ingenious wheeling and dealing required to get a new bridge funded; about the mocking note from the stranger in sunglasses at Swain's, probably the damn dognapper himself; about the severed ear arriving soon after, by FedEx, followed by the paw in the cigar box; about the governor agreeing to veto the bridge; about how Stoat was expecting the lunatic to free his beloved Labrador any day now, and also his wife—

Here he was interrupted by the man with the crimson eye.

"Hold on, sport. Nobody said anything about a woman hostage."

"Well, he's got her," Stoat said. "I'm ninety-nine percent sure. That's why the situation is so dicey, why it would be better for you to wait until after he lets Desie go."

The man said, "What makes you so sure she'll want to come home?"

Palmer Stoat frowned. "Why wouldn't she?" Then, as an afterthought: "You don't know my wife."

"No, but I know these situations." The man handed a towel to Stoat and said: "Show me this room where you keep your dead animals."

Stoat wrapped the towel around his waist and tiptoed through the shattered glass. He led the bearded man down the hall to the den. Stoat began giving a stalk-by-stalk history of each mount, but he was barely into the Canadian lynx saga when "the captain" ordered him to shut up.

"All I want to know," the man said to Stoat, "is what exactly he did in here."

"Pried out the eyes and left them on my desk."

"Just the mammals, or the fish, too?"

"All of them." Stoat shook his head somberly. "Every single eyeball. He arranged them in a pattern. A pentagram, according to Desie."

"No shit?" The captain grinned.

"You don't find that sick?"

"Actually, I admire the boy's style."

Palmer Stoat thought: He *would* think it's cute. Him with his moldy rain suit and funky fifty-cent shower cap and weird fake eye. But then again, Stoat mused, who better to track down a perverted sicko than another perverted sicko?

"You shot all these critters for what reason, exactly?" The

man was at the long wall, appraising the stuffed Cape buffalo head. Being so tall, he stood nearly nose-to-nose with the great horned ungulate.

"You shot them, why—for fun or food or what, exactly?" he asked again, twirling the bird beaks on the platted ends of his beard.

"Sport," Stoat answered warily. "For the sport of it."

"Ah."

"You look like you do some hunting yourself."

"On occasion, yes," the man said.

"Whereabouts?"

"The road, usually. Any busy road. Most of what I'm after is already dead. You understand."

Dear God, thought Palmer Stoat: *Another* professional hit man. This one shoots his victims on the highway, while they're stuck in traffic!

"But certain times of the year," the visitor added, "I'll take a buck deer or a turkey."

Stoat felt a wavelet of relief, perceived a sliver of common ground. "I got my first whitetail when I was seventeen," he volunteered. "An eight-pointer."

The one-eyed man said, "That's a good animal."

"It was. It really was. From then on I was hooked on hunting." Stoat thickly laid on the good-ole-boy routine, and with it the southern accent. "And now, hell, lookit me. I'm runnin' outta wall space! The other day I got a black rhino—"

"A rhino! Well, congratulations."

"Thank you, cap'n. My first ever. It was quite a thrill."

"Oh, I'll bet. You cook him?"

Stoat wasn't sure he'd heard right. "I'm gettin' the head mounted," he went on, "but I jest don't know where to hang the dang thing—"

"On account a ya'll runnin' outta gawdamn wall space!"

"Right." Stoat gave a brittle chuckle. The big sonofabitch was making fun of him.

"Sit your ass down," the man said, pointing toward the desk. The leather chair felt cool against Palmer Stoat's bare back; he tried to cross his flabby thighs but the bath towel was wrapped too snugly. The bearded one-eyed man walked around the desk and stood directly behind the leather chair. The only way Stoat could see the man was to cock his head straight back. From that upside-down vantage, the captain's visage appeared amiable enough.

"So you're a lobbyist," he said to Stoat.

"That's right." Stoat began to explain his unsung role in the machinations of representative government, but the one-eyed man slammed a fist so hard on the polished wood that Stoat's picture frames toppled.

"I know what you do," the man said mildly. "I know all about the likes of you."

Palmer Stoat made a mental note to call a Realtor first thing tomorrow and put his house on the market; it had become a chamber of torture, practically every room violated by demented intruders—first the dognapper, then the sadistic Mr. Gash and now this nutty bald cyclops. . . .

"I've only got one question," the man said to Stoat. "Where is this Toad Island?"

"Up the Gulf Coast. I'm not exactly sure where."

"You're not sure?"

"No . . . captain . . . I've never been there," Stoat said.

"That's beautiful. You sold the place out. Single-handedly greased the skids so it could be 'transformed' into a golfer's paradise—isn't that what you told me?"

Stoat nodded wanly. Those had been his exact words.

"Another fabulous golfer's paradise. Just what the world needs," the one-eyed man said, "and you did all this having never set foot on the island, having never laid eyes on the place. Correct?"

In a voice so timorous that he scarcely recognized it, Palmer Stoat said: "That's how it goes down. I work the political side of the street, that's all. I've got nothing to do with the thing itself."

The man laughed barrenly. " 'The thing itself'! You mean the monstrosity?"

Stoat swallowed hard. His neck muscles hurt from looking upward at such a steep angle.

"A client calls me about some piece of legislation he's got an interest in," he said. "So I make a phone call or two. Maybe take some senator and his secretary out for a nice dinner. That's all I do. That's how it goes down."

"And for that you get paid how much?"

"Depends," Stoat replied.

"For the Shearwater bridge?"

"A hundred thousand dollars was the agreement." Palmer Stoat could not help himself, he was such a peacock. Even when faced with a life-threatening situation, he couldn't resist broadcasting his obscenely exorbitant fees.

The captain said, "And you have no trouble looking at yourself in the mirror every morning?"

Stoat reddened.

"Incredible," the man said. He came purposefully around the leather chair and with one hand easily overturned the heavy desk. Then he kicked the chair out from under Stoat, dumping him on his butt. The towel came untied and Stoat lunged for it, but the one-eyed man snatched it away and, with a theatrical flair, flung it cape-like across the horns of the stuffed buffalo.

Then he wheeled to stand over Stoat, a bloated harp seal wriggling across the carpet. "I'm going to do this job for your buddy Dick," the man growled, "only because I don't see how *not* to."

"Thank you," cheeped the cowering lobbyist.

"As for your dog, if he's really missing an ear or a paw or even a toenail, I'll deal appropriately with the young fellow who did it." The captain paused in contemplation.

"As for your wife—is that her?"—pointing at the upended picture frame on the floor, and not waiting for Stoat's answer. "If I find her alive," the man said, pacing now, "I'll set her loose. What she does then, that's up to her. But I do intend to advise her to consider all options. I intend to tell her she can surely do better, much better, than the sorry likes of you."

Palmer Stoat had crawled into a corner, beneath a stacked glass display of antique cigar boxes. The bearded man approached, his legs bare and grime-streaked below the hem of the kilt. Stoat shielded his head with his arms. He heard the big man humming. It was a tune Stoat recognized from an old Beach Boys album—"Wouldn't It Be Great," or something like that.

He peeked out to see, inches from his face, the intruder's muddy boots.

"What I ought to do," Palmer Stoat heard the man say, "I ought to kick the living shit out of you. That's what would lift my spirits. That's what would put a spring in my step, ha! But I suppose I won't." The man dropped to one knee, his good eye settling piercingly on Stoat while the crimson orb wandered.

"Don't hurt me," said Stoat, lowering his arms.

"It's so tempting."

"Please don't."

The bearded man dangled the two bird beaks for Stoat to examine. "Vultures," he said. "They caught me in a bad mood."

Stoat closed his eyes and held them shut until he was alone. He didn't move from the floor for two hours, long after the intruder had departed. He remained bunched in the corner, his chin propped on his pallid knees, and tried to gather himself. Every time he thought about the last thing the captain had said, Palmer Stoat shuddered.

"Your wife is a very attractive woman."

17

The dog was having a grand time.

That's the thing about being a Labrador retriever—you were born for fun. Seldom was your loopy, freewheeling mind cluttered by contemplation, and never at all by somber worry; every day was a romp. What else could there possibly be to life? Eating was a thrill. Pissing was a treat. Shitting was a joy. And licking your own balls? Bliss. And everywhere you went were gullible humans who patted and hugged and fussed over you.

So the dog was having a blast, cruising in the station wagon with Twilly Spree and Desirata Stoat. The new name? Fine. McGuinn was just fine. Boodle had been OK, too. Truthfully, the dog didn't care *what* they called him; he would've answered to anything. "Come on, Buttface, it's dinnertime!"—and he would've come galloping just as rapturously, his truncheon of a tail wagging just as fast. He couldn't help it. Labradors operated by the philosophy that life was too brief for anything but fun and mischief and spontaneous carnality.

Did he miss Palmer Stoat? It was impossible to know, the canine memory being more sensually absorbent than sentimental; more stocked with sounds and smells than emotions. McGuinn's brain was forever imprinted with the smell of Stoat's cigars, for example, and the jangle of his drunken late-night fumbling at the front door. And just as surely he could recall those brisk dawns in the duck blind, when Stoat was still trying to make a legitimate retriever out of him—the frenzied flutter of bird wings, the *pop-pop-pop* of shotguns, the ring of men's voices. Lodged in McGuinn's memory bank was every path he'd ever run, every tomcat he'd ever treed, every leg he'd tried to hump. But whether he truly missed his master's companionship, who could say. Labradors tended to live exclusively, gleefully, obliviously in the moment.

And at the moment McGuinn was happy. He had always liked Desie, who was warm and adoring and smelled absolutely glorious. And the strong young man, the one who had carried him from Palmer Stoat's house, he was friendly and caring and tolerable, aroma-wise. As for that morbid bit with the dog in the steamer trunk—well, McGuinn already had put the incident behind him. Out of sight, out of mind. That was the Lab credo.

For now he was glad to be back at Toad Island, where he could run the long beach and gnaw on driftwood and go bounding at will into the cool salty surf. He loped effortlessly, scattering the seabirds, with scarcely a twinge of pain from the place on his tummy where the stitches had been removed. So energetic were his shoreline frolics that McGuinn exhausted himself by day's end, and fell asleep as soon as they got back to the room. Someone stroked his flank and he knew, without looking, that the sweetly perfumed hand belonged to Desie. In gratitude the dog thumped his tail but elected not to rise—he wasn't in the mood for another pill, and it was usually Desie who administered the pills.

But what was this? Something being draped across his face—a piece of cloth smelling vaguely of soap. The dog blinked open one eye: blackness. What had she done? McGuinn was too pooped to investigate. Like all Labradors, he frequently was puzzled by human behavior, and spent almost no time trying to figure it out. Soon there were unfamiliar noises from the bed, murmurs between Desie and the young man, but this was of no immediate concern to McGuinn, who was fast asleep and chasing seagulls by the surf.

Twilly Spree said: "I can't believe you blindfolded him."

Desie tugged the sheet to her chin. "He's Palmer's dog. I'm sorry, but I feel funny about this."

She moved closer, and Twilly slipped an arm around her. He said, "I guess this means we have to be extra quiet, too."

"We have to be quiet, anyway. Mrs. Stinson is in the next room," Desie said.

Mrs. Stinson was the proprietress of Toad Island's only bed-and-breakfast. She stiffly had declared a no-dogs policy, and was in the process of turning them away when Twilly had produced a one-hundred-dollar bill and offered it as a "pet surcharge." Not only did Mrs. Stinson rent them the nicest room in the house but she brought McGuinn his own platter of beef Stroganoff.

Twilly said, "Mrs. Stinson is downstairs watching wrestling on Pay-Per-View."

"We should be quiet, just the same," said Desie. "Now I think you ought to kiss me."

"Look at the dog."

"I don't want to look at the dog."

"A purple bandanna."

"It's mauve," Desie said.

Twilly was trying not to laugh.

"You're making fun of me," said Desie.

"No, I'm not. I think you're fantastic. I think I could search a thousand years and not find another woman who felt guilty about fooling around in front of her husband's dog."

"They're very intuitive, animals are. So would you please stop?"

"I'm not laughing. But just look at him," Twilly said. "If only we had a camera."

"That's it." Desie reached over and turned off the lamp. Then she climbed on top of Twilly, lifted his hands and placed them on her breasts. "Now, you listen," she said, keeping her voice low. "You told me you wanted to make love."

"I do." McGuinn looked outrageous. It was all Twilly could do not to crack up.

Desie said, "Did you notice I'm in my birthday suit?"

"Yup."

"And what am I doing?"

"Straddling me?"

"That's correct. And are those your hands on my boobs?"

"They are."

"And did you happen to notice," Desie said, "where *my* hand is?"

"I most certainly did."

"So can we please get on with this," she said, "because it's one of the big unanswered questions about this whole deal, about me running off with you, Twilly—this subject."

"The sex?"

Desie sighed. "Right. The sex. Thank God I don't have to spell everything out." She squeezed him playfully under the covers.

He smiled up at her. "Nothing like a little pressure the first time out."

"Oh, you can handle it." Desie, squeezing him harder. "You can *definitely* handle it."

"Hey! Watch those fingernails."

"Hush," she said, and kissed him on the mouth.

They were not so quiet, and not so still. Afterward, Desie rolled off and put her head next to Twilly's on Mrs. Stinson's handmade linen pillowcases. Desie could tell by the frequent rise and fall of his chest that he wasn't drowsy; he was wired. She switched on the lamp and he burst out laughing.

"Now what?" She snapped upright and saw McGuinn sitting wide-awake at the foot of the bed. His tail was bebopping and his ears were cocked and he looked like the happiest creature in the whole world, even with a ludicrous mauve blindfold.

Twilly whispered: "Dear God, we've traumatized him for life."

Desie broke into a giggle. Twilly removed the bandanna from the dog and put out the light. In the darkness he was soothed by the soft syncopations of their breathing, Desie's and McGuinn's, but he didn't fall asleep. At dawn he rose and pulled on a pair of jeans and a sweatshirt. Desie stirred when she heard him murmur: "Time for a walk."

She propped herself on one elbow. "Come back to bed. He doesn't need a walk."

"Not him. Me."

She sat up, the sheet falling away from her breasts. "Where you going?"

"The bridge," said Twilly.

"Why?"

"You coming?"

"It's nippy out, Twilly. And I'm beat."

He turned to McGuinn. "Well, how about you?"

The dog was up in an instant, spinning euphorically at Twilly's feet. A walk—was he kidding? Did he even *have* to ask?

*   *   *

Krimmler had worked nineteen years for Roger Roothaus. He had been hired because of his reputation as a relentless prick. When Krimmler was on-site, construction moved along swiftly because Krimmler whipped it along. The faster a project got completed, the less money it cost the developer, and the more profit and glory accrued to the engineering firm of Roothaus and Son. Krimmler abhorred sloth and delay, and would let nothing—including, on occasion, the law—stand in the path of his bulldozers. Unless otherwise instructed by Roger Roothaus personally, Krimmler began each day with the mission of flattening, burying or excavating something substantial. Nothing gladdened his soul so much as the sharp crack of an oak tree toppling under a steel blade. Nothing fogged him in gloom so much as the sight of earth-moving machinery sitting idle.

Krimmler's antipathy toward nature was traceable to one seminal event: At age six, while attending a Lutheran church picnic, he'd been bitten on the scrotum by a wild chipmunk. The incident was not unprovoked—Krimmler's mischievous older brother had snatched the frightened animal from a log and dropped it down Krimmler's corduroy trousers—and the bite itself had barely drawn blood. Nevertheless, Krimmler was traumatized to such a degree that he became phobic about the outdoors and all creatures dwelling there. In his imagination every uncut tree loomed as a musky, mysterious hideout for savage scrotum-nipping chipmunks, not to mention snakes and raccoons and spiders and bobcats . . . even bats!

Young Krimmler felt truly safe only in the city, shielded by concrete and steel and glass. It was the comfort drawn there—in the cool sterile shadows of skyscrapers—that propelled him toward a career in engineering. Krimmler proved ideally suited to work for land developers, each new mall and subdivision and high-rise and warehouse park bringing him that much closer to his secret fantasy of a world without trees, without wilderness; a world of bricks and pavement and perfect order; a world, in short, without chipmunks. It was inevitable Krimmler would end up in Florida, where developers and bankers bought the politicians who ran the government. The state was urbanizing itself faster than any other place on the planet, faster than any other place in the history of man. Each day 450 acres of wild forest disappeared beneath bulldozers across Florida, and Krimmler was pleased to be on the forefront, proud to be doing his part.

Early on, Roger Roothaus had recognized the value of placing such a zealot on-site as a project supervisor. So long as a single sapling remained upright, Krimmler was impatient, irascible and darkly obsessed. The construction foremen hated him because he never let up, and would accept none of the standard excuses for delay. To Krimmler, a lightning storm was no reason to shut down and run for shelter, but rather a splendid opportunity to perform unauthorized land clearing, later to be blamed on the violent weather. He would permit nothing to waylay the machines, which he regarded with the same paternal fondness that George Patton had felt for his tanks.

Krimmler regarded each new construction project as a battle, one step in a martial conquest. And so it was with the Shearwater Island resort. Krimmler lost no sleep over the fate of the oak toads, nor did he derive particular joy from it; burying the little critters was simply the most practical way to deal with the situation. As for the sudden disappearance of Brinkman, the pain-in-the-ass biologist, Krimmler couldn't be bothered to organize a search.

What'm I now, a goddamn babysitter? he'd griped to Roothaus. The guy's a lush. Probably got all tanked up on vodka and fell off that old bridge—speaking of which, what's all this shit I see in the newspaper. . . .

"Not to worry," Roger Roothaus had assured him.

"But is it true? The governor vetoed the bridge money!"

"A technicality," Roger Roothaus had said. "We get it back in a month or two. All twenty-eight mil."

"But what about the meantime?"

"Just chill for a while."

"But I got a survey crew coming over from Gainesville this week—"

"Calm down. It's a political thing," Roger Roothaus had said. "A long story, and nothing you've got to worry about. We just need to chill out for a spell. Take some time off. Go up to Cedar Key and do some fishing."

"Like hell," Krimmler had said. "Forget the bridge, I've still got serious acreage to clear. I've got the drivers ready to—"

"No. Not now." The words of Roger Roothaus had hit Krimmler like a punch in the gut. "Mr. Clapley says to lay low for now, OK? No activity on-site, he says. There's a small problem, he's handling it. Says it shouldn't take long."

"What kind a problem?" Krimmler had protested. "What in the hell kind a problem could shut down the whole job?"

"Mr. Clapley didn't say. But he's the boss chief, OK? He's paying the bills. So I don't want no trouble."

Krimmler had hung up, fuming. He was fuming when he went to bed, alone in the luxury camper that he drove from site to site. And he was still fuming the next morning when he woke up and heard the goddamned mockingbirds singing in the tops of the goddamned pines, heard the footsteps of a goddamned squirrel scampering across the camper's aluminum roof—a *squirrel*, which was a second goddamned cousin to a chipmunk, only bolder and bigger and filthier!

Wretched was the only way to describe Krimmler's state after the Roothaus phone call; wretched in the milky tranquillity of the island morning, wretched without the growling, grinding gears of his beloved front-end loaders and backhoes and bulldozers. And when the surveyors showed up at the construction trailer at 7:00 a.m. sharp (a minor miracle in itself!), Krimmler could not bring himself to send them away, just because some shithead politicians were monkeying around with the bridge deal. Because the bridge was absolutely crucial to the project; without it, Shearwater Island would forever remain Toad Island. It had been hairy enough (and plenty expensive!) hauling the earth-moving equipment, one piece at a time, across the old wooden span. A fully loaded cement truck would never make it, and without cement you've got no goddamned seaside resort. Without cement you've got jack.

So why not get the bridge surveying out of the way? Krimmler reasoned. What harm could come of *that*? It would be one less chore for later, one less delay after the money finally shook loose in Tallahassee. To hell with "laying low," Krimmler thought. Roger'll thank me for this later.

So he led the surveyors to the old bridge and sat on the hood of the truck and watched them work—moving their tripod back and forth, calling coordinates to one another, spray-painting orange X's on the ground to mark critical locations. It was tedious and boring, but Krimmler hung around because the alternative was to sulk by himself in the trailer, listening to the goddamned birds and hydrophobic squirrels. The bridge survey was the closest thing to progress that was happening on Toad Island at the moment, and Krimmler felt a powerful need to be there. Once the surveyors were gone, that would be all for . . . well, who knew for *how* long. Krimmler willed himself not to fret about that. For now, perched on the hood of a Roothaus and Son F-150 pickup, he would be sustained by the click of the tripod and the sibilant *ffffitt* of the aerosol spray-paint cans. Briefly he closed his eyes to envision the gleaming new bridge, fastened to the bottom muck of the Gulf with stupendous concrete pillars, each as big around as a goddamn sequoia. . . .

"Hello there."

Krimmler stiffened, his eyes opening to a leery squint. "Who're *you*?"

It was a young man with a deep weathered tan and sun-bleached hair. He wore a navy sweatshirt and jeans, but no shoes. His feet were caramel brown.

"Just a tourist," he said.

"You don't look like a tourist."

"Really. Then what do I look like?" The young man gave a grin that put Krimmler on edge.

"All I meant," said the engineer, "was, you know, the suntan. Any darker and you'd be speaking Jamaican. Whereas most of the tourists we see around here are white as a fish belly."

"Well, I'm what you call a professional tourist," the young man said, "so I'm out in the sunshine all the time. What're you guys doing?" He jerked his chin in the direction of the surveyors. "Is this for that big golfing resort everybody's talking about?"

Krimmler said, "You play golf?"

"Where do you think I got this tan."

From the young man's air of casual confidence, Krimmler sensed that he might be living off a trust fund, or possibly socked-away dope earnings. Krimmler began to address him not as a scruffy pest but as a potential customer and future member of the Shearwater Island Country Club.

"We're building two championship courses," Krimmler said, "one designed by Nicklaus, the other by Raymond Floyd."

The young man whistled, turning to gaze at the island. "Two golf courses," he marveled. "Where you gonna put 'em?"

"Oh, there's plenty of space," Krimmler said, "once you re-arrange a few trees."

"Ah." The young man looked back, again with the odd weightless grin.

"We'll have condos, town houses and custom estate homes," Krimmler went on. "The fairway lots are selling like Beanie Babies. You're interested, they've got some color handouts at the sales trailer."

"Raymond Floyd, you say?"

"That's right. He's doing the south course."

"Well, I'm impressed," the young man said. "And all this?"

"For the new bridge," said Krimmler. "Four lanes. Sixty-foot clearance."

"But isn't this the one I read about in the paper?"

"Naw."

"The one the governor just vetoed?"

"Forget what you see in the news," Krimmler told the young man. "The bridge is a done deal. The resort's a done deal. We're good to go."

"Is that right."

"Soon," Krimmler said, with a wink. "Real soon."

He heard a cry and, wheeling, saw one of the surveyors huffing after a big black dog. The dog somehow had gotten its leash caught up with the instrument tripod and was dragging the thing across the pavement like a crippled mantis.

"Hey, stop!" Krimmler yelled. "Stop, goddammit!"

The tan young man stepped away from Krimmler's side and broke into a run. He chased down the dopey dog and untangled the tripod, which he returned with its broken Sokkia transit to the slow-footed surveyor. Krimmler got there in time to hear the young man apologizing, and to watch him press a crisp wad of cash into the surveyor's palm. Then off they went, the black dog at the young man's heels, crossing the old wooden bridge toward the island.

"Hey!" Krimmler called brightly after them. "Don't forget to swing by the sales office and pick up a brochure!"

18

When Krimmler returned to the travel trailer, he was alarmed to see lights in the windows. Approaching the front door, he heard a throb of excited voices.

She's stabbing me! The crazy . . . ugh! . . . bitch is . . . agh! . . . stabbing me!!!

Calm down. Please try to calm down.

Stay calm? There's a fondue . . . ugh! . . . fork in my ass! HELP!

Sir, we've got units on the way.

No, Debbie, not there! You promised, NOT THERE! Yaaaggghh—Jesus, look whatchu done now! You crazy damn bitch!!

Krimmler was turning to flee when the trailer door flew open. In a blur he was tackled, dragged inside and heaved like a sack of fertilizer onto the sour carpet. He expected to behold chaos, a deranged harpy with a bloody cheese fork poised over a dying boyfriend. . . .

But the only person in Krimmler's Winnebago was a powerfully built man with blond hair, which had been moussed into peculiar white-tipped spikes. The man wore a houndstooth suit and brown leather shoes with zippers down the ankles, like Gerry and the Pacemakers might have worn in 1964.

The interior of the trailer showed no evidence of a savage stabbing. The cries and shrieks of crazed Debbie's victim had come from Krimmler's stereo speakers. The spiky-haired stranger twisted down the volume knob and positioned himself in a captain's chair, which he spun to face Krimmler.

"I work for Mr. Clapley," the man said. He had a deceptively gentle voice.

"I work for Mr. Clapley, too." Krimmler began to rise from the floor, but the spiky-haired man produced a handgun and motioned him to be still.

"You were talking to a guy this morning. Barefoot guy with a dog," said the stranger. "Over by the bridge, remember?"

"Sure."

"I was watching. Who was he?"

Krimmler shrugged. "Just some tourist. He wanted to know about the new golf courses. I sent him to the sales office."

"What else?"

"That's it. Why'd you bust into my place? Can't I get up now?"

"Nope," said the man in the houndstooth suit. "Did he ask about the new bridge?"

Krimmler nodded.

"Well?"

"I told him it was a done deal."

"Why'd you tell him that?"

"Because he acted like he had money," Krimmler said. "Mr. Clapley *is* still in the business of selling property, isn't he?"

The stranger popped a cassette out of Krimmler's stereo console. He placed it in an inside pocket of his suit jacket, all the time keeping the gun on display in his other hand. Krimmler wondered why Robert Clapley would employ such a thug. Possibly the stranger was lying about that, though it didn't really matter at the moment. Krimmler was unfailingly respectful of firearms.

"I never saw this goddamned guy before," he told the spiky-haired stranger. "He didn't say his name, and I didn't think to ask."

"Is he with a woman?"

"I got no idea."

"Yesterday I saw a couple in a Buick station wagon crossing to the island," the stranger said. "They had a dog in the car."

"Anything's possible," Krimmler said restlessly. "Look, I told you everything I know."

"Well, he acts like a troublemaker. Didn't he strike you as a troublemaker?" The man went into Krimmler's refrigerator for a beer. "Was he pissed when you told him about the new bridge?"

"Not that I could tell," Krimmler said. "Why the hell would he care about a bridge?"

The man with the gun was silent for a few moments. Then he said: "It's a helluva sound system you got in this cozy little tin can."

"Yeah. Thanks."

"You can actually hear the people *out of breath* on those tapes. You can hear them wheezing and gasping and shit. It's just amazing what's possible on a first-rate sound system."

"The speakers are brand-new," Krimmler said. "From Germany."

The spiky-haired man opened the beer and took a swallow. "So. This troublemaker with the black dog—where would he be staying on the island?"

"If he's not camping out, then he's probably at Mrs. Stinson's bed-and-breakfast."

"And where's that?"

Krimmler gave directions. The man holstered his gun. He told Krimmler it was all right to get up off the floor.

"Can I ask your name?"

"Gash."

"You really work for Clapley?"

"I do. Ask him yourself." The stranger turned for the door.

"That tape you were listening to," said Krimmler, "was that for real? Was that you on there, calling for help?"

The man laughed—a creepy and unsettling gurgle that made Krimmler sorry he'd asked.

"That's good," Mr. Gash said. "That's really rich."

"Look, I didn't mean anything."

"Hey, it's OK. I'm laughing because the man on that tape, he's dead. Dead as a fucking doornail. Those were his last mortal words you heard: 'You crazy damn bitch!!' The last living breath out of his mouth."

Mr. Gash chuckled again, then stepped into the night.

It was nine-thirty, and Lisa June Peterson was alone in her office, which adjoined the governor's own. When the phone rang, she assumed it was Douglas, the probate attorney she'd been dating. Every time Douglas called, the first question was: "What're you wearing, Lisa June?"

So tonight, being in a frisky mood, she picked up the phone and said: "No panties!"

And a male voice, deeper and older-sounding than Douglas's, responded: "Me neither, hon."

The governor's executive assistant gasped.

"Ah, sweet youth," the voice said.

Lisa June Peterson stammered an apology. "I'm so—I thought you were somebody else."

"Some days I think the same thing."

"What can I do for you?" Lisa June asked.

"Get me an appointment with the governor."

"I'm afraid he's out of town." Lisa June, trying to recover, hoping to sound cool and professional.

The caller said: "Then I'll catch up with him later."

She was troubled by something in the man's tone—not menace, exactly, but a blunt certainty of purpose. "Maybe I can help," she said.

"I seriously doubt it."

"I can try to reach him. Does Governor Artemus know you?"

"Apparently so," the man said.

"May I have your name?"

"Tyree. You need me to spell it?"

"No." Lisa June Peterson was floored. "Is this some kind of a joke?"

"Anything but."

"You're *Governor* Tyree—no bullshit?"

"Since when do fine young ladies use that word in formal conversation? I am shocked to the marrow."

Lisa June Peterson already was on her feet, collecting her purse and car keys. "Where are you now?" she asked the caller.

"Pay phone down on Monroe."

"Meet me in front of the capitol. Ten minutes."

"Why?"

She said, "I drive a Taurus wagon. I'm wearing a blue dress and glasses."

"And no panties, 'member?"

Nothing in Lisa June Peterson's experience prepared her for the sight of Clinton Tyree. First his size—he looked as big as a refrigerator. Then the wardrobe—he was dressed like a squeegee man: boots, homemade kilt and shower cap. As he got in her car, the dome light offered an egg-white glimpse of shaved scalp, a ruby glint from a prosthetic eye. But it wasn't until they were seated side by side on upturned cinder blocks in front of a campfire that Lisa June Peterson got a good look at the lush cheek braids and the bleached bird beaks adorning them.

"Buzzards," the former governor said. "Bad day."

His face was saddle-brown and creased, but it opened to the same killer smile Lisa June remembered from her research; from those early newspaper photographs, before things went weird. The inaugural smile.

She said, "It's really you."

"Just the chassis, hon."

They were in a wooded lot outside of town, near the municipal airport. The ex-governor was skinning out a dead fox he'd scavenged on the Apalachee Parkway. He said it had been struck by a motorcycle; said he could tell by the nature of the dent in the animal's skull.

"What should I call you?" Lisa June Peterson asked.

"Let me think on that. You hungry?"

"I was." She turned away while he worked at the haunches of the dead fox with a small knife.

He said, "This is my first time back to Tallahassee."

"Where do you live now?"

"You know what's tasty? Possum done right."

Lisa June said, "I'll keep my eyes peeled."

"Tell me again what it is you do for Mr. Richard Artemus."

She told him.

Clinton Tyree said: "I had an 'executive assistant,' too. She tried, she honestly did. But I was pretty much an impossible case."

"I know all about it."

"How? You were just a baby."

Lisa June Peterson told him about the research that Governor Artemus had asked her to do. She did not tell him the scheme that had been kicking around her head, keeping her up nights;

her idea to do a book about Clinton Tyree, Florida's lost governor.

"Did your boss say what he wanted with my files?" The grin again. "No, I didn't think so."

"Tell me," said Lisa June.

"You poor thing."

"What is it?"

"Your Governor Dickie has an errand for me, darling, and not a pleasant one. If I don't oblige, he's going to throw my poor helpless brother out on the street, where he will surely succumb to confusion. So here I am."

Lisa June felt a stab of guilt. "Doyle?"

Clinton Tyree raised a furry eyebrow. "Yes. My brother Doyle. I suppose *that* was in your damn research, too."

"I'm so sorry." But she was thinking: Dick Artemus isn't capable of such a cold-blooded extortion.

The ex-governor speared the sliced pieces of fox on the point of a whittled oak branch, balancing it over the flames. "The reason I came to see him—your boss—is to let him know the dire ramifications of a double cross. He needs to be aware of how seriously I regard the terms of this deal."

Lisa June Peterson said: "Isn't it possible you misunderstood?"

Clinton Tyree gazed down at her with a ragged weariness. Then he dug into a dusty backpack and brought out a brown envelope crookedly folded and dappled with stains. Lisa June opened it and read the typed letter that had been delivered to Clinton Tyree by his best friend, Lt. Jim Tile. It didn't matter that there was no signature at the bottom—Lisa June recognized the bloated phrasing, the comical misspellings, the plodding run-on sentences. The author of the threat could only be the Honorable Richard Artemus, governor of Florida.

"My God." Despondently she folded the letter. "I can't hardly believe it."

Clinton Tyree snatched her under the arms, drawing her face close to his. "What *I* can't believe," he rumbled, "is that your boss had the piss-poor, shit-for-brains judgment to come fuck with *me*. Me of all people."

His crimson eye jittered up toward the stars, but the good eye was fixed steady and lucid with wrath. "Anything bad happens to my brother from all this nonsense, someone's going to die a slow, wretched death involving multiple orifices. You get the picture, don't you?"

Lisa June Peterson nodded. The ex-governor eased her to the ground. "Try some fox leg," he said.

"No, thanks."

"I advise you to eat."

"Maybe just a bite."

"People speak of me as Skink. You call me captain."

"OK," said Lisa June.

"Any reason you need to be home tonight?"

"No. Not really."

"Dandy," said Clinton Tyree, stoking the campfire. "That'll give us time to get to know each other."

The flight from Fort Lauderdale to Gainesville took ninety minutes, plenty of time for Palmer Stoat to reflect on a productive half day of work. With a two-minute phone call he'd made forty grand. The woman on the other end was the chairperson of the Miami–Dade County Commission, who had obligingly moved to the bottom of the night's agenda an item of large importance to Palmer Stoat. It was a motion to award the exclusive fried-banana concession at Miami International Airport to a person named Lester "Large Louie" Buccione, who for the purpose of subverting minority set-aside requirements was now representing himself as Lestorino Luis Banderas, Hispanic-American.

To avoid the unappetizing prospect of competitive bidding, Lester/Lestorino had procured the lobbying services of Palmer Stoat, whose sway with Miami-Dade commissioners was well known. Once he had identified the necessary loophole and lined up the requisite voting majority, all that remained for Stoat was to make sure the fried-banana contract was placed far down on the agenda, so that the "debate" would be held no sooner than midnight. The strategy was to minimize public input by minimizing public attendance. A sparse crowd meant sparse opposition, reducing the likelihood that some skittish commissioner might get cold feet and screw up the whole thing.

It was a cardinal rule of political deal fixing: The later the vote, the better. So stultifying was the average government meeting that not even the hardiest of civic gadflies could endure from gavel to gavel. Generally, the only souls who remained to the wee hours were being paid to sit there—lawyers, lobbyists, stenographers and a few drowsy reporters. And since the shadiest deals were saved for the end, when the chamber was emptiest, competition was fierce for space at the tail of the agenda.

Lester Buccione had been elated to learn that the fried-banana contract would be taken up last, in tomb-like tranquillity, and that for this favor the chairperson of the Miami-Dade Commission had demanded only that one of her deadbeat cousins be hired as a part-time cashier at one of Lester's new fried-banana kiosks. So pleased was "Lestorino" that he had promptly messengered to Palmer Stoat's home a cashier's check for the $40,000 fee, which divinely had mended Stoat's tattered confidence—five-digit reassurance that the planet had not skittered off its axis, that the rightful order of the urban food chain had not been perverted, despite the harrowing madness that had ruptured Stoat's personal universe.

He had been fingering the check from Lester Buccione, savoring its crisp affirmation, when out of the blue his missing wife had telephoned and asked him to charter another plane to Gainesville. Right away! And Palmer Stoat had thought: Thank God she's finally come to her senses. He would fly up to get her and then they would go away for a while, somewhere secluded and safe from the demented dog dismemberer, the lascivious bald cyclops, the sadistic Blond Porcupine Man, the doll-stroking Clapley. . . .

The plane landed at half-past two. Stoat searched for Desie inside the terminal but she wasn't there. One of his cell phones rang—Stoat carried three—and he snatched it from a pocket. Durgess was on the line: No luck so far with the rhino, but good news about Robert Clapley's cheetah! They'd found one in Hamburg, of all places, at a children's zoo. The cat would arrive within days at the Wilderness Veldt Plantation, where it would be caged, washed and fattened up in advance of the big hunt. Anytime you're ready! said Durgess, more perky than Stoat had ever heard him. I'll inform Mr. Clapley, Stoat said, and get back to you.

He walked to the airport parking lot and squinted into the sunlight, not knowing exactly what to look for. A horn honked twice. Stoat turned and saw a white Buick station wagon approaching slowly. A man was driving; no sign of Desie. The car stopped beside Palmer Stoat and the passenger door swung open. Stoat got in. In the backseat lay Boodle, an orange-and-blue sponge football pinned beneath his two front paws. His tail thwapped playfully when he saw Stoat, but he clung to the toy. Stoat reached back and stroked the dog's head.

"That's the best you can do?" the driver said.

"He stinks," said Stoat.

"Damn right he stinks. He spent the morning running cows. Now give him a hug."

Not in a two-thousand-dollar suit I won't, thought Stoat.

"You're the one from Swain's," he said to the driver. "Where the hell's my wife?"

The station wagon started moving.

"You hear me?"

"Patience," said the driver, who looked about twenty years old. He wore a dark blue sweatshirt and loose faded jeans and sunglasses. He had shaggy bleached-out hair, and his skin was as brown as a surfer's. He drove barefoot.

Palmer Stoat said, "You tried to scare me into thinking you cut up my dog. What kind of sick bastard would do that?"

"The determined kind."

"Where'd you get the ear and the paw?"

"Not important," the young man said.

"Where's Desie?"

"Whew, that cologne you're wearing. . . ."

"WHERE IS MY WIFE?"

The Roadmaster was heading north, toward Starke, at seventy-five miles an hour. Stoat angrily clenched his hands; moist, soft fists that looked about as menacing as biscuits.

"Where the hell are you taking me? What's your name?" Stoat was emboldened by the fact that the dognapper appeared to be unarmed. "You're going to jail, you know that, junior? And the longer you keep my wife and dog, the longer your sorry ass is gonna be locked up."

The driver said: "That blonde you sometimes travel with, the one with the Gucci bag—does Desie know about her?"

"What!" Stoat, straining to sound indignant but thinking: How in the world does he know about Roberta?

"The one I saw you with at the Lauderdale airport, the one who tickled your tonsils with her tongue."

Stoat wilted. He felt a thousand years old. "All right. You made your damn point."

"You hungry?" the driver asked.

He turned into a McDonald's and ordered chocolate shakes, fries and double cheeseburgers. As he pulled back on the highway, he handed the bag to Palmer Stoat and said, "Help yourself."

The food smelled glorious. Stoat came to life, and he quickly went to work on the cheeseburgers. Boodle dropped the foam football and sat up to mooch handouts. The driver warned Stoat not to feed the dog anything from the McDonald's bag.

"Doctor's orders," the young man said.

"It's all your fault he got sick in the first place." Stoat spoke through bulging, blue-veined, burger-filled cheeks. "You're the one who yanked all the glass eyeballs out of my trophy heads. That's what he ate, the big dope—those taxidermy eyes."

"From the trophy heads. Yes, I know."

"And did Desie tell you what his surgery cost?"

The driver fiddled with the knobs on the stereo system. Stoat recognized the music; a rock song he'd heard a few times on the radio.

"I tell you what," the young man said, "these speakers aren't half-bad."

"Why'd you steal my dog?" Stoat swiped at his lips with a paper napkin. "Let's hear it. This ought to be good." He finished engulfing one double cheeseburger, then wadded the greasy wax wrapper.

The young man's eyebrows arched, but he didn't look away from the highway. He said to Stoat: "Don't tell me you haven't figured it out."

"Figured *what* out?"

"How I chose you. How all this rough stuff got started—you honestly don't know?"

"All I know," Stoat said with a snort, "is that you're some kinda goddamn psycho and I did what you wanted and now I'm here to collect my wife and my dog." He fumbled on the door panel for the window switch.

"Oh brother," said the driver.

Stoat looked annoyed. "What now?"

The driver groaned. "I don't believe this."

"Believe what?" said Palmer Stoat, clueless. Casually he tossed the balled-up cheeseburger wrapper out of the speeding car.

"Believe what?" he asked again, a split second before his brainpain detonated and the world went black as pitch.

19

In Twilly Spree's next dream he was down in the Everglades and it was raining hawks. He was running again, running the shoreline of Cape Sable, and the birds were falling everywhere, shot from the sky. In the dream Desie was running barefoot beside him. They were snatching up the bloodied hawks from the sugar white sand, hoping to find one still alive; one they could save. McGuinn was in Twilly's dream, too, being chased in circles by a scrawny three-legged bobcat—it might have been hilarious, except for all the birds hitting the beach like russet feather bombs. In the dream Twilly saw a speck on the horizon, and as he drew closer the speck became the figure of a man on the crest of a dune; a man with a long gun pointed at the sky. Heedlessly Twilly ran on, shouting for the hawk killer to stop. The man lowered his weapon and spun around to see who was coming. He went rigid and raised the barrel again, this time taking aim at Twilly. In the dream Twilly lowered his shoulders and ran as fast as he could toward the hawk killer. He was astonished when he heard Desie coming up the dune behind him, running even faster. Twilly saw the muzzle flash at the instant Desie's hand touched his shoulder.

Except it wasn't Desie's hand, it was his mother's. Amy Spree gently shook her son awake, saying, "My Lord, Twilly, were you dreaming? When did *this* start?"

Twilly sat up, chilled with sweat. "About a week ago."

"And what do you dream about?"

"Running on beaches."

"After all these years! How wonderful."

"And dead birds," Twilly said.

"Oh my. You want a drink?"

"No thanks, Mom."

"Your friend is relaxing out on the deck," said Amy Spree.

"I'm coming."

"The man with the pillowcase over his head?"

"Yes, Mom."

"She says it's her husband."

"Correct."

"Oh, Twilly. What next?"

Amy Spree was a stunning woman of fifty-five. She had flawless white skin and shy sea-green eyes and elegant silver-streaked hair. Twilly found it ironic that in divorcehood his mother had chosen Flagler Beach, given both her aversion to tropical sunlight and her previous attachment to a philandering swine who hawked oceanfront property for a living. But Amy Spree said she was soothed by the Atlantic sunrises (which were too brief to inflict facial wrinkles), and harbored no lingering bitterness toward Little Phil (whom she dismissed as "confused and insecure"). Furthermore, Amy Spree said, the shore was a perfect place to practice her dance and clarinet and yoga, all of which required solitude.

Which her son interrupted once a year, on her birthday.

"I never know what to get you," Twilly said.

"Nonsense," his mother clucked. "I got the best present in the world when you knocked on the door."

They were in the kitchen. Amy Spree was preparing a pitcher of unsweetened iced tea for Twilly, his new lady friend and her husband, who was trussed to a white wicker rocking chair once favored by Twilly's father.

"How about a dog?" Twilly asked his mother. "Wouldn't you like a dog?"

"*That* dog?" Amy Spree eyed McGuinn, who had hungrily positioned himself at the refrigerator door. "I don't think so," said Amy Spree. "I'm happy with my bonsai trees. But thank you just the same."

She put on a straw hat as broad as a garbage-can lid. Then she carried a glass of tea outside to Desirata Stoat, on the deck overlooking the ocean. Twilly came out later, dragging Palmer Stoat in the rocking chair. Twilly placed him on the deck, next to Desie. Twilly sat down on a cedar bench with his mother.

Amy Spree said, "I am not by nature a nosy person."

"It's all right," said Desie, "you deserve to know." She looked questioningly at Twilly, as if to say: Where do we start?

He shrugged. "Mrs. Stoat's husband is a congenital litterbug, mother. An irredeemable slob and defiler. I can't seem to teach him any manners."

Desie cut in: "There's an island over on the Gulf Coast. My husband's clients intend to bulldoze it into a golf retirement resort. A pretty little island."

Twilly's mother nodded. "I was married to such a man," she said with a frown. "I was young. I went along."

An unhappy noise came from Palmer Stoat. The pillowcase puckered in and out at his mouth. Desie put one foot on the chair and began to rock him slowly.

"What's the matter?" she asked her husband. "You getting thirsty?"

Twilly said, "His gourd hurts. I whacked him pretty hard."

"For tossing garbage out of the car," Desie explained to Twilly's mother.

"Oh dear," said Amy Spree. "He's always had trouble controlling his anger. Ever since he was a boy."

"He's still a boy," Desie said fondly.

Amy Spree smiled.

"That's enough of *that*," said Twilly. He jerked the pillowcase from Palmer Stoat's head and peeled the hurricane tape off his mouth. "Say hello to my mom," Twilly told him.

"Hello," Stoat mumbled, squinting into the sunlight.

"How are you?" said Amy Spree.

"Shitty." Stoat's cheeks were flushed and his lips were gnawed. His left temple featured a knot the size of a plum.

"Mr. Stoat," said Twilly, "please tell my mother about the bridge."

Palmer Stoat blinked slowly, like a bullfrog waking out of hibernation. Desie continued to rock him with her foot.

"Tell her how you lied to me about the bridge," Twilly said, "lied about the governor killing the bridge so the island would be saved. Mother, Mr. Stoat is a close personal friend of Governor Richard Artemus."

"Really?" said Amy Spree.

Stoat worked up a glower for Twilly. "You don't know what you're talking about."

Twilly raised his hands in disgust. "You said the bridge was dead but, lo and behold, what do I encounter this very morning on Toad Island? A survey team, Mother. Measuring for—surprise, surprise!—a new bridge."

"Uh-oh," said Amy Spree.

"Without it, Mr. Stoat's clients can't build their fancy resort, because they can't get their cement trucks across the water."

"Yes, son, I understand."

McGuinn ambled onto the deck. He sniffed the knots at Palmer Stoat's wrists, then leisurely poked his nose in his master's groin.

"Boodle, no!" Stoat bucked in the rocking chair. "Stop, goddammit!"

Amy Spree turned her head, stifling a giggle. On the beach behind the deck were half a dozen young surfers, shirtless, with their boards under their arms. They were staring out morosely at the flat water. Amy Spree thought the scene would make a good picture, photography being her newest hobby. McGuinn trotted down the steps to make friends.

"So what now?" Twilly slapped his palms loudly against his thighs. "That's the question of the day, Desie. What do I do with this lying, littering shithead of a husband you've got?"

Desie looked at Twilly's mother, who looked at Palmer Stoat. Stoat cleared his throat and said: "Give me another chance."

"Are you talking to me," said Twilly, "or your wife?"

"Both."

"Palmer," Desie said, "I'm not sure I want to come home."

"Oh, for God's sake." Stoat huffed impatiently. "What is it you want, Desie?"

"Honestly I don't know."

"You want to be Bonnie Parker, is that it? Or maybe Patty Hearst? You want to end up a newspaper headline."

"I just want—"

"Fine. Then don't come home," said Palmer Stoat. "Don't even bother."

Amy Spree rose. "Son, I need some help downstairs in the garage."

"Relax, Mom," Twilly said. "It's all right."

Amy Spree sat down. Desie Stoat took her foot off the chair, and her husband rocked to a stop.

"Do whatever you want," he snarled at his wife. "Fuck you. Fuck that stupid Labrador retriever. To hell with the both of you."

Twilly's mother said: "There's no need for profanity."

"Lady, I'm tied to a goddamn chair!"

Desie said, "Oh please. It's not like you've been a model husband the last two years."

Stoat made a noise like a football going flat. "You'll be hearing from my lawyers, Desirata. Now: One of you fruitcakes better untie me." He twisted his neck to get a fix on Twilly Spree. "And with regard to the Toad Island bridge, junior, there's not a damn thing you or anyone else on God's green earth can do to stop it. You can have my wife and you can have my dog, but that new bridge is going up whether you like it or not. It's what we call a foregone conclusion, junior—no matter how many paws and ears and dog balls you send out. So take off these ropes this minute, before I start raising holy hell."

Never had Desie seen her husband so infuriated. His face was swollen up like an eggplant.

She said, "Palmer, why did you have to lie?"

Before Stoat could tee off on her again, Twilly slapped a fresh strip of hurricane tape across his lips. The pillowcase came down over wide hate-filled eyes.

Amy Spree said, "Son, don't be too rough with the man."

Twilly hauled the rocking chair indoors while Desie whistled for McGuinn. Later Amy Spree served dinner, broiled shrimp over rice under a homemade tomato-basil sauce. They brought Palmer Stoat to the table but he made clear, with a series of snide-sounding grunts, that he wasn't particularly hungry.

"There's plenty more," said Twilly's mother, "if you change your mind. And I apologize, kids, for not having wine."

"Mom gave up drinking," Twilly explained to Desie.

"But if I'd known you were coming, I would have picked up a bottle of nice merlot," said Amy Spree.

"We're just fine. The food is fantastic," Desie said.

"What about your puppy?"

"He'll eat later, Mrs. Spree. There's a bag of chow in the car."

Dessert was a chocolate cheesecake. Twilly was cutting a second slice when his mother said, "Your father was asking about you."

"You still talk to him?"

"He calls now and again. Between flings."

"So how's waterfront moving out on the West Coast?" Twilly said.

"That's what I wanted to tell you. He quit the business!"

"I don't believe that. Quit, or retired?"

"Actually, they took away his real estate license."

"In California?"

"He didn't go into all the gory details."

Twilly was incredulous. "Don't you have to disembowel somebody to lose your real estate license in California?"

"Son, I couldn't believe it, either. Know what he's selling now? Digital home entertainment systems. He mailed me a color brochure but I can't make sense of it."

Twilly said, "You know what gets me, Mom? He could've quit the business after Big Phil died. All that money—Dad didn't need to hawk one more lousy foot of beach. He could've moved to the Bahamas and gone fishing."

"No, he could not," said Amy Spree. "Because it's in his blood, Twilly. Selling oceanfront is in his blood."

"Please don't say that."

"Excuse me," Desie interjected, "but Palmer acts like he needs to use the little boys' room."

"Again?" Twilly rose irritably. "Jesus, his bladder's smaller than his conscience."

Later Amy Spree walked them downstairs, where her son hoisted the rocking chair (with Palmer Stoat, squirming against the ropes) into the station wagon.

She said, "Twilly, what're you going to do with him? For heaven's sake, think about this. You're twenty-six years old."

"You want to take his picture, Mother? He likes to get his picture made. Isn't that right, Palmer?"

From under the puckering pillowcase came a snort.

"Polaroids especially," said Twilly.

Desie blushed. From the rocker came a dejected moan.

Amy Spree said: "Twilly, please don't do something you'll come to regret." Then, turning to Desie: "You stay on his case, all right? He's got to buckle down and work on that anger."

Twilly slid behind the wheel, with Desie on the other side and McGuinn hunkered between them, drooling on the dashboard.

"I love you, son," said Amy Spree. "Here, I wrapped the rest of the cheesecake."

"I love you, too, Mom. Happy birthday."

"Thanks for remembering."

"And I'll bring back the rocking chair."

"No hurry."

"Might be next year," said Twilly, "maybe sooner."

"Whenever," said his mother. "I know you're busy."

Word of the governor's veto somehow reached Switzerland. Robert Clapley was floored when one of the bankers financing Shearwater Island called him up in the middle of the night. "Vot hippen to ze bridge?" All the way from Geneva at two-thirty in the morning—like he'd never heard of international time zones, the icy-blooded bastard.

Yet Clapley was wide-awake, skull abuzz, when the phone rang.

All night long he'd been trying to contact Palmer Stoat, as the Barbies were on a bimbo rampage for more rhinoceros powder. Clapley had returned from Tampa and found them locked in the bathroom, a boom box blasting fusion dance music from behind the door. An hour later the two women emerged arm in arm, giggling. Katya's hair was tinted electric-pink to match her tube top, and from the sun-bronzed cleft between her breasts arose an ornate henna fer-de-lance, fangs bared and dripping venom. By contrast, Tish had dressed up as a man, complete with a costume mustache, in Clapley's favorite charcoal gray Armani.

He was struck helpless with horror. The women looked vulgar and deviant—anti-Barbies! They announced they were going to a strip club near the airport for amateur night. First prize: a thousand bucks.

"I'll give you two thousand," Clapley pleaded, "to stay home with me."

"You got horn?" Katya, with a cruel wink. "No? Then we go score some." And merrily they had breezed out the door.

On the telephone, the banker from Geneva was saying: "Ze bridge, Mr. Clapley, vot hippen?"

And over and over Robert Clapley tried to make the stubborn blockhead understand there was no cause for alarm. Honest. Trust me. The governor's a close personal friend. The veto was nothing but a sly deception. The new bridge is good to go. Shearwater Island is a done fucking deal.

"So relax, Rolf, for God's sake." Clapley was fuming. He'd answered the phone only because he thought it might be that fuckweasel Stoat, finally returning his calls, or possibly the Palm Beach County vice squad, with precious Katya and Tish in custody. . . .

"But ze newspaper said—"

"I told you, Rolf, it's just politics. Jerkwater Florida politics, that's all."

"Yes, but you see, Mr. Clapley, with a line of credit as large as vot ve extended to you—"

"Yeah, I know what you ex-shtended—"

"Von hundred ten million, U.S."

"I'm keenly aware of the amount, Rolf."

"News such as this vood naturally cause some concern. It is understandable, no? Given our exposure."

"Sure. So let me say it *one more time.* And feel free to pass this along to all your associates at the bank: There's nothing to worry about, OK? Now you say it."

From the other end: "Vot?"

"Your turn," said Robert Clapley. "Repeat after me: THERE IS NOTHING TO WORRY ABOUT. Come on, Rolf, let me hear you."

The problem was: Clapley was unaccustomed to dealing with bankers. He was used to dealing with dopers—criminals, to be sure, but far more flexible and pragmatic when something went wrong. The average drug smuggler lived in a world crawling with fuckoffs, deadbeats and screwups; not a day of his life unfolded exactly as planned. He transacted narcotics, guns and cash, routinely taking insane risks that young Rolf in Geneva could not possibly fathom. Exposure? thought Robert Clapley. This cheesebrain doesn't know the meaning of the word.

"Oh, Rolf?"

"Dere is nutting to vorry bout."

"Thattaboy," said Clapley.

He had resorted to Swiss bankers only because the Shearwater project had become too big for dope money—or at least Robert Clapley's kind of dope money. Oh, Toad Island he'd bought up all by himself, no sweat. However, more serious dough was needed to clear the place and remake it into a world-class golf and leisure community. Clapley's only other project, a seventeen-story apartment tower off Brickell Avenue in Miami, had been financed entirely with marijuana and cocaine profits, which Clapley had washed and loaned to himself through a phony Dutch holding company. He would have loved to work the same scam with Shearwater Island but he didn't have $100-odd million in loose cash lying around, and the only people who did were people who didn't need Robert Clapley to invest it for them: seasoned Colombian money launderers who favored commercial real estate over residential.

So Clapley had gone looking for his first-ever legitimate partners and wound up with the Swiss bankers, who had been so impressed by the balance sheet on the Brickell Avenue tower that they'd offered him a generous line of credit for developing and marketing his scenic island getaway on Florida's Gulf Coast. Afterward, the bankers mostly had left Clapley alone—so much so that he'd been lulled into complacency.

Because, obviously, they'd been keeping a cold blue Aryan eye on his ass. How else would they have found out that Dick Artemus had vetoed the damn Shearwater bridge?

Still, Clapley sensed that young Rolf was uncomfortable in the role of edgy inquisitor, that he wanted very much to be stoic and unflappable in the Swiss banker tradition. . . .

"Surely this sort of minor snafu has come up before."

Rolf said, "Yah, shore. Snafus all ze time."

"So there's no cause to get all hot and bothered," said Clapley. "And Rolf?"

"Yah."

"Next time, don't call at such a wicked hour. I've got ladies here."

"Oh."

"That's ladies, plural." Clapley, with a suggestive chuckle.

"Again, sir, my apologies. But ve can hope for no more surprises? That vood be good."

"Oh, that vood be vunderful," chided Robert Clapley, perceiving starch in the young banker's tone, and not liking it. "Now it's time to say good-bye. Somebody's knocking at the door."

"Ah. Perhaps one of your ladies plural."

"Good night, again, Rolf."

Clapley put on a silk robe that almost matched his pajamas. He hurried to the peephole and let out a burble of glee. Palmer Stoat!

Clapley snatched open the door. "You got my rhino dust!"

"No, Bob. Something better."

As Stoat walked past him, Clapley inhaled a foul wave of heat, halitosis and perspiration. The lobbyist looked awful; blotchy and damp-skinned, a nasty purple bruise shining on his head.

"It's about Toad Island," he said, trudging uninvited toward the kitchen. "Where are the future twins?"

"Mass," said Clapley.

"What for—to show off their kneeling?" Stoat was wheezing as if he'd walked all sixteen flights. "By the way, I lined up your cheetah hunt."

"Swell. But what I need right now, more than oxygen, is the horn off a dead rhinoceros."

Palmer Stoat waved a sticky-looking palm. "It's in the works, Bob. On my mother's grave. But that's not what I came here to tell you." He removed a carton of orange juice from the refrigerator and a bottle of Absolut from the liquor cabinet. He fixed himself an extremely tall screwdriver and told Robert Clapley all that had happened to him in the clutches of the maniac dognapper.

"Plus, now he's brainwashed my wife. So here's what I did, Bob. Here's your big news. I advised this fucker—whose name is Twilly, by the way—I told him to keep Desie, keep the damn dog and quit wasting our time. The bridge is going up, I told him. Toad Island's history. So fuck off!" Palmer Stoat smacked his liver-colored lips and smiled.

Clapley shrugged. "That's it?"

Stoat's piggy wet eyes narrowed. "Yes, Bob, and that's plenty. No more extortion. The guy's got nothing I care about. He can't stop us and he can't hurt us."

"You're only half-right," said Clapley, "as usual."

"No, Bob. He's pathetic."

"Really."

"He doesn't matter anymore." Palmer Stoat made this a pronouncement. "He's a gnat. He's a no-place man."

"That's 'nowhere man.' "

"What can he do to us now? What's he got left?" Stoat gave a sickly grin. "He shot his wad, Bob."

Robert Clapley was thinking how unwell Stoat looked. He was reminded of the day Stoat almost swallowed the baby rat.

"So what're you saying, Palmer?"

"Onward and upward is what I'm saying." Stoat tipped another shot of vodka into his drink. "From now on, it's full speed ahead. You build your bridge and dig those pretty golf courses—me, I'm getting a divorce and a new dog."

"You say this diseased cocksucker's name is Twilly."

"Forget about him, Bob. He's Desie's headache now."

Clapley frowned. "No, Palmer, I can't forget about him. He went to a lot of trouble to make his point with you. I expect he's not done screwing with Shearwater yet."

"For God's sake, what's he gonna do—throw himself in front of the bulldozers? Let him be," Stoat said. "It's over, Bob. Call off Mr. Gash and send him back to Liquid, or whatever-the-hell club you found him at."

"I'm afraid that's not possible."

Stoat gingerly pressed the chilled tumbler of vodka to the knot on his head. "Meaning you don't want to, right?"

"Meaning it's not possible, Palmer. Even if I *did* want to," Clapley said. "Mr. Gash isn't communicating with me at the moment. He gets these moods."

Palmer Stoat shut his eyes. Down one pallid cheek rolled a single clear droplet from the vodka glass. "Would he hurt Desie?"

"Under certain conditions, sure," Clapley said. "Hell, you met the man. He's a primitive. Take a hot shower, Palmer, you'll feel better. Later we'll go look for the twins."

All night he waited in vain for the Buick station wagon. He was parked in a grove of pines not far from Mrs. Stinson's bed-and-breakfast. Playing over and over in the tape deck was one of his most prized 911s—a private bootleg not for sale anywhere at any price, not even on the Internet. Mr. Gash had learned of the recording one afternoon while hanging in his custom iguana-skin sex harness from the rafters of his air-conditioned South Beach apartment. One of the three women in bed below him fortuitously turned out to be a police dispatcher trainee from Winnipeg, Canada, who had a friend who had a friend who worked fire rescue in Duluth, Minnesota, where the bizarre in-cident was rumored to have occurred.

For three hundred dollars Mr. Gash had procured the tape recording, raw and unedited. He set the conversation to Mozart's Offertory in D Minor, "Misericordias Domini."

CALLER: I've got an emergency!
DISPATCHER: Go ahead.
CALLER: My wife thinks I'm in Eau Claire!
DISPATCHER: Sir?
CALLER: But I'm eighteen thousand feet over Duluth and dropping like a fucking stone!

DISPATCHER: Sir, this is Duluth fire rescue. Please state your emergency.

CALLER: OK, here's my emergency. I'm on an airplane that's about to fucking crash. We lost an engine, maybe both engines—whoaaaaa, Jesus!—and we're coming down, and my wife thinks I'm in Eau Claire, Wisconsin.

DISPATCHER: You're on a plane?

CALLER: Yes! Yes! I'm calling from a cellular.

DISPATCHER: And you're in Duluth?

CALLER: No, but I'm getting closer every second. Oh God! Oh God, we're ro—ro—rolling!

DISPATCHER: Hold on, sir, hold on. . . .

CALLER: Please, you gotta call my wife. Tell her the company sent me upstate at the last minute. Tell her . . . I dunno, make something up, I don't give a shit . . . anything!

DISPATCHER: Sir, I'm . . . sir, did your pilot have a heart attack?

CALLER: No! I'd let you talk to him but he's kinda busy right now, trying to pull us outta this nosedive . . . whooaaaaa . . . Mother Mary . . . whooaaaaaaa!!!

DISPATCHER: What type of aircraft? Can you give me a flight number?

CALLER: I don't know. . . . Oh God, it's so dizzy, so dizzy, oh Jesus . . . I think I see, uh, cornfields. . . . My wife's name is Miriam, OK? Phone number is area . . . uh, area code—

DISPATCHER: Cornfields? Anything else? Can you see Duluth yet?

CALLER: Oooooeeeeeeeehhhhh. . . .

DISPATCHER: Sir, I need a location or I can't assign units.

CALLER: It's way too late for units, mister. . . . Whoaaaaaaa
. . . you just . . . whoaaaaaa, Jesus, you just tell 'em to
look for the giant smoking hole in the ground. That'll
be us. . . . Oh fuck me, FUCK MEEEEEEEEE! . . .
DISPATCHER: Sir, I have to put you on hold but don't hang
up. Sir? You there?

Mr. Gash was tantalized by the call—the idea that a cheating
husband aboard a crashing airplane would find the composure
to dial 911 just to cover his doomed ass. What admirable futil-
ity! What charming desperation!

A dozen times he replayed the tape. Everything was on there,
eighteen thousand feet of gut-heaving panic. Everything was
there but the fatal impact and explosion.

Too late for units.

Man, thought Mr. Gash, was that poor bastard ever right.

Mr. Gash's Duluth connection had enclosed a newspaper
clipping with the cassette. The flight was a twin-engine com-
muter out of St. Paul. It went down in a farm field; twenty-one
dead, no survivors. Local authorities didn't release the name of
the passenger who had placed the telephone call from the cabin;
they said it would upset the relatives. The original 911 tape was
turned over to the National Transportation Safety Board and
sealed as evidence in the accident investigation. The version sent
to Mr. Gash was a second-generation copy of high quality.

Suddenly he thought of something to make the recording
even more dramatic: Redub it with a symphonic piece, one that
ended with a crashlike crescendo of cymbals—a musical simu-
lation of an aircraft breaking up as it smashes into the ground.

Sir? You there?

Boom, booooooom, KA-BOOOOOOOM!

"Oh, yeah," Mr. Gash murmured. He got out of the car to
stretch. It was nearly daylight on Toad Island, and still there was

no sign of the troublemaker, the woman, the black dog or the Buick Roadmaster.

Mr. Gash went down the street to the bed-and-breakfast. He ambled up the porch steps and knocked. Mrs. Stinson called him around to the kitchen, where she was making muffins. At the screen door she greeted him warily, studying his oily spiked hair with unmasked disapproval.

Mr. Gash said, "I'm looking for a guy with a black dog."

"Who're you?"

"He's driving a big station wagon. Might have a woman along."

"I said, who are you?"

"The guy owes me some money," said Mr. Gash. "He owes everybody money, so if I were you I'd be careful."

Mrs. Stinson offered a chilly smile through the screen. "Well, he paid me cash. In advance."

"I'll be damned."

"So get on outta here before I call the law. You two settle this some other time, 'cause I don't allow no trouble."

Mr. Gash put one hand against the door. He made it appear casual, as if he was only leaning. "Is he here now? That dog is dangerous, by the way. Killed some little girl down in Clewiston. Ripped her throat out. That's another reason this guy's on the run. Was he here last night?"

"I don't know where they went, mister. All I know is, the room's paid for and I'm doing my muffins, because breakfast is part of the package." Mrs. Stinson took a step back, positioning herself (Mr. Gash noticed) within reach of a wall phone.

"As for that dog of his," she said, "he's about as scary as a goldfish, and not much smarter. So you get on outta here. I mean it."

"You don't know this guy, ma'am. He's bad news."

"I don't know *you*," Mrs. Stinson barked. "Now go! You and your fairy hairdo."

Mr. Gash was about to punch through the screen when he heard a car turn the corner. He spun around, his heartbeat quickening because he thought it was the young troublemaker, returning in the Buick woody.

It wasn't. It was a black-and-tan Highway Patrol cruiser.

"How about that!" said Mrs. Stinson.

Mr. Gash edged away from her door. He watched the state police car go by the house, a black uniformed trooper at the wheel. In the backseat cage of the car was the form of a man, a prisoner slumped sideways against a door as if he had passed out. Mr. Gash wasn't sure, but it seemed like the trooper slowed down a little when he passed the bed-and-breakfast.

From behind him, Mr. Gash heard Mrs. Stinson chortle: "Ha! You still wanna chat, smart-mouth?"

As soon as the police cruiser was out of sight, Mr. Gash stepped off the porch and began to walk. He had a story ready, just in case: The car wouldn't start. He went to the bed-and-breakfast to use the phone. Next thing he knows, the old hag starts raving at him like some nut. . . .

On the road Mr. Gash saw no sign of the Highway Patrolman. He got to his car and kept walking; circled the block at an easygoing pace and returned. Better safe than sorry, he thought. It was probably nothing at all. Probably just some DUI that the state trooper was carting off to jail. That's about all they were good for, Mr. Gash mused, busting drunks.

He pulled off his houndstooth jacket and laid it on the front seat. Then he stepped behind a pine tree to take a leak. He was zipping up when he heard movement—something on the edge of the trees, near the car. Mr. Gash took out his gun and peered around the trunk of the pine. He saw a bum crouched by the side of the road.

Mr. Gash stole out from behind the tree. The bum had his back to him; a big sonofabitch, too. When he stood up, he was nearly a foot taller than Mr. Gash. He appeared to be wearing a white-and-black checkered skirt over bare legs and hiking boots.

With confidence Mr. Gash returned the gun to his shoulder holster. He smiled to himself, thinking: This dolly would be a hit on Ocean Drive.

When the bum turned around, Mr. Gash reconsidered his assessment.

"Take it easy, pops." Hoping the man took notice of the gun under his arm.

The bum said nothing. He wore a cheap shower cap on his head, and he had a jittery red eyeball that looked like a party gag. A silvery beard hung off his cheeks in two ropy braids, each decorated with a hooked beak. In one of his huge hands the bum held by its tail an opossum, its jaw slack and its fur crusty with blood. In the other hand was a paperback book.

Mr. Gash said, "Where'd you come from?"

The man smiled broadly, startling Mr. Gash. He had never seen a bum with such perfect teeth, much whiter than his own.

"Nice dress." Mr. Gash, testing the guy.

"Actually it's a kilt. Made it myself."

"You got a name?"

"Not today," said the bum.

"I hope you weren't planning to steal my car."

The bum grinned again. He shook his head no, in a manner suggesting that Mr. Gash's car wasn't worth stealing.

Mr. Gash pointed at the opossum and said, "Your little pal got a name?"

"Yeah: Lunch. He got hit by a dirt bike."

Mr. Gash thought the bum seemed oddly at ease, being interrogated by a stranger with a handgun.

"You didn't answer my question, pops. Where'd you come from?"

The bum held up the book. "You should read this."

"What is it?" Mr. Gash said.

"*The Comedians.* By Graham Greene."

"Never heard of him."

"He would have enjoyed meeting you."

"The hell's *that* supposed to mean?" Mr. Gash took two steps toward the car. He was creeped out by the guy's attitude, the nonchalant way he handled the dead opossum.

The bum said, "I'll loan you my copy."

Mr. Gash got in his car and started the engine. The bum came closer.

"Stop right there, pops." Mr. Gash, whipping out the semi-automatic. The guy stopped. His weird red iris was aimed upward the treetops, while his normal eye regarded Mr. Gash with a blank and unnerving indifference.

Mr. Gash waggled the gun barrel and said, "You never saw me, understand?"

"Sure."

"Or the car."

"Fine."

"The fuck are you staring at?"

There it was again—that toothpaste-commercial smile.

"Nice hair," the bum said to Mr. Gash.

"I ought to kill you, pops. Just for that I ought to shoot your sorry homeless ass. . . ."

But the bum in the homemade checkered skirt turned away. Toting his paperback book and his roadkill opossum, he slowly made his way into the pines, as if Mr. Gash wasn't there; wasn't pointing a loaded gun at his back, threatening to blow him away on the count of six.

Mr. Gash sped off, burning rubber. What a mother-freaking nutcase! he thought. I hate this place and I hate this job.

A whole goddamn island full of troublemakers!

Mr. Gash turned on the tape and punched the REWIND button.

Very soon, he reminded himself. Then I get to go home.

20

The first few times Twilly and Desie made love, McGuinn paid no attention; just curled up on the floor and snoozed. Then one night—the night they freed Palmer—the dog suddenly displayed a rambunctious interest in what was happening up on the mattress. Desie was on the verge of what promised to be a memorable moment when the bed frame heaved violently, and Twilly let out a groan that was notably devoid of rapture. All movement ceased, and the springs fell dolefully silent. Desie felt hot liver-biscuit breath on her cheeks and a crushing weight upon her chest. By the quavering glow of the motel-room television, she saw that the Labrador had leapt upon Twilly's bare back and planted himself there, all 128 pounds. That alone would have distracted Twilly (who was nothing if not focused while in Desie's embrace), but the dog had made himself impossible to ignore by clamping his jaws to the base of Twilly's neck, as if snatching an unsuspecting jackrabbit.

"Bad boy," Twilly scolded through clenched teeth.

McGuinn was not biting hard, and he didn't seem angry or even agitated. He was, however, intent.

"Bad dog," Twilly tried again.

Desie whispered, "I think he's feeling left out."

"What do you suggest?"

"Are you hurt?"

"Only my concentration," Twilly said.

Desie released the headboard and slipped her arms around Twilly's shoulders. She hooked her fingertips inside the Labrador's cheeks and tugged gently. McGuinn compliantly let go. Ears pricked in curiosity, the huge dog stared down at Desie. She could hear his tail thwumping cheerfully against Twilly's thighs.

"Good boy," Twilly said, the words muffled by Desie's right breast. "Wanna go for a w-a-l-k?"

McGuinn scrambled off the bed and bounded to the door. Desie used a corner of the top sheet to sop the dog slobber from Twilly's neck, which also featured a detailed imprint of canine dentition.

"No bleeding," Desie reported.

"How about hickeys?"

"Maybe he was having a bad dream."

"Or a really good one."

They tried again later, after McGuinn's walk. They waited until they heard him snoring on the carpet near the television. This time it was Twilly whose promising climax got thwarted— the dog flew in out of nowhere, knocking the wind out of Twilly, and knocking Twilly out of Desie.

"Bad boy," Twilly rasped. He was highly annoyed. "You're a bad, bad boy. A rotten, miserable, worthless boy."

"He's biting your neck again!"

"He certainly is."

"Maybe I'm making too much noise when we do it," Desie said. "Maybe he thinks you're hurting me."

"No excuses. He's not a puppy anymore."

But the more strenuously Desie tried to prize open the dog's jaws, the more intractable his grip became. To McGuinn it was a new game, and Labradors loved to play games.

"Well, I intend to get some rest," Twilly said. "If the dumb bastard doesn't let go of me by morning, I'm killing him."

And to sleep Twilly went, a jumbo-sized Labrador retriever attached to his neck. Soon the dog was sleeping, too, as placidly as if he'd dozed off with his favorite rubber ball in his mouth. Desie lay rigid in the bed, listening to both of them enjoy a deep, restful slumber. She thought: So this is my status at age thirty-two and a half—alone with a kinky dog and my kidnap-per-lover in a twenty-nine-dollar motel room in Fort Pierce, Florida. What interesting choices I've made! Roll the highlights, please, starting with untrustworthy Gorbak Didovlic, the not-so-gifted NBA rookie; brilliant Andrew Beck, the self-perforating producer of deceptive political commercials; slick-talking Palmer Stoat, the tiresomely devious husband whom we dumped only two hours earlier at a Cracker Barrel restaurant off Interstate 95.

And finally young Twilly Spree, who would probably love me faithfully and forever in his own charming adolescent way, but who has no ambition beyond wreaking havoc, and no imaginable future that doesn't include felony prison time. The man of my dreams!

Fun? Big fun. Major adrenaline rush. Mysteriously wealthy, and other surprises galore. Then what? Desie wondered. Then he'll be gone, of course.

Well, there was still Palmer. Deceitful asshole though he was,

Desie nonetheless had felt a twinge of pity at the sight of him tied up and hooded in the rocking chair. And the expression on his pie-shaped face when Twilly removed the sweat-stained pillowcase and cut the ropes—a look of malignant contempt, manufactured for Desie's benefit. See how serious I am!

But he'd take her back in a heartbeat, her husband would. Palmer required a sharp-looking wife, one who would put up with his conveniently ambiguous travel plans and his unsportsmanlike hunting trips and all that Polaroid weirdness in the bedroom. Palmer knew he had a good thing in Desie, and he also knew what divorces cost. So, sure, he'd take her back.

That would be the easiest road for Desie, too, but she couldn't take it. She would not be able to look at her husband without thinking of tiny orange-striped toads, bulldozed into goop.

Her folks in Atlanta—they'd be glad to have her home for a while. Mom was busy with her medical practice, but Dad would be retiring soon from Delta. Maybe I could start back at GSU, Desie thought, finish up on my teaching degree.

Yeah, right. And afterward I'll move to Appalachia and live in a tin shanty and do volunteer work with the learning disabled. Who the hell am I kidding?

Twilly stirred when Desie stroked his brow.

"You awake?"

"Am now," he said.

"Dreaming?"

"I dunno. Is there a giant black dog on my back?"

"I'm afraid so."

"Then I wasn't dreaming," Twilly said.

"I've been lying here wondering . . . what happens now?"

"The itinerary, you mean."

"The agenda," she said.

"Well, first, I intend to seriously fuck things up so Shearwater never gets built."

Desie cupped his chin in her hands. "You can't stop it."

"I can try."

"They'll fix it so you can't. Palmer and the governor. I'm sorry but that's a fact," said Desie. "If they say the bridge is a done deal, it's done."

"Just watch."

"There's nothing you can do, Twilly, short of killing somebody."

"I agree."

"My God."

"What?"

"Don't even joke about that," Desie said. "Nothing like this is worth taking a human life."

"No? What's the life of an island worth? I'd be curious to know." Twilly reached behind his head and flicked McGuinn smartly on the tip of the nose. The dog awoke with a startled yelp, releasing his hold on Twilly's neck. He jumped to the floor and began to paw, optimistically, at the doorjamb.

Twilly rose on one arm to face Desie. "Ever been to Marco Island? You can't imagine how they mauled that place."

"I know, honey, but—"

"If you'd seen it when you were a kid and then now, you'd say it was a crime. You'd say somebody ought to have their nuts shot off for what they did. And you'd be right."

Desie said, "If you're trying to scare me off, you're doing a fine job."

"You asked me a question."

Desie pulled him into her arms. "I'm sorry. We can talk about this in the morning."

As if it could end differently.

"The whole damn island," she heard him murmur. "I can't let that happen again."

Dick Artemus offered Lisa June Peterson a drink. He was on his third. She said no thanks.

"Still drivin' that Taurus?" he asked her.

"Yes, sir."

"You break my heart, Lisa June. I can put you in a brand-new Camry coupe, at cost."

"I'm fine, Governor. Thanks, just the same."

The phone on his desk rang and rang. Dick Artemus made no move to pick it up. "Is Dorothy gone home already? Jesus Christ."

"It's six-thirty. She's got kids," Lisa June Peterson said. She reached across the desk and punched a button on the telephone console. Instantly the ringer went mute.

The governor savored his bourbon. He winked and said: "Whaddya got for me?"

Lisa June thought: Great, he's half-trashed. "Two things. About this special session—before we send out the press release, you should know that Willie Vasquez-Washington is pitching a conniption. He says he doesn't want to fly back to Tallahassee next week, doesn't want his vacation interrupted. He says he's going to make himself a royal pain in the ass if you drag the House and Senate back into session—"

"Those his words?" Dick Artemus grimaced. " 'Royal pain in the ass.' But you told him this was for schools, right? For the education budget."

Lisa June Peterson patiently explained to the bleary governor that Willie Vasquez-Washington was no fool; that he'd quickly figured out the true purpose for the special legislative session, namely to revive the Toad Island bridge project on behalf of the governor's buddies—

"Hell, they aren't my buddies!" Dick Artemus spluttered. "They aren't my pals, they aren't my partners. They're just some solid business folks who contributed to the campaign. Goddamn that Willie, he ain't no saint himself. . . ."

Lisa June Peterson informed her boss that Willie Vasquez-Washington didn't know (or care) why the governor had vetoed the bridge appropriation in the first place, but he promised to make the governor suffer dearly for screwing up his travel plans.

"He's going skiing in Banff," Lisa June reported. "Taking the whole family."

Dick Artemus sniffed. "Who's payin' for *that*?"

"I can find out."

"Naw. Hell." The governor puffed his cheeks in disgust. "Y'know, I never had to deal with shit like this in Toyota Land. What else, Lisa June? Let's have it."

"Clinton Tyree came to see you the other night, when you were in Orlando."

Dick Artemus straightened in the chair. "Damn. What'd he want? What'd he say?"

"He said he'll do what you asked him to—"

"Fannnnn-tastic!"

"—but he'll come back to Tallahassee and murder you if anything happens to his brother Doyle. Murder you slowly, he asked me to emphasize."

"Oh, for God's sake." The governor forced out a chuckle.

Lisa June said, "He mentioned the following items: a pitchfork, handcuffs, a fifty-five-gallon drum of lye and a coral snake."

"He's a nut," the governor said.

"He's also serious."

"Well, don't worry, 'cause nuthin's gonna happen to brother

Doyle. For God's sake." Dick Artemus groped distractedly for the bourbon bottle. "Poor Lisa June, you're probably wonderin' what the hell you got yourself into with this crazy job. You can't figger out what the heck's goin' on."

Lisa June Peterson said, "I know what's going on. He showed me the letter you wrote."

"What letter!" Dick Artemus protested. Then, sheepishly: "Ok, scratch that. Yeah, I wrote it. See, sometimes. . . ."

He gazed with a drowsy bemusement into his glass.

Lisa June said, "Sometimes what?"

"Sometimes in this world you gotta do things that aren't so nice."

"For the sake of a golf course."

"Don't get me started, darling. It's a lot more complicated than that." The governor raised his face to offer a paternal smile. "There's a natural order to consider. A certain way things work. You know that, Lisa June. That's how it's always been. You can't change it and I can't change it and some crazy old homicidal hermit—Skink, isn't that what he calls himself?—well, he damn sure can't change it, neither."

Lisa June Peterson stood up, smoothing her skirt. "Thanks for the pep talk, Governor."

"Aw, don't get sulky on me. Sit down, now. Tell me what he looked like. Tell me what happened, I'm dyin' to hear."

But even if Dick Artemus had been sober, Lisa June couldn't have brought herself to share what had happened at the campfire—that the ex-governor had kept her up all night with a fevered monologue; that he had told her true stories of old Florida, that he had ranted and incanted and bellowed at the stars, stomping back and forth, weeping from one eye while the other smoldered as red as a coal; that he had painted teardrops on his bare scalp with fox blood; that he had torn his queer checkered kilt while scrambling up a tree, and that she'd put it back together with three safety pins that she'd found in a corner of her purse; that he'd kissed her, and she'd kissed him back.

Lisa June Peterson couldn't have brought herself to tell her boss that she'd left Clinton Tyree snoring naked and sweaty in the woods a mere ten miles from the capitol, or that she'd rushed home with the intention of putting it all down on paper—everything he'd said and done, and *said* he'd done—saving it for the book she planned to write. Because when she got home to her apartment, showered, fixed a cup of hot tea and sat down with a legal pad, she could not put down a word. Not one.

"Nothing much happened," Lisa June Peterson told the governor.

Dick Artemus rocked forward and planted his elbows on his desk. "Well, what does he look like? He's a big fucker, according to the files."

"He's big," Lisa June confirmed.

"Taller'n me?"

"He looks old," Lisa June said.

"He *is* old. What else?"

"And sad."

"But he's still freaky, I bet."

"I've seen freakier," said Lisa June.

"Aw, you're pissed at me. Don't be like this." Dick Artemus held out his arms imploringly. "I wasn't really gonna evict the man's brother from that lighthouse, Lisa June. You honestly think I'd do something as shitty as that?"

"The letter was enough."

"Oh, for God's sake." The governor grabbed his bourbon and leaned back, balancing the glass on his lap. "All I want him to do is find that crazy kid with the dog. That's all."

"Oh, he'll find him," Lisa June Peterson said. "Now, how do you want to deal with the Honorable Representative Vasquez-Washington?"

"That fucking Willie." Dick Artemus hacked out a bitter laugh. "You know what to do, Lisa June. Call Palmer Stoat. Get him to make things right."

"Yes, sir."

"Hey. What happened to your knee?" The governor, craning his neck for a better angle.

"Just a scrape." Lisa June thinking: I knew I should've worn hose today, Dick Artemus being an incorrigible ogler of legs.

"Ooooch," he said. "How'd that happen?"

"Climbing a tree," said Lisa June Peterson.

"This I gotta hear."

"No, you don't."

The name of the strip club was Pube's.

Upon bribing the bouncer, Robert Clapley was dismayed to be informed that the Barbies had easily won first place in the amateur contest, snatched up the thousand-dollar cash prize and departed the premises with an individual named Avalon Brown, who claimed to be an independent film producer from Jamaica.

"I feel sick," Clapley said to Palmer Stoat.

"Don't. It's the best thing that could happen to you," Stoat said, "getting rid of those two junkie sluts."

"Knock it off, Palmer. I need those girls."

"Yeah, like you need rectal polyps."

Stoat was in a sour and restless mood. All around him were frisky nude women, dancing on tabletops, yet he couldn't stop thinking about Desie and the Polaroid.

But those nights were over, as was his marriage.

"Let's go," Clapley said. "Maybe they went back to the apartment."

Palmer Stoat raised a hand. "Hang on." The stage announcer

was introducing the entrants for the final event, a Pamela Anderson Lee look-alike contest.

"Whoa, momma!" Stoat piped.

"If I had a grapefruit knife," said Robert Clapley, "I'd gouge out my eyeballs."

"Bob, are you kidding? They're gorgeous."

"They're grotesque. Cheap trash."

"As opposed to your classy twins," Stoat said archly, "Princess Grace and Princess Di, who are presently double-fellating some Rastafarian pornographer in exchange for a whole half a gram of Bolivian talc."

Clapley seized Stoat by the collar. "Palmer, you're a goddamn pig."

"We're both pigs, Bob, so relax. Chill out. I'll get you a rhino horn and then you'll win your precious Barbies back." Stoat pulled free of Clapley's clutch. "Anyway, there's nothing you can do to me that hasn't already been done—starting with that fucking rodent your charming Mr. Gash gagged me with."

"That was after you tried to rip me off," Clapley reminded him, "double-billing me for the bridge fix. Or was it triple-billing?"

"So maybe I got a little greedy. But still. . . ."

Onstage, thirteen Pamela Anderson Lees were dancing, or at least bobbling, to the theme music from the *Baywatch* television series. Palmer Stoat sighed in glassy wonderment. "Man, we live in incredible times. Look at all that!"

"I'm outta here."

"Go ahead. I'll grab a taxi." Stoat's gaze was riveted to the pneumatic spectacle onstage. It was just what he needed to take his mind off Desie.

"Don't call me again until Governor Dickhead signs over the bridge money and you've got your hands on some rhinoceros dust. Those are the only two goddamn news bulletins I want from you. Understand?"

Stoat grunted a vague assent. "Bob, before you take off. . . ."

"What now, Palmer?"

"How about another Cuban?"

Robert Clapley slapped a cigar on the table. "Turd fondler," he said.

"Sweet dreams, Bob."

21

On a cool May night, an unmarked panel truck delivered a plywood crate to the Wilderness Veldt Plantation. The crate had been shipped directly to a private airstrip in Ocala, Florida, thereby avoiding port-of-entry inspections by the U.S. Customs Service, Fish and Wildlife and other agencies that would have claimed a jurisdictional interest.

At the Wilderness Veldt Plantation, the scuffed box was loaded onto a flatbed and transported to a low-slung, windowless barn known as Quarantine One. Less than an hour later, Durgess was summoned from home. He was met outside the facility by a man named Asa Lando, whose job title at the hunting ranch was Supervisor of Game.

"How bad?" Durgess asked.

Asa Lando spat in the dirt.

Durgess frowned. "All right, lemme take a look."

The barn was divided into eight gated stalls, fenced with heavy-gauge mesh from the ground to the beams. Each stall had an overhead fan, a heater and a galvanized steel trough for food and water. The Hamburg delivery was in stall number three.

Durgess said: "You gotta be kiddin'."

"I wish." Asa Lando knew he was in trouble. It was his responsibility to procure animals for the hunts.

"First off," Durgess began, "this ain't no cheetah."

"I know—"

"It's a ocelot or a margay. Hell, it can't weigh no more'n thirty-five pounds."

Asa Lando said, "No shit, Durge. I got eyes. I can see it ain't no cheetah. That's why I woke you outta bed."

"Second of all," said Durgess, "it's only got two goddamn legs."

"I can *count,* too." Asa sullenly poked the toe of his boot into the sawdust. "Could be worse."

Durgess glared. "How? If he came in a jar?"

"Look, this ain't the first time we run into this sorta situation," Asa reminded him. "We got plenty clients happy to shoot gimped-out game."

"Not this client," Durgess said. One time they'd gotten away with a three-legged wildebeest, but two legs was out of the question, especially for a big cat.

Morosely the men stared through the fencing. With plucky agility, the ocelot hopped over and began rubbing its butt against the links.

"I wonder what the hell happened to him," Durgess said.

"Doc Terrell says he was likely a-born that way—one front leg, one back leg. All things considered, he's got an awful decent disposition."

Durgess cheerlessly agreed. "Tell me again where you got him."

"Uncle Wilhelm's Petting Zoo," Asa said. "They got rid of him on account he was eatin' all their parrots. Don't ast me how he caught the damn things, but I guess he taught hisself to jump like a motherfucker."

"And how much did we pay?" Durgess braced himself.

"Five grand, minus freight."

"Sweet Jesus."

"C.O.D."

"Asa, buddy, we got a serious problem." Durgess explained that one of their best customers, Palmer Stoat, was bringing a bigshot business associate to Wilderness Veldt to shoot a cheetah, a full-grown African cheetah.

"It's a big kill," Durgess said gravely. "Big money."

Asa eyed the wiry cat. "Maybe we can fatten him up 'tween now and then."

"Sure," Durgess said. "Staple on a couple fake legs while we're at it. Lord, Asa, sometimes I wonder 'bout you."

But the Supervisor of Game wasn't ready to admit failure. "Three hundred yards, Durge, one cat looks like another to these bozos. Remember Gummy the Lion?"

Durgess flicked his hand in disgust. Formerly known as Maximilian III, Gummy the Lion had been the star of a trained-animal act at a roadside casino outside Reno, Nevada. Old age and a lifelong affinity for chocolate-chip ice cream claimed first the big cat's canines and eventually all its teeth, so Max had been retired and sold to a wildlife wholesaler, who had in turn peddled the animal to the Wilderness Veldt Plantation. Even Asa Lando had been aghast when they'd uncrated it. Durgess had figured they were stuck with a new pet—who'd pay good money to shoot a senile, toothless lion?

A moron named Nick Teeble, it turned out. Eighteen thousand dollars he'd paid. That was how badly the retired tobacco executive had wanted a lion skin for the stone fireplace in his Costa Rican vacation chalet. It had been Asa who had sized up Nick Teeble for the phony he was; Asa who had persuaded

Durgess to use the enfeebled Gummy in the canned hunt. And Asa had been right: Nick Teeble was both oblivious and incompetent, an ideal combination for Wilderness Veldt. It had taken Nick Teeble seven shots to hit the lion, whose disinclination to run or even stir from its nap was attributable to a complete and irreversible deafness (brought about by twenty-one years of performing in front of a very loud, very bad casino brass combo).

Durgess said to Asa London: "That was different. Teeble was a chump."

"*All* our customers are chumps," Asa Lando pointed out. "They damn sure ain't hunters. They just want somethin' large and dead for the wall. Talk about chumps, you can start with your Mr. Stoat."

"The man he's bringing here has done real big-game trips. He won't go for no Gummy routine," Durgess asserted. "He ain't gonna buy it if we tell him he *shot* two legs off that cat."

Asa Lando said, unflaggingly: "Don't be so sure."

"Hey, the man wants a cheetah, which is the fastest land mammal in the whole entire world. This poor critter here"— Durgess gestured at the lopsided ocelot—"couldn't outrun my granny's wheelchair."

As if on cue, the cat hip-hopped itself in a clockwise motion, hoisted its tail and sprayed through the mesh of the cage, dappling both men's pants.

"Damn!" cried Asa Lando, jumping back from the stall.

Durgess turned and trudged out of the building.

Riding in silence, they crossed the old bridge in late afternoon. Twilly Spree headed for the beach instead of the bed-and-breakfast, even though they were hungry. He hoped a sunset would improve Desie's spirits.

But a front was pushing through, and the horizon disappeared behind rolling purple-tinged clouds. A grayness fell suddenly over the shore and a cool, wet-smelling breeze sprung off the Gulf. Twilly and Desie held hands loosely as they walked. McGuinn loped ahead to harass the terns and gulls.

"Rain's coming," Twilly said.

"It feels great." Desie took a long deep breath.

"At each end of this beach is where they want to put those condos," said Twilly, "like sixteen-story bookends. 'Luxury units starting in the low two hundreds!' " This was straight off a new billboard that Robert Clapley had erected on U.S. 19. Twilly had noticed it that morning while driving back to the island.

Desie said, "I've got a question. You don't have to answer if you don't want."

"OK."

"Two questions, actually. Have you ever killed a person?"

Twilly thought of Vecker Darby's house exploding in a chemical cloud with Vecker Darby, slow-footed toxic dumper, still inside.

"Have you?" Desie asked.

"Indirectly."

"What kind of answer is that?"

"A careful one," Twilly said.

"Would you do it again? Over toads? Honey, you *arrest* somebody for mushing toads. You don't murder them."

Twilly let her hand slip from his fingers. "Desie, it's not just the toads, and you know it."

"Then what—over condos? Two lousy high-rises? You act like they're paving the whole coast."

"And you're beginning to sound like your husband."

Desie stopped in her tracks, the tail of a wave washing over the tops of her feet. A gust of wind blew the hair away from her neck, her astonishingly lovely neck, and Twilly fought the impulse to kiss her there.

She said, "This is all my fault."

"What is?"

"I should never have told you about this island, about what they're planning to do."

"Why not? It's horrible what they're planning."

"Yes, but now you're talking about killing people, which is also wrong," said Desie, "not to mention a crime, and I don't particularly want to see you go to jail. Jail would not be good for this relationship, Twilly."

He said, "If it wasn't Shearwater, it'd be something else. If it wasn't this island, it would be another. That's what you need to understand."

"And if it wasn't me with you here on this beach, it would be someone else. Right?"

"Please don't." Twilly reached for her waist but she spun away, heading back (he assumed) toward the car.

"Desie!"

"Not now," she called over her shoulder.

From the other direction came an outburst of barking. At first Twilly thought it was another big dog, because he'd never heard McGuinn make such a racket.

But it was him. Twilly could see the familiar black hulk far down the beach, alternately crouching and dashing circles around somebody on the sand. The behavior looked anything but playful.

Twilly broke into a run. A nasty dog-bite episode was the last thing he needed to deal with—the ambulance, the cops, the wailing victim. Just my luck, Twilly thought glumly. How can you possibly piss off a Labrador retriever? Short of hammering them with a baseball bat, they'd put up with just about anything. Yet someone had managed to piss off ultramellow McGuinn. Probably some idiot tourist, Twilly fumed, or his idiot kids.

He jogged faster, kicking up water whenever a wave slid across his path. The run reminded him of his two dreams, without all the dead birds and the panic. Ahead on the beach, McGuinn continued to carry on. Twilly now could see what was upsetting the dog—a stocky, sawed-off guy in a suit. The man was lunging with both arms at the Labrador, which kept darting out of reach.

What now? Twilly wondered.

As he drew closer, he shouted for the dog to come. But McGuinn was in manic mode and scarcely turned his head to acknowledge Twilly's voice. The stranger reacted, though. He stopped grabbing for the dog and arranged himself into a pose of calm and casual waitfulness.

Twilly prepared for trouble. He pulled up and walked the last twenty yards, to catch his breath and assess the situation. Immediately, McGuinn positioned himself between Twilly and the stranger, who clearly was no tourist. The man wore a rumpled houndstooth suit and ankle-high leather shoes with zippers. He had a blond dye job and a chopped haircut that belonged on somebody with pimples and a runny nose.

"Down!" Twilly said to McGuinn.

But the Lab kept snapping and snarling, his lush coat bristling like a boar's. Twilly was impressed. Like Desie, he believed animals possessed an innate sense of danger—and he believed McGuinn's intuition was correct about the out-of-place stranger.

"Obedience school," the man said. "Or try one of those electrified collars. That'll do the trick."

"He bite you?" Twilly's tone made it clear he was not stricken with concern for the stranger's health.

"Naw. We're just playing. What's his name?"

"You might be playing," Twilly said to the man, "but he's not."

McGuinn lowered himself on all fours. He rumbled a low growl and panted unblinkingly. His haunches remained bunched and taut, as if readying to launch at the stranger.

"What's his name?" the man asked again.

Twilly told him.

"Sounds Irish," the man remarked. His eyes cut back and forth between Twilly and the dog. "You Irish?" he said to Twilly.

"You'll have to do better than this."

The stranger acted innocent. "What do you mean? I'm just trying to be friendly."

Twilly said, "Cut the shit."

The weather was coming up on them fast. A cold raindrop hit the side of Twilly's neck. The man with the spiky hair took a fat one on the nose. He wiped it dry with the sleeve of his jacket.

"Rain'll ruin those shoes of yours," Twilly said, "in about two minutes flat."

"Let me worry about the footwear," the stranger said, but he glanced down anyway at his feet. Twilly knew he was thinking about how much the brown leather shoes had cost.

"McGuinn! Let's go." Twilly clapped his hands loudly.

The dog wouldn't move, wouldn't shift his stare from the man in the musty-smelling suit. The Labrador had retained little from his short-lived time as a hunting dog in training, but one thing that had stayed with him was an alertness to guns. A human with a gun carried himself in a distinctly different manner. The Palmer Stoat who clomped through the marsh with a 20-gauge propped on his shoulder practically was a separate species from the Palmer Stoat who each night clipped McGuinn to a leash and covertly led him next door to crap on the neighbor's garden. To Stoat and his human hunter friends, the transformation in themselves—bearing, gait, demeanor and voice—was so subtle they didn't notice, yet it was glaringly obvious to McGuinn. A visual sighting of the gun itself was superfluous; humans who carried them had an unmistakable presence. Even their perspiration smelled different—not worse, for in the ever-ripe world of dogs there was hardly such a thing as a bad odor. Just different ones.

For a moment the stranger acted as if he wanted to make friends. He reached a hand beneath his moldy-smelling coat and said, "Here, boy. I've got something you'll like. . . ."

McGuinn, cocking his head, licking his chops, never taking his hopeful brown eyes off the stranger's hand, which emerged from under the coat with . . .

The gun. Had to be.

Now, from behind, the Labrador heard the young man say: "Stay, boy. Don't move!"

Never had McGuinn detected such urgency in a command. He decided, on a whim, to obey.

There was another gun-toting human on Toad Island: Krimmler, who had taken to carrying a loaded .357 after Robert Clapley's hired freak accosted him in the Winnebago.

The pistol added to Krimmler's nervousness, and he had plenty of time to be nervous. Construction on the Shearwater resort project remained suspended, and the lush new quiet on the island made Krimmler restless and edgy—it was the very sound of Nature, gradually reclaiming the ground plowed up by his beloved bulldozers. One morning he was appalled to find a green shoot sprouting in the old dirt tracks of a front-end loader. A baby tree! Krimmler thought, ripping it from the soil. A baby tree that would otherwise grow to be a tall chipmunk-harboring tree!

The tranquillity that had once merely annoyed Krimmler now turned him into a paranoid basket case. At night he slept with the .357 under his pillow, half-certain he accidentally would shoot off his own ear while groping for the gun in a moment of dire need. By day he tucked it in the front of his pants, half-certain he accidentally would shoot off his genitals if danger surfaced.

Krimmler did not, as it turned out, shoot off any of his own body parts. He went for the .357 exactly once, dislodging it from his waistband and knocking it all the way down his baggy right pants leg. It landed with a clunk on the flimsy floor of the construction trailer, where it was retrieved by the smiling bald-headed bum with the racing flag around his waist.

"You rascal," the bum said to Krimmler.

"Gimme that!" Krimmler exclaimed.

The bum tapped the bullets out of the cylinder, then handed the empty gun to the engineer.

"Good way to shoot off your pecker," the bum remarked.

"What do you want!"

"I'm looking for a young man, a woman and a dog. A black Labrador retriever."

Krimmler said, "What is this! Don't tell me you work for Mr. Clapley, too?"

The bald bum began twirling the long, grungy-looking braids of his beard. Some sort of shrunken-looking artifact was attached to each end.

He said, "The Lab might be missing an ear. Other parts, too."

"I'll you tell you the same thing I told that other guy," Krimmler said. This bounty hunter was even bigger and worse-dressed than Mr. Gash. He also had a bad eye, which made him appear even more unstable.

"I don't know where your boy is," Krimmler said, "or his goddamned dog, either. If he's not camping at the beach, he's probably at the b-and-b. Or maybe he left the island. Tourists sometimes do, you know."

The bum said, "I don't work for Clapley."

"I knew it, you asshole!"

"I work for Governor Richard Artemus."

"Right," said Krimmler, "and I'm Tipper Gore."

"One question, sir."

"Go fuck yourself," Krimmler said, "but first go take a bath."

That's when the bum slapped Krimmler. He slapped him with an open hand—Krimmler saw it coming. Slapped him with an open hand so hard it knocked Krimmler unconscious for forty-five minutes. When he awoke, he was naked and halfway up a tall pine tree, wedged loosely in the crotch of three branches. The scratchy bark was murder on his armpits and balls. His jaw throbbed from the blow.

The sky had clouded and the wind had kicked up cold from the west. Krimmler felt himself swaying with the tree. On a nearby limb sat the bum in the racing-flag skirt. He was sipping a cream soda and reading (with his normal eye) a paperback book.

He glanced up at Krimmler and said: "One question, sir."

"Anything," Krimmler said weakly. He had never been more terrified. The treetops undoubtedly were full of goddamned squirrels, mean as timber wolves!

The bum said, "What 'other guy'?"

"The one with the snuff tape."

"Tell me more." The bum closed his book and put it in the pocket of his rain jacket, along with his empty cream-soda can.

"He had a tape of some poor slob dying. Getting stabbed to death by his girlfriend. Live, as it happened." Krimmler was scared to look down, as he was afraid of heights. He was also scared to look up, for fear of seeing one of those squirrels or possibly even a band of mutant chipmunks. So he squeezed his eyes shut.

The bum said: "What'd this other guy look like?"

"Short. Muscle-bound. Bad suit, and hair to match."

"Blondish?" the bum inquired. "Spiked out like a hedgehog?"

"That's him!" Krimmler felt relieved. Now the bum knew he was being truthful, and therefore had no compelling reason (other than Krimmler's general obnoxiousness) to push him out of the tree. The bum rose to stretch his arms, the pine bough creaking under his considerable weight. At the sound, Krimmler opened his eyes.

The bum asked, "What's the guy's name?"

"Gash," Krimmler replied. A chilly raindrop landed on his bare thigh, causing him to shiver. Another drop fell on his back.

"Last name or first?"

"Mr. Gash is what he called himself."

"What did he want with the young man and the dog?"

"He said Mr. Clapley had sent him. He said the kid was a troublemaker. I didn't ask him what he meant." The rising wind made the pine needles thrum. Krimmler clawed his fingernails into the bark. "Can you please get me down from here?"

"I can," said the bum, hopping to a lower branch, "but I don't believe I will."

"Why the hell not! What're you doing!"

"Gotta go," the bum informed the quaking Krimmler. "Bath time."

22

The man in the zippered shoes said, "I've killed my share of dogs."

"I don't doubt it," said Twilly.

"Kitty cats, too."

"Oh, I believe you."

"And one time, some jerkwad's pet monkey. Bernardo was his name. Bernardo the baboon. Came right out of his halter and went for my scalp," the man said. "They say monkeys are so smart? Bullshit. Dogs're smarter."

"Yeah," said Twilly.

"But I'll shoot this one, you try and get cute."

"Well, he's not mine."

"What're you saying?" The rain was flattening the spikes in the man's hair. He held his right arm straight, the gun trained on the Labrador's brow. "You don't care if I pop this mutt?"

Twilly said, "I didn't say that. I said he doesn't belong to me. He belongs to the guy who sent you here."

"Wrong!" The man made a noise like the buzzer on a TV game show. "He belongs to a major asshole named Palmer Stoat."

"Didn't he hire you?"

The man cackled and made the sarcastic buzzer noise again. "Would I work for a fuckhead like that? Ha!"

"What was I thinking," Twilly said.

"Mr. Clapley's the one that hired me."

"Ah."

"To clean out the troublemakers. Now, how about you get a move on. Call the damn dog and let's go," the man said, "before we get soaked. Where's your car?"

"That way." Twilly nodded down the beach.

"Your lady friend?"

"Gone." Twilly thinking: God, I hope so. "We had a fight. She split."

"Too bad. I had some plans."

Twilly changed the subject. "Can I ask you something?"

"My name is Mr. Gash."

That's when Twilly became aware that the man in the brown zippered shoes intended to kill him. The man would not have offered his name unless he knew Twilly wouldn't be alive to repeat it.

"Can I ask you something?"

"Long as your feet keep moving," said the man.

They were walking along the windswept shoreline, Twilly with McGuinn at his heels. Mr. Gash followed a few feet behind. He was taking care not to get his shoes wet in the surf.

"Why are you pointing the gun at the dog," Twilly said, "and not at me?"

"Because I saw how you hauled ass up here when you thought Fido was in trouble. You care more about that dumb hound than you do about yourself," Mr. Gash said. "So I figure you won't try any crazy shit long as I keep the piece aimed at Fido's brain, which I'm sure is no bigger than a stick of Dentyne."

Twilly reached down and scratched the crown of McGuinn's head. The Lab wagged his tail appreciatively. He seemed to have lost interest in the strange-smelling human with the gun.

"Also," said Mr. Gash, "it'll be cool to watch you watch the dog die. Because that's what has to happen. I gotta do Fido first."

"How come?"

"Think about it, man. I shoot you first, the dog goes batshit. I shoot the dog first, what the hell're *you* going to do—bite me in the balls? I seriously doubt it."

Twilly said, "Good point."

His legs felt leaden and his arms were cold; the temperature was dropping rapidly ahead of the weather front. The salt spray stung, so Twilly kept his eyes lowered as he walked. He could see Desie's footprints in the sand, pointing in the same direction.

Mr. Gash was saying: "I got tape of a hellacious dog attack. Chow named Brutus. The owner's on the phone yelling for help and Brutus gets him by the nuts and will not let go. The 911 operator tells the guy to, quick, try and distract the dog. So the poor fucker, he dumps a pot of Folger's decaf on Brutus and the last thing on the tape is this scream that goes on forever. Damn dog took everything! I mean the whole package."

"Ouch," said Twilly.

"You should hear it."

"How'd you get a tape of something like that?" Twilly thinking: The more pertinent question is: Why?

Mr. Gash said, "I got my sources. Where's your goddamned car, anyway? I'm getting drenched."

"Not far."

Twilly was crestfallen to spy the Roadmaster behind a scrub-covered sand dune, where he had parked it. He had hoped Desie would see the keys in the ignition and drive back to the bed-and-breakfast, to sulk or pack her bag or whatever.

Maybe she decided to walk, thought Twilly. The important thing was that she was somewhere else, somewhere safe. . . .

But she wasn't. She was lying down in the backseat. Mr. Gash tapped the gun barrel against the rain-streaked window. Desie sat up quizzically and put her face near the glass. Mr. Gash showed her the semiautomatic and told her to unlock the door. When she hesitated, he grabbed McGuinn's collar, jerked the dog off the ground and jammed the gun to its neck.

The door flew open.

Mr. Gash beamed. "Lookie there, Fido. She loves you, too."

The trooper got to the old bridge before he changed his mind. He whipped the cruiser around and drove back to look for his friend. Thirty minutes later he found him, naked on a dune. The governor stood with his face upturned, his arms out-stretched—letting the rain and wind beat him clean.

Jim Tile honked and flashed his headlights. The man who called himself Skink peered indignantly through the slashing downpour. When he saw the Highway Patrol car, he stalked across the sand and heaved himself, dripping luxuriantly, into the front seat.

"I thought we said our good-byes," he growled, wringing out his beard.

"I forgot to give you something."

The man nodded absently. "FYI: Governor Dickhead was right. They sent someone after this boy. The boy with the dog."

Jim Tile said, "He's twenty-six years old."

"Still a boy," Skink said. "And he's here on the island, like we figured. I believe I met the man they sent to kill him."

"Then I'm glad I came back."

"You can't stay."

"I know," said the trooper.

"You've got Brenda to consider. Pensions and medical benefits and such. You can't be mixed up in shit like this."

"Nothing says I can't take off the uniform, Governor, at least for a few minutes."

"Nothing except for common sense."

"Where's your damn clothes?"

"Hung in a tree," said Skink. "What'd you bring me, Jim?"

The trooper jerked a thumb toward the trunk of the cruiser.

"Pop it open for me, would you?" Skink got out in the rain and went to the rear of the car. He returned with the package, which Jim Tile had wrapped in butcher's paper.

Skink smiled, hefting the item up and down in one hand. "You old rascal! I'm guessing Smith & Wesson."

The trooper told him the gun was clean; no serial numbers. "One of my men took it off a coke mule in Okaloosa County. Very slick operation, too—eighteen-year-old Cuban kid driving a yellow Land Rover thirty-seven miles per hour at three in the morning on Interstate 10. It's a wonder we noticed him."

Skink borrowed a handkerchief to swipe the condensation off his glass eye. "I don't get it. You're the one told me not to bring the AK-47."

"Guess I'm getting nervous in my old age," the trooper said. "There's something else in the glove compartment. You go ahead and take it."

Skink opened the latch and scowled. "No, Jim, I hate these damn things." It was a cellular phone.

"Please. As a favor," the trooper said. "It will significantly improve my response time."

Skink closed his palm around the phone. "You better hit the

road," he said grumpily. "This damn car stands out like the proverbial turd in the punch bowl."

"And you don't?"

"I'll be getting dressed momentarily."

"Oh, then you'll *really* blend in," Jim Tile said.

Skink got out of the police cruiser and tucked the heavy brown package under one arm. Before closing the door, he leaned in and said, "My love to your bride."

"Governor, I don't hear from you in twenty-four hours," the trooper said, "I'm coming back to this damn island."

"You don't hear from me in eight, don't even bother."

Skink gave a thumbs-up. Then he turned and began to run across the windblown dunes. It was a meandering, waggle-stepped, butt-wiggling run, and Jim Tile couldn't help but laugh.

He watched his friend disappear into the hazy yellow-gray of the storm. Then he wheeled the car around and headed for the mainland.

CALLER: Help me! Help me, God, please, oh God, help. . . .

DISPATCHER: What's the problem, sir?

CALLER: She set fire to my hair! I'm burning up, oh God, please!

DISPATCHER: Hang on, sir, we've got a truck on the way. We've got help coming. Can you make it to the bathroom? Try to get to the bathroom and turn on the shower.

CALLER: I can't, I can't move. . . . She tied me to the damn bed. She . . . I'm tied to the bed with, like—oh Jesus, my hair!—clothesline. Aaaggggg-hhhoooooohhhh. . . .

DISPATCHER: Can you roll over? Sir, can you turn over?

CALLER: Cindy, no! Cindy, don't! CINDY!

DISPATCHER: Sir, if you're tied to the bed, then how—
CALLER: She held the phone to my ear, the sick bitch. She
    dialed 911 and put the phone to my ear and now . . .
    ooohhhhhhh. . . . Stop! . . . Now she's doing marsh-
    mallows. My hair's on fire and she's cooking. . . . Stop,
    God, stop, I'm burning up, Cindy! . . . Marsh—oh
    Jesus!—mallows. . . . Cindy, you crazy psycho bitch. . . .

Mr. Gash turned down the volume and said, "See? That's
what love gets you. Man's wife ties him to the bedposts, pretending like she's gonna screw his brains out. Instead she puts a
lighter to his hair and roasts marshmallows in the flames."

Desie said, "That was real?"

"Oh yes, Virginia." Mr. Gash popped the tape out of the console, and read from the stick-on label. "Tacoma, Washington.
March tenth, 1994. Victim's name was Appleman. Junior Appleman."

"Did he die?"

"Eventually," Mr. Gash reported. "Took about six weeks. According to the newspaper, the Applemans had been having serious domestic problems. The best part: He lied to the dispatcher.
It wasn't clothesline she tied him up with, it was panty hose. He
was too embarrassed to say so. Even on fire! But my point is, romance is fucking deadly. Look at you two!"

Twilly and Desie traded glances.

"You wouldn't be here right now, about to die," Mr. Gash
added, "if you guys hadn't gotten romantically involved. I'd bet
the farm on it."

They were all in the station wagon, parked among the bulldozers in the woods. Desie recognized the place from Dr.
Brinkman's tour of the island. Night had fallen, and the rain had
ebbed to a drizzle. The only light inside the car came from the
dome lamp, which Mr. Gash had illuminated while playing the

911 cassette for his captives. He was next to Twilly Spree in the front seat. Desie sat behind them with McGuinn, who noisily had buried his snout in a sack of dry dog food and was therefore heedless of the semiautomatic pointed at his head.

Mr. Gash said to Desie, "What's your name, babe?"

"Never mind."

Mr. Gash held the gun in his right hand, propped against the headrest. With his other hand he pawed through Desie's purse until he found her driver's license. When he saw the name on it, he said, "Shit."

Desie shrunk in her seat.

"Nobody told me. I wonder why," Mr. Gash mused. "They told me about the dog but not the wife!"

Twilly said, "Her husband didn't know."

"Didn't care is more like it."

"You're making a mistake," said Twilly. Of course the man in the brown zippered shoes ignored him.

"Well, 'Mrs. Stoat,' I had big plans for tonight. I was going to drive you back to the mainland and hook up with a couple party girls. Introduce you to the wonderful world of multiple sex partners." Mr. Gash was studying Desie's photograph on the license. "I like the highlighting job on these bangs. It's a good look for you."

Desie resisted the impulse to comment upon the killer's platinum-tinted eyebrows.

"How exactly do you pronounce your name?" Mr. Gash asked. "Dez-eye-rotta? Is that close?"

" 'Desie' is fine."

"Like the Cuban guy on the old Lucy show."

"Close enough."

"Take off your earrings," Mr. Gash told her. "I've got a friend in Miami, an Italian girl, she'll look wicked hot in those. Almost as hot as you."

Desie removed the pearl studs and handed them over.

Mr. Gash said, "You're way too pretty for that crybaby porker of a husband. And since I haven't been laid in six days, I say what the hell. I say go for it."

Twilly tensed. "Don't be an idiot. Clapley isn't paying you to molest the wives of his friends."

"Friend? According to Mr. Clapley, Stoat's nothing—and I quote—but a 'turd fondler.' Besides," said Mr. Gash, "my job is cleaning out the troublemakers. And, Mrs. Stoat, sleeping with a troublemaker makes you a troublemaker, too."

Desie pretended to stare out the fogged-up windows. A tear crawled down one cheek.

"The way I see it," Mr. Gash went on, "is a murder-suicide. The young hothead boyfriend. The married woman who refuses to leave her rich husband. The lovers argue. Boyfriend goes postal. Whacks the broad, whacks the puppy dog, and then finally he whacks himself. Of course, they find the weapon"—Mr. Gash, nodding at his own—"at the scene."

Twilly said, "Not very original."

"The murdered dog makes it different. That's what the cops'll be talking about," said Mr. Gash. " 'What kind of creep would hurt an innocent dog?' Speaking of which, before I shoot you I've gotta ask: Where'd you get that damn ear, the one you sent to Stoat? Jesus, was he freaked!"

Twilly shifted slightly in the driver's seat. He braced his back against the door and casually took his right arm off the steering wheel.

"You really collect those horrible tapes?" Desie's voice was like acid.

"By the trunkload." Mr. Gash flashed a savage smile.

For a few moments, a chorus of ragged breathing was the only sound in the car; all three humans, including Mr. Gash, were on edge. Twilly glanced over the seat to check on

McGuinn, who had finished off the dog food and was now mouthing the paper sack. The Lab wore an all-too-familiar expression of postprandial contentment.

God, Twilly thought, please don't let him fart. This psycho punk would shoot him in a heartbeat.

Mr. Gash was saying, "Whoever finds your bodies, the first thing they'll do is call 911. You could be nothing but skeletons and still they'll call emergency." Mr. Gash paused to relish the irony. "Know what I'm going to do, Mrs. Stoat? I'm going to get the tape of that phone call, as a remembrance of our one and only night together. What do you think of that?"

"I think you're a monster."

" 'Possible human remains.' That's what the cops call those cases."

Desie Stoat said, "Please don't shoot my dog."

"You crack me up," said Mr. Gash.

"I'll do anything you want. Anything."

Desie sat forward and pinched the damp sleeve of Mr. Gash's houndstooth coat.

"*Anything*, Mrs. Stoat? Because I've got a very active imagination."

"Yes, we can tell by your wardrobe," said Twilly. He drew his right hand into a fist, mentally calibrating the distance to Mr. Gash's chin.

Desie was saying, "Please. There's no need to do that."

Mr. Gash shrugged. "Sorry, babe. The mutt dies first."

"Then I hope you're into necrophilia," she told him, trembling, "because if you shoot McGuinn, you're in for the worst sex of your whole life. That's a promise."

Mr. Gash pursed his waxy-looking lips and grew pensive. Twilly could tell that Desie's threat had hit home; the killer's kinky fantasies were in ruins.

Finally he said, "OK, I'll let him go."

Desie frowned. "Here? You can't just let him go."

"Why the hell not."

Twilly said, "He's been sick. He's on medicine."

"Better sick than dead."

"He's a dog, not a turtle. You don't just let him go," Desie protested. "He doesn't know how to hunt for himself—what's he going to eat out here?"

"You guys, for starters," said Mr. Gash. "Dogs go for fresh meat, is my understanding."

Desie blanched. Mr. Gash was paying close attention to her reaction, savoring it. Twilly saw an opportunity. He coiled his shoulder muscles, drew a deep breath and—

Then it hit him, rank and unmistakable. McGuinn!

Mr. Gash's nose twitched. His face contorted into a gargoyle scowl. "Aw, who cut the cheese? Did *he* do that!"

"What are you talking about?" Twilly, laboring to breathe through his mouth.

"I don't smell anything," insisted Desie, though her eyes had begun to well.

"Your damn dog passed gas!"

Mr. Gash was up on his knees, cursing furiously and waving the semiautomatic. McGuinn wore that liquid expression of pure lovable innocence well known to all owners of Labrador retrievers. The Look had evolved over hundreds of years as an essential survival trait, to charm exasperated humans into forgiveness.

Unfortunately, Mr. Gash was immune. "Roll down the goddamn windows!" he gasped at Twilly.

"I can't. They're electric and you took the car keys."

Mr. Gash dug the ignition key out of his pocket and twisted it into the switch on the steering column. Then he threw himself across Twilly's lap and feverishly began mashing all the window buttons on the door panel. Mr. Gash remained in that position long enough to gag Twilly with a miasmal body funk that, by comparison, made dog flatulence smell like orange blossoms.

Had Twilly been able to draw an untainted breath, he likely could have reached around and broken Mr. Gash's neck, or at least his firing arm. But the stench off the gamy houndstooth suit had a paralyzing effect, and by the time Twilly recovered, Mr. Gash had thrust the upper half of his torso across the front seat and placed the gun barrel squarely between McGuinn's calm, still-guileless eyes.

"You were home free, Fido. Then you had to go and fart."

Desie cried out and threw both arms around the Lab's trunk-like neck.

For several moments, nobody moved. A piney breeze rushed through the open windows of the Roadmaster. Twilly hoped it might refresh Mr. Gash and cool his fury.

It did not. He cocked the hammer.

"Back to Plan A," he said.

Twilly dove across the seat and slammed his right fist into Mr. Gash's rib cage, the nearest availing target. The punch didn't land right—Twilly had expected the sting of bone against bone but the impact was softer, as if he'd slugged a sofa. He could not have foreseen that Mr. Gash would be wearing, beneath the jacket, holster and long-sleeved shirt, a padded corset of cured rattlesnake hides.

The device had been fashioned by the same Washington Avenue upholstery wizard who'd customized Mr. Gash's iguana-skin sex harness. Why Mr. Gash would don a corset undergarment was a question Twilly never would get to ask. The answer: The killer had a vain streak when it came to his physique. He was driven to take measures that artificially streamlined his midsection, which in recent years had shown signs of incipient tubbiness—an unnerving development that Mr. Gash bitterly blamed on the dull sedentary lifestyle of a hit man. It was an occupation that neither required nor allowed much physical exercise; plane trips, car rides, endless stakeouts in motel rooms and bars. For Mr. Gash, already self-conscious about his short stature, the sight of a marbled, thickening belly was intolerable. A discreetly tailored corset seemed a good temporary solution, at least until he found time to join a spa. And because he lived on South Beach, not just any corset would do. Yet that's all Mr. Gash could find when he went shopping: starchy medical corsets, white or beige; no colors, no patterns. Mr. Gash wanted something with élan, something that didn't look like a flab-binding swathe, something he wouldn't be ashamed to display when stripping off his clothes for the women he took home, something intriguing enough to divert their eyes away from his gelatinous tummy.

Snakeskin was the obvious choice. With snakeskin you couldn't go wrong anywhere on Ocean Drive. Mr. Gash had chosen Eastern diamondback because the women who consented to go home with him typically were danger freaks and would therefore (Mr. Gash reasoned) be more aroused by the remains of a venomous serpent than those of a common boa or python. And over time the rattlesnake-hide corset had served Mr. Gash very well, both socially and cosmetically. When he wasn't wearing it, he felt shy and bloated—and, oddly, shorter! Without the corset, Mr. Gash would not have fit comfortably (or even attempted to fit) into his trademark houndstooth ensemble.

None of this was known to Twilly Spree. All he knew was that he hit the man with an exceptionally good punch and that the man sagged but did not keel, gulped but did not cry out, grimaced but did not roll his eyes in the manner of the soon-to-be unconscious. So Twilly clutched Mr. Gash desperately around the waist, struggling to flip him backward and get at the gun. That's when a bomb went off in Twilly's right eardrum, and white-hot starbursts exploded in his eye sockets. He hoped it was the beginning of another dream, but it wasn't.

23

The breeze felt good. More important to McGuinn, it *tasted* good; a tantalizing smorgasbord for doggy senses. There was the tangy trace of boar raccoon, the musky whiff of mother opossum, the familiar fumes of randy tomcat—and a host of intriguing new woodland scents that required immediate investigation. The night beckoned McGuinn and, once the dog food was gone, he saw no reason not to answer the call.

Except for Desie.

Desie kept hugging him, and nothing in the world was more pleasurable to a Labrador retriever than the cooing affection of a female human. They smelled fantastic! So McGuinn was torn between the primal urge to prowl and mark territory and the not-so-primal urge to be coddled and stroked.

The gunshot clinched it—so loud it made him jump, yet nevertheless triggering one of the few learned responses to have lodged for more than a day or two in his quicksand memory. A gunshot meant McGuinn was supposed to run! This he explicitly recalled from all those frosty dawns in the marsh with Palmer Stoat. A gunshot meant ducks falling from the sky! Warm, wet, tasty ducks! Ducks to be scented out and snapped floating from the pond, carried off at a gallop to be eagerly gnawed upon until hollering male humans up and snatched them away. That's what gunfire meant to McGuinn.

So he vaulted from the station wagon—out of Desie's loving arms, through an open window (yipping as his surgical wound grazed the lock button), into the misting darkness in quest of . . . ducks? But where?

Mr. Gash watched him run away and said, "That solves the dog problem."

He pushed Twilly Spree's lifeless form out of the car, pulled the door shut, and climbed into the backseat with Desie. He considered moving her to the rear cargo bed, but it was cluttered with mangled chew toys and carpeted with Labrador sheddings. Mr. Gash preferred sex that did not require a head-to-toe vacuuming afterward.

"Take off your clothes." He placed the gun to Desie's temple. Mechanically she removed her sweatshirt, bra and jeans. Mr. Gash shook himself out of the houndstooth coat and with his free hand folded it neatly into a square.

"Stick this under your head," he told Desie.

"What about your pants?" She was so frightened, so strung out with terror that her own voice seemed to be echoing from a cavern; some remote, untouchable part of her consciousness that urged her to stall, drag it out, keep the monster occupied as long as you can.

As awful as it might get.

"My pants?" said Mr. Gash.

"They're wet."

"Yeah, they are. From the *rain*."

"I know," Desie said, "but it's cold on my skin. Could you please take them off? The shirt, too." She was lying on her back, covering her nipples with her hands. Now it was purely about survival; nothing could be done for Twilly, who was either dead or dying. Desie would cry for him later, if she made it.

Mr. Gash sat poised on the edge of the seat. "Don't you move," he told her. "Don't you even blink."

He unzipped his brown shoes and placed them under the seat. Then he tugged off his damp trousers and laid them across one of the headrests. Next came the shoulder holster, then the shirt.

"What's that?" Desie asked. Even in the dark she could tell it was a most unusual garment.

"Bulletproof vest," Mr. Gash lied.

"Is that from a snake?"

"Sure is. Wanna touch?"

"No."

"It's dead. Go on and touch it."

Desie did what she was told, tracing her fingertips across the corrugated scales of the hide. She shivered not at the sensation but at the thought of where it had come from.

"Please take that off, too," she said.

As Mr. Gash fumbled to unlace the corset, he said, "Mrs. Stoat, I don't think you get it. This isn't a goddamn honeymoon, it's what the cops would call an aggravated sexual battery. And you're making me more damn aggravated by the minute."

When he climbed on top of her, she robotically positioned a hand on each of his shoulders, which felt greased and lumpy. Something hard poked her neck, and she correctly assumed it was the handgun.

Mr. Gash said, "Oh shit."

"What?"

"There's a leak in this damned car."

Desie looked up and noticed a dime-sized hole in the Road-master's roof. The hole was from the bullet that accidentally fired from the killer's gun when he smacked it against Twilly Spree's head. Now water was dripping from the hole onto Mr. Gash's bare torso.

"Right down the crack of my ass," he reported sourly.

He sat up and hastily plugged the leak with a wadded-up dis-count coupon for chicken-flavored Purina. Then he again low-ered himself on Desie, saying, "Now. *Finally.*"

She resolved not to fight; Mr. Gash was too muscular. But she had another plan: to will herself paralyzed from the neck down, so she wouldn't feel him. It was a technique Desie had developed while engaged to the multi-baubled Andrew Beck. Later, the self-numbing hypnosis had proved useful with Palmer Stoat, during the nights when his Polaroid antics became tedious.

Her trick was to imagine she was living in a borrowed body, through which she could see and speak but not feel. And at first she didn't feel anything of Mr. Gash.

"Gimme second." His breathing came in a heavy rhythm, as if he was practicing a meditation. "Just hang on," he said.

Elatedly, Desie thought: The creep can't get it up!

But relief gave way to gloom, for she realized he would kill her anyway—probably even sooner now, in a violent rage of frustration.

"Help me out here, babe."

He was grinding against her with somber determination. His hipbones banged into her hipbones, his chest slapped against her breasts, his chin dug into her forehead. . . .

Desie fought off waves of nausea—the man stank of rancid perspiration, syrupy cologne and unlaundered clothes.

"I'm not . . . used to . . . this." Mr. Gash, panting gaseously.

The rank heat of his breath made Desie shudder.

"Used to what—women?" she said. "You bi?"

"No! What I'm not . . . used to . . . is *one* woman. I'm used to . . . more."

"How many more?"

"Two . . . three. Sometimes four." He told her what he liked to do (and have done to him) while hanging in his lizard-skin sling from the ceiling.

"Whew," Desie said. "Can't help you there, chief."

Mr. Gash stopped grinding and pushed himself up on his arms. "Sure you can. There's lots of things you can do, Mrs. Stoat."

Twilly awoke facedown in mud. He blew clods out both nostrils when he lifted his head.

His head! He'd never known such pain. He tried to spit and again nearly blacked out. His left ear clanged like a fire alarm. The whole side of his skull felt flaming hot; liquid and distended.

Twilly thought: I guess I've finally been shot. He was incensed but not especially afraid, which was a chronic problem in his life—anger supplanting normal, well-founded fears. Twilly had an unhealthy lack of concern for his own safety.

He rolled over and saw stars. They vanished behind a wispy curtain of fast-moving clouds. It was nighttime and a hard rain was ending. Twilly didn't know where he was, or what he was doing there, but he had a hunch somebody would bring him up to speed. He raised an exploratory hand to his head and located a large raw knot, but no bullet wound. His fingers came back sticky so he held them in front of his face to check the color of the blood; the brighter the better. That's when he knew he'd lost the vision in his left eye.

"Hell," he muttered.

With a forefinger Twilly gingerly probed the socket and was relieved to find the eyeball externally intact. Slowly he raised on his forearms, teetering in the sloppy mud. Overhead the stars and clouds spun madly around the treetops. Twilly waited patiently for the world to slow down. With his good eye he discerned bulky motionless shapes on either side of him—to his left, a bulldozer; to his right, a boat-sized station wagon.

Progress, he told himself.

Gradually the locomotive ringing subsided and Twilly could make out distinct noises—the wind in the pines, an incongruous jingling in the understory, almost like sleigh bells. . . .

And, from inside the car, a muffled struggle.

Twilly tried to stand, bracing himself on the fender. He noticed it was shimmying. Once on his feet, he felt dizzy and sick to his stomach. Meanwhile the jingling sounded closer, causing him to speculate it was all inside his head; something loose or broken.

But the station wagon *was* rocking—not much, but enough to keep Twilly's shaky equilibrium in flux. Miserably he sunk to his knees and listed against the car, his cheek mashed against the cool steel. He groped for purchase and found a door handle.

There he hung like a drunken rock climber until the latch clicked and the heavy door swung open. Twilly lost his grip and slid limply to the mud. He lay blinking at the heavens as his eardrums pealed with the jingle bells of the oncoming sleigh. Where's the snow? he wondered sleepily.

Moments later, Twilly saw the sleigh shoot over him, a hulking black shadow that momentarily blotted out the stars and the clouds. He smelled it, too, though it didn't smell like Christmas. It smelled like a big wet dog. From inside the car came a startled cry, and suddenly Twilly remembered where he was, and what was happening. He remembered everything.

"He thinks it's a game," Desie explained.

"Make him let go!"

"He won't hurt you."

"Get him off me, goddammit, so I can kill him."

The mutt was riding Mr. Gash as if he were a pony. The wet, filthy mutt! Its yellow fangs were planted on his neck—not hard enough to break the skin, but firmly enough to bring severe distress to Mr. Gash, who was not an animal lover. (He regarded the 911 tape of the testicle-chomping chow as one of the most harrowing in his extensive collection.)

"I've shot dogs," he hissed at Desie, "for a lot less than this."

"He thinks we're playing."

"You mean he's pulled this shit before? While you were screwing?"

"To him it's wrestling. He hates to be left out." The combined weight and aromas of the two animals, the Lab and Mr. Gash, made it difficult for Desie to speak up.

"Who taught him how to open a car door?" Mr. Gash said snidely.

"I dunno. That's a new one."

"Make him get off! He weighs a fucking ton."

Weakly, Desie said, "McGuinn, down!"

The dog held its position. They heard a tail flopping mirthfully against the upholstery.

"Jesus, he's drooling all over me!" Mr. Gash cried.

Desie saw a strand of slobber glistening from one of his earlobes. He swung the gun away from her neck and reached it behind his own head, so the barrel was jammed to the Labrador's jaw.

"Big mistake," said Desie.

"What?" The dumb mutt *had* to die—first, because he had interrupted Mr. Gash's strenuous efforts to achieve an erection; second, because he had fouled Mr. Gash's hair with spit.

"You have any idea," Desie said, "how hard that dog's head is?"

"What're you saying, Mrs. Stoat? This is a forty-five-caliber handgun."

"I'm saying his noggin is like a cinder block. The bullet could bounce off him and wind up in you or me. It's something to think about, that's all."

Mr. Gash did think about it. She had a point. The beast was glommed to his very spine, after all. Plus, it would be a blind shot, backhanded over the shoulder. Very risky.

"Shit," said Mr. Gash. The evening was not playing out as he had hoped. "How long does he usually hang on?"

"Till he gets bored. Or hungry." Desie felt suffocated and claustrophobic.

"He farts again, I'm definitely pulling the trigger."

"Tell that to *him*," she muttered at Mr. Gash, "not me."

Twilly Spree was on all fours in the slop, peering up into the backseat through the open door. In the greenish glow of the dome light he saw Desirata Stoat and her dog, with Mr. Gash sandwiched obscenely between them. None of them could see Twilly, who listened only briefly to the taut conversation before scooting like a water bug underneath the Roadmaster.

He thought: Crazy damn dog, he'll get her killed.

It wouldn't take much for Mr. Gash to blow a gasket and start shooting. The challenge was to get McGuinn off the killer, then somehow get the killer off Desie.

"Let go a me, you dumb bastard! Let go a me!" The rising fury of Mr. Gash.

Twilly licked his lips and tried to whistle. Nothing came out—he was trembling too much from the damp cold.

He heard Desie cry out: "What're you doing!"

Then Mr. Gash: "Making do."

The car began rocking again. Twilly vigorously rubbed the clamminess from his cheeks. He was striving for a specific two-note whistle; the whistle used to summon McGuinn for supper. Twilly puckered and blew. This time it worked.

The station wagon stopped shaking. There was a shout, a splash, an inquisitive bark. The dog had let go of the killer and was out of the car, hunting for the source of the dinner call. Twilly could track McGuinn's pacing by the tinkling of his collar. It was only a matter of moments before the ever-hungry Lab sniffed out Twilly's hiding place.

"Who made that noise!" Mr. Gash bellowed from the back-seat.

"What noise?" came Desie's voice. "That bird, you mean."

"It was no goddamned bird."

Twilly whistled again, this time with a whimsical lilt. He saw McGuinn's legs stiffen—all senses on full alert. The dog was zeroing in.

Not yet, Twilly thought, please. He heard more movement above him: Mr. Gash, scrambling from the station wagon.

"That's it," the killer was saying, "somebody's out there. Some asshole troublemaker."

Twilly sucked in his breath as McGuinn's twitching snout appeared below the rear bumper. The dog began to whine and scratch at the ground. No! Twilly thought. *Stay!*

Finally, the two pale feet Twilly was awaiting emerged from the car and descended into view. They disappeared into the mud as the killer stood up.

"Damn," Mr. Gash rasped. "That's cold."

From Twilly's vantage, the bony white ankles looked like aspen saplings. He clasped a hand around each one and jerked. The killer went down hard and unquietly. McGuinn retreated, moon-howling in confusion.

Twilly wriggled from under the car and hurled himself upon the thrashing Mr. Gash. The resulting splatter of muck glooped uncannily into Twilly's good eye, completing his decline to full sightlessness. Wild punches landed harmlessly upon the brawny arms and shoulders of Mr. Gash, who simply bucked Twilly aside, raised his gun and fired.

This time Twilly knew it for a fact: He was shot. The slug slammed into the right side of his chest and knocked him goony. He didn't fall so much as fold.

He heard the wind blowing. Desie sobbing. That weird sleigh-bell jingling in the trees. His own heart pounding.

Twilly believed he could even hear the blood squirting from the hole in his ribs.

And a strange new voice, possibly imaginary.

"I'll take it from here," it said, very deeply.

"What? Like hell you will." That was Mr. Gash, the killer.

"The boy comes with me."

"Ha! Pops, I should've shot your ass, back up the road. Now get the fuck outta here."

"Mister, run! Go get help! Please." That would be Desie.

"Shut up, Mrs. Stoat"—the killer again—"while I blow this sorry old fart's head off."

"I said, the boy's mine." The deep voice, astoundingly calm.

"You mental or what? I guess maybe so," Mr. Gash said. "Whatever. It's just one more dead troublemaker to me."

Twilly felt himself sliding away, as if he were on a raft spinning languidly downriver. If this was dying, it wasn't half-bad.

And if it was only a dream, he had no desire to awaken. Twenty-six years of unspent dreams is what they owed him.

On impulse he decided to summon McGuinn—a dog was always good company on a river.

"I said, the boy is mine."

Who's he talking about? Twilly wondered. What boy?

He also wondered why he could no longer hear himself whistling, why suddenly he couldn't hear anything at all.

24

W hat is it you want, Willie?"

The age-old question. Palmer Stoat tinkled the ice cubes in his glass and awaited a reply from the vice chairman of the House Appropriations Committee.

"You and your rude-ass manners," Willie Vasquez-Washington said. "Man, I'll tell you what I want. I want the Honorable Richard Artemus to not fuck with my spring snow skiing, Palmer. I want to be in Canada next week. I do *not* want to be in Tallahassee for some bullshit 'special session.' "

"Now, Willie, it's too late—"

"Don't 'now Willie' me. This isn't about the schools budget, amigo, it's about that dumb-ass bridge to that dumb-ass Cracker island, which I thought—no, which you *told* me!—was all ironed out a few weeks ago. And then. . . ." Willie Vasquez-Washington paused to sip his Long Island iced tea. "Then your Governor Dick goes and vetoes the item. His own baby! Why?"

Palmer Stoat responded with his standard you-don't-really-

want-to-know roll of the eyes. They were sitting at the bar in
Swain's, the last place on the planet where Stoat wanted to retell
the squalid dognapping saga. After all, it was here the lunatic
had sent the infamous phantom paw. The bartender was even
rumored to have named a new drink after it, to Stoat's mortifi-
cation.

"Fine. Don't tell me," said Willie Vasquez-Washington. "But
guess what? It ain't my problem, Palmer."

"Hey, you got your inner-city community center."

"Don't start with that."

"Excuse me. Community *Outreach* Center," said Stoat.
"Nine million bucks, wasn't it?"

"Back off!"

"Look, all I'm saying. . . ." The lobbyist dropped his voice,
for he did not wish to appear to be insulting an Afro-Haitian-
Hispanic-Asian-Native American, or any combination thereof
(assuming Willie Vasquez-Washington was telling the truth
about at least one of the many minorities he professed to be). In
any case, the upscale cigar-savoring clientele at Swain's was re-
lentlessly Anglo-Saxon, so the presence of a person of color (especially one as impeccably attired as Representative
Vasquez-Washington) raised almost as many eyebrows as had
the sight of the severed Labrador paw.

"Willie, all I'm saying," Palmer Stoat continued, "is that the
governor kept his end of the deal. He did right by you. Can't
you help him out of this one lousy jam? These were circumstances beyond his control."

"Sorry, man."

"We can't pull this off without you."

"I'm aware of that." Willie Vasquez-Washington, drumming
his fingernails on the oak. "Any other time, Palmer, but not
now. I've been planning this vacation for years."

Which was a complete crock, Stoat knew. The junket was

being paid for secretly by a big HMO as a show of gratitude to Willie Vasquez-Washington, whose timely intervention had aborted a potentially embarrassing investigation of certain questionable medical practices; to wit, the HMO encouraging its minimum-wage switchboard operators to make over-the-phone surgical decisions for critically ill patients. What a stroke of good fortune (Stoat reflected wryly) that Willie Vasquez-Washington played golf every Saturday with the State Insurance Commissioner.

"Willie, how's this? We fly you in for the Toad Island vote, then fly you straight back to Banff. We'll get a Lear."

Willie Vasquez-Washington eyed Stoat as if he were a worm on a Triscuit. "And you're supposed to be so damn sharp? Lemme spell it out for you, my brother: I cannot skip the special session and go skiing, like I want. Why? Because they would crucify my ass in the newspapers, on account of the newspapers have bought into the governor's bullshit. They think we're all headed back to the capital to vote more money for poor little schoolkids. Because, see, the papers don't know jack about your bridge scam. So I am one stuck-ass motherfucker, you follow?"

Now it was Willie Vasquez-Washington's turn to lower his voice. "I'm stuck, man. I gotta go to this session, which means no skiing, which means the wife and kids will be supremely hacked off, which means—sorry!—no new bridge for Honorable Dick and his friends."

Palmer Stoat calmly waved for another round. He handed a genuine Montecristo Especial No. 2 to Willie Vasquez-Washington, and lighted it for him. Stoat was mildly annoyed by this impasse, but not greatly worried. He was adept at smoothing over problems among self-important shitheads. Stoat hoped someday to be doing it full-time in Washington, D.C., where self-importance was the prevailing culture, but for now he was content to hone his skills in the swamp of teeming greed known as Florida. Access, influence, introductions—that's what all lobbyists peddled. But the best of them also were fast-thinking, resourceful and creative; crisis solvers. And Palmer Stoat regarded himself as one of the very best in the business. A virtuoso.

Shearwater! Jesus H. Christ, what a cluster fuck. It had cost him his wife and his dog and nearly his life, but he would not let it cost him his reputation as a fixer. No, this cursed deal *would* get done. The bridge would get funded. The cement trucks would roll and the high-rises would rise and the golf courses would get sodded. The governor would be happy, Robert Clapley would be happy, everybody would be happy— even Willie Vasquez-Washington, the maggot. And afterward they would all say it never would have come together except for the wizardly lobbying of Palmer Stoat.

Who now whispered through a tingling blue haze to the vice chairman of the House Appropriations Committee: "He wants to talk to you, Willie."

"I thought that was your job."

"Face-to-face."

"What the hell for?"

"Dick's a people person," Stoat said.

"He's a damn Toyota salesman."

"He wants to make this up to you, Willie. He wants to know what he can do to make things right."

"Before the session starts, I bet."

Stoat nodded conspiratorially. "They'll be some money floating around next week. How's your district fixed for schools? You need another school?"

"Man. You serious?" Willie Vasquez-Washington laughed harshly. "Suburbs get all the new schools."

"Not necessarily," said Palmer Stoat. "There's state pie, federal matching, lottery spill. Listen, you think about it."

"I am not believin' this shit."

Stoat took out a fountain pen and wrote something in neat block letters on a paper cocktail napkin. He slid it down the bar to Willie Vasquez-Washington, who chuckled and rolled the cigar from one corner of his mouth to the other.

Then he said: "OK, OK, I'll meet with him. Where?"

"I've got an idea. You ever been on a real big-game safari?"

"Not since I took the bone out of my nose, you asshole."

"No, Willie, this you'll dig. Trust me." Stoat winked and signaled for the check.

Willie Vasquez-Washington's gaze once more fell upon the cocktail napkin, which he discreetly palmed and deposited in an ashtray. On the drive back to Miami, he thought about the words Palmer Stoat had written down, and envisioned them five feet high, chiseled into a marble façade.

WILLIE VASQUEZ-WASHINGTON SENIOR HIGH SCHOOL.

Asa Lando urged Durgess to check out the horn; the horn was first-rate. Durgess could not disagree. However. . . .

"This rhino is how old?" he asked.

"I don't honestly know," said Asa Lando. "They said nineteen."

"Yeah? Then I'm still in diapers."

It was the most ancient rhinoceros Durgess had ever seen; even older and more feeble than the one procured for Palmer Stoat. This one was heavier by at least five hundred pounds, which was but a small consolation to Durgess. The animal had come to the Wilderness Veldt Plantation from a wildlife theme park outside Buenos Aires. The park had "retired" the rhino because it was now sleeping, on average, twenty-one hours a day. Tourists assumed it was made from plaster of paris.

"You said money was no object."

Durgess raised a hand. "You're right. I won't even ask."

"His name's El Jefe." Asa Lando pronounced it "Jeffy," with a hard *J*.

"Why'd you tell me that?" Durgess snapped. "I don't wanna know his name." The guide slept better by pretending that the animals at Wilderness Veldt actually were wild, making the hunts less of a charade. But named quarry usually meant tamed quarry, and even Durgess could not delude himself into believing there was a shred of sport to the chase. It was no more suspenseful, or dangerous, than stalking a pet hamster.

"El Jeffy means 'the boss,' " Asa Lando elaborated, "in Spanish. They also had a name for him in American but I forgot what."

"Knock it off. Just knock it off."

Durgess leaned glumly against the gate of the rhino's stall in Quarantine One. The giant creature was on its knees, in a bed of straw, wheezing in a deep and potentially unwakable slumber. Its hide was splotched floridly with some exotic seeping strain of eczema. Bottleflies buzzed around its parchment-like ears, and its crusted eyelids were scrunched into slits.

Asa Lando said: "What'd ya expect, Durge? He's been locked in a box for five damn days."

With a mop handle Durgess gingerly prodded the narcoleptic pachyderm. Its crinkled gray skin twitched, but no cognitive response was evident.

"Besides," said Asa Lando, "you said it didn't matter, long as the horns was OK. Any rhinoceros I could find, is what you said."

Durgess cracked his knuckles. "I know, Asa. It ain't your fault."

"On short notice, you can't hope for much. Not with endangereds such as rhinos and elephants. You pretty much gotta take what's out there, Durge."

"It's awright." Durgess could see that El Jefe once had been a strapping specimen, well fed and well cared for. Now it was just old, impossibly old, and physically wasted from the long sweltering flight.

"Can he run," Durgess asked, "even a little bit?"

Asa Lando shook his head solemnly.

"Well, can he *walk*?"

"Now and again," said Asa Lando. "He walked outta the travel crate."

"Hooray."

"Course, that was downhill."

"Well, hell," Durgess said impatiently. "He must move around enough to eat. Lookit the size of the bastard."

Asa Lando cleared his throat. "See, they, uh, brought all his food to him—branches and shrubs and such. He pretty much just stood in the same spot all day long, eatin' whatever they dumped in front of his face. Give him a big shady tree, they told me, and he won't go nowheres."

Durgess said, "I'm sure."

"Which is how I figure we'll set up the kill shot. Under one a them giant live oaks."

"Oaks we got," Durgess sighed.

He thought: Maybe we can get us two birds with one stone. Maybe Mr. Stoat's big-shot hunter would go for a jenna-wine African rhinoceros over a cheetah; even a sleepy rhino was an impressive sight. And El Jefe's front horn *was* primo—fifty grand is what Stoat said he could get for a decent one. Durgess idly wondered if the mysterious Mr. Yee might be enticed into a bidding war. . . .

"I gotta make a phone call," Durgess said to Asa Lando.

"One more thing. It might could help."

"What?"

"He stomped a man to death, Durge."

"No shit!"

"Six, seven years ago. Some superdumb tourist," Asa Lando said, "hopped on his back so the wife could take a picture. Like he was ridin' a bronco. Old El Jeffy went nuts is what them Argentinos told me. Threw the tourist fellow to the ground and mushed his head like a tangelo. Made all the papers in South America."

Durgess smiled crookedly. "So it ain't just any rhino we got here, Asa. It's a *killer* rhino. A world-famous killer rhino."

"Exactly right. That help?"

"You bet your ass," Durgess said. "Call me when he wakes up."

Mr. Gash couldn't believe that the bum with the crimson eye and the weird checkered skirt had showed up in the dead of night, in the middle of the woods. And packing a pistol!

"I said, the boy is mine."

Mr. Gash leered. "You're into *that,* huh, pops? A rump ranger."

"I'll take the woman, too." The bum motioned with the gun toward the station wagon containing Desirata Stoat.

"Pops, you can have the 'boy.' He's dying anyway. But the lady," said Mr. Gash, waving with his own gun, "she stays with me. Now get the fuck outta here. I'm counting to six."

The bum flashed his teeth. The braids of his beard were dripping after his jog through the rain; tiny perfect globes, rolling off the bleached buzzard beaks. Mr. Gash was unnerved by the sight, as he was by the man's eerie calm. Being cold and unclothed had put Mr. Gash at a psychological disadvantage in the standoff. By rights he should have felt cocksure, a single-action Smith being no match for his trusty semiautomatic. Yet all it would take would be one lucky shot in the dark—and even a bum could get lucky.

Mr. Gash elected to proceed carefully, lest his pecker be blown off.

He said to the bum: "You can have the dog, too."

"I was hungry enough, Mr. Gash, I just might."

"What kinda sick kink you into, pops?" Mr. Gash levered himself to one knee. His foot made a sucking sound when he tugged it out of the mud. He was somewhat flattered that the bum knew his name.

"The governor sent me, Mr. Gash. I'll take over from here."

"Hooo! The governor!"

"Yessir. To fetch that young man."

"Well, Mr. Robert Clapley sent *me,*" said Mr. Gash, "to do the exact same thing. And my guess is Mr. Clapley pays a whole lot handsomer than the governor. So we got a conflict, don't we?"

A jingling came from the pines, and McGuinn's shadow appeared at the edge of the clearing. The second gunshot had launched the dog on another fruitless search for falling ducks, and he had returned only to encounter yet another human with a gun; an uncommonly large human who smelled of fried opossum and wood smoke. McGuinn's mouth began to water. Unspooling his tongue, he trotted forward to greet the stranger in the customary Labrador manner.

Mr. Gash saw what was coming and steadied his arm, preparing to fire. Here was the opportunity he'd been awaiting: The bum wouldn't be able to ignore the dog. *Nobody* could ignore that loony pain-in-the-ass mutt. And the moment the bum got distracted, Mr. Gash would shoot him in the heart.

From the car, Desie called out: "McGuinn! Come, boy!"

Naturally the dog paid no attention. On his way to meet the stranger, he stepped blithely over Twilly Spree, sprawled bleeding on the ground.

"Bad boy! Come!" Desie shouted, to no avail.

McGuinn sensed that the extra-large human with the gun presented no menace, but rather the promise of an opossum snack. It was imperative to make friends. . . .

As the dog's nose disappeared beneath the hem of the bum's checkered kilt, Mr. Gash's forefinger tightened on the trigger. He was waiting for the bum to react—to recoil in surprise, yell in protest, shove the dog away. Something. Anything.

But the bum didn't even flinch; wouldn't take his good eye (or the .357) off Mr. Gash. He merely stood there smiling, a smile so luminous as to be visible on a moonless night.

Smiling, while a filthy 128-pound hairball sniffed at his privates! Mr. Gash was disgusted.

"You're one sick bastard," he spat at the bum.

A voice from behind Mr. Gash: "Look who's talking."

He turned to see Desie at the car door, modeling his snakeskin corset. Assuming that the perverted bum would be transfixed by Mrs. Stoat, Mr. Gash decided to seize his chance.

"You're all sick!" he snarled.

In the moment between uttering those words and pulling the trigger, something unexpected happened to Mr. Gash. The bum shot him twice. The first slug clipped off his right kneecap, toppling him sideways. The second slug, striking him on the way down, went through one cheek and out the other.

Flopping about, Mr. Gash felt a large boot descend firmly on his throat, and the semiautomatic being pried from his fingers. He began to choke violently on a gob of mud, and he was slipping into blackness when a huge fist snatched him by the hair and jerked him upright to a sitting position. There he coughed volcanically until he was able to expel the gob.

But it wasn't mud. It was an important segment of Mr. Gash's tongue, raggedly severed by the bum's second bullet. Only when he endeavored to speak did Mr. Gash comprehend the debilitating nature of his wound.

"Zhhooo zhhaa off mah fugghy ung!"

The bum tweaked Mr. Gash's chin. "Not bad, sport. You could've been a rap star."

"Zhoooo zhhuuhh of a bizhhh!"

The bum hoisted Mr. Gash by the armpits and heaved him headfirst into the leering grille of the Buick. Mr. Gash crumpled into a grimy naked heap on the ground, and he would have preferred to remain there indefinitely until his multitude of fiery pains abated. The bum, however, had other plans.

Twilly was no longer floating down a river. He was lying flat on a tailgate. The good news was, his vision had returned, more or less. Two silhouettes hovered over him: Mrs. Desirata Stoat and a tall hoary stranger with silvery twines growing from each side of his face. The stranger was using a finger to probe the gurgling hole in Twilly's thorax.

"Hold still, son," the man advised.

"Who are you?"

"You call me captain, but for now shut up."

Desie said, "Honey, you lost some blood."

Twilly nodded dully. It wouldn't have surprised him to learn he'd lost every drop. He could barely hoist his eyelids. "You OK?" he asked Desie. "He hurt you?"

"Nothing that three or four months in a scalding bath won't cure. But no, he didn't get what he was after," she said, "thanks to you and McGuinn and this gentleman."

Twilly swallowed a deep breath. "Somebody's been shooting a gun. I smell it."

"Son, I told you to hush," the captain said. Then to Desie: "You got something clean I can use on him?"

She retrieved her bra from inside the car. With a pocketknife, the captain cut a swatch of padding from one of the cups. He folded the foam into a makeshift plug, which he gently worked into Twilly's wound.

"Somewhere in my raincoat," the captain said to Desie, "there's a phone. Can you get it for me?"

Twilly shut his eyes. Moments later Desie took his hands, her touch supernaturally hot. He was losing it; slipping under. He heard the beeps of a keypad, followed by half a conversation. The captain's voice trailed Twilly into a dream, his third ever. He believed it might be his last.

"Jim, you awake?"

In the dream Twilly was on a beach that looked very much like Toad Island. It was straight-up noon.

"Listen, how many helicopters they got waiting around on the governor these days? . . . Because I need to borrow one. The fastest they got."

In the dream Twilly was chasing after a black dog, and the dog was chasing after a man. They all were running hard.

"It's the kid, Jim. . . . Gunshot to the chest. Be nice if they could round up a doctor for the ride."

In Twilly's dream he somehow caught up with the dog, passing it with a terrific kick of speed. Rapidly he gained ground on the man who was running away. Drawing closer, Twilly saw that the man was wearing baggy Jockey shorts and a sleeveless undershirt. He looked scrawny and old, too old to be moving so fast.

"We're still on the island. He can set the chopper down on the beach."

Twilly tackled the man from behind. He rolled him over in the sand and was about to uncork a punch when he saw it was his father. In the dream, Little Phil Spree blinked up at his son and chirped, "The coast is clear! The coast is clear!"

"I've got the man who shot the boy. . . . I haven't decided yet, Jim, but don't you worry your pretty head."

In the dream the dog began to bark madly and spin; a frantic feral spell. Twilly Spree pulled away from his father and sprung to his feet. All along the shore, as far as he could see in both directions, were shiny mustard-yellow bulldozers. Poised on every dune! Blades glinting in the sun, the dozers were aligned in ready position at identical angles, like a division of panzers. "The coast is clear!" crooned Twilly's father.

"The woman's doing all right. I expect she'll want to ride along in the whirlybird. . . . She's nodding yes. Also, there's a station wagon here that oughta be disposed of pretty quick."

Twilly ran headlong for the water. The black dog followed him in, baying insanely. The Gulf was chilly and mirror-calm. When the dog finally quit barking, Twilly could hear his father chanting mindlessly on the beach—and also the fearsome rumble of the bulldozers, chewing up the island. In the dream Twilly waited for the dog to catch up, and together they struck out for the horizon. The sky over the water darkened with birds that were spooked from the island by the din of the earth-moving machines. As he swam farther and farther out to sea, Twilly grew afraid that the gulls and terns and skimmers would start tumbling down like before, blood-spattered and broken. If that happened, he wouldn't be able to bear it—he was too weak and too lost. If the birds came down again, it would be over, Twilly knew. In such a morbid rain, he would drown. He would not survive his own dream.

"Good news. I'm coming in on that chopper, too. . . . I got a little errand to run and you're gonna help me, Lieutenant. . . . Because you wouldn't want to miss it for the world, that's why."

25

Oh, Mr. Gash put up a fight.

Not a great fight, but then again, he was minus a kneecap and most of his tongue. So pain was a factor. Plus he was stark naked, which seriously compromised his freewheeling style of personal combat. Nonetheless, he managed to get off a couple of right hooks that would have knocked most men to their knees.

The punches had no discernible effect upon the bum in the checkered skirt, who at the time was lugging Mr. Gash down the slope of a hill. The hill was not a natural formation, for Toad Island was as flat as a skillet. The hill had been created by earthmoving machines. It was a steep mound of scraped-up soil, scrub and tree stumps; the debris of a road-grading incursion through the pine woods. The bum had slung Mr. Gash over one shoulder, like a sack of lime, and charged down the soft-packed bank. He seemed to be in a hurry. Mr. Gash slugged at him frenetically, landing at least two monster blows—one to the ribs, one to the kidneys. Nothing; not even a grunt of acknowledgment. The bum kept to his mission. Mr. Gash flailed and spluttered incoherently. He knew something bad was coming. He just didn't know what.

At the bottom of the hill, the bum dumped him and turned to go back up.

Now what? thought Mr. Gash. He made one last ferocious swipe at the man but came away with only the pinned-together checkered skirt, which turned out to be a flag of the sort waved at the finish line of automobile races. Mr. Gash used it to sop the blood from the holes in his cheeks. The stump of his tongue stung like a mother. He lay in the mulch and pondered his options, which were limited. Because his mangled right leg was useless, escape by running, walking or crawling was impossible. He would have to wriggle, and wriggle swiftly, assuming the bum was not finished with him.

With a mournful effort, Mr. Gash rolled himself over. He reached out both arms, dug his fingers into the sodden grit and pulled himself forward until his chin touched his knuckles. Total linear progress: Two feet, max.

Mr. Gash thought: This sucks. He felt the tickle of an insect on his buttocks and flogged at it awkwardly. From the other side of the man-made hill came the *chug-chugging* of an engine, too rackety to be a car. Steadily it got louder. Mr. Gash craned his neck, squinting into the gloom. Of course he knew what he was hearing. He'd driven one of the damn things himself, the night he took care of that troublemaker Brinkman. Now the rig loomed directly above him, on the crest of the slope. Mr. Gash recognized the blocky square-edged outline. He could smell the acrid exhaust. A tall figure emerged from the cab, then reached back inside—undoubtedly to release the brake.

"Fuugghh me," Mr. Gash groaned.

The bulldozer jolted clangorously downhill. Rabidly, Mr. Gash tried to drag himself out of its path, and he almost made it. Only half of him got pinned under the track; the lower half.

So his lungs still worked, which was encouraging. Another positive sign was the surprising lack of pain below his waist. Mr. Gash concluded that the bulldozer had not crushed his torso so much as embedded it in the spongy turf. His immediate concern were the diesel fumes being belched into his face. His eyes burned and his stomach roiled—obviously the dozer's exhaust pipes had been damaged in the descent. Eventually the machine would run out of fuel and its engine would cut off, but Mr. Gash wondered if he could stay conscious until then, inhaling from a noxious cloud. He felt simultaneously sleepy and convulsive.

A pair of dirt-caked hiking boots appeared before him. Then the bulldozer hiccuped once and went silent. As the smoke dissipated, Mr. Gash raised up on his forearms and drank in the fresh breeze. Crouched beside him was the bum, his glass eye gleaming like a polished ruby in the starlight.

"You're gonna die out here," he said to Mr. Gash.

"Ungh-ungh."

"Yeah, you are, Iggy. It's all over."

'Iggy'? Now the fucker's making fun of my hair! Mr. Gash boiled.

"You're dying even as we speak," the bum said. "Trust me. I know a thing or two about roadkill. You qualify."

"Ungh-ungh!"

"In case you haven't noticed, your ass is lying under a Cat D6. That's twenty tons of serious steel," said the bum. "I don't know about making peace with God, but it might be a good time to tell the young lady you're sorry for trying to hurt her. Want me to go get her?"

Mr. Gash said, "Fuugghh oooh, popff."

The bum stood up. "That's a mighty poor attitude," he said, "for a man who's bleeding out of both ears. Now, if you'll excuse me, Iggy, I've gotta go track down some fool dog."

"FUUGGHH OOOOH!"

Mr. Gash's head sagged. Soon he heard the crunch of the bum's heavy footsteps fading into the woods.

What an idiot, thought Mr. Gash. He should've shot me! I'll be out of here by dawn!

Hastily he began trying to dig himself out from beneath the track of the bulldozer. The task was arduous. Being pinned on his tummy, Mr. Gash was forced to reach behind himself and work his arms like turtle flippers. After twenty grueling minutes Mr. Gash quit in exhaustion. He fell asleep with a centipede skittling across his shoulder blade. He was too weary to slap it away.

Hours later a helicopter awakened him. It was daylight; a high rose-tinged sky. Mr. Gash couldn't see the chopꞁer but he could hear the eggbeater percussion of the rotors as it landed nearby. He lifted his head and gave an unholy wail; pain had found him. Horrible, nerve-shearing, bone-snapping pain. He observed, despairingly, that all his frantic digging had accomplished little. A pitiable few handfuls of dirt had been scalloped around each leg, upon which the Caterpillar D6 remained steadfastly parked. Mr. Gash could not drag himself a single millimeter out from under it. After a third attempt, he gave up.

Instead of escape, he now focused on survival. The helicopter, of course. It would be lifting off soon—Mr. Gash could tell by the accelerating whine of the engines. Anxiously he scanned the ground within his reach, searching for something, anything, to draw the pilot's attention. His eyes fixed upon a silky-looking wad in the muck. It was the crazy bum's skirt—the checkered racing flag, now lavishly spotted with Mr. Gash's dried blood. He snatched it up and shook off the loose dirt.

With a head-splitting roar, a black-and-gray jet helicopter appeared over the spires of the pines. With both hands Mr. Gash raised the checkered flag. He began a wildly exaggerated wave, flopping his upper body back and forth like a rubber windshield wiper. It was a completely new experience for Mr. Gash: desperation. He swung the flag with the fervor of a drunken soccer hooligan, for he feared the pilot couldn't see him, grime-smeared and half-interred beneath a bulldozer.

He was right. The chopper circled the clearing once but didn't hover. It banked sharply to the north and hummed off.

The flag dropped from Mr. Gash's hands. He was in the purest mortal agony. From the waist down: dead. From the waist up: every cell a burning cinder. His head thundered. His arms were cement. His throat was broken glass on the scabby nub of his tongue. Sickening trickles ran down the fuzz of both jawlines, all the way to Mr. Gash's chin—warm blood from his ears.

That fucking troublemaker of a bum had been right. It was over.

Or maybe not.

Mr. Gash noticed a small object on the ground, something he couldn't have spotted in the dark. It lay a few precious feet out of reach, partially hidden by a palmetto frond. It was black and rectangular and plastic-looking, like the remote control of a VCR, or the clip to a Glock.

Or a cellular telephone.

Mr. Gash used a broken branch to retrieve it. Woozily, he

mashed at the POWER button with his forefinger. The phone emitted a perky bleep and lit up with a peachy glow. Mr. Gash stared at the numbers on the keypad. A desolate smirk came to his whitening lips.

Palmer Stoat said, "Good news, Bob."

"Better be."

They met at noon in Pube's; this time in a champagne booth reserved for private friction dancing.

Stoat said, "Remember the other night we were here? Well, I got a date afterward with one of the Pamela Anderson Lees."

"You're a pig," Robert Clapley remarked mirthlessly.

"Back to the bachelor life for me. I'm moving on!"

"That's your news?"

"No," said Palmer Stoat. "The news is big."

Clapley looked as if he hadn't slept in a year. Sullenly he fingered the gold link chain on his neck. A dancer approached the table and introduced herself as Cindi with an *i*. Clapley gave her a ten and sent her away.

Stoat said, "I take it you haven't found your Barbies."

"They called me."

"Hey! It's a start."

"From the residence of Mr. Avalon Brown." Robert Clapley took a slug of bourbon. "Mr. Brown is recruiting investors for his newest feature-film project. Katya and Tish thought it would be nice of me to help out. They, of course, would get starring roles in the movie."

"Which is titled . . ."

"*Double Your Pleasure.*"

"Ah. An art film." Palmer Stoat smiled commiseratingly. "And how much have you agreed to invest?"

"For a hundred thousand dollars, Mr. Avalon Brown promises to make me a full partner," Clapley said. "For a tenth of that, I could have him killed."

Inwardly, Stoat shuddered. A messy homicide scandal could wreck everything: the Shearwater deal, Dick Artemus's reelection chances and (last but not least) Stoat's own career.

He lay a consoling hand on Clapley's shoulder. "Bob, for the last time, forget about those two tramps. You've got to move on, the way I'm moving on."

"I can't."

"Sure you can. Join me on the Palmer pussy patrol."

Clapley said, "Know what I've got in my pants?"

"Dolls?"

"Righto."

"How many?" Stoat asked dispiritedly.

"Two in each pocket."

"These would be the Vibrator Barbies?"

"Screw you, Palmer. I miss the twins. I want them back," Robert Clapley said, waving off another dancer. "They say I don't help with the movie, they're cutting off all their hair and moving to Kingston."

"Sunny Jamaica."

"World headquarters of Avalon Brown Productions."

"Let 'em go," Stoat said. "I'm begging you."

"Are you deaf? It's *not* going to happen." Clapley gave a brittle laugh. "That's why men like Mr. Gash exist—and prosper. Because of situations like this."

Stoat said, "Speaking of which, here's some of that good news I promised. That pesky problem we've been having up at Toad Island is all taken care of. The kid who grabbed my dog is in the hospital with a forty-five-caliber hole in his chest."

"Fantastic! That means Mr. Gash is available for a new job."

"I don't know about Mr. Gash. My information comes directly from the governor," Stoat said, "and he wasn't too clear on the details. The important thing is, that nutty kid is finally out of the picture. And, oh yeah, Desie and Boodle are OK, too. Not that I give a shit."

Robert Clapley found himself gazing past Stoat, at a dancer performing in a nearby booth. She had long golden hair, high conical breasts and pouty lacquered lips.

"Close." Clapley was talking strictly to himself. "If only she was taller."

"Jesus Hubbard Christ. You want to hear the rest, or you want to go diddle with your dollies?" Palmer Stoat unsheathed a Cohiba and fired it up with a flourish. He took his sweet time.

Without looking away from the woman, Clapley said, "Tell me about the bridge money. Tell me it's all set."

"We're almost there, Bob. It's ninety-nine percent a done deal."

"Who's the one percent?"

"Willie Vasquez-Washington."

"Again!"

"Don't worry. He's almost there."

Robert Clapley sneered. "I've heard that one before. How tall you think that girl is? The blonde."

"Gee, Bob, it's awful hard to tell while she's got her feet hooked behind her ears."

"I assume you've got another plan."

"Oh, a good one."

"Do tell."

"We're taking Rainbow Willie on a hunting trip. You, me, and Governor Dick. At that private game reserve I told you about up in Marion County," Stoat said. "We're gonna hunt, drink, smoke and tell stories. And we're gonna make friends with Willie, whatever it takes."

Clapley scowled. "Whoa. That little prick is *not* getting my trophy cat."

"That's the other thing I came to tell you. Durgess, my guide, he says they sent the ranch a bum cheetah. A stone gimp."

"That's good news?"

"No, Bob, the good news is, he's got a rhinoceros instead. A genuine killer rhino." Stoat paused suspensefully. "Stomped a man to death a few years back."

Robert Clapley's head snapped around. Tremulously he sat forward. "And the horn?"

"Huge," Stoat whispered. "Major stud dust."

"God. That's fantastic."

Clapley's hands dove under the table, into his pockets. Stoat pretended not to notice.

"When's the hunt?" Clapley was breathless.

"This weekend. Durgess said the sooner the better."

"Yes! They'll come back to me now, for sure. Katya and Tish, I know they will." Clapley was radiant. "They'll come running home for the good stuff—especially when they find out I'm going to shoot the big bastard myself. A killer rhino. Can you imagine? They'll dump that ganja turd in a heartbeat."

"In which case, you wouldn't have to kill him, right?" Stoat cringed whenever he thought of Porcupine Head amok.

Clapley shrugged. "Frankly, I'd rather spend my money on something else. Mr. Gash isn't cheap." Clapley snatched a cigar out of Stoat's pocket. "And neither are you, Palmer. How much is all this extra fun going to cost me? Remember, you owed me the cheetah and then some. So . . . how much?"

"Not a dime, Bob. The hunt is on me."

"That's mighty kind."

"But the horn you've got to buy separately," Stoat said, "at the price we discussed. Rules of the house."

"Glad to do it," said Clapley. "Oh, by the way, these Cohibas of yours are counterfeit."

"What! No way."

"You can tell by the labels, Palmer. See these tiny black dots? They're supposed to be raised up, so you can feel 'em with your fingertips. That's how they come from the factory in La Habana. But these you got"—Clapley, wagging one in front of Stoat's nose—"see, the dots are smooth to the touch. That means they're el fake-o."

"No way," Stoat huffed. "Three hundred dollars a box at the Marina Hemingway. No way they're knockoffs." He removed the cigar from his lips and set it, unaffectionately, on the table's edge. He hunched close to examine the label.

Robert Clapley stood to leave. He patted Stoat on the back and said, "Don't worry, buddy. I'll get us some real McCoys, for the big rhinoceros hunt."

At that moment, a Florida Highway Patrol car entered the black wrought-iron gate of the governor's mansion in Tallahassee. At the door, a plainclothes FDLE agent waved Lt. Jim Tile inside, but not before giving his two companions a hard skeptical look. One was a black dog. The other was a man who was not properly attired for lunch with the chief executive.

Lisa June Peterson was waiting for them.

"Nice to see you again," Skink said, kissing her cheek. "You look ever-lovely."

Lisa June's cheeks flushed. Jim Tile shot a laser glare at his friend, who beamed innocently.

"I got him to shower," the trooper said, "but that's all."

"He looks fine," said Lisa June Peterson.

Former Governor Clinton Tyree wore hiking boots, his

blaze orange rain jacket with matching trousers, a new shower cap (with a daisy pattern) and a vest made from Chihuahua pelts.

"For special occasions," he explained.

"Dear Lord," Jim Tile said.

"It's truly one of a kind."

Lisa June said nothing; surely there was a story behind the vest, and just as surely she didn't want to hear it. She knelt to scratch McGuinn's chin. "Aw, what a handsome boy."

"An OK dog," Skink conceded, "but definitely not the brightest bulb in the chandelier."

Lisa June took the former governor's arm. "Come on. He's waiting for you."

"Oh, I'm tingling with excitement."

"Don't start," Jim Tile said. "You promised."

Skink told Lisa June: "Hon, don't mind Jim. He's just pissed because I lost his cell phone."

She led them to the dining room. Lunch was hearts-of-palm salad, conch chowder, medallions of venison and Key lime pie.

"An all-Florida menu," Lisa June announced with a whimsical curtsy, "in yore onna, suh!"

Skink parked himself at the head of the long table. The trooper said, without irony, "That's the governor's place, Governor."

"Yes, Jim, I remember."

"Don't do this."

"Do what?"

Lisa June said, "It's fine, Lieutenant. Governor Artemus has been fully briefed."

"With all due respect, I seriously doubt that."

Through a side door burst Dick Artemus; dapper, energized and primed to charm. His face was fresh-scrubbed and ruddy, his hair lustrous and ardently brushed, his green eyes clear and twinkling. When Clinton Tyree stood up, the governor bear-hugged him as if he were a long-lost twin.

"The one and only! I can't believe you're here!" Dick Artemus looked positively misty.

Dropping to one knee, he fondly grabbed McGuinn by the ruff and made *coo-cheee-coo* sounds. "Hey, boy, I'm glad to see you still got both ears. That bad man didn't hurt you after all!"

Skink glanced skeptically at Jim Tile.

"This is quite an honor," Dick Artemus said, rising.

"Why?" Skink asked.

"Because you're a legend, Governor."

"I'm a goddamned footnote in a history book. That's all."

"How about a glass of orange juice?" Lisa June Peterson suggested.

"Thanks. Heavy on the pulp," Skink said.

Dick Artemus exclaimed: "Me, too! The best OJ is the kind you gotta chew. What're those little beauties tied to the ends of your beard—may I ask?"

"Buzzard beaks."

"Ah! I was gonna guess eagles." Dick Artemus signaled to one of the stewards. "Sean, an orange juice for the governor and how about a screwdriver for me. And you folks?"

In unison, Jim Tile and Lisa June Peterson declined a beverage.

"So, tell me," Dick Artemus burbled to Skink, "how's the old place look? Seven hundred North Adams Street."

"About the same."

"Bring back memories?"

"More like hives."

The governor was undaunted. "Was the gym built when you were here? Would you like a tour?"

Skink looked at Lisa June. "Is he for real?" He threw back his head and cackled. "A tour!"

Lunch was more small talk; Dick Artemus was the world champion of small talkers. Lt. Jim Tile was strung drum-tight, and he finished his meal as rapidly as decent manners allowed. He had argued vigorously against such a meeting, as there was no telling how Clinton Tyree would react upon returning to the mansion after so many years. The trooper also held no expectation that the ex-governor would take a liking to the present governor, or for that matter show him even a trace of respect. Nothing good could come of the visit, Jim Tile had warned Lisa June Peterson, who had promised to warn the governor.

But Dick Artemus wasn't worried, for he believed he was the most irresistible sonofabitch in the whole world. He believed he could make *anyone* like him. And he had been flattered to learn that the legendary Clinton Tyree wanted to meet him.

"Tell me about your eye," he chirped.

"If you tell me about your hair."

Lisa June, helpfully: "Governor Tyree lost the eye many years ago, during a violent robbery."

"Actually, it was more of an old-fashioned assault," Skink said, inhaling a frothy sliver of pie. "I go through glass eyeballs like underwear. A friend of mine found this one in Belgrade." He tapped the crimson iris with a tine of his silver dessert fork. "Said she got it off a Gypsy king, and I choose to believe her. She had quite a circus background."

The governor nodded as if this were conversation he heard every day. His attention was broken by something poking him between his legs—the Labrador, lobbying for a handout. Dick Artemus genially slipped the dog a chunk of corn bread.

"Let's talk turkey," he said. "First, I want to thank you, Governor, for finding this troubled young man."

"Unfortunately, someone else found him first."

"Yes. Lieutenant Tile notified me as soon as he heard. He also told me how you risked your life to get the kid out alive."

"A promise is a promise." Skink put down the fork with a sharp clink. "I kept mine."

"Yes. You sure did." The governor shifted uneasily, then pretended it was because of the dog nosing him beneath the table. Lisa June Peterson knew better. So did Jim Tile.

Skink said, "You said you're going to get the boy some counseling."

"That's right."

"Where?"

"Uh . . . well, wherever he wants," Dick Artemus fumbled. "How's he doing, by the way? How bad was he hit?"

"He'll make it. He's tough," Skink said. "Why're all those cops outside his hospital room?"

"For his own protection," the governor replied matter-of-factly. "Somebody tried to kill him, remember?"

"So he's not under arrest?"

"Not to my knowledge. Mr. Stoat isn't interested in prosecuting. He says the publicity of a trial would be unwelcome, and I couldn't agree more."

"All right." Skink, planting his elbows on the table. "Now, what about my brother?"

"Yes?" The governor snuck an anxious glance at Lisa June Peterson.

"Doyle," she said.

"Right. Doyle Tyree!" Dick Artemus, awash with relief. "The lighthouse keeper. Certainly he can stay there as long as he wants. Hillsborough Inlet, right?"

"Peregrine Bay." Again Skink turned to Lisa June Peterson. "Would you and Jim mind if I spoke to the governor in private?"

Lisa June tried to object and Jim Tile weighed in with a grave sigh, but Dick Artemus brushed them off. "Of course they don't mind. Lisa June, why don't you take this puppy out back and introduce him to some of our magnificent old Leon County pine trees." Dick Artemus had a speech to give in thirty minutes, and he didn't wish to be seen with dog snot on his inseam.

Once they were alone, the former governor said to the present governor: "What about that island?"

"It'll be real nice when they're done."

"It's real nice now," Skink said. "Ever been there?"

Dick Artemus said he hadn't. "Look, you remember how this stuff works." He drained his glass down to the ice cubes, chasing the last of the vodka. "The guy wrote some major checks to my campaign. In return, he expects a little consideration. Slack, if you want to call it that. And I've gotta say, he's done most everything by the book with this Shearwater thing. The zoning, the permits, the wildlife surveys—it all looks kosher. That's what my people say."

"You oughta at least see the place before you let 'em wreck it."

"Governor, I appreciate how you feel."

"You don't appreciate shit."

"What're you doing? Hey, let go!"

The bulldozer dream kept rerunning itself, the snarling chorus of machines chasing Twilly Spree farther and farther from shore. The way it finally ended was: The gulls began falling from the sky, just as Twilly had dreaded. The birds were stiff before they hit the water and they hurtled down like rocks, splashing around his head. He dove to escape, but whenever he surfaced for a breath he got struck; a sickening *thwock* against his skull. Twilly soon lost the strength to swim, and he found himself sinking into an icy whorl of cobalt and foam. It felt like talons pulling him down, death clawing at his bare legs. Then something powerful took hold of him and tugged him upward, out of the swirling cold and free of the grasping claws.

The black dog! It was like a damn Disney flick, a plucky hound swimming to the rescue, dragging him to the top for air. . . .

Except it wasn't a dog bringing him up. It was Desie, one arm behind his head, holding him upright while she adjusted the pillows. The first thing Twilly saw when he opened his eyes was the pale cleft at the base of her neck. He leaned forward to kiss it, a deed that (judging by the pain) split open his chest.

Desie was smiling. "Somebody's feeling better."

"Lots," Twilly gasped.

"Don't try to talk," she said, "or smooch."

She pecked him on the forehead; not a good sign. They always pecked him on the forehead right before they said good-bye.

"I'm sorry about everything," he told her.

"Why? I was there because I wanted to be."

"You leaving?"

She nodded. "Hot-lanta. Spend some catch-up time with the folks."

"I love you," Twilly said blearily, though it was absolutely true. It was also true he would fall in love with the next woman who slept with him, as always.

Desie Stoat said, "I know you do."

"You look incredible."

"It's the Demerol, darling. I look like hell. Get some rest now."

"What about that man. . . ."

"Oh!" Desie tweaked his ankle through the blanket. "You'll never guess who he is!"

When she told him, Twilly acted as if he'd been mainlined

with pure adrenaline. His head rocked off the bed and he blurted: "I know that name! From my mother."

"Clinton Tyree?"

"The whole story! She thought he was a hero. My father said he was a nut."

Desie said, "Well, he hit on me in the helicopter."

"See? That proves he's sane." Twilly flashed a weak smile before sinking back on the pillows.

"He also expressed an extremely low opinion of my husband. He said a school-yard flasher would be a step up."

Twilly chuckled. A nurse bustled in to fiddle with the drip on his IV bag. She told him to get some sleep, and on her way out favored Desie with a scalding glare.

"I spoke to Palmer this morning. Just to let him know I'm OK," Desie said. "He sounded happy as a clam. He's going hunting this weekend with Governor Dick and—guess who else—Robert Clapley. I suppose they're celebrating Shearwater."

Twilly grunted curiously. "Hunting for what? Where?"

"Honey, even if I knew, I'd never tell." Desie wore a sad smile. She traced a finger lightly down his cheek. "All that crazy talk about killing somebody—you keep it up, hotshot, you're headed for an early grave. Call me selfish but I don't want to be around when it happens."

Twilly Spree spoke out of a fog. "Have faith," he said.

Desie laughed ruefully. "Faith I've got. It's good sense I'm dangerously short of."

When she stood up to go, Twilly saw she was wearing a new sundress: sea green with spaghetti straps. It put a knot in his heart.

"I need a favor. It's McGuinn," Desie said. "Could you keep him until I get squared away? My mom's deathly allergic to dogs."

"What about Palmer?"

"Nossir. I might not get much out of this divorce, Twilly, but my husband is *not* keeping McGuinn. Please, can you take care of him?"

"Sure." Twilly liked the dog and he liked the idea of seeing Desie again, when she came to collect him. "Where is he now?"

"With Lieutenant Tile and you-know-who. The motel where I'm staying won't take pets." Desie picked up her purse. "I've got a flight to catch. Promise me one more thing."

"Shoot."

She put one knee on the edge of the bed and leaned forward to kiss him; a proper kiss this time. Then she whispered, "Don't make love to anyone else in front of the dog. He'll be so confused."

"Promise." Playfully, Twilly tried to grab her straps, but she slipped away.

"Be good. There're four humongous cops outside your door with nobody to pound on."

Twilly tried a feeble salute. He could barely lift his arm.

"Good-bye, hon," Desie said.

"Wait. That other guy, Gash. . . ."

Her eyes hardened. "Freak accident," she said.

"It happens." Suddenly Twilly was very sleepy. "Love you, Desie."

"So long, tiger."

CALLER: Hep meh! Peezh!

DISPATCHER: Do you have an emergency?

CALLER: Yeah, I gah a emoozhezhee! I gah a fugghy boo-gozer oh meh azzhhh!

DISPATCHER: 'Boo-gozer'? Sir, I'm sorry, but you'll have to speak more clearly. This is Levy County Fire Rescue, do you have an emergency to report?

CALLER: Yeah! Hep! Mah baggh is boge! Ah bing zzhaa eng mah fay! I ngee hep!

DISPATCHER: Sir, do you speak English?

CALLER: Eh izzh Engizh! Mah ung gaw zzha off! Whif ah gung!

DISPATCHER: Hang on, Mr. Boogozer, I'm transferring you to someone who can take the information. . . .

CALLER: Ngooohh! Hep! Peezh!

DISPATCHER TWO: Diga. ¿Dónde estás?

CALLER: Aaaaaagghh!!!

DISPATCHER TWO: ¿Tienes un emergencia?

CALLER: Oh fugghh. I gaw die.

DISPATCHER TWO: Señor, por favor, no entiendo nada que estás diciendo.

CALLER: Hep! . . . Hep!

26

As a car salesman Dick Artemus encountered plenty of pissed-off folks—furious, frothing, beet-faced customers who believed they'd been gypped, deceived, baited, switched or otherwise butt-fucked. They were brought to Dick Artemus because of his silky demeanor, his indefatigable geniality, his astounding knack for making the most distraught saps feel good about themselves—indeed, about the whole human race! Regardless of how egregiously they'd been screwed over, no customers walked out of Dick Artemus's office angry; they emerged placid, if not radiantly serene. It was a gift, the other car salesmen would marvel. A guy like Dick came along maybe once every fifty years.

As governor of Florida, this preternatural talent for bullshitting had served Dick Artemus exquisitely. Even his most virulent political enemies conceded he was impossible not to like, one-on-one. So how could it be, Dick Artemus wondered abjectly, that Clinton Tyree alone was immune to his personal magnetism? The man did *not* like him; detested him, in fact. Dick Artemus could draw no other conclusion, given that the ex-governor now held him by the throat, pinned to the wood-paneled wall of the gubernatorial dining room. It had happened so fast—dragged like a rag doll across the table, through the remaining tangy crescent of Key lime pie—that Dick Artemus had not had time to ring for Sean or the bodyguards.

Clinton Tyree's brows twitched and his glass eyeball fluttered, and his grip was so hateful that the governor could not gulp out a word. That's the problem, Dick Artemus lamented. If only this crazy bastard would ease up, maybe I could talk my way out of this mess.

In the tumult Clinton Tyree had lost his shower cap, and his refulgent bullet-headed baldness further enhanced the aura of menace. Looming inches from the governor's meringue-smudged nose, he said: "I oughta open you up like a mackerel."

It hurt Dick Artemus to blink, his face was so pinched.

"Nothing must happen to disturb my brother. *Ever,*" the ex-governor whispered hoarsely.

Dick Artemus managed a nod, the hinges of his jaw painfully obstructed by the brute's thumb and forefinger.

"What exactly do you believe in, sir?"

"Uh?" peeped Dick Artemus.

"The vision thing. What's yours—tract homes and shopping malls and trailer parks as far as the eye can see? More, more, more? More people, more cars, more roads, more houses." Clinton Tyree's breath was hot on the governor's cheeks. "More, more, more," he said. "More, more, more, more, more, more, more. . . ."

Dick Artemus felt his feet dangling—the madman was hoisting him one-handed by the neck. A terrified squeak escaped from the governor.

"I didn't fit here, Dick," Clinton Tyree was saying. "But you!

This is your place and your time. Selling is what you do best, and every blessed inch of this state is for sale. Same as when I had your job, Dickie, only the stakes are higher now because there's less of the good stuff to divvy up. How many islands are left untouched?"

Clinton Tyree laughed mordantly and let Dick Artemus slide down the wall. He hunched over him like a grave digger. "I know what I *ought* to do to you," he said. "But that might get my friends in hot water, so instead. . . ."

And the next thing the governor knew, he had been stripped of his coat, shirt and necktie. He lay bare-chested on the floor, with 240 pounds of one-eyed psychopath kneeling on his spine.

"What the hell're you doing?" he cried, then his head was roughly jerked backward until he could see the pitiless vermilion glow of Clinton Tyree's dead eye.

"Hush now, Governor Dick."

So Dick Artemus shut up and concentrated on bladder control, to preserve his dignity as well as the gubernatorial carpet. If Clinton Tyree did not intend to kill him, then what was he up to? Dick Artemus shivered when he felt his trousers being loosened and yanked down.

He thought: Aw Jesus, it's just like *Deliverance.*

Involuntarily his anus puckered, and he found himself suddenly ambivalent about the possibility of being rescued midsodomy—the headlines might be more excruciating than the crime. The only governor of Florida to be boned by a former governor on the floor of the governor's mansion! There's one for the history books, Dick Artemus thought disconsolately, and more than just a damn footnote.

Even worse than the threat of public humiliation was the potential political fallout. Was Florida ready to reelect a defiled chief executive? Dick Artemus had his doubts. He remembered how the audience felt about the Ned Beatty character at the end of the movie—you were sorry for the guy, but no one was standing in line for his next canoe trip.

A calloused paw grabbed one of the governor's buttocks and he girded for the worst. Then: an unexpected sensation, like a dry twig scratching up and down his flesh, or the lusty play of a woman's fingernails—sharp, yet pleasing. Dick Artemus remained motionless and oddly becalmed. He wondered what the big freak was doing, straddling his cheeks and humming so quietly to himself.

The bizarre proceeding was disrupted when a door opened and a woman shouted Clinton Tyree's name. Dick Artemus twisted his neck and saw Lisa June Peterson and Lt. Jim Tile each fastening themselves to one of the ex-governor's arms, pulling him away—the madman grinning yet submissive—out of the dining room.

Dick Artemus lurched to his feet and tugged up his pants and smoothed his tousled hair. Not a word would be said about this—Lisa June and the trooper could be counted upon for that. No one would ever know! He hurried to the bedroom for a freshly pressed shirt and notified his driver he was ready. And in the car on the way to the Planters Club, Dick Artemus breezily reviewed the notes for his speech, as if nothing out of the ordinary had happened. It was only later, after leaving the dais to a round of polite applause, that Dick Artemus discovered what Clinton Tyree had done to him. The FDLE agent standing outside the men's room heard a sob and flung open the door to see the governor of Florida with blood-flecked boxer shorts bunched at his ankles, his milk-white bum thrust toward the mirror. He was appraising himself woefully over one shoulder.

"Sir?" the agent said.

"Go away!" croaked Dick Artemus. "Out!"

But the agent already had seen it. And he could read it, too, even backward in the mirror:

The word SHAME in scabbing pink letters across the governor's bare ass, where it had been meticulously etched with a buzzard beak.

Jim Tile said, "This time you've outdone yourself."

"Jail?" Skink asked.

"Or the nuthouse."

Lisa June Peterson said, "Are you kidding? Nobody's going to jail. This never happened."

They were heading to the hospital in Jim Tile's patrol car. The trooper and Lisa June sat up front. McGuinn and the ex-governor were curled in two aromatic heaps—one black and one fluorescent orange—on the backseat, in the prisoner cage.

"Imagine if Governor Artemus orders Governor Tyree prosecuted," Lisa June was saying. "Once the story leaks out, Lord, it's front-page news all over the country—and not the kind you clip out for the family scrapbook, if you're Dick Artemus."

From the backseat: "What's the big deal? He won't scar."

Jim Tile said, "I believe you're missing the point."

"Two weeks, his scrawny butt'll be as good as new. What?" Skink perked up. "Lisa June, are you giggling?"

"No."

"Yes, you are!"

"Well, it was . . ."

"Funny?" Skink prompted.

"Not what I expected to see, that's all." Lisa June Peterson tried to compose herself. "You on top of him. Him with his fanny showing. . . ."

Thinking about the scene, Jim Tile had to chuckle, as well. "When can I go home?" he said.

From the backseat: "Soon as we spring the boy."

Lisa June addressed both of them. "If anyone asks, here's

what happened today: Governor Richard Artemus held a cordial, uneventful private lunch with former Governor Clinton Tyree. They discussed—let's see—bass fishing, Florida history, the restructuring of the state Cabinet—and the strenuous job demands of the office of chief executive. The meeting lasted less than an hour, after which former Governor Tyree declined a tour of the refurbished residence, due to a previous commitment to visit a friend in a local hospital. All agreed?"

"Sounds good to me," Jim Tile said.

"It will sound even better to Governor Artemus. Trust me." Skink sat up in the cage. "But what about that bridge?"

Jim Tile said, "Don't even think about it."

"Hell, I'm just curious."

"Your work is done here, Governor."

"Oh, relax, Lieutenant."

Lisa June Peterson said, "They'll reappropriate the bridge funding next week, during the special session. Once that happens, Shearwater is a go."

Skink sagged forward, hooking sun-bronzed fingers in the steel mesh. "So the veto was bullshit. They lied to the boy."

"Of course they did. They thought he was going to kill your buddy." Lisa June nodded toward the dozing dog. "It was extortion, captain. They couldn't cave in."

"Plus the bridge is a twenty-eight-million-dollar item."

"There's that, yes."

"And let's not forget that Governor Pencil Dick is dearly beholden to Shearwater's developer."

"Agreed," Lisa June Peterson said, "but the point is, everything worked out. Mr. Stoat's dog is safe. Mr. Stoat's wife is safe. And the young man, Mr. Spree, will get the professional help he needs. . . ."

Skink snorted. "The island, however, is fucked."

A cheerless silence settled over the occupants of the patrol car.

Jim Tile thought: This is precisely what I was afraid of. This was the danger they risked, bringing him out of the swamp on such heartless terms.

The trooper said, "Governor, where will you take the kid?"

"A safe place. Don't you worry."

"Until he's feeling better?"

"Sure."

"Then what?" Lisa June asked.

"Then he's free to burn down the goddamn capitol building if he wants. I'm not his father," Skink groused, "and I'm not his rabbi." Once again he drew himself caterpillar-like into a ball, resting his shaved dome on the car seat. The Labrador awoke briefly and licked him on the brow.

As Jim Tile wheeled up to the hospital entrance, Lisa June Peterson asked: "You sure about this? He's OK to travel?"

The trooper explained that Twilly Spree's gunshot wound was a through-and-through; minor damage to the right lung, two fractured ribs, no major veins or arteries nicked.

"Lucky fella," Jim Tile said. "In any case, he's safer with him"—cutting his eyes toward the backseat—"than anyplace else. Somebody wanted the young man dead. Maybe still does."

"What if those officers upstairs won't let him out?"

"Miss Peterson, three of those troopers are being evaluated next month for promotions. Guess who's one of the evaluators?" Jim Tile removed his mirrored sunglasses and folded them into a breast pocket. "I don't think they'll raise a fuss if Mr. Spree decides to check himself out."

From the backseat: "You ever been there?"

"Excuse me, Governor?"

"Jim, I'm talking to Lisa June. Darling, you ever been down to Toad Island?"

"No."

"You just might like it."

"I'm sure I would," she said.

"No, I meant you might like it *the way it is*. Without the fairways and yacht basins and all the touristy crap."

Lisa June Peterson turned to face him. "I know exactly what you meant, captain."

Jim Tile parked in the shade and left the back windows cracked, so the dog could get some fresh air. While a nurse changed Twilly Spree's dressing, the three of them—Skink, Lisa June and Jim Tile—waited outside the hospital room. Jim Tile spoke quietly to the four young troopers posted at the door, then led them down the hall for coffee. Skink flopped crosslegged on the bare floor. Lisa June borrowed a spring-backed chair from the nursing station and sat next to him.

He eyed her with an avuncular amusement. "So, you're going to stay put here in Tallahassee. Learn the ropes. Be a star." The ex-governor winked.

"Maybe I'll write a book about you instead."

"I enjoy Graham Greene. I'd like to think he would have found me interesting," Skink mused, "or at least moral."

"I do," Lisa June said.

"No, you write a book about Governor Dickless instead— and publish it before the next election. Wouldn't that be a kick in the kumquats!" Skink's mandrill howl startled a middle-aged patient wearing a neck brace and rolling an IV rig down the hallway. The man made a wobbly U-turn and steamed back toward the safety of his room.

Lisa June Peterson lowered her voice. "Look, I was thinking. . . ."

"Me, too." The captain, playfully pinching one of her ankles.

"Not about *that*."

"Well, you should. It'll do you good."

"The new bridge," Lisa June whispered. "Shearwater."

"Yeah?"

"The deal's not sewn up yet. There's one more meeting." She told him who would be there. "And Palmer Stoat, too, of course. He set the whole thing up. It's a hunting trip."

Skink's thatched eyebrows hopped. "Where?"

"That's the problem. They're going to a private game ranch outside Ocala. You need an invitation to get in."

"Darling, please."

"But let's say you did get in," Lisa June continued. "I was thinking you could talk to them about Toad Island. Talk to them the way you talked to me about Florida that night by the campfire. Who knows, maybe they'd agree to scale down the project. Leave some free beach and a few trees at least. If you can just get Dick on your side—"

"Oh, Lisa June—"

"Listen! If you can get Dick on your side, the others might go along. He can be incredibly persuasive, believe me. You haven't seen him at his best."

"I should hope not." Skink, toying with his buzzard beaks. "Lisa June, I just whittled a serious insult into the man's rear end. He ain't never *ever* gonna be on my side. And you know that." The captain leaned sideways and smooched one of her kneecaps. "But I sincerely appreciate the information."

The door to Twilly Spree's room opened and they both got up. A pleasant freckle-faced nurse reported that Mr. Spree was improving by the hour.

Lisa June Peterson tugged Skink's sleeve. "I'd better be getting back to the capitol. The boss has a busy afternoon."

"Don't you want to meet the notorious psycho dognapper?"

"Better not. I just might like him."

Skink nodded. "That would be confusing, wouldn't it?"

"Heartbreaking is more like it," she said, "if something bad were to happen."

When he wrapped his great arms around her, Lisa June felt

bundled and hidden; safe. He told her: "Between you and Jim, I've never seen such worriers."

From somewhere in the deep crinkly folds of his embrace he heard her ask: "But it wouldn't hurt to try, would it? Talking sense to them, I mean. What could it hurt?"

"It's a hunting trip, darling. Can't be talking out loud during a hunt. You gotta stay real quiet, in order to sneak up on the varmints." Skink pressed his lips to her forehead. "Sorry for making a mess of lunch. How about a rain check?"

"Anytime."

"Bye now, Lisa June."

"Good-bye, Governor."

They had sex on the lion-skin rug in the den, under the dull glassy gaze of the fish and wild animals Palmer Stoat had killed: the Cape buffalo, the timber wolf, the tuft-eared lynx, the bull elk, the striped marlin, the tarpon. . . .

Afterward, Estella, the right-wing prostitute from Swain's, asked: "You miss her?"

"Miss her? I booted her!" Stoat proclaimed. "The dog's a different story. Boodle was good company."

"You're fulla shit."

"How about another drink?"

"Why not," she said.

They were both nude, and smoking Havana's finest. Romeo y Julieta was the brand. Palmer Stoat was delighted to have found a partner who would keep a lit cigar in her mouth during athletic intercourse. Later, if he could get it up again, he would snap some pictures—the two of them going at it, stogie-to-stogie, like dueling smokestacks!

Her scotch freshened, Estella rolled on one side and stroked the frizzy auburn mane of the lion skin. "You shot this stud muffin yourself?"

"I told you, sweetheart. I shot all of 'em." Stoat fondly patted the tawny hide, as if it were the flank of a favorite saddle horse. "This sumbitch was tough, too. Took me three slugs at point-blank."

It would have taken only one had Stoat not been bowled off his feet by the pack of fourteen half-starved hounds that Durgess had deployed to tree the exhausted cat. While falling, Stoat had squeezed off two wild rounds that struck a hapless grackle and a cabbage palm, respectively. These colorful details were not shared with rapt Estella.

"Tell me about Africa," she said, pursing her painted lips to launch a halo of blue smoke.

"Africa. Yes." Most everything he knew about Africa came from *National Geographic* TV specials.

"Where did you go to 'bag' this lion—Kenya?"

"That's right. Kenya." Stoat ran a dry tongue across his lips, dawbing at the honeyed sheen of Johnnie Walker. "Africa is . . . amazing," he ventured. "Incredible."

"Oh, I'd give anything to go there someday." Estella said it dreamily, with a shake of her hair.

Balancing a drink in one hand, Stoat carefully pivoted on his side and fitted himself to the slope of her bottom, spoon-style. "It's so big," he said quietly. "Africa is."

"Big. Yes." Estella arched seductively and Stoat deftly drew back, so as not to ignite her multi-hued locks with his cigar.

"Sweetheart, it would take years to see it all."

"We should go together, Palmer. You could hunt and I could go antiquing," she said. "No charge for the sex, either. You pay for my plane tickets, the nookie is free."

Stoat was tempted to say yes. God knows he needed to get away. And as soon as the legislature finished its final bit of nonsense next week . . . well, why not a safari vacation to Africa? By the time he returned, the movers would have cleaned out Desie's stuff and the house would feel like his own again. Stoat could begin remodeling for bachelorhood. (He had changed his mind about moving; it would take years to find a place with such an ideal trophy room.)

"Let me see what I can do with my schedule," he told Estella, meaning he first wanted to float the Africa idea past his preferred choice of an overseas companion, the Pamela Anderson look-alike from Pube's. At the moment Stoat could not recall her Christian name, though he was sure he'd copied it on a cocktail napkin and saved it in his billfold.

"What's that empty spot?" Estella, pointing at a conspicuous space on the animal wall.

"That's for my black rhino. I bagged it a couple weeks ago."

"A rhinoceros!"

"Magnificent beast," Palmer Stoat said, taking a prodigious drag. "You'll see for yourself, when the mount is finished."

"You went *back* to Africa? When was this?" Estella asked. "How come you never told me?"

"That's because we're always talking politics, babe. Anyway, it was a quickie trip, just for a couple days," he added dismissively. "I believe it was the same weekend you went to that Quayle-for-President brunch."

She wriggled around to face him on the lion skin. "Let me get this straight. You went all the way to Kenya for a weekend? God, you must really love to hunt."

"Oh, I do. And I'm going back Saturday." Instantly, Stoat was sorry he'd said it.

Estella sat up excitedly, sloshing scotch on both of them. "Can I go, too, Palmer? Please?"

"No, honey, it's business this time. I'm taking along an important client. I promised him a rhino like mine."

"Aw, come on. I'll stay out of your way."

"Sorry, sweetheart."

"Then bring me back a nice present, all right? And not just cheapo beads or a grass skirt. A cool wood carving, or maybe— I know!—a Masai spear."

"Consider it done." Stoat, thinking dismally: Where am I going to find something like *that* in Ocala, Florida?

"Wow. All the way to Africa." Estella raised her violet-rimmed lashes to the long wall of stuffed animal heads and laminated fish—Stoat's prize trophies. She said: "I've never even fired a cap pistol, Palmer, but every year I give a little money to the NRA. I am totally behind the Second Amendment."

"Me, too. As you can tell." Stoat airily swept his arm toward the blank-eyed taxidermy. "Like the song says, happiness is a hot gun."

Estella smiled inquisitively. "I don't think I ever heard that one."

27

Krimmler couldn't sleep.

I might never sleep again, he thought.

And Roger Roothaus had not believed the "bum in the tree" story!

Asked Krimmler if he'd been drinking. Suggested he take a vacation, drive the Winnebago up to Cedar Key or Destin.

"Nothing's happening on the island anyway," Roger Roothaus had said. "Not until we hear otherwise from Mr. Clapley. So go enjoy yourself. It's on me."

Krimmler protested. Insisted he felt fine. A bum really *did* break into my camper and beat me up and drag me up a god-damn tree. And left me stranded there, Roger! I had to crawl down in a blinding rainstorm. Nearly broke my ass.

Man, I'm worried about you, Roothaus had said.

You should be!

Don't say a word about this to Mr. Clapley, OK?

But Clapley sent a guy, too, another freak who busted into my place and roughed me up. He had snuff tapes—

I gotta take another call, Roothaus had said curtly. You get off the rock for a while, Karl. I'm serious.

But Krimmler had no intention of leaving Toad Island, because a general never abandoned the battleground, even for an all-expenses-paid beach vacation. So Krimmler loaded his .357 and hunkered down in the Winnebago to await the next intruder.

Hours passed and nobody came, but the pulse of the island murmured ominously at his door. The breeze. The seabirds. The rustle and sigh of the leaves. Krimmler was a haunted man. Besieged by Nature, he possessed the will and armaments to fight back—but no troops. Truly he was alone.

Oh, to hear the familiar backfire of an overloaded dump truck, the plangent buzz of chain saws, the metallic spine-jolting *ploink* of a pile driver . . . how Krimmler's soul would have cartwheeled with joy!

But the earth-moving machines he so loved sat mute and untended, and with each passing moment the cursed island resurged; stirred, blossomed, flexed to life. Locked inside the dank-smelling travel camper, Krimmler began to worry for his own sanity. He was teased and tormented by every cry of a sandpiper, every trill of a raccoon, every emboldened bark of a squirrel (which he had come to dread nearly as much as he dreaded chipmunks). The onset of a blustery dusk only seemed to amplify the primeval racket at Krimmler's door, and to drown the din he slammed a Tom Jones CD into the stereo. He turned on all the lights, wedged a deck chair under the doorknob, crawled under the covers—and waited for a slumber that would not come.

Outside the window, Toad Island mocked him.

Krimmler plugged his ears and thought: I might never sleep again.

He squeezed his eyelids together and spun a plot. At dawn he would commandeer one of the bulldozers and start mowing down trees, purely for therapy. Jump into a D-6 and plow a wide dusty trench through some quiet, piney thicket. Fuck you, squirrels. Welcome to your future.

Krimmler smirked at the idea.

After a while he sat up and listened. The Winnebago had fallen silent except for a steady dripping on the roof from wet branches overhead. Hurriedly Krimmler snatched up the .357 and went to put in another CD.

That's when he heard the cry, unlike anything he'd heard before. It began as a low guttural moan and built to a winding, slow-waning scream. The hair rose on Krimmler's forearms and his tongue turned to chalk. The scream was mighty enough to be that of a large cat, such as a panther, but nerdy Dr. Brinkman had said all panthers had long ago been shot or driven out of northwest Florida. In fact (Krimmler recalled), Roger Roothaus had explicitly inquired about the possibility of panthers on Toad Island, because the animals were listed as a protected species. One measly lump of scat and Uncle Sam could padlock the whole Shearwater operation, possibly forever.

Again the unearthly cry arose. Krimmler shuddered. What else could it possibly be but a panther? That goddamn Brinkman! He lied to us, Krimmler thought—a closet bunny-hugger, as I always suspected! That would explain why he disappeared all of a sudden; probably ran off to squeal to the feds.

Krimmler jerked open the door of the Winnebago and glared into the blue fog and drizzle. The cat scream seemed to be coming from the same upland grove where he had ordered the oak toads buried. The quavering yowl sounded almost human, like a man slowly dying.

Heppppppppppppppppmeeeeeeeeeeeeeeeeeeeeeee!!!

Well, sort of human, Krimmler mused. If you let your imagination run wild.

He stepped into a pair of canvas work trousers and pulled on a windbreaker. Grabbing the pistol and a flashlight, he stalked into the mist. To hell with that drunken snitch Brinkman, wherever he is, Krimmler seethed. This bugshit island *will* be tamed; cleared, dredged, drained, graded, platted, paved, stuccoed, painted and reborn as something of tangible, enduring human value—a world-class golf and leisure resort.

To Krimmler, the screaming in the night was a call to arms. He would not cower and he would not retreat, and he would not allow Shearwater to be thwarted by some smelly, spavined, tick-infested feline. Not after so much work and so much money and so much bullshit politics.

I'll kill the damn thing myself, Krimmler vowed.

Again the night was cleaved by wailing, and Krimmler struck out toward it in a defiant rage. This panther is beyond endangered, he thought. This fucker is doomed.

His charge was halted momentarily when he slipped on a log, the fall shattering his flashlight. Quickly he gathered himself and marched on, slashing with his gun arm to clear a path through the silhouetted trees. The feral cry drew him to the clearing where the toad-mulching bulldozers were parked, and in a frenzy Krimmler started firing the moment he burst from the woods.

"Here, kitty, kitty!" he exulted with a mad leer.

Heppppppppppppppppmeeeeeeeeeeeeeeeeeeeeeee!!!

Besides the money, what Robert Clapley missed most about the drug business was the respect. If you were known to be a smuggler of serious weight, the average low-life schmuck wouldn't dream of screwing with you.

A schmuck such as Avalon Brown, for instance—making Clapley stew for forty-five minutes in the lobby of the Marlin Hotel while he attended to "important business" upstairs with the two Barbies.

Although Avalon Brown obviously found it amusing to be rude to a wealthy American real-estate developer, he would never (Clapley was certain) treat a major importer of cocaine with such reckless disrespect. The longer Clapley had to wait, the more his thoughts turned to Mr. Gash—now, there was a fellow who could teach Avalon Brown some manners, and would be pleased to do so.

Clapley wondered why Mr. Gash had not phoned from Toad Island. Shootings, even if not fatal to the target, customarily resulted in a first-person report from the field. Maybe Mr. Gash was sulking, Clapley speculated, because the dognapper had survived. Mr. Gash took a great deal of pride in his work.

Still, he ought to call soon, Clapley thought. Wait'll I tell him about Avalon Brown—a turd fondler like that would be just the thing to brighten Mr. Gash's spirits; the sort of assignment he'd been known to do for free.

"Bobby?"

In the lobby stood Katya and Tish, aloof but not outwardly sullen. There was no sign of Jamaica's answer to Stanley Kubrick.

"Bobby, Mr. Brown vonts to know vere is movie money."

"My lawyers are drawing up the partnership papers. Let's go eat lunch," Robert Clapley said.

As they strolled to the News Café, Clapley was nearly overcome by distress. The Barbies looked ghoulish. They had frizzed their hair and dyed it as black as onyx, shading lips and eyelids to match. They wore musty lace shawls over loose diaphanous halters, tight leather pants and buckled, open-toed shoes as clunky as tugboats. It was criminal, Clapley lamented silently. The women were *made* for short skirts and high heels; hell, he ought to know. He was the design engineer! At no small expense, he had re-formed Katya and Tish into perfect twin images of *the* American beauty icon. And here was the thanks he got: rebellion. Toenails painted black!

Over cappuccinos and bagels, he asked: "You girls miss me?"

"Shore, Bobby," Tish said.

"Score any rhino dust yet?"

Tish shook her head tightly. Katya dropped her eyes.

"No luck, huh?" Clapley clucked in mock sympathy.

"Just cocaine. Cocaine is bo-rink." Katya, crunching into a toasted raisin bagel.

"Very boring," Robert Clapley agreed. "What's with the new look? Is that for your movie?"

"Is casual Goth, Bobby." By way of explanation, Tish pointed to a silver crucifix hanging from her neck. Katya was wearing one, too, Clapley noticed.

"Goth? You mean bats and vampires and shit like that."

"Ya," Katya said, "and blude vership."

"Also, good dance clubs," Tish added.

Clapley chuckled caustically. "Blood worship and rave. You're definitely in the right town."

His whole body twitched and perspired with wanton anxiety. Every ounce of concentration was required to steady the coffee cup in his hands. Meanwhile, the Barbies were giddily diverted by a shirtless young man racing backward on Rollerblades; the requisite ponytail, Oakley shades and a white cockatoo on one shoulder.

"Girls." Robert Clapley felt like a teacher who hears giggling in the back of the classroom. "Katya! Tish!"

Their naughty smiles evaporated.

"Do you still want some rhino dust?"

Tish glanced at Katya, who cocked an unplucked eyebrow.

"Vere?" she asked suspiciously.

"The condo in Palm Beach."

"Ven? You have now?"

"Not today," Clapley said. "Day after tomorrow."

Tish said, "No boolshit, Bobby? You got horn?"

"I will."

"How you find? Vere it is?" Katya demanded.

Clapley could hardly bear to look at them, their hair and makeup were so appalling. Plus, they were noshing like a pair of starved heifers!

"Vere you get dis horn?" Katya persisted.

"From a real rhinoceros. I'll be shooting it myself."

Tish froze, her waxy cheeks bulging with bagel. Katya sat forward, the pink tip of tongue showing between her front teeth, like a kitten's.

"Black rhino. A monster," Robert Clapley said. "The hunt is all set for Saturday morning."

"You shoot rhino? No boolshit?"

"That's right."

"What if you don't hit?"

"Then it will probably kill me. Just like it killed another man a few years ago." Clapley affected a rueful sigh. "A truly awful thing, it was. The guide says this is an extremely dangerous animal. A rogue."

The Barbies sat big-eyed and transfixed. Another teenaged Rollerblader skated past, swinging his spandex-covered buns, but the women remained riveted upon the great white hunter.

"Don't you worry. I *won't* miss," Clapley told them. "I never miss."

Katya said, "Big gun, ya?"

"The biggest."

"Then, after, you bring home horn!"

"Only if you'll be there waiting."

The women nodded in syncopated enthusiasm.

"Fantastic. But you can't tell anyone, especially not Mr. Brown," Clapley warned. "This is very risky, what I'm doing for you. I could get in lots of trouble."

"OK, Bobby."

"Not to mention trampled to death."

Katya tenderly put a hand on top of Clapley's. "We love, Bobby, that you would do such risky things for us. To shoot so dangerous rhino."

"Haven't I always given you whatever you wanted? Haven't I? You and Tish asked for more horn, and this is the only way I can get it for you. Putting my life on the line."

"Thank you, Bobby."

"So, I'll see you both Saturday night? With *blond* hair. Please?"

Tish tittered. "Tall shoes, too."

"That would be fantastic." So much for the Goth shit, Robert Clapley thought. He was rapturous with triumph and longing; soon his twins would be home.

In the lobby of the Marlin, he hugged both of them and said: "I trust Mr. Avalon Brown got you a nice oceanfront suite."

Tish looked questioningly at Katya, who seemed embarrassed.

"No? Well, maybe after the movie's a big hit." Clapley leaned in for good-bye kisses, wincing at the fumes of a sickly, unfamiliar perfume.

"What is that?" he wheezed politely.

"Name is called Undead," Katya replied. "I think by Calvin."

"Lovely. Tell Mr. Brown I'll be in touch."

"Be careful to shoot rhino, Bobby."

"Don't worry about me," Clapley said. "Oh, I almost forgot. Dr. Mujera will be flying in from South America next week. Just a reminder." He tapped an index finger on his chin. "Assuming you girls are still interested."

"Maybe," Katya said, guardedly.

"Ya, maybe," Tish said.

"Only the best for you two. Right? He's the top guy in the whole world."

"But Mr. Brown says he loves our chins, like is now."

"Is that so," Clapley said thinly.

"Good chins for movie light-ink," Tish elaborated.

"Soft," Katya added. "He says soft angles look better. Not sharp, like on American models."

"Dr. Mujera has operated on many, many international movie stars."

"For real, Bobby? Chins of movie stars?"

"I'll speak to Mr. Brown myself. I believe he'll be very pleased with the doctor's qualifications." Robert Clapley looked at his wristwatch. "As a matter of fact, I've got some time now. Why don't you girls phone the room and ask Mr. Brown to join us for a drink?"

"No," Katya said. "Massage lady is there."

"Two o'clock every day," said Tish.

"The massage lady?"

"He says is for stress," Katya explained.

Clapley offered an understanding smile. "Mr. Brown must be under a lot of pressure."

"See you Saturday, Bobby. We party like before, OK?"

"Baby, I can't wait."

"And good lucks with black rhino!"

"Don't worry about me," Robert Clapley told his future

Barbie twins. "You just get busy fixing that beautiful hair of yours."

When they put him in the Highway Patrol car, Twilly Spree was loaded on painkillers, which worked out fine because McGuinn immediately pounced on his chest to say hello. It still hurt like hell, but not enough to make Twilly pass out.

The first stop was a Barnett bank, where he made a cash withdrawal that by chance equaled, almost to the dollar, three whole years of Lt. Jim Tile's Highway Patrol salary. Even the former governor was taken aback.

"Inheritance," Twilly said thickly. "My grandfather's spinning in his grave."

The next stop was a GM dealership on the way out of Tallahassee.

"What for?" the captain demanded.

"We need a car."

"I walk most everywhere."

"Well, I don't," Twilly said, "not with a hole in my lung."

Jim Tile appeared highly entertained. Twilly sensed that Clinton Tyree was accustomed to running the show.

"Can I call you Governor?"

"Rather you didn't."

"Mr. Tyree? Or how about Skink?"

"Neither."

"All right, *captain*," Twilly said, "I just wanted to thank you for what you did on the island."

"You're most welcome."

"But I was wondering how you happened to be there."

"Spring break," Skink said. "Now, let's get you some wheels."

With McGuinn in mind, Twilly picked out another used Roadmaster wagon, this one navy blue. While he filled out the paperwork in the salesman's cubicle, the trooper, the captain and the big dog ambled around the showroom. None of the other salesmen dared to go near them. Afterward, in the parking lot, Jim Tile admired the big Buick. McGuinn was sprawled in the back, Twilly was in the front passenger seat and Skink was behind the wheel.

"I don't really want to know where you three are headed," the trooper said, "but, Governor, I do want to know what you did with that gun I gave you."

"Gulf of Mexico, Jim."

"You wouldn't lie to me?"

"I threw it out of the chopper. Ask the boy."

Twilly nodded. It was true. The pilot wisely had asked no questions.

"But the cell phone is a sad story, Jim. I must've dropped it in the woods," Skink said. "The great state of Florida should buy you a new one. Tell Governor Dick I said so."

Jim Tile circled to Twilly's side of the car and leaned down at the window. "I assume you know whom you're traveling with."

"I do," Twilly said.

"He is a dear friend of mine, son, but he's not necessarily a role model."

Skink cut in: "Another public service announcement from the Highway Patrol!"

Twilly shrugged. "I'm just looking for peace and quiet, Lieutenant. My whole mortal being aches."

"Then you should take it easy. Real easy." The trooper returned to the driver's side. Clearly something was bothering him.

Skink said, "Jim, you believe the size of this thing!"

"How long since you drove a car?"

"Been awhile."

"Yeah, and how long since you had a license?"

"Twenty-two years. Maybe twenty-three. Why?" The captain idly walked his fingers along the steering wheel. Twilly had to grin.

"Tell you what I'm going to do," Jim Tile said. "I'm going to leave right now, so that I don't see you actually steer this boat off the lot. Because then I'd have to pull you over and write you a damn ticket."

Skink's eye danced mischievously. "I would frame it, Jim."

"Do me a favor, Governor. This young man's already been through one shitstorm and nearly didn't make it. Don't give him any crazy new ideas."

"There's no room in his head for more. Am I right, boy?"

Twilly, deadpan: "I've turned over a new leaf."

The trooper put on his wire-rimmed sunglasses. "Might as well be talking to the damn dog," he muttered.

Clinton Tyree reached up and chucked him on the shoulder. Jim Tile gravely appraised his road Stetson, the brim of which had been nibbled ragged by McGuinn.

"Governor, I'll say it again: I'm too old for this shit."

"You are, Jim. Now, go home to your bride."

"I don't want to read about you two in the paper. Please."

Skink plucked off the trooper's shades and bent them to fit his face. "Elusive and reclusive! That's us."

"Just take care. Please," Jim Tile said.

As soon as he was gone, they drove straight for the interstate. Twilly drifted in and out of codeine heaven, never dreaming. Near Lake City the captain excitedly awakened him to point out a dead hog on the shoulder of the highway.

"We could live off that for two weeks!"

Twilly sat up, rubbing his eyes. "Why are you stopping?"

"Waste not, want not."

"You love bacon that much, let me buy you a Denny's franchise," Twilly said. "But I'll be damned if you're stashing a four-hundred-pound pig corpse in my new station wagon. No offense, captain."

In the back of the car, McGuinn whined and fidgeted.

"Probably gotta pee," Skink concluded.

"Makes two of us," Twilly said.

"No, makes three."

They all got out and walked toward the fringe of the woods. The ex-governor glanced longingly over his shoulder, toward the roadkill hog. McGuinn sniffed at it briefly before loping off to explore a rabbit trail. Twilly decided to let him roam for a few minutes.

When they got back to the car, the captain asked Twilly how he felt.

"Stoned. Sore." With a grunt, Twilly boosted himself onto the hood. "And lucky," he added.

Skink rested one boot on the bumper. He peeled off the shower cap and rubbed a bronze knuckle back and forth across the stubble of his scalp. He said, "We've got some decisions to make, Master Spree."

"My mother saved all the clippings from when you disappeared. Every time there was a new story, she'd read it to us over breakfast," Twilly recalled. "Drove my father up a wall. My father sold beachfront."

Skink whistled sarcastically. "The big leagues. More, more, more."

"He said you must be some kind of Communist. He said anybody who was anti-development was anti-American."

"So your daddy's a patriot, huh? Life, liberty and the pursuit of real estate commissions."

"My mother said you were just a man trying to save a place he loved."

"And failing spectacularly."

"A folk hero, she said."

Skink seemed amused. "Your mother sounds like a romantic." He refitted the shower cap snugly on his skull. "You were in, what, kindergarten? First grade? You can't possibly remember back that far."

"For years afterward she talked about you," Twilly said, "maybe just to give my dad the needle. Or maybe because she was secretly on your side. She voted for you, that I know."

"Jesus, stop right there—"

"I think you'd like her. My mother."

Skink pried off the sunglasses and studied his own reflection in the shine off the car's fender. With two fingers he repositioned the crimson eye, more or less aligning it with his real one. Then he set his gaze on Twilly Spree and said, "Son, I can't tell you what to do with your life—hell, you've seen what I've done with mine. But I will tell you there's probably no peace for people like you and me in this world. Somebody's got to be angry or nothing gets fixed. That's what we were put here for, to stay pissed off."

Twilly said, "They made me take a class for it, captain. I was not cured."

"A class?"

"Anger management. I'm perfectly serious."

Skink hooted. "For Christ's sake, what about *greed* management? Everybody in this state should get a course in *that*. You fail, they haul your sorry ass to the border and throw you out of Florida."

"I blew up my uncle's bank," Twilly said.

"So what!" Skink exclaimed. "Nothing shameful about anger, boy. Sometimes it's the only sane and logical and moral reaction. Jesus, you don't take a class to make it go away! You take a drink or a goddamn bullet. Or you stand and fight the bastards."

The ex-governor canted his chin to the sky and boomed:

"Know ye the land where the cypress and myrtle
Are emblems of deeds that are done in their clime;
Where the rage of the vultures, the love of the turtle,
Now melt into sorrow, now madden to crime?"

Quietly, Twilly said, "But I'm already there, captain."

"I know you are, son." Slowly he lowered his head, the braids of his beard trailing down like strands of silver moss. The two bird beaks touched hooks as they dangled at his chest.

"Lord Byron?" Twilly asked.

Skink nodded, looking pleased. "The Bride of Abydos."

With a thumb Twilly tested his bandaged wound. The pain was bearable, even though the dope was wearing off. He said, "I suppose you heard about this big-game trip."

"Yes, sir."

"You wouldn't happen to know where it is."

Here was Skink's chance to end it. He could not.

"I do know where," he said, and repeated what Lisa June Peterson had told him.

"So, what do you think?" Twilly asked.

"I think a canned hunt is as low as it gets."

"That's not what I mean."

"Ah. You mean as the potential scene of an ambush?"

"Well, I keep thinking about Toad Island," Twilly said, "and how to stop that damn bridge."

Skink's blazing eye was fixed on the highway, the cars and trucks streaking past. "Look at these fuckers," he said softly, as if to himself. "Where could they all be going?"

Twilly slid off the hood of the station wagon. "I'll tell you where *I'm* going, Governor, I'm going to Ocala. And on the way I intend to stop at a friendly firearms retailer and purchase a high-powered rifle. Want one?"

"The recoil will do wonders for your shoulder."

"Yeah, it'll hurt like a sonofabitch, I imagine." Twilly plucked the car keys from Skink's fingers. "You don't want to come, I can drop you in Lake City."

"That's how you treat a folk hero? Lake City?"

"It's hot out here. Let's get back on the road."

Skink said, "Did I miss something? Is there a plan?"

"Not just yet." Twilly Spree licked his lips and whistled for the dog.

28

Durgess warmed his hands on a cup of coffee while Asa Lando gassed up the big forklift. It was three hours until sunrise.

"You sure about this?" Durgess asked.

"He ain't moved since yesterday noon."

"You mean he ain't woke up."

"No, Durge. He ain't *moved*."

"But he's still breathin', right?"

Asa Lando said, "For sure. They said he even took a dump."

"Glory be."

"Point is, it's perfectly safe. Jeffy isn't going anywheres."

Durgess poured his coffee in the dirt and entered the building marked Quarantine One. Asa Lando drove the forklift around from the rear. The rhinoceros was on its chest and knees, a position the veterinarian had described as "sternal recumbency." The vet had also estimated the animal's age at thirty-plus and used the word *dottering*, which Asa Lando took to mean "at death's door." Time was of the essence.

Durgess opened the stall and Asa Lando rolled in atop the forklift. They couldn't tell if the rhino was awake or asleep, but Durgess kept a rifle ready. El Jefe exhibited no awareness of the advancing machine. Durgess thought he saw one of the ears twitch as Asa Lando cautiously slid the steel tines beneath the rhino's massive underbelly. Slowly the fork began to rise, and a tired gassy sigh escaped the animal's bristly nostrils. Hoisted off the matted straw, the great armored head sagged and the stringy tail swatted listlessly at a swarm of horseflies. The stumpy legs hung motionless, like four scuffed gray drums.

"Easy now," Durgess called, as Asa Lando backed out the forklift and headed for the flatbed truck. Durgess was astounded: Suspended eight feet in the air, the rhinoceros was as docile as a dime-store turtle. A tranquilizer dart would have put the damn thing into a coma.

In preparation for the fragile cargo, Asa Lando had padded the truck bed with two layers of king-sized mattresses. Upon being deposited there, the pachyderm blinked twice (which Durgess optimistically interpreted as a sign of curiosity). Asa tossed up an armful of fresh-cut branches and said, "Here go, Mr. El Jeffy. Breakfast time!"

Durgess himself had selected the location for the kill: an ancient moss-covered live oak that stood alone at the blue-green cleft of two vast grassy slopes, about a mile from the Wilderness Veldt lodge. A hundred years ago the land had produced citrus and cotton, but back-to-back winter freezes had prompted a switch to more durable crops—watermelon, cabbage and crookneck squash. It was the sons and grandsons of those early vegetable growers who eventually abandoned the farm fields and sold out to the Wilderness Veldt Plantation Corporation, which turned out to be co-owned by a Tokyo-based shellfish cartel and a Miami Beach swimsuit designer named Minton Tweeze.

In the dark it took Durgess a half hour to find the designated oak tree—he was driving the flatbed slowly so as not to lose Asa Lando, who was following with the forklift. Durgess parked the truck so that its headlights illuminated the clearing around the craggy trunk of the old tree. Before unloading the rhino, Durgess looped one end of a heavy cattle rope around its neck. The other end he secured to the trailer hitch of the flatbed.

"Why bother?" Asa Lando said.

"I got fifty thousand excellent reasons."

But the rhino never made a move to break free; in fact, it made no movement at all. When Asa lowered the animal to the ground, it settled immediately to its knees, its drowsy demeanor unchanged. If it was happy to be outdoors again, neither Durgess nor Asa Lando could tell. They might as well have been rearranging statuary.

Uneasily, Durgess studied Robert Clapley's high-priced quarry in the twin beams of the truck lights. "Asa, he don't look so good."

"Old age. That's what he's dyin' from."

"Long as he makes it till morning." Durgess cocked his head and put a tobacco-stained finger to his lips. "You hear a dog bark?"

"No, but I heard a wheeze." Asa Lando jerked a thumb toward the rhino. "Chest cold. Doc Terrell says he probably picked it up on the aeroplane."

Durgess hastily stubbed out his cigarette. "Christ. A rhinoceros with fucking asthma."

"Comes and goes, Durge. Same with the arthritis."

"To hell with that. I heard a dog out there, I swear I did."

He cupped a hand to his ear and listened: Nothing. Asa Lando shrugged. "I'm tellin' you, it's Jeffy got a chest wheeze. That's all."

Durgess edged toward the somnolent load and unslipped the rope. It seemed unnecessarily harsh to keep the aged creature tied down, as some prey had to be (due to the incompetent riflery of Wilderness Veldt clients, most of whom had no reasonable chance of hitting anything that wasn't tethered to a stake).

Asa Lando took out a camera and snapped a picture of the rhinoceros, for posting on the Wilderness Veldt's Web site. Then he heaved a bale of wheat in front of the animal, which acknowledged the gesture with a gravelly sniff.

"Well, Durge, that's it. All we can do now is go back to the lodge until dawn."

"And say our prayers," Durgess said. "What if he up and dies, Asa? You think he'll fall over on one side, or will he stay . . . you know. . . ."

"Upright? That's a good question."

"Because if he don't fall, I mean, if he just sorta keeps on his knees. . . ."

Asa Lando brightened. "They won't even know!"

"There's a strong possibility," Durgess agreed. "The damn thing could be stone-dead and. . . ."

"From fifty yards away, how could they tell?"

"That's what I'm sayin', Asa. These clowns'll never figger it out. Long as Jeffy here don't keel over before they actually squeeze off a shot."

Durgess took a step closer, into the spear of white light and swirling insects. He peered skeptically at the motionless rhino. "You still with us, old-timer?"

"He is," Asa Lando said. "Unless that's a puddle of *your* piss on the grass."

The hunting party had come in the night before and, against Durgess's advice, celebrated into the late hours with rich desserts, cognac and Cuban cigars. It was rare that the governor was able to cut loose and relax without fear of ending up in a snarky newspaper column—ordinarily he was careful not to be seen socializing so intimately with insider lobbyists such as Palmer Stoat or shady campaign donors such as Robert Clapley. And upon first arriving at the Wilderness Veldt, Dick Artemus had been subdued and remote, his wariness heightened by a recent unsettling event inside the governor's mansion.

Gradually, however, the chief executive began to feel at ease within the gated privacy of the Wilderness Veldt Plantation, drinking fine whiskey and trading bawdy stories in cracked leather chairs by a cozy stone fireplace. This was what it must have been like in the good old days, the governor thought wistfully, when the state's most important business was conducted far from the stuffy, sterile confines of the capitol—hammered into law by sporting men, over smoky poker games at saloons and fish camps and hunting lodges; convivial settings that encouraged frank language and unabashed horse trading, free from the scrutiny of overzealous journalists and an uninformed public.

Willie Vasquez-Washington, however, wasn't so comfortable among the walnut gun cabinets and the stuffed animal heads, which unblinkingly stared down at him from their stations high on the log walls. Like the governor, Willie Vasquez-Washington also felt as if he'd taken a step backward to another time—a time when a person of his color would not have been welcome at the Wilderness Veldt Plantation unless he wore burgundy doublets and waistcoats, and carried trays of Apalachicola oysters (as efficient young Ramon was doing now). Nor was Willie Vasquez-Washington especially enthralled by the company at the lodge. He had yet to succumb to the famous charms of Dick Artemus, while Palmer Stoat was, well, Palmer Stoat—solicitous, amiably transparent and as interesting as cold grits. Willie Vasquez-Washington was no more favorably impressed by Robert Clapley, the cocky young developer of Shearwater, who had greeted him with a conspicuously firm handshake and a growl: "So you're the guy who's trying to fuck me out of a new bridge."

It was Willie Vasquez-Washington's fervent wish that the political deal could be settled that night, over dinner and drinks, so he would be spared the next day's rhinoceros hunt. Half-drunk white men with high-powered firearms made him extremely nervous. And while Willie Vasquez-Washington was not, in any sense of the term, a nature freak, he had no particular desire to watch some poor animal get shot by the likes of Clapley.

So Willie Vasquez-Washington attempted on several occasions to draw the governor aside, in order to state his simple proposal: A new high school in exchange for a yea vote on the Toad Island bridge appropriation. But Dick Artemus was caught up in the frothy mood of the pre-hunt festivities, and he was unwilling to tear himself away from the hearth. Nor was Palmer Stoat a helpful intermediary; whenever Willie Vasquez-Washington approached him, the man's face was so crammed with food that his response was indecipherable. In the soft cast of the firelight, Stoat's damp bloated countenance resembled that of an immense albino blowfish. What meager table manners he had maintained while sober deteriorated vividly under the double-barreled effects of Rémy Martin and baby back ribs. The ripe spray erupting from Stoat's churning mouth presented not only an unsavory visual spectacle but also (Willie Vasquez-Washington suspected) a health hazard. The prudent move was to back off, safely out of range.

At 1:00 a.m., Willie Vasquez-Washington gave up. He headed upstairs to bed just as Stoat and Clapley broke into besotted song:

"You can't always do who you want,
No, you can't always do who you want. . . ."

They stopped at a shop with a Confederate flag nailed to the door, on U.S. 301 between Starke and Waldo. Twilly Spree purchased a Remington 30.06 with a scope and a box of bullets. Clinton Tyree got Zeiss night-scope binoculars and a secondhand army Colt .45, for use at close range. A five-hundred-dollar cash "donation" toward the new Moose Lodge served to expedite the paperwork and inspire a suddenly genial clerk to overlook the brief waiting period normally required for handgun purchases in Florida.

Skink and Twilly stopped for dog food, camo garb and other supplies in the town of McIntosh, seventeen miles outside Ocala. At a diner there, a shy ponderous waitress named Beverly blossomed before their very eyes into a svelte southern version of Rosie O'Donnell—a transformation hastened by a hundred-dollar tip and the gift of a one-of-a-kind Chihuahua-hide vest, which Skink good-naturedly took off and presented to her on the spot. Beverly pulled up a chair and offered numerous scandalous anecdotes about what went on at the Wilderness Veldt Plantation and, more importantly, flawless directions to it. By nightfall Twilly and Skink were comfortably encamped on the north end of the spread, having conquered the barbed ten-foot fence with a bolt cutter. The ex-governor built a small fire ring in a concealed palmetto thicket, while Twilly took McGuinn to scout the area. The dog was like a dervish on the leash, pulling so hard in so many different directions that it nearly dislocated Twilly's acutely tender right shoulder. By the time they returned to the campsite, Skink had dinner cooking over the flames—for Twilly, a rib-eye steak and two baked potatoes; for himself, braised rabbit, alligator tail and fried water moccasin, all plucked, freshly smote, off a bountiful two-mile stretch of pavement south of Micanopy.

Skink said, "Any sign of the warriors?"

"No, but I could see the lights of the main lodge at the top of a hill. I'm guessing it's three-quarters of a mile from here." Twilly looped McGuinn's leash over one ankle and sat down with a jug of water by the fire. The dog rested its chin on its paws, gazing up longingly at the sizzling meat.

"Still no brainstorm?" Skink inquired.

"Truth is, we ought to just shoot the fuckers."

"It's your call, son."

"How about some input?" Twilly wanted the captain to assure him there was another way to save Toad Island, besides committing murder.

Instead Skink said, "I've tried everything else and look where it's got me."

"You're just tired is all."

"You don't know the half of it."

They ate in restive silence, the night settling upon them like a dewy gray shroud. Even McGuinn inched closer to the fire. Twilly thought of Desie—he missed her, but he was glad she wasn't with him now.

"I propose we sleep on it." Skink, crunching on the last curl of snake.

Twilly shook his head. "I won't be sleeping tonight."

"We could always just snatch 'em, I suppose."

"Yeah."

"Make a political statement."

"Oh yeah. Just what the world needs," Twilly said.

"Plus, hostages are a lot of work. You've gotta feed 'em and take 'em to the john and wash their dirty underwear so they don't stink up the car. And listen to all their goddamn whining, sweet Jesus!" Skink laughed contemptuously.

"On the other hand," Twilly said, "if we kill them, then the entire Federal Bureau of Investigation will be chasing us. That's not a happy prospect."

The ex-governor pried loose his glass eye and tossed it to Twilly, who held it up before the fire. The thing appeared surreal and distant, a glowering red sun.

"Beats a plain old patch," Skink said, swabbing the empty socket.

Twilly handed the prosthetic eye back to him. "What do you think they'll be hunting tomorrow?"

"Something big and slow."

"And when it's over, they'll gather around the fireplace, drink a toast to the dead animal and then get down to business. Make their greedy deal and shake hands. And that gorgeous little island on the Gulf will be permanently fucked."

"That's how it usually goes."

"I can't sit still for that, captain."

Skink tugged off his boots and placed them next to the binoculars case. In a pocket of his rain suit he found a joint, which he wedged into his mouth. He lowered his face to the edge of the flames until the end of the doobie began to glow.

"Son, I can't sit still for it, either," he said. "Never could. Want a hit?"

Twilly said no thanks.

"You ever licked toads to get high?" Skink asked.

"Nope."

"Don't."

Twilly said, "I should warn you, I'm not much of a shot."

"Maybe you won't have to be." Skink dragged heavily on the joint. "All kinds of bad shit can happen to foolish men in the woods."

"Still, a plan would be helpful."

"It would, son."

Twilly stretched out, using McGuinn as a pillow. The rhythmic rise and fall of the dog's chest was soothing. Skink dumped water on the fire, and the aroma of wood smoke mingled sweetly with the marijuana.

"What time is it, Governor?"

"Late. You get some rest, we'll figure something out."

"They've got more guns than we do."

"That's undoubtedly true."

The Labrador stirred slightly beneath Twilly's head, and he reached up to scratch the dog's chin. One of McGuinn's hind legs started to kick spasmodically.

Twilly said, "There's him to consider, too."

"No need to bring him along. We can tie him to a tree, where he'll be safe."

"And what happens to him if we don't make it back?"

The captain exhaled heavily. "Good point."

Twilly Spree fell asleep and had another dream. This time he dreamed he was falling. There was a bullet hole in his chest, and as he fell he leaked a curlicued contrail of blood. Far below him were a break of green waves and a long white beach, and in the sky all around him were the seabirds, falling at the same velocity; lifeless clumps of bent feathers and twisted beaks. Somewhere above was the faint, fading sound of a helicopter. In the dream Twilly snatched wildly at the falling gulls until he got one. Clutching the broken bird to his breast, he plummeted in a clockwise spin toward the beach. He landed hard on his back, and was knocked momentarily senseless. When he awoke, Twilly glanced down and saw that the gull had come to life and flown away, out of his hands. It was dark.

And Clinton Tyree was looming over him. Around his neck was a pair of binoculars. Hefted in his arms like an overstuffed duffel was McGuinn, looking chastened.

Twilly raised his head. "What?"

"A flatbed and a forklift. You won't believe it."

Skink rekindled the fire and made coffee. Wordlessly they changed into camouflage jumpsuits and broke out the guns and ammunition. Twilly removed the dog's collar, so it wouldn't jingle.

"Hey, captain, I got one for you. Not a plan but a poem."

"Good man."

" 'I should have been a pair of ragged claws,' " Twilly said, " 'Scuttling across the floors of silent seas.' "

The former governor of Florida clapped his hands in delight. "More!" he exhorted. "More, more, more!" His laughter crashed like a hailstorm through the tall trees and scrub.

Durgess awoke everybody an hour before dawn. No one in the hunting party had the stomach for a hearty breakfast, so the four men gathered quietly around the table for coffee, aspirins, Imodium and, in Robert Clapley's case, two Bloody Marys. Willie Vasquez-Washington had correctly guessed that khaki would be the fashion order of the day. He wondered if Clapley, Stoat and Governor Dick had purchased their nearly identical big-game wardrobes at a sale (although Stoat's absurd cowboy hat somewhat set him apart).

The mood at the table was subdued; a few lame hangover jokes, and halfhearted inquiries about the weather. Durgess sat down to explain how the hunt would be organized. Because the rhinoceros was Clapley's kill, he and Durgess would go first into the bush. Asa Lando would follow twenty or so yards behind, accompanied by the governor, Palmer Stoat and Willie Vasquez-Washington. Ten yards behind them would be the governor's two regular bodyguards.

Weaponry was the next subject, Robert Clapley announcing

he had come armed with a .460 Weatherby, "the Testarrosa of hunting rifles."

Durgess said, "That's all we'll need." Thinking: A slingshot and a pebble would probably do the job.

Not to be outdone, Stoat declared he was bringing his .458 Winchester Magnum.

"My choice, too," interjected Dick Artemus, who had never shot at anything larger, or more menacing, than a grouse. The governor had yet to fire the powerful Winchester, which he had received as a bribe six years earlier while serving on the Jacksonville City Council.

It was hopeless to object, but Durgess felt obliged. "Mr. Clapley's gun is plenty. I'll be armed and so will Asa, in case the animal gives us any trouble. And so will the governor's men." The FDLE bodyguards had lightweight Ruger assault rifles, semiautomatics.

"He's right," Clapley chimed in. He didn't want anybody else sneaking a shot at his trophy rhino.

"Just hold on," Palmer Stoat said to Durgess. "You said this was a killer, right? A rogue."

"Yessir."

"Then—no disrespect meant to you, Bob, or to Dick's security people—but I intend to protect myself out there. I'm bringing my own rifle."

"Me, too," the governor said. "The more the merrier."

Durgess relented without comment. It was always the same story with these big-city shitheads, always a dick-measuring contest. One guy gets a gun, they *all* gotta have one.

The guide turned to Willie Vasquez-Washington. "You a Winchester man, too?"

"Nikon. Pictures is all I'm shooting."

"That's cool." Once Durgess had turned down an offer to guide big-game photo safaris in South Africa because he'd heard that hunters tipped better than photographers. Sometimes, on mornings such as this, Durgess wished he'd taken the gig anyway.

Robert Clapley said, "One thing we've got to get straight right now. It's about the horn—I'm taking that sucker home with me. *Today.*"

Durgess thought: Sure, tough guy. Soon as we see the dough. Otherwise Mr. Yee awaits, cash in hand.

"The horn? What in the world you gonna do with that?" Willie Vasquez-Washington asked.

Palmer Stoat explained how rhinoceros horn was ground into an illicit powder that was sold as an aphrodisiac. "It didn't put any extra lead in Bob's pencil, but his two blond babeniks went animal for the stuff."

Willie Vasquez-Washington chortled in astonishment.

"They got so wet, Bob needed a spatula to scrape 'em off the sheets." Stoat winked archly at Clapley, who turned as red as his tomato cocktail.

Still hollow-eyed from the night before, Dick Artemus gamely looked up from his coffee cup. "I heard about that stuff from a buddy works for Toyota HQ. These horns are very pricey, he says, plus you've got to go all the way to Hong Kong or Bangkok to find one. Supposedly you sprinkle it in your *sake* and get a hard-on that lasts longer than a hockey season."

"Some men do, but not Bob," Palmer Stoat chirped.

Willie Vasquez-Washington couldn't believe what he was hearing—Clapley clearly was more excited about scoring the sex powder than stalking the formidable African rhinoceros. White guys were truly pathetic, the worst, when it came to fretting about their dicks.

Addressing the table, Robert Clapley said, "Palmer disapproves of my two ladies, though I suspect he's just jealous. They have exotic tastes, it's true—and talents to match."

There was a ripple of appreciative laughter.

"So bring a hacksaw for the horn," Clapley instructed Durgess firmly.

"Yessir."

"You know what's also supposed to be good for boners? Bull testicles," the governor volunteered informatively. "Rocky Mountain oysters is what they call 'em out West. Can you imagine eating barbecued bull's balls?"

Durgess rose sluggishly, as if cloaked in cast iron. "We best be movin' out now," he told the men. "I'll go fetch Asa. You fellas meet us in front."

"With our guns," Palmer Stoat added.

"Yessir. With your guns," Durgess said, with dull resignation.

29

They found a knoll with a clear downhill view of the towering moss-draped oak, which stood alone at the confluence of two slopes. The men lay down in the tallest grass to wait, Twilly sighting with the Remington while Skink scanned with the field glasses. McGuinn sat restlessly between them, nosing the foggy dawn air. The end of his leash was looped once around Skink's ax-handle wrist.

"Is it alive?" Twilly, squinting through the rifle scope.

"Hard to say," Skink said.

They were talking about the black rhinoceros.

"Lookie there!"

"What?"

Skink, who needed only half of the binoculars, said: "It's eating. See for yourself."

Twilly positioned the crosshairs and saw twin puffs of mist rising from the beast's horned snout. Its prehensile upper lip browsed feebly at a bale of hay.

"Looks about a thousand years old," Twilly said.

Skink sounded somber. "If we're going to do this thing, whatever it is, it's gotta happen before they plug that poor sonofabitch. That I won't watch, you understand?"

McGuinn edged cagily toward the slope, but Skink yanked him on his butt. Twilly pointed on a line with his rifle: "Here they come, captain."

The hunting party arrived in a zebra-striped Chevy Suburban, parking no more than two hundred yards from the solitary oak. Eight men in all, the group made no effort at stealth. The great El Jefe, masticating serenely beneath the tree, seemed oblivious to the slamming doors, clicking gun bolts and unmuffled male voices.

At the front of the truck they held a brief huddle—Skink spotted the orange flare of a match—before the stalk began in earnest. Two men headed out first, both armed. Twilly didn't recognize either of them but he knew one had to be Robert Clapley.

Four men followed in a second group. Twilly didn't need a scope to pick out Desie's husband. He remembered Palmer Stoat's oversized cowboy hat from that first day, when he had pursued the obnoxious litterbug down the Florida Turnpike. Another giveaway was the bobbing cigar; downwind or upwind, only a stooge such as Stoat would smoke while tracking big game.

Skink said, "There's your boy." He recognized Stoat's doughball physique from the night he'd broken into the lobbyist's house and usurped his bathroom. Seeing him again now, in such an inexcusable circumstance, Skink was even less inclined toward mercy. Twilly Spree had related how all the madness had started—Stoat blithely chucking hamburger cartons out the window of his Range Rover. The ex-governor had understood perfectly Twilly's infuriated reaction, for such atrocious misbe-

havior could not be overlooked. In Skink's view, which he kept
to himself, Twilly had shown uncommon restraint.

In the same contingent of hunters as Palmer Stoat marched
the governor, looking theatrically chipper in an Aussie bush hat.
Dick Artemus carried his gun in a way that suggested he practiced everything except shooting. A third man, leaner and
darker, held a long-lensed camera but no weapon. The fourth
man in the group walked out front with a rifle at the ready; he
was older and wiry-looking, dressed more like a mechanic than
a hunter.

The last two members of the motley safari stayed many paces
behind and shouldered shorter rifles—semiautomatics, Skink
somberly informed Twilly. The men wore jeans, running shoes
and navy blue windbreakers with the letters FDLE visible on the
back.

"Governor Dick's bodyguards," Skink said, "with Mini-14s,
if I'm not mistaken."

Twilly didn't like the odds. The sun was rising behind the
knoll, which meant he and the captain would get some cover
from the glare. But still. . . .

Skink nudged him. "Make the call, son. I'm not getting any
younger."

Like a disjointed centipede, the hunting party advanced tentatively along the cleft at the base of the grassy slopes. Drawing
closer to their prey, the two men out front altered their walk to
a furtive stoop, pausing every few steps to rest on their haunches
and strategize. The one doing all the pointing would be the
guide, Twilly figured, while Robert Clapley would be the one
bedecked like an Eddie Bauer model.

Viewed from a distant perch, the stalk unfolded as comic
mime of a true wild hunt. Whenever the lead duo halted and
crouched, the men trailing behind would do the same. The bare
grass offered the trackers neither protection nor concealment,

but none was necessary. The killer rhinoceros continued chewing, unperturbed.

"If you had to take out one of them," Twilly said to Skink, "who would it be—Governor Dickless?"

"Waste of ammo. They got assembly lines that crank out assholes like him. He wouldn't even be missed."

"Stoat, then?"

"Maybe, but purely for the entertainment. Tallahassee has more lobbyists than termites," Skink said.

"That leaves only Mr. Clapley." Twilly closed one eye and framed the developer square in the crosshairs. Clapley's face appeared intent with predatory concentration. Twilly carefully rested a forefinger on the Remington's trigger.

Skink said: "It's his project. His goddamned bridge. His hired goon who tried to kill you."

Twilly exhaled slowly, to relax his shooting arm. The hunting guide and Clapley had approached to within forty yards of the rhinoceros.

"On the other hand," Skink was saying, "it might be more productive just to snatch the bastard and haul him down to the Glades for three or four months. Just you and me, re-educating his ass on the Shark River."

Twilly turned his head. "Captain?"

"Could be fun. Like a high-school field trip for young Bob Clapley, or holiday camp!" Skink mused. "We'll send him home a new man—after the banks have called in his construction loans, of course. . . ."

"Captain!"

"It's your call, son."

"I *know* it's my call. Where's the damn dog?"

"The dog?" Skink sprung up and looked around anxiously. "Oh Jesus."

*   *   *

So many enthralling smells!

McGuinn reveled in the country morning: Sunrise, on the crest of a green hill, where seemingly everything—leaves, rocks, blades of grass, the dew itself—was laced with strange intoxicating scents. Large animals, McGuinn concluded from their potent musks; jumbos. What could they be? And what sort of place was this?

Although most of the smells that reached the hill were too faint to merit more than a cursory sniff or a territorial spritz of pee, one scent in particular hung fresh and warm, cutting pungently through the light fog. McGuinn was itching to bolt loose and track it.

The scent was not that of a domestic cat or another dog. Definitely not duck or seagull. Negative also for deer, rabbit, raccoon, skunk, muskrat, mouse, toad, turtle or snake. This earthy new animal odor was unlike any the dog had previously encountered. It made his hair bristle and his nose quiver, and it was so heavy in the air that it must have been exuded by a creature of massive proportion. McGuinn yearned to chase down this primordial behemoth and thrash it mercilessly . . . or at least pester it for a while, until he found something better to do.

In the distance a vehicle stopped and emptied out a new bunch of humans, and soon McGuinn detected other aromas—gasoline exhaust, sunblock, aftershave, coffee, cigar smoke and gun oil. But it was the smell of the mystery beast that beckoned irresistibly. The dog glanced around and saw that nobody was paying attention to him. The young man, Desie's friend, was preoccupied with pointing a gun down the hill. Similarly distracted was his travel companion, the hairy-faced man who was perfumed indelibly with burnt wood and dead opossum, and on whose wrist was limply fastened the cursed leash.

McGuinn levered his butt imperceptibly off the grass,

scooted backward a couple of inches, then sat down again. Neither of the men looked up. So McGuinn did it again, and still again, until the slack in the leash was gone and all that remained was to coil his muscles and execute The Lunge—a heedless, headlong escape maneuver familiar to all owners of Labrador retrievers. During many an evening walk, McGuinn had employed The Lunge to excellent effect, leaving Palmer Stoat or Desie standing empty-handed, snatching at thin air, while he dashed off to deal with an insolent Siamese, or to take a dip in the New River. The dog was well aware he was exceptionally fast, and virtually impossible for humans to overtake on foot.

Once he made his break.

This time it happened so smoothly that it was anticlimactic. McGuinn surged forward and the leash simply came free, slipping so cleanly off the hand of the hairy-faced man that he didn't feel it. The next thing the dog knew, he was barreling away, unnoticed and unpursued. Down the long slope he ran—ears unfurled, tongue streaming, velvet nose to the grass—faster and faster until he was but a black streak, hurtling past the dumbstruck hunters. He heard a flurry of agitated voices, then a familiar angry command—"Boodle, no!"—which he gleefully disregarded. Onward he sped, the leash flopping at his heels, the powerful alien fragrance reeling him in as if he were a barracuda hooked on a wire. Directly ahead loomed a gnarled mossy tree, and beneath it stood a great horned creature so immense and unflinching, McGuinn thought at first that it was made of stone.

But, no, smell it! A piquant blend of mulchy digestive vapors, sour body mold and steaming shit. With a self-congratulatory howl, the dog bore in. He circled first one way and then the other before dropping to a snarling crouch behind the animal's gargantuan armor-plated flanks. McGuinn expected the beast to wheel in self-defense, yet the stately rump remained motionless.

McGuinn inched around cautiously to confront the snouted end, where he initiated a sequence of spirited head fakes, left and right, to feign a charge. Yet the creature did not shirk, bridle or jump at its tormentor's well-choreographed hysterics. The creature did not move; merely stared at the dog through crinkled, gnat-covered slits.

McGuinn was flabbergasted. Even the laziest, stupidest dairy cow would have spooked by now! The dog backed off to catch his breath and sort through his options (which, given a Lab's cognitive limitations, were modest and few). He affected a baleful pearly drool, only to stare in bewilderment as the monster placidly resumed nibbling from its bale of forage. Incredible!

Then came the approach of measured footsteps, followed by urgent human whispers. McGuinn knew what that meant: No more fun here. Soon someone would be snatching up his leash and jerking the choke chain. Time was running out. One last try: The dog growled, flattened his ears and insinuated himself into a wolf-like slink. Once more he began circling the torpid brute, which (McGuinn noticed) had ceased chewing, its jaws bewhiskered with sodden sprouts. But now the dog directed his focus at the stern of his prey: a sparse cord of a tail, dangling invitingly.

A leap, a flash of fangs and McGuinn had it!

Instantly the beast erupted, whirling with such hellish might that the dog was flung off, landing hard against the trunk of the sturdy old oak. He scrambled upright and shook himself vigorously from head to tail. With a mixture of surprise and elation, he observed that the monster was running away—and pretty darn fast, too!

McGuinn broke into lusty pursuit, driven by ancient instincts but also by sheer joy. Was there a better way to spend a spring morning, racing free through cool green meadows, snapping at a pair of fleeing hindquarters while slow-footed humans yammered helplessly in protest?

Every dog dreamed of such adventure.

No one was more rattled than Palmer Stoat to see a black Labrador charging into the line of fire, because it looked like his dog—Jesus H. Christ, it *was* his dog!—gone for all these days, only to surface at the worst possible time in the worst possible place. Stoat felt an upswell of despair, knowing the dog wasn't running downhill to greet him, but rather to flush Robert Clapley's prize rhinoceros, thereby disrupting the hunt and possibly mucking up (yet again!) the Shearwater deal.

It was no less than a curse.

"Boodle, no!" Stoat yelled, cigar waggling. "Bad boy!"

A few yards ahead stood Clapley, his aggrieved expression revealing all: He wanted to shoot the dog, but Durgess wouldn't permit it. In fact, the guide was signaling all of them to remain still.

"Hold up here," Asa Lando dutifully instructed Stoat's group.

Dick Artemus leaned in and whispered, "Palmer, is that your damn fool dog?" Willie Vasquez-Washington chuckled and began shooting pictures. In mute wonderment the guides and hunters watched the Labrador circle and taunt the rhinoceros; even Asa Lando found it difficult not to be entertained. The dog really was a piece of work!

Palmer Stoat shaded a nervous eye toward Clapley, huddled in a heated discussion with Durgess. Of all those present, Stoat alone knew of Clapley's peculiar obsession. Stoat alone knew without asking that the man had brought dolls, and probably a miniature pearl-handled hairbrush, concealed inside his ammo vest. Stoat alone knew the wanton seed of Clapley's motivation (which had nothing to do with sport), and understood the true base nature of his panic. No rhino, no horn; no horn, no live Barbies! In such a fraught equation, one frolicsome Labrador carried zero weight.

Only too late did it dawn on Stoat that he should have taken Bob aside the night before and explained that the "killer" rhinoceros would not and could not escape, due to the insurmountable barbed fence that enclosed the Wilderness Veldt Plantation. And though the news might have taken a bit of luster off the hunt, it might also have lowered Robert Clapley's buggy anxiety to a saner level, at which he might not have attempted to sight his Weatherby on something so inconsequential as a pesky hound. From the spot where Stoat knelt, he could see Clapley trying again and again to raise the gun barrel, only to have it slapped down by Durgess.

In desperation Stoat bellowed: "Boodle! Come!"

Dick Artemus stuck two fingers in his cheeks and gave a whistle that sounded like the screak of a tubercular macaw. The Labrador failed to respond. Peering at the confrontation through a 500-mm lens, Willie Vasquez-Washington could make out amazing details—the electric green bottleflies buzzing about the rhino's rear end, the shining strands of spittle on the dog's chin. . . .

And when the Lab suddenly leapt forward and seized the rhino's tail, it was Willie Vasquez-Washington who loudly piped: "Look at that crazy sonofabitch!"

Palmer Stoat saw the rhinoceros spin. He saw Boodle windmilling through the air. He saw Robert Clapley shake free of Durgess and jump to his feet. And then he saw the rhino take off, his idiot dog biting at its heels. The beast vectored first one direction and then another, ascending halfway up the northernmost slope before deferring to gravity. With a resolute snort, the rhino arced back downhill toward the three groups of men, whom it might easily have mistaken for shrubbery or grazing antelopes (given the rhinoceros's notoriously poor vision). Arbitrarily it picked for an escape route the twenty-yard gap between the first two groups. The dog bayed merrily in pursuit.

Because of the rhino's barge-like girth and laconic-looking trot, the swiftness of its advance was misjudged by both Stoat and Clapley—though not by the two guides, whose awe at the decrepit pachyderm's resurgence was outweighed by their aversion to violent death. Durgess, who anticipated the next phase of the fiasco, grimly flattened himself to the ground. Asa Lando spun on one heel and ran for the live oak. Governor Dick Artemus took the cue; dropped his gun and hit the grass ass-first. His two bodyguards dashed forward, seizing him roughly under the armpits and dragging him toward the zebra-striped truck. Meanwhile, Willie Vasquez-Washington backpedaled, snapping pictures in hasty retreat.

And Palmer Stoat, faced with a charging African rhinoceros, raised his rifle and took aim. Exactly sixty-six feet away, Robert Clapley did the same. Both men were too adrenalized to recognize their respective vulnerabilities in the lethal geometry of a cross fire. Both were too caught up in the heart-pounding maleness of the moment to sidestep manifest disaster.

It had been years since Stoat had shot an animal that was more or less ambulatory, and he trembled excitedly as he drew a bead on the grizzled brow of the lumbering rhino. As for Clapley, killing it would be more than a display of *machismo*—it would fulfill a fantasy that consumed him night and day. Through his rifle scope (laughably unnecessary at such close range), Clapley breathlessly admired the rhino's immense horn. He imagined presenting the hair-encrusted totem—upright and daunting—on a satin pillow to the twin Barbies, who would be curled up nude and perfumed and (he fervidly hoped) blond. He envisioned a grateful glow in their nearly completed faces. Next week: the chins. By Christmas: perfection.

As the rhinoceros thundered on a straight line between them, Clapley and Stoat swung their gun barrels to lead the beast, as they would a dove on the wing. Except, of course, they were not aiming upward, but level.

"Hold your fire!" Durgess shouted, strictly for the record.

That night, drinking heavily at a bar in McIntosh, neither he nor Asa Lando would be able to say which of the fools had fired first. Judging by the stereophonic roar of gunfire—and the instantaneous results—Robert Clapley and Palmer Stoat could have pulled their triggers simultaneously. Both of them completely missed the rhinoceros, naturally, and both went down very hard—Clapley, from the Weatherby's bone-jarring recoil; Stoat, from a combination of recoil and shrapnel.

Reconstructing the split-second mishap wasn't easy but, with some help from Master Jack Daniel, Durgess and Asa Lando would conclude that Stoat's slug must have struck the trunk of the oak at the instant Clapley's slug struck Stoat's Winchester, which more or less exploded in Stoat's arms. At that point the lobbyist was not dead, although his right shoulder had been seriously pulped by splintered gun stock.

Asa Lando would recall looking down from the tree and seeing Stoat, hatless and dazed, struggling to his knees. Likewise, Durgess would remember helping Robert Clapley to an identical position, so that the two hunters were facing each other like rival prairie dogs. But the guides well knew that Stoat wasn't staring at Clapley, and Clapley wasn't staring at Stoat—both men were scanning intently for a fresh rhinoceros corpse.

"You missed," Durgess informed Clapley.

"What?" Clapley's ears ringing from the gunshot.

"Mr. Stoat missed, too," Durgess added, by way of consolation.

"What?"

As Durgess stood up to scout for the runaway rhino, he heard frantic shouting from high in the live oak: Asa Lando, trying to warn him. The ground under Durgess's boots began to shake—that's what he would talk about later.

Like a damn earthquake, Asa. Could you feel it, too?

The rhinoceros had cut back unexpectedly and now was rumbling up from behind the scattered hunting party; prey turned predator. There was no time to flee. Asa squawked from the tree. Palmer Stoat spit his broken cigar and gaped. Durgess dove for Robert Clapley but Clapley wasn't there; he was down on all fours, scrambling after his rifle. Helplessly Durgess rolled himself into a ball and waited to be crushed. Beneath him the earth was coming unsprung, a demonic trampoline.

Durgess felt the rhinoceros blow past like a steam locomotive, wheezing and huffing. He peeked up in time to see an outstretched black shape silhouetted briefly against the creamy pink sky, and to feel Labrador toenails scuff his forehead. Durgess decided he was in no hurry to get up, a decision reinforced by the sound of Clapley shrieking.

The guide would remember remaining motionless until hearing a man's heavy footsteps, and feeling a shadow settle over him. He would remember rocking up slowly, expecting to see Asa, but facing instead a bearded apparition with a gleaming grin and a molten red eye that might have been plucked from the skull of the devil himself.

"We've come for the dog," the apparition said.

While being dragged to safety, the governor lost the tender scabs on his buttocks. By the time the bodyguards got him to the Suburban, he had bled through his khaki trousers—the word SHAME appearing chimerically across his ass, like stigmata. If Willie Vasquez-Washington noticed, he didn't say so. He and Dick Artemus were hustled into the backseat. The FDLE agents hopped up front, locked the doors and radioed for a helicopter and ambulances.

Riding back to the lodge, the governor looked drained and shaken, his great cliff of silver hair now a tornadic nest. He sank low in the seat. Willie Vasquez-Washington rode ramrod-straight, a fervent amazement on his face.

"Sweet Jesus," he said. "Did you see that!"

"Willie?"

"Those poor fuckers."

"Willie!"

"Yeah?"

"I was never here. You were never here." The governor placed a clammy hand on Willie Vasquez-Washington's knee. "Can we agree on that?"

The vice chairman of the House Appropriations Committee rubbed his jaw thoughtfully. With his other hand he touched a button on the Nikon, still hanging from his neck, and set off the automatic rewind. The hum from a swarm of wasps would not have been more unsettling to Dick Artemus.

Ruefully his eyes fell on the camera. "You got some pictures, huh?"

Willie Vasquez-Washington nodded. "A whole roll."

"Color or black-and-white?"

"Oh, color."

Dick Artemus turned and stared straight ahead. Just then, a white-tailed buck crashed out of the cabbage palms and entered the path in front of the truck. The agent who was driving stomped the accelerator and swerved expertly around the deer.

"Nice move!" Willie Vasquez-Washington cheered, bouncing in the seat.

The governor never flinched, never blinked.

"Willie," he said, wearily.

"Yeah?"

"What is it you want?"

Twilly Spree tried to go after McGuinn but he was chased down and tackled by Clinton Tyree, who whispered in his ear: "Let it happen, son."

Said it with such a startling serenity that Twilly understood, finally, what sustained the man—an indefatigable faith that Nature eventually settles all scores, sets all things straight.

So they let the dog go, then watched as the rhinoceros snorted to action. It ran halfway up the slope before turning back toward the hunting party, which dissolved in bedlam. Viewed from the bank of the knoll, the debacle unfolded with eerie, slow-motion inevitability—the two idiots swinging their rifles as the beleaguered rhino attempted to cut between them, a triangulated aim turning linear and deadly. And when the shots rang out, it indeed appeared that Palmer Stoat and Robert Clapley had managed to blast one another in a brainless cross fire.

Skink and Twilly were quite surprised to see both men lever to their knees. They were somewhat less surprised to see the rhino swing around once more, this time charging blind from behind the shooters.

Skink sucked in his breath. "Say good night, Gracie."

Clapley was groping inanely in the grass when the rhinoceros scooped him up at a full trot. His screams carried up the slope, echoing among the caws of grumpy crows. Like a frog on a gig, Clapley frantically tried to push himself off the rhino's horn (which at forty-nine centimeters would have been considered truly a splendid prize). Furiously the animal bucked its head, tossing and goring Clapley as it ran.

Ran directly at the injured Palmer Stoat, whose Winchester

was in pieces and whose reflexes were in disarray. Stoat spastically waved one pudgy arm in an attempt to intimidate the beast (which, Skink later noted, couldn't possibly have seen him anyway; not with Robert Clapley's body impaled so obtrusively on its nose). With McGuinn nipping at its hocks, the rhinoceros—all two and one-quarter tons of it—flattened Stoat as effortlessly as a beer truck.

Twilly and Skink waited to come down off the hill until the animal had run out of steam, and the zebra-striped Suburban carrying the governor and his bodyguards had sped away. One of the guides remained on the ground, balled up like an armadillo. Skink checked on him first, while Twilly went through the messy formality of examining Palmer Stoat. The lobbyist's eyes were open, fixed somewhere infinite and unreachable. They reminded Twilly of the glassy orbs he'd removed from Stoat's animal heads.

The exhausted rhinoceros had returned to the shade of the live oak and collapsed to its knees. From thirty yards away, Skink and Twilly could hear the animal wheezing and see the heat rippling off its thick hide. Across the prow-like snout hung Robert Clapley, limp and contorted.

Skink asked Twilly: "What's with the dog?"

Once the armor-plated behemoth had quit playing runaway, McGuinn had grown bored and sniffed elsewhere for mischief: The tree. A human was up in the tree! The dog decisively stationed himself beneath the tall oak and commenced a barking fit, punctuated by the occasional lunge.

To the man in the branches, Twilly said: "You OK up there?"

"Pretty much. Anyway, who the hell are you?" It was the other hunting guide, the one dressed like a mechanic.

"Nobody. We just came for the dog."

"That's yours? You see what all he did?" The man in the tree was highly upset. "You see the holy shitstorm he caused, your damn dog!"

"I know, I know. He's been a very bad boy."

Twilly whistled the dinner whistle. McGuinn, having already lost track of the time of day, fell for it. Sheepishly he lowered his head, tucked his tail and sidled toward Twilly in a well-practiced pose of contrition. Twilly grabbed the leash and held on tight. He didn't want the dog to see what had happened to his former master.

Skink ambled up and seized McGuinn in a jovial bear hug. The Labrador chomped one of Skink's cheek braids and began to tug, Skink giggling like a schoolboy.

Twilly said, "We'd better go."

"No, son. Not just yet."

He got up, took out the .45 and strode purposefully toward the rhinoceros.

"What are you doing?" Twilly called out. In the tumult he'd left his Remington up on the knoll. "Don't!"

As Skink approached the rhinoceros, a voice from the tree inquired: "Are you fuckin' nuts?"

"Hush up," said the former governor of Florida.

The rhino sensed him coming and struggled to rise.

"Easy there. Easy." Skink stepped gingerly, edging closer. His arm gradually reached out, the blue barrel of the Colt pointing squarely at the animal's brainpan—or so it appeared to Twilly, who had kept back. Morosely he wondered why Skink would kill the old rhino now; perhaps to spare it from being shot by somebody else, a cop or a game warden. Meanwhile, McGuinn bucked at the leash, thinking the opossum-smelling man had cooked up a fun new game.

"Hey, what're you doing?" Twilly shouted again at Skink.

The rhino's view remained obstructed by the lumpy object snagged on its horn. El Jefe could not clearly see either the silver-bearded man or the gun at its face, which was just as well, though the man had no intention of harm.

Watching Skink's arm stiffen, Twilly braced for the clap of a gunshot. None came, for Skink didn't place the weapon to the ancient animal's brow. Instead he touched it firmly to Robert Clapley's unblinking right eye, to make absolutely sure the fucker was dead. Satisfied, he stepped back and lowered the gun. The man in the tree hopped down and scampered away. McGuinn barked indignantly, which made the rhinoceros stir once more. With a volcanic grunt and a violent head shake, it launched Robert Clapley's beanbag body, which landed in a khaki heap.

Skink went over and poked it with a boot. Twilly saw him bend over and pick something up off the ground. Later, striding up the slope, he removed the article from his pocket and showed it to Twilly. "What do you make of *this*?" he asked.

It was a voluptuous blond doll, dressed in a skimpy deerhide outfit of the style Maureen O'Sullivan wore in the old Johnny Weismuller movies. Barbie as Jane.

"Came off Clapley," Skink reported, with a troubled frown. "A girl's doll."

Twilly Spree nodded. "Sick world."

30

It was seventy-seven steps to the top of the lighthouse. He counted each one as he went up the circular stairwell. Where the steps ended stood a warped door with flaking barn-red paint and no outside knob. The former governor of Florida gave three hard raps, waited a few moments, then knocked again. Eventually he heard movement on the other side; more a shuffling than a footfall.

"Doyle?"

Nothing.

"Doyle, it's me. Clint."

He could hear his brother breathing.

"Are you all right?"

The only light slanting into the stone column came from a row of narrow salt-caked windows. Littering the floor from wall to wall were envelopes—hundreds of identical envelopes, yellowed and unopened. Payroll checks from the State of Florida. It had been a very long time since Clinton Tyree had seen one.

In the shadows he noticed a crate of fresh oranges, three one-gallon water jugs and, stacked nearby like library books, two dozen boxes of Minute rice. It was rice he smelled now, cooking on the other side of the door.

"Doyle?"

He so wanted to lay eyes on his brother.

"I'm not going to stay. I just need to know you're all right."

Clinton Tyree leaned his shoulder to the wood. The door held fast. He heard more shuffling; the scrape of metal chair legs across a pine floor, the sibilant protest of a cheap cushion being sat upon, emphatically. His brother had taken a position.

"The park rangers said there are people bringing you food. Doyle, is that true?"

Nothing.

"Because if there's anything you need, I'll get it for you. Groceries, medicine, whatever. Anything at all."

Books, magazines, paintings, a VCR, a grand piano . . . how about a whole new life? Jesus, Clinton Tyree thought, who am I kidding here.

He heard the chair scoot closer to the door. Then came a metallic click, like a Zippo lighter or a pocketknife being opened. Then he thought he heard a murmur.

"Doyle?"

Still not a word.

"The reason I came—look, I just wanted to tell you that you never have to leave this place if you don't want. It's all been taken care of. Don't be frightened ever again, because you're safe here, OK? For as long as you want. I give you my word."

There was another click behind the door, and then two solid footsteps. Clinton Tyree pressed a cheek to the briny wood and sensed more than heard his brother on the other side, doing the same.

"Doyle, please," he whispered. "Please."

He heard a bolt slide, and he stepped back. The door cracked and an arm came out slowly; an old man's arm, pallid and spidered with violet veins. On the underside, between the wrist and the elbow, were faded striations of an old scar. The hand was large, but bony and raw-looking. Clinton Tyree grabbed it and squeezed with all his heart, and found his brother still strong. The pale wrist twisted back and forth against his grip, and that's when he noticed the new wound on the meat of the forearm, letters etched into flesh—*i love you*—blooming in droplets as bright as rose petals.

Then Doyle Tyree snatched his hand away and closed the door in his brother's face.

As he descended the lighthouse, the former governor of Florida counted all seventy-seven steps again. When he reached the bottom he got on his belly and wedged through a gap in the plywood that had been nailed over the entrance to keep out vandals and curious tourists.

From the darkness of the beaconage, Clinton Tyree emerged, squinting like a newborn, into a stunning spring morning. He stood and turned his tear-streaked face to the cool breeze blowing in off the Atlantic. He could see tarpon crashing a school of mullet beyond the break.

The plywood barricade to the tower was papered with official notices, faded and salt-curled:

NO TRESPASSING

CLOSED TO THE PUBLIC UNTIL FURTHER NOTICE

STATE PROPERTY—KEEP OUT

But someone recently had tacked a business card to the plywood. The tack was shiny, not rusted, and the card stood out white and crisp. Clinton Tyree put his good eye to it and smiled. The inaugural smile.

LISA JUNE PETERSON
Executive Assistant
Office of the Governor

He took the card off the board and slipped it under the elastic band of his shower cap. Then he trudged down the beach, over the dunes and through the sea oats, across the street to the Peregrine Bay Visitor Center and Scenic Boardwalk, where the navy blue Roadmaster was parked.

Palmer Stoat was buried with his favorite Ping putter, a Polaroid camera and a box of Cuban Montecristo #2s, a cause for authentic mourning among the cigar buffs at the ceremony. The funeral service was held at a Presbyterian church in Tallahassee, the minister eulogizing Stoat as a civic pillar, champion of the democratic process, dedicated family man, lover of animals, and devoted friend to the powerful and common folk alike. Those attending the service included a prostitute, the night bartender from Swain's, a taxidermist, three United States congressmen, one retired senator, six sitting circuit judges, three dozen past and present municipal commissioners from throughout Florida, the lieutenant governor and forty-one current members of the state Legislature (most of whom had been elected with campaign funds raised by Stoat, and not because he admired their politics). Those sending lavish sprays of flowers included the Philip Morris Company, Shell Oil, Roothaus and Son Engineering, Magnusson Phosphate Company, the Lake County Citrus Cooperative, U.S. Sugar, MatsibuCom Construction of Tokyo, Port Marco Properties, the Southern Timber Alliance, the National Rifle Association, University of Florida Blue Key, the Republican Executive Committee and the Democratic Executive Committee. Messages of regret arrived from Representative

Willie Vasquez-Washington and Governor Richard Artemus, neither of whom could make it to the service.

"Our grief today should be assuaged," the minister said, in closing, "by the knowledge that Palmer's last day among us was spent happily at sport, with his close friend Bob Clapley—just the two of them, walking the great outdoors they loved so much."

Burial was at a nearby cemetery, which, fittingly, served as the final resting place for no less than twenty-one of Florida's all-time crookedest politicians. The joke around town was that the grave digger needed an auger instead of a shovel. The Stoats had attended the funerals of several of the dead thieves, including some convicted ones, so Desie was familiar with the layout. For Palmer she selected an unshaded plot on a bald mound overlooking Interstate 10. Since he had so often (and enthusiastically) predicted Florida would someday be as bustling as New York or California, she figured he would appreciate a roadside view of it coming to pass.

At the grave, more kind words were spoken. Desie, who sat in front with her parents and Palmer's only cousin, a defrocked podiatrist from Jacksonville, found herself weeping tears of true aching sadness—not over the eulogies (which were largely fiction), but over the unraveling of her own feelings about her husband, and how that had contributed to his untimely death. While she could take no blame for the freakish hunting mishap, it was also indisputable that the doomed rhino expedition had been precipitated by the dognapping crisis—and that the dognapping had been complicated by Desie's attraction to, and abetment of, Twilly Spree.

True, Palmer would still have been alive had he, early on, done the honorable thing and bailed out of the Shearwater fix. But there had been no chance of that, no reasonable expectation that her husband would suddenly discover an inner moral compass—and Desie should have known it.

So she was feeling guilt. And grief, too, because even as she kept no romantic love for Palmer, she also kept no hate. He was what he was, and it wasn't all rotten or she wouldn't have married him. There was a companionable, eager-to-please side of the man that, while it couldn't have been called warm, was lively enough to be missed and even grieved for. Putting the Polaroid in his coffin had been Desie's idea, an inside joke. Palmer would have laughed, she thought, although he undoubtedly would have preferred the bedroom snapshots. Those, she had destroyed.

As the casket was lowered, a murmuring rippled lightly through the mourners. Desie heard panting and felt something wet and velvety brush her fingers. She looked down to see McGuinn, nuzzling her clasped hands. The big dog had a black satin bow on his neck, and a chew toy clamped in his teeth. The toy was a rubber bullfrog with an orange stripe down its back. The frog croaked whenever McGuinn bit down on it, which was every ten or twelve seconds. A few people chuckled gently, grateful for the distraction, but the minister (who was busy walking through the valley of the shadow of death) raised his glacial eyes with no hint of amusement.

Not a dog person, Desie decided, and extracted the chew toy from McGuinn's jaws. The Labrador curled up at her feet and watched, curiously, as another big wooden box disappeared into the ground. He assumed it contained a one-eared dog, like the one in the box that had been buried on the beach. But if there was death in the air, McGuinn couldn't smell it for all the flowers.

Meanwhile, the widow Stoat glanced expectantly first over one shoulder and then the other, scanning the faces of the mourners. He wasn't there. She opened her hand and looked at the rubber toy, which actually resembled a toad more than a bullfrog. She turned it over in her palm and saw that someone had written in ballpoint ink across its pale yellow belly: *I dreamt of you!*

And then a postal box number in Everglades City, not far from Marco Island.

The sneeze set his lungs afire.

Twilly Spree grimaced. "You sure didn't have to jump on me like that."

"Oh, I damn sure did," Skink said. "I'd never catch you on a dead run downhill. You're way too fast for an old fart like me."

"Yeah, right. How much did you say you weigh?"

"I just figured you might not want to get shot again, so soon after the first time. And that's likely what would have happened out there with those two peckerheads blasting away with their cannons. Either that or the damn rhino would have stomped you into a tortilla."

"All right, all right—thank you," Twilly said sarcastically. "Thank you very much for jumping on my broken ribs. I'd forgotten how good that feels."

He sneezed again, the pain causing his eyes to well.

Skink said, "I've got an idea. Pull off at the next exit."

At a gas station they vacuumed the dog hair out of the station wagon—enough of it, Skink observed, for a whole new Labrador. Twilly's sneezing was cured. They headed southbound on the Florida Turnpike, which recently had been renamed (for reasons no one could adequately explain) after Ronald Reagan.

"Name a rest stop after him. *That* would make sense," Skink groused. "But the whole turnpike? Christ, he was still making cowboy movies when the damn thing was built."

Twilly said he didn't care if they dedicated the road to Kathie

Lee Gifford, as long as they raised the toll to one hundred dollars per car.

"Not nearly high enough. Make it half a grand," Skink decreed. "Twice as much for Winnebagos."

Traffic was, as usual, rotten. Twilly felt a familiar downward skid in his mood.

"Where you headed now?" he asked the captain.

"Back to Crocodile Lakes, I suppose. My current residence is a cozy but well-ventilated NASCAR Dodge. You?"

"Everglades City."

Skink canted an eyebrow. "What for?"

"Strategic positioning," Twilly said. "Or maybe just to catch some redfish. Who knows."

"Oh man."

"Hey, there's something I've been meaning to ask: All these years, you never thought about leaving?"

"Every single day, son."

"Where to?" Twilly said.

"Bahamas. Turks and Caicos. Find some flyspeck island too small for a Club Med. Once I bought a ticket to the Grenadines and got all the way to Miami International—"

"But you couldn't get on the plane."

"No, I could not. It felt like I was sneaking out the back door on a dying friend."

Twilly said, "I know."

Skink hung his head out the car and roared like a gut-shot bear. "Damn Florida," he said.

For ten miles they rode in silence. Then Twilly felt the heat of that gaze—and from the corner of an eye he saw the buzzard beaks, twirling counterclockwise on the tails of the burnished braids.

Skink said, "Son, I can't tell you how to handle the pain, or where to find a season of peace—or even one night's worth. I just hope you have better luck at it than I did."

"Governor, I hope I do half as well."

With a tired smile, Skink said, "Then I've got only one piece of advice: If she's crazy enough to write you, be sure to write back."

"Gee. I'll try to force myself. By the way, how'd it go with your brother?"

"You've been so good not to ask."

"Yeah, well, it's been a hundred miles," Twilly said, "so I'm asking now."

"It went fine. We had a good talk." And, in a way, they had. Skink dug out Jim Tile's mirrored sunglasses and pinched them to the bridge of his nose. "You taking the Trail across?"

Twilly nodded. "I thought I would. Nice straight shot."

"And an awful pretty drive. Drop me at Krome Avenue, I'll hitch to the Keys."

"Like hell. I want to see this alleged race car." Twilly reached for the stereo. "Is Neil Young OK with you?"

"Neil Young would be superb."

So they flew past the exit for the Tamiami Trail and remained on the Ronald Reagan Turnpike. It was the tail of rush hour and the traffic was still clotted; frenzied. The unspoken question bubbling like nitroglycerin inside the Buick Roadmaster was whether they could make it through Miami, whether they could actually get out of the godforsaken city before somebody did *something* that simply couldn't be overlooked. . . .

And somehow they did get out, navigating onward through the turgid hellhole of west Kendall toward Snapper Creek, Cutler Ridge, Homestead—until finally the highway delivered them, more or less sane, to Florida City. They glowered at the blighted dreck of mini-marts and fast-food pits until escaping on Card Sound Road, bounded only by scrub and wetlands, and aiming the prow of the Buick toward North Key Largo; both men breathing easier, Twilly humming and Skink even tapping his boots to the music, when—

"You see that?" Twilly stiffened at the wheel.

"See what?"

"That black Firebird ahead."

"What about it," Skink said.

But of course he had seen what Twilly had seen: a beer bottle fly out the front passenger's window, spooking a great blue heron off the canal bank.

"Asshole," Twilly muttered, knuckles tightening on the wheel.

Another airborne beer bottle, this time from the driver's side. Skink counted four bobbing heads inside the Firebird—two couples, launching a festive vacation. They looked young. The car was a rental.

"Unbelievable," Twilly said.

No, it's not, Skink thought dismally. More, more, more. . . .

The next item of litter from the Firebird was a plastic go-cup, followed by a lighted cigarette butt, which skittered into the crackling dry grass along the shoulder of the road.

Skink swore. Twilly hit the brakes, threw the station wagon into reverse and backed up to the spot where the cigarette had landed. He jumped from the car and stomped out the small flame, and kept on stomping in tight circles for a full minute. It looked like excellent therapy. Skink felt like joining him.

When Twilly got back in the driver's seat, he calmly put the pedal to the floor. Skink watched the speedometer tick all the way up to 110. The Firebird was no longer a distant speck on the blacktop; it was getting bigger rapidly.

"I was wondering," Twilly said, perfectly composed. "You in a rush to get home?"

Skink thought about it; thought about everything. Palmer

Stoat. Dick Artemus. Doyle. Twilly. The hardworking heron whose supper was so rudely interrupted by a beer bottle.

And he thought of the two couples in the Firebird, laughing and drinking but plainly oblivious to the two unkempt, deeply disturbed men riding their bumper. How else to explain what happened next—an Altoids tin casually ejected through the Firebird's sunroof. It glanced off the windshield of the pursuing station wagon and landed, as trash, in the water.

Twilly clicked his tongue impatiently. "Well, Governor? Shall we?"

He thought: Oh, what the hell.

"Anytime you're ready, son."

EPILOGUE

With the death of ROBERT CLAPLEY, the Zurich-based SwissOne Banc Group withdrew all lines of credit for the Shearwater Island Development Corporation, which immediately folded. At a bankruptcy auction arranged by Clapley's estate, his extensive waterfront holdings on Toad Island were sold to an anonymous buyer, who eventually renamed it Amy Island and deeded every parcel for preservation. No new bridge was built.

NORVA STINSON, the only remaining private landowner on Toad Island, staunchly refused to sell her tiny bed-and-breakfast to the Nature Conservancy for any sum less than $575,000— six times its appraised value. Her demand was politely rejected, and Mrs. Stinson still lives in the house today, subsisting mainly on canned donations from a local church group.

Three months after the collapse of the Shearwater project, bird-watchers hiking on Toad Island discovered a man's skeleton. The legs had been crushed by an enormous weight, and a Nokia cellular telephone was clutched in the bones of one hand. FBI pathologists later identified the remains as DARIAN LEE GASH, a convicted felon, registered sex offender and well-known player on the South Beach club scene. The cause of death was determined to be bullet wounds from two different .357-caliber handguns, only one of which was ever recovered.

The 911 tape recording of Mr. Gash's frantic, though largely unintelligible, plea for help has been included in Volume Four of *The World's Most Bloodcurdling Emergency Calls*, and widely marketed on television and the Internet. The cassette is priced at $9.95 and the compact disc is $13.95, not including shipping and handling.

The body of KARL KRIMMLER was found in the shallows of a brackish marsh in the pine uplands of Toad Island. He was pinned inside the cab of a Caterpillar D-6 bulldozer that he inexplicably had driven at full throttle into the water. An autopsy determined he had drowned, the pathologist noting "a large number of viable tadpoles in the victim's upper trachea." In the same marsh, police divers discovered a Smith & Wesson model .357 pistol that was later linked to the shooting of Darian Lee Gash. Because of Mr. Gash's checkered past, detectives theorized that the deaths of the two men were a sordid murder-suicide. The remains of DR. STEVEN BRINKMAN were never recovered.

Following the botched rhinoceros "hunt," the WILDERNESS VELDT PLANTATION was raided by federal wildlife agents, who broke into the compounds and discovered twelve impalas, eight Thompson's gazelles, a defanged Malaysian cobra, a juvenile

Cape buffalo, three missing circus chimpanzees, a troop of heavily sedated baboons, a mule painted to resemble a zebra, and a feisty two-legged ocelot. The facility was swiftly shut down by the U.S. Attorney's Office, which alleged multiple violations of the Endangered Species Act and other statutes. The rhinoceros known as EL JEFE was safely recaptured, tranquilized and transported to a protected game reserve in Kenya, not far from where it had been born thirty-one years earlier. Its massive front horn was painlessly removed, so that the animal would have no value to poachers or hunters.

JOHN RANDOLPH DURGESS relocated to West Texas, where he took a job as a guide on a private 22,000-acre hunting reserve called Serengeti Pines. There he was killed and partially devoured by a wild cougar, which had jumped the fence to feast on imported dik-diks.

ASA LANDO was hired as an animal handler at Walt Disney World's Animal Kingdom theme park, near Orlando. Two months later he was quietly dismissed, following the unexplained disappearance of the attraction's only male cheetah.

Double Your Pleasure, Double Your Pain, featuring KATYA GUDONOV and TISH KARPINSKI, was released by Avalon Brown Productions and went instantly to home video. Within weeks, the Mattel Corporation obtained an emergency injunction prohibiting the two stars of the film from "performing, portraying, attiring, advertising or in any way representing themselves as Barbie dolls, a trademarked symbol; this order to include but not expressly be limited to such oral and visual depictions as 'Goth Barbies,' 'Undead Barbies,' and 'Double-Jointed Vampire Barbies.'" Both women received unfriendly visits from agents of the U.S. Immigration and Naturalization Service, and soon thereafter left the United States on an extended working vacation to the Caribbean.

ESTELLA HYDE, also known to Fort Lauderdale vice officers as Crystal Barr, Raven McCollum and Raven Bush, became volunteer treasurer of the Broward County Chapter of Citizens for Quayle. During a fund-raising brunch for the former vice president at Pier 66, she met and befriended Governor Dick Artemus, who soon afterward invited her to Tallahassee to serve on the Public Service Commission.

After surrendering his California real estate license to avoid prosecution, PHILLIP SPREE, JR., moved to Beaufort, South Carolina, where he specialized in peddling oceanfront property on low-lying barrier islands. Before long, Little Phil came to believe his own bubbly sales pitch, and built himself a getaway house on pilings at the edge of the Atlantic. He, his fourth wife and their architect perished there one summer, when Hurricane Barbara smashed the beach bungalow to matchsticks.

AMY SPREE married her yoga instructor and moved to Cassadaga, Florida, where she is faithfully visited by her son every year on her birthday.

LT. JIM TILE retired from the Florida Highway Patrol and opened a fish camp and diner near Apalachicola. The following Christmas, he received in the mail a gaily wrapped package. Inside was a new Nokia cellular phone, the speed dial programmed to an unlisted number in North Key Largo. Callers are treated to a voice-mail greeting that consists entirely of the solo guitar lead-in to "Fortunate Son," by Creedence Clearwater Revival.

LISA JUNE PETERSON resigned her job as executive assistant to Governor Dick Artemus and went to work as a lobbyist for the Clean Water Action Group. The following spring, she was instrumental in pushing for a new anti-pollution law that resulted in a $5,000-a-day fine against a notoriously virulent Magnusson Phosphate plant in Polk County. As a result, mine owner Dag Magnusson angrily switched political parties and spent the rest of his days bitterly funneling thousands of dollars in illicit campaign contributions to Democratic candidates.

Ten months after the hunting fiasco at Wilderness Veldt, a groundbreaking ceremony was held in Miami on the future site of the WILLIE VASQUEZ-WASHINGTON SENIOR HIGH SCHOOL. Governor Dick Artemus attended the event and posed graciously with the honoree, both men wielding gold-painted shovels while photographers took their picture.

The PEREGRINE BAY LIGHTHOUSE remains closed to the public, though on occasion mariners along Florida's southeast coast claim to see a bright light flashing at the dome of the barber-striped tower. The Coast Guard routinely discounts these sightings as an illusion caused by foul weather, since the lighthouse is known to be empty and out of service.

ABOUT THE AUTHOR

CARL HIAASEN was born and raised in Florida. He is the author of eleven novels, including *Skinny Dip, Lucky You, Stormy Weather, Basket Case,* and, for young readers, *Hoot.* He also writes a regular column for the *Miami Herald.* You can visit him at www.CarlHiaasen.com.

WANT MORE
SKINK?
CARL HIAASEN
A MISSING GIRL,
A HUNGRY GATOR,
ONLY ONE WAY OUT...
SKINK
NO
SURRENDER
A MISSING GIRL,
A HUNGRY GATOR,
ONLY ONE WAY OUT...
SkinkNoSurrender.com